FEUCHTWANGER STUDIES

Patrons

EDGAR FEUCHTWANGER

FEUCHTWANGER MEMORIAL LIBRARY,
UNIVERSITY OF SOUTHERN CALIFORNIA

General Editor

FRANK STERN

Volume 9

PETERLANG

Oxford · Berlin · Bruxelles · Chennai · Lausanne · New York

Birgit Maier-Katkin,
Marje Schuetze-Coburn
and Michaela Ullmann (eds)

Women in Exile

Feuchtwanger and Gender Dynamics in Exile and Exile Literature

PETERLANG

Oxford · Berlin · Bruxelles · Chennai · Lausanne · New York

Bibliographic information published by the Deutsche Nationalbibliothek. The German National Library lists this publication in the German National Bibliography; detailed bibliographic data is available on the Internet at http://dnb.d-nb.de.

A catalogue record for this book is available from the British Library.

Library of Congress Cataloging-in-Publication Data

Names: Maier-Katkin, Birgit, 1962- editor. | Schuetze-Coburn, Marje, 1959- editor. | Ullmann, Michaela, editor.
Title: Women in exile : Feuchtwanger and gender dynamics in exile and exile literature / Birgit Maier-Katkin, Marje Schuetze-Coburn, Michaela Ullmann.
Description: Oxford ; New York : Peter Lang, 2024. | Series: Feuchtwanger studies, 1662-9965 ; volume no. 9 | Includes bibliographical references and index.
Identifiers: LCCN 2024024561 (print) | LCCN 2024024562 (ebook) | ISBN 9781803742977 (paperback) | ISBN 9781803742984 (ebook) | ISBN 9781803742991 (epub)
Subjects: LCSH: Feuchtwanger, Lion, 1884-1958—Relations with women. | Feuchtwanger, Lion, 1884-1958—Criticism and interpretation. | Women in literature. | Exiles in literature. | Women—Social conditions—History— 20th century. | Exiles—History—20th century. | LCGFT: Literary criticism. | Essays.
Classification: LCC PT2611.E85 Z964 2024 (print) | LCC PT2611.E85 (ebook) | DDC 833/.912—dc23/eng/20240607
LC record available at https://lccn.loc.gov/2024024561
LC ebook record available at https://lccn.loc.gov/2024024562

With thanks to the University of Southern California Libraries.

Cover design by Peter Lang Group AG

ISSN 1622-9965
ISBN 978-1-80374-297-7 (print)
ISBN 978-1-80374-298-4 (ePDF)
ISBN 978-1-80374-299-1 (ePub)
DOI 10.3726/b21187

© 2024 Peter Lang Group AG, Lausanne
Published by Peter Lang Ltd, Oxford, United Kingdom
info@peterlang.com – www.peterlang.com

This publication has been peer reviewed.

This volume is dedicated to Marta Feuchtwanger and all women in exile.

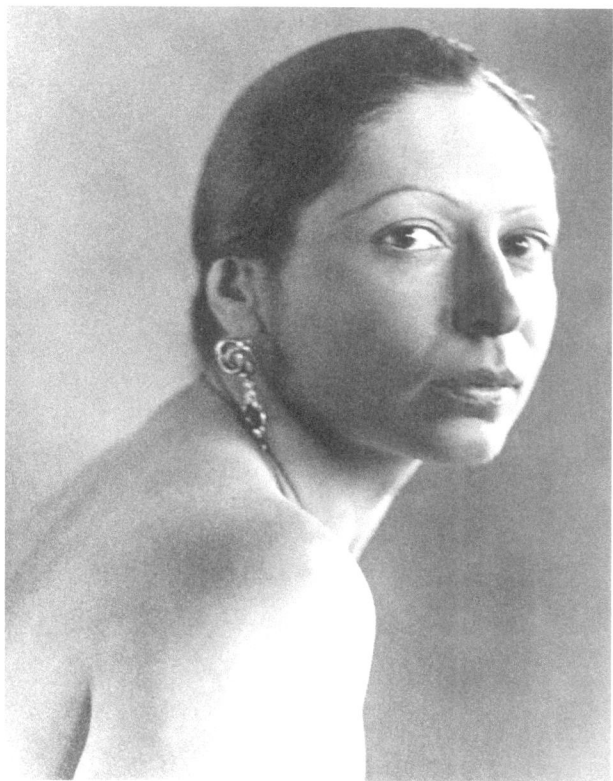

Figure 1. Portrait of Marta Feuchtwanger, ca. 1920s.

Contents

Figures

Acknowledgments

The International Feuchtwanger Society (IFS) gratefully acknowledges the support of our sponsors whose generosity made possible the success of the tenth biennial conference of the IFS "Women in Exile: Feuchtwanger and Gender Dynamics in Exile and in Exile Literature": USC Libraries, Interim Dean Andrew T. Guzman, and Dean Melissa Just at the University of Southern California; Villa Aurora in Pacific Palisades; and the Austrian and German Consulates in Los Angeles. We also wish to thank all the colleagues who participated and attended the conference, especially those who shared their final research papers for inclusion in this volume.

BIRGIT MAIER-KATKIN, MARJE SCHUETZE-COBURN, AND
MICHAELA ULLMANN

Introduction

Wenn ich mit Freunden zusammensitze und sie mich über mein Leben mit Lion ausfragen, erzähle ich von unseren kleinen und manchmal auch nicht so kleinen Erlebnissen oder von turbulenten Ereignissen, die über uns zusammenbrachen und wie wir sie dann durchgestanden haben.

[When I spend time with friends and they ask about my life with Lion, I tell them about our small and at times not so small experiences or about the dramatic events that came down on us and how we got through it all]
— Marta Feuchtwanger, *Nur eine Frau* (Berlin und Weimar: Aufbau Verlag, 1984).

With its focus on women in exile and particularly with Feuchtwanger and Gender Dynamics, this volume aims to participate in the ongoing discourse about women's presence, contribution, and experience of historical events. The Nazi period not only affected the lives of men but also challenged women to forge a path outside their home country. Regarding the well-known Lion Feuchtwanger, it was his wife, Marta Feuchtwanger, who worked diligently in the background and was involved in promoting his success and legacy. To the inner circles of friends and family, Marta was well known for her social gatherings, her skill of storytelling, her sherry and *Apfelstrudel* (apple pie), and her vibrant and energetic personality. This reveals that behind a famous and celebrated man, there tend to be multiple, often unacknowledged, contributions from women that play a large part in their success and continued recognition. A closer look at female participation during the period of exile from Nazi Germany reveals a nuanced understanding of historical experience. Women in exile have been instrumental in adjusting to and succeeding in the new, often unbearable environment of foreign surroundings. Many exiled women joined their men in exile; they were homemakers, secretaries, chefs, translators, drivers, personal assistants, artists, musicians, scholars, and much more. Some had their own successful careers and professional accomplishments while at the same time taking care of family business.

This volume aims to connect Lion Feuchtwanger's work to the gendered experience of exile from Nazi Germany and is divided into five parts. Part I offers a detailed exploration of select women who—in some way or another—shared their life with Lion Feuchtwanger. Part II examines women's influence on Feuchtwanger's work and exile experience. Part III explores the depiction of women characters in Lion Feuchtwanger's work, Part IV branches out to explore select women (unrelated to Feuchtwanger) who exemplify noteworthy perspectives of women in exile, and Part V offers Edgar Feuchtwanger's insider view on Lion Feuchtwanger's diaries. The volume offers an interdisciplinary discussion of how women represent, experience, and are depicted within a life in exile. Contributions to this volume arose from the International Feuchtwanger Society conference held in Los Angeles, Southern California on September 15–17, 2023, along with additional solicited papers. The topic of women in exile is not unique to this volume. It has been approached by scholars including Charmian Brinson, Judith Gerson, Atina Grossmann, Hiltrud Häntzschel, Marion Kaplan, Dagmar Lorenz, Sybille Quack, Inge Hansen-Schaberg, or exile organizations such as *Frauen im Exil* (Women in Exile), to name a few. What differentiates this volume is a focus on women in exile that draws connections to the Feuchtwanger family and to Lion Feuchtwanger's work, but also seeks to shed light on some select unique gendered exile perspectives unrelated to the Feuchtwangers.

All five parts in this book aim to connect three elements of gendered literary analysis: (1) to promote and make women visible who typically remain hidden behind their male counterparts, (2) to explore how women are depicted in literature, and (3) to connect forced exile from Nazi Germany to gendered experiences and perspectives that shaped women's lives and that of the wider (often male dominant) exile community.

The following gives a more detailed overview regarding each part and chapter contributions.

Part I begins with biographical studies of women who either have a personal connection with or are related to Lion Feuchtwanger. Birgit Maier-Katkin takes a closer look at Lion's First Lady Marta Feuchtwanger who after Lion's death began to manage his literary heritage and successfully promoted his legacy across two continents (Germany and the United States). Maier-Katkin argues that it is due to Marta's ingenious, unrelenting, and diligent efforts that Lion's work is still remembered today and that their house in Los Angeles became a famous residence for artists and exiles. Heike Specht sheds light on several women in the Feuchtwanger family who not only played a decisive role in promoting the family wealth but also showed great intuition and socio-political understanding when the family was under attack by the Nazi government and had to initiate new ways to survive in exile outside of Germany. Specht reveals how the Feuchtwanger family's ascent from *Wirtschafts- to Bildungsbürgertum* (economic to educated bourgeoisie) explains the unique contribution Feuchtwanger women added to the public success of Lion Feuchtwanger's generation.

Part II treats biographical connections between Feuchtwanger and the women who played an instrumental role during his exile. Roland Jaeger looks at the extensive correspondence between Lion Feuchtwanger and Lola Humm-Sernau (his long-time secretary in Berlin and Sanary-sur-Mer, France) to show not only the importance of written correspondence but also to point to Sernau's own career and work in exile that so far has received little acknowledgment. William Katin writes about two women Ingrid Warburg and Eleanor Roosevelt who were influential in Lion Feuchtwanger's successful escape to the United States. His essay points to the fact that some women worked behind the scenes, hidden from public and official recognition, in order to offer their skills and help in the fight against Nazi Germany.

Part III offers literary explorations of select Feuchtwanger novels with a particular focus on gendered depiction. Both Franziska Wolf and Helga Schreckenberger discuss Feuchtwanger's novel *Exil* which is part of the *Wartesaal Trilogy*. Wolf addresses the poetics of female death in Feuchtwanger's novel and investigates how these deaths are used to create narrative effects that reinforce gender stereotypes. She argues that in Feuchtwanger's depiction of the moment of death, this is particularly noticeable as the author engineers a dialectic between passive female suffering and active male positioning. Helga Schreckenberger examines the precarious economic and emotional situation that is depicted in Feuchtwanger's novel *Exil* as it reflects on the German exile community in 1935 Paris. Schreckenberger argues that the novel assigns to the concept of exile two different gendered meanings embodied in Sepp and Anna. Sepp exemplifies the nomadic, active, and successful spirit of exile, the figure of "Recke" and Anna embodies the condition of "Elend" as she remains rooted to her pre-exile existence, unsuccessfully searching for financial and domestic stability. In her essay about the *Josephus Trilogy*, Tanja Kinkel explores high-ranking female personalities from Ancient Rome. Kinkel connects Feuchtwanger's depiction of Berenice, Dorion, Mara, and Lucia to questions of acculturation, identity formation, and the experience of exile. Kinkel points out that all three novels reveal an interesting power dynamic between men and women, and argues that in the final analysis, Feuchtwanger reveals an inherent gendered miscommunication that is manifested in the inability to understand each other. Frank Stern continues Kinkel's discussion of Feuchtwanger's female legends and mythologies in ancient times with a Midrash reading of Feuchtwanger's novel *Jephthah and His Daughter*. He shows how Feuchtwanger was aware of the Jewish written and oral tradition and the Midrashim that dealt intensively with daughter and father. Stern argues that Feuchtwanger's work indicates his ongoing literary fascination with female personalities in biblical and later times.

Part IV expands the discussion about women and Lion Feuchtwanger to include a select group of exile women whose exile experience in different parts of the world demonstrates not only gendered challenges that needed to be overcome but also unique artistic and social perspectives that women introduced to their communities and contributed to their surroundings in exile. Jacqueline Vansant discusses exile networks in Minna Lachs' autobiographical reflections to reveal how various networks function in a time of crises. Her essay shows the important role of a variety of formal and informal networks played in Lachs' successful preparations to leave and eventual escape from Nazi Austria. Through the genre of the memoir, Käthe Erichsen offers a reading of exile and gender in Sonia Wachstein's *Hagenberggasse 49* in which she examines the simultaneous conveying of lyrical storytelling and historical testimony. Erichsen's essay explores how the status of exile prompts a negotiation between home and displacement to compose a new identity. Christina Wieder looks at gendered exile in

Argentina. Her essay focuses on Hedy Crilla and Irena Dodal whose film creations provide insight into the kind of concrete emancipation images artists brought from their homelands. Wieder argues that through a form of self-translation their film creations represent their country of origin and simultaneously make elements of their exile country visible. Wieder reads this as a way to offset personal and professional fragmentation caused by the experience of exile. Examining Lotte Lenya, a star performer in the 1920s in some of Bertolt Brecht's plays during the Weimar Republic, Margrit Fröhlich shows how after a slow and almost failed start, Lenya attained a near cult status in America. She became a musical and film star and was known for her genial interpretations of Brecht's and Kurt Weill's work. Camille Jenn-Gastal traces the German-Jewish musicologist Annelise Landau through exile. Although Landau struggled after her arrival in New York, she was able to reestablish her career and ultimately succeeded in her mission to make German-Jewish composers known to the American public. Katrin Sippel addresses women's exile experience in Portugal from the perspective of women's fashion. The essay shows how from the male viewpoint of influential and powerful Portuguese male community leaders, the presence of Jewish women from Germany and Austria was seen as a threat to the more conservative moral values imposed (by state policies) on Portuguese women. Sippel argues that while some women exiles were castigated for their fashion and public assertive behavior, and came into conflict with the law, in the final analysis their presence began to modernize the stringent male–female divide and subsequently allowed Portuguese women to adopt a more independent manner in the public space. In Part V, the book concludes with a return to gendered biographical information as Edgar Feuchtwanger shares his insider commentary on his grand-uncle's relationship with women. By mostly focusing on Lion Feuchtwanger's recently published diaries, he provides a comprehensive review from the perspective of a survivor and softens the tone that sharply criticizes Lion's objectification of women.

 The authors in this volume investigate biographical, historical, literary, cross-cultural, and cross-gender aspects of women and female characters and their influence on Lion Feuchtwanger's personal biography, his writings, and the world in which he lived, as well as women's experience in exile in a more general way. These fifteen chapters written by authors from Austria, England, France, Germany, and the United States provide new insights and evidence of women who had a direct and profound impact on Lion Feuchtwanger's life and creative impulses, as well as women whose contributions impacted the exile experience more broadly. This volume advances exile studies scholarship through its focus on gender, women's roles, and the use of innovative approaches that move beyond traditional biographical surveys by incorporating fashion, art, and popular culture.

PART I

Marta Feuchtwanger and the Feuchtwanger Women

BIRGIT MAIER-KATKIN

1 Marta Feuchtwanger's Ingenuity: Memorializing Lion Feuchtwanger

ABSTRACT

This chapter explores Marta Feuchtwanger's support and personal investment in the literary career of her husband Lion Feuchtwanger. From the beginning of their relationship, Marta gave Lion her undivided support and this continued well beyond his death. The main focus of this chapter will be on the years after Lion's death when Marta began to manage Lion's literary legacy. From her place of exile in Los Angeles, she reached out to a widespread international community to promote Lion's work and to keep exile themes at the center of postwar discourse. The chapter examines how Marta memorialized Lion. It looks at the initiatives she started, the contacts she promoted, and the legacy she created for Lion, for herself, and the field of exile studies. This allows us to examine how the woman who stood by her husband's side throughout their forty-six years of marriage became one of the most outspoken proponents of his work and shaped Lion's legacy well after his death.

Marta Löffler, like Lion Feuchtwanger a native of Munich, encountered Lion for the first time in 1909, shortly before her nineteenth birthday when she attended a house party at the Feuchtwanger home at the invitation of her friend Franziska Feuchtwanger (Lion's sister).[1] Three years later on May 22, 1912, the couple married and shared life together until Lion's death in 1958. Throughout their forty-six years of marriage, Marta gave Lion her undivided support. Marta's interest in promoting her husband's work continued well beyond his death. From her place

---

[1] Andreas Heusler, *Lion Feuchtwanger: München—Emigrant—Weltbürger* (St. Pölten: Residenz Verlag, 2014), 104. See also: Marta Feuchtwanger, *Nur eine Frau: Jahre—Tage—Stunden* (Munich: Knaur, 1983), 7. For more information on the young couple in Munich, see Birgit Maier-Katkin, "Lion und Marta Feuchtwanger: Ein junges Paar in München", in *Feuchtwanger und München*, ed. Tamara Fröhler and Andreas Heusler, vol. 8 (Oxford: Peter Lang, 2022), 27–47.

of exile in Los Angeles, she reached out to a widespread international community not only to promote Lion's literary work but also to create research opportunities for future exile scholars. After an introduction to Marta's life, this chapter focuses on the years after Lion's death when Marta began to manage Lion's literary heritage and promoted his legacy as a major German writer. Looking at Marta's dedication to Lion's work, it explores how Marta influenced Lion's legacy. In particular, it examines what initiatives she started, which contacts she cultivated, and what institutions arose from her relentless effort to promote Lion's work.

Early Years

In 1891 Marta Feuchtwanger was born the third child to a family of Jewish textile merchants in Munich. Starting in her youth, she was a passionate athlete, interested in gymnastics and all sorts of sports activities which lasted into her old age.[2] Three years after Marta met Lion, the couple decided to get married when it became apparent that Marta was pregnant. Sadly, their baby girl died shortly after her birth. After a long honeymoon through Europe and Africa, Lion began to devote himself to writing novels.[3] Marta organized the more practical aspects of married life and showed great interest in Lion's work. She was the first to read his texts; in turn he respected her thoughts and critique. During Hitler's quick rise to power in January 1933, Lion was on a reading tour in America. At that time, he was known as an outspoken critic of Hitler's regime and warned against his return. Marta was skiing in Austria. Both recognized the imminent danger and decided not to return to Germany. Lion first joined Marta in St. Anton, then the couple made their way to

2   Spurred on by his wife, even Lion engaged in daily exercise until the end of his life.
3   Lion Feuchtwanger, *Ein möglichst intensives Leben: Die Tagebücher*, ed. Nele Holdack, Marje Schuetze-Coburn, and Michaela Ullmann (Berlin: Aufbau, 2018), 128–9. Lion's first major success was the novel *Jud Süss* (1925) which launched his international success, followed by *Erfolg* (Success; 1930).

Bern in Switzerland, and from there fled to Southern France. Eventually in 1941, they reached America as part of an adventurous rescue mission. Lion would never return to Germany.[4]

Exile in America

In France as well as in the United States, the Feuchtwanger home became a renowned meeting place for many emigrants. Marta arranged events around Lion's literary activities. She organized public readings, evenings with music, and nurtured the atmosphere of a literary salon. After relocating several times, in 1943 Marta fell in love with a house on 520 Paseo Miramar in the Pacific Palisades which later became known as Villa Aurora.[5] In her interview with Lawrence Weschler, Marta recalls, "[M]y husband and I wanted always to be nearer to the ocean, to have a view to the ocean."[6] The area was still underdeveloped, there were only

4   For more detail, see Marta Feuchtwanger, "The Escape," trans., Adrian Feuchtwanger, in *The Devil in France: My Encounter with Him in the Summer of 1940*, ed. Bill Dotson, Marje Schuetze-Coburn, and Michaela Ullmann (Berlin: Aufbau, 1997), 265–76.

5   Although the Feuchtwanger home is nowadays referred to as Villa Aurora, the origin of the name "Villa Aurora" is unclear. Marta seldomly referred to the house this way and was not sure about the origin. Lamont Johnson a good friend and neighbor of the Feuchtwangers seemed to recall that in the early 1960s the neighborhood began to assign French and Italian names to the Mediterranean-style homes. Marble plates with romantic sounding names were attached to the houses, the names were arbitrarily chosen from a dictionary or map book. This is what happened to the Feuchtwanger house. Randy Young, "Exil im Paradies—Die Feuchtwangers in Pacific Palisades/Exiles in Paradise—The Feuchtwangers in Pacific Palisades," in *10 Jahre Years Villa Aurora 1995–2005*, ed. Villa Aurora (Munich: Dölling und Galitz Verla, 2005), 12–21. Here 13–14.

6   Lawrence Weschler, Assistant Editor, UCLA, Oral History Program, Los Angeles, CA, 1978, in An Émigré Life: Munich, Berlin, Sanary, Pacific Palisades: Marta Feuchtwanger, vol. 1, interviewed by Lawrence M. Weschler, Oral History Program (Los Angeles: University of California, 1976), Tape Number: XXII, Side One, August 22, 1975. 1144–5.

nine houses at the time. The house, Marta and Lion were interested in,
had stood empty after the bankruptcy of its developer and did not attract buyers. At that time gas was rationed, gas prices were high, and few
homeowners were willing to live in the steep hills far from downtown Los
Angeles, far from schools, stores, and doctors.[7] Marta was neither bothered by the remoteness from Los Angeles nor the horrible condition of
the house, she recalls, "[the look of t]he house was terrible. But I fell in
love of the view: that was the only thing I liked about the house. Because
the other things—in the basement, the spider webs were so thick, you
needed an axe to go through. You couldn't see anything, it was just so
neglected …"[8] Despite the initial dilapidated state of the home, Marta
and Lion immediately fell in love with the phenomenal ocean view onto
the Pacific Ocean and Santa Monica Bay. After the dirt was removed,
the couple enjoyed the Spanish-style home (a recreation of a small castle
in Spain) as well as the building materials that had been brought from
Europe[9] (Figure 2). Marta explains, "The ceilings, the wood of the ceilings, they brought from Spain, and the fountain in the patio is from
Italy."[10] The neighborhood of Pacific Palisades with its Mediterranean
flora and climate reminded the couple of Europe.[11] Marta and Lion were

---

7   Young, *10 Jahre*, 16.
8   Weschler, Tape Number: XXII, Side One, August 22, 1975. 1147.
9   Marta comments on the fact that the builder used blueprints which belonged to a
     house in Spain "in the neighborhood of Seville which was an old castle … . It was
     not a big castle. They found not only the castle, which was the style which they
     wanted, but also they found the blueprints there … They build the house here ex-
     actly after the blueprints," in Weschler, Tape Number: XXII, Side One, August 22,
     1975. 1150–1.
10   Weschler, Tape Number: XXII, Side One, August 22, 1975. 1151.
11   Marta's real estate agent was an Englishman. She recalls, "All the others couldn't
     understand that I was insisting on a view over the ocean … . But this man from
     England—the English people always went to Italy to have a good time, so he knew
     what that means—he found this hill." Tape Number: XXII, Side One, August 22,
     1975, 1145. Marta recalls that the builder brought electricity, gas, and water to the
     area and began to build houses in Spanish style, "[T]he whole area has Spanish
     names all around—Miramar and all those names, and Castellammare." Weschler,
     Tape Number: XXII, Side One, August 22, 1975. 1150.

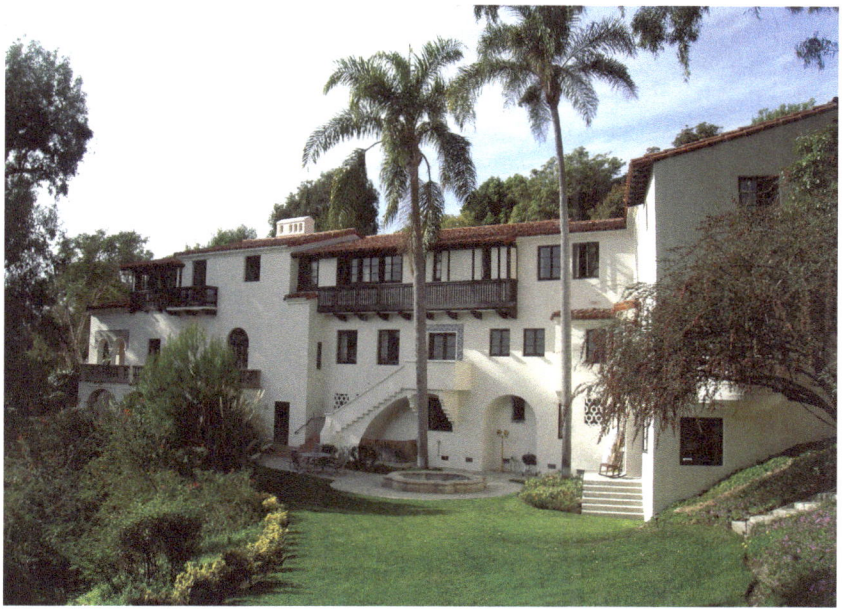

Figure 2. Villa Aurora. Photograph by Boris Schaarschmidt.

excited about the prospect of a large garden.[12] Randy Young writes, "They purchased more lots for privacy, built paths down the hillside and bridges over the ravines; Marta planted trees and designed flowerbeds, with roses and seasonal varieties. The garden was a delight to them both."[13] For Marta—who was a passionate swimmer—this was an ideal location.[14]

Even in exile, Lion enjoyed a successful writing career and so the couple was able to afford the necessary repair work and the long car rides. Marta organized parties and social engagements in their home. The Feuchtwangers sent invitations to public readings and evenings of music. At times, the visitors were treated to Marta's legendary homemade apple strudel. Among

12 Marta explains, "Later on we bought even … more lots … . I planted trees, I said, because you make paper out of trees and a writer needs paper …" Weschler, Tape Number: XXII, Side One, August 22, 1975. 1162. See also, Young, *10 Jahre*, 15.
13 Young, *10 Jahre*, 16.
14 Ibid.

the guests, one could find famous artists and prominent people such as Charlie Chaplin, Bertolt Brecht, Ludwig Marcuse, Charles Laughton, Ingrid Bergmann, Thomas, and Katja Mann.[15] Due to Lion's international success, as well as Marta's lively spirit, and a large circle of friends, the couple enjoyed a productive and busy social life. After Lion Feuchtwanger died in December 1958, his wife Marta survived him by almost thirty years.

Marta the Executor of Lion's Literary Heritage

Marta was a person who self-confidently pursued her path in life. In the face of severe challenges, such as the loss of her child, the experiences of two world wars, exile from Nazi Germany, and even Lion's countless affairs, she had an ability to continue despite setbacks.[15] Marta's biographer Manfred Flügge maintains that while financially and socially dependent on her husband, Marta nevertheless held on to her own freedoms. The life Lion offered her was extraordinary and, in many ways, a blessing as she could construct her own independent life. By accepting his literary heritage and shaping it after Lion's death, Marta completed his story.[17] Flügge writes:

> Zuletzt führte sie eine ironische Existenz, ein abgeleitetes Leben. Sie wusste genau, dass das Dasein als »Dichterwitwe« etwas Groteskes haben kann. Witwe ist kein Beruf, soll sie gesagt haben. Sie akzeptierte diese Rolle mit Selbstironie. Lions Leben und Werk, abgeschlossen und zum akademischen Forschungsgegenstand geworden, waren auch ein Teil ihres Lebens und wie ihr Haus zum Ausstellungsstück geworden. Sie äußerte ihre Sicht der Dinge, kannte sich blendend aus in seinem Werk, als wäre es das ihre. In gewissem Sinne war es das auch.[18]

15   Ingo Herman, ed., *Marta Feuchtwanger Leben mit Lion: Gespräch mit Reinhart Hoffmeister in der Reihe "Zeugen des Jahrhunderts"* (Göttingen: Lamuv Verlag, 1991), footnote 45, 105.

16   Manfred Flügge, *Die vier Leben der Marta Feuchtwanger: Biographie* (Berlin: Aufbau, 2008), 394.

17   Ibid., 395.

18   Ibid., 397–8. All translations are mine, unless otherwise indicated.

[In the end, Marta lived an ironic existence, a strange life. She was keenly aware that the life of a poet's widow can be fraught with grotesqueness. She claimed that to be a widow is not a profession. She accepted this role with self-irony. Lion's life and work, now finished and subject to academic research, was also part of her life and like her house had become an item to be exhibited. She offered her opinion, was well acquainted with his work, as if it were her own. In a way, it was just that.]

After her husband's death, Marta was determined to promote Lion's cultural legacy, to preserve his success and literary contributions for posterity (Figure 3). In this she succeeded, even though she lived abroad and in exile far away from the two newly emerging postwar German nations.

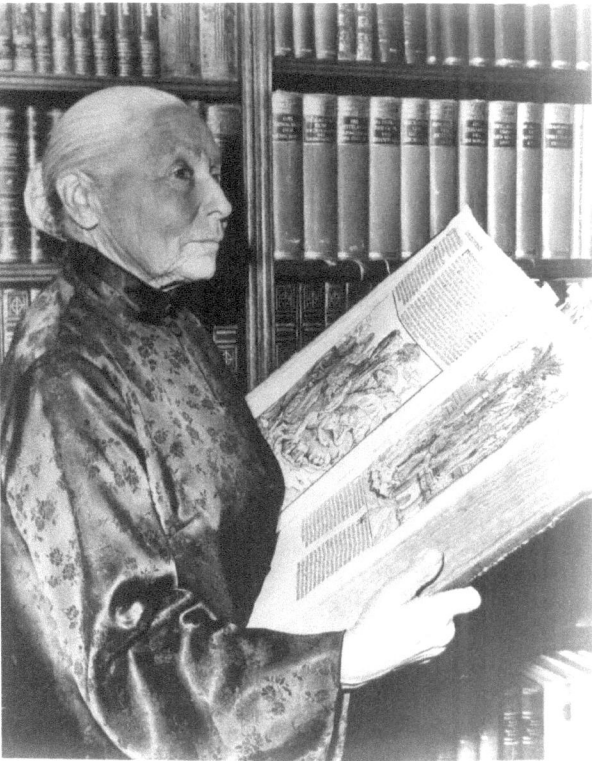

Figure 3. Marta Feuchtwanger holding *Nuremberg Chronicle* (1493) in Villa Aurora. Feuchtwanger Papers, USC Libraries, University of Southern California.

Administering Lion's Literary Legacy

In his last will and testament, Lion left his wife the house and all possessions.[19] For Marta, the moment had come to secure Lion's success and
fame by networking with the literary community and securing the books
and property that Lion had left behind. Lion and Marta had no heirs.
Marta was worried about the future of Lion's extensive book collection
that had grown steadily. Just between 1941 to Lion's death in 1958, approximately 30,000 books had been added.[20] Marta had various options to
consider since there were several universities in and around Los Angeles.
Harold von Hofe, a personal friend of Marta's and professor at the
University of Southern California (USC), stepped in and offered to establish a connection with his institution. Marta happily accepted. Several
months after Lion's death, von Hofe convinced Marta to sign over the
books and the house to USC.[21] In 1959 the following agreement between
Marta and the University was established: the house and property (except
Marta's clothing and jewelry) as well as Lion's extensive library was to be
administered by USC. The university agreed to take on all the costs for
insurance and upkeep of the house. The contract also included that after
Marta's death, USC would be able to sell the house and use the money
to create a space on university grounds to house Lion's book collection.
Together with Lion's former secretary, Hilde Waldo, Marta managed
Lion's literary heritage, the library, and house; while the university took

19   Lion's will from September 22, 1952, states: "I give, devise and bequeath all the
      property and estate of every kind and description […] to my wife, Marta Loeffler
      Feuchtwanger." Ibid., 359.
20   Schuetze-Coburn writes that between the year 1941 (when Lion arrived in
      Southern California) and his death, "During these seventeen years, he acquired
      nearly 30,000 volumes, meaning that he added an average of roughly 1,700 books
      each year." Marje Schuetze-Coburn, "The History of the Feuchtwanger Memorial
      Library," in *Against the Eternal Yesterday: Essays Commemorating the Legacy of Lion
      Feuchtwanger*, eds, Bill Dotson, Marje Schuetze-Coburn and Michaela Ullmann
      (Los Angeles: USC Libraries, 2009), 66–79. Here 71.
21   Ibid., 71.

on responsibility for the home and Lion's most valuable books.[22] With this arrangement, Marta was able to live in her home until the end of her life. She was employed as the first curator of the Feuchtwanger Memorial Library and received a monthly salary from the university.[23] Marta was happy that the house and Lion's books would be preserved and that with the financial assistance of the university, she was able to administer and watch over Lion's legacy. With the help of Lion's former secretary, Hilde Waldo, Marta managed the library and house, and welcomed visitors from all over the world. She shaped Lion's image by corresponding with publishing houses, scholars, and journalists worldwide and was willing to speak out whenever literary and biographical questions arose. She managed book and film rights, and accepted invitations to symposia about Lion's work or more generally about the topic of exile.[24]

Guided Tours: Marta Memorializes Lion

Marta became well known for her personally guided house tours (Figure 4). Visitors from all over the world enjoyed the individual attention as Marta offered a narrated tour throughout the Feuchtwanger home to keep the memory of Lion alive.[25] The demand for tours was so high that she had to create a waiting list for her visitors.[26] Her dedication to this task is reflected in the many thank you letters written to Marta. Diplomats from Germany as well as England were impressed by Marta's skills. They noticed how she played her charm to memorialize Lion's work and her life with him. The sherry that Marta served became legendary among the

22 Flügge, *Vier Leben*, 360–1.
23 Flügge, *Vier Leben*, 360.
24 Ibid., 361.
25 University of Southern California Library, Special Collections, Marta Feuchtwanger Papers, Box 7a, Folder 3.
26 For a sample of a waiting list, see University of Southern California Library, Special Collections, Marta Feuchtwanger Papers, Box 7a, Folder 6.

guests. In a letter from 1968, the General Consul of Germany, Werner Montag, expresses his appreciation for the warm hospitality and conveys his fascination with Marta's well-crafted tour. To accentuate his gratitude, the Consul gifts Marta a bottle of sherry to replenish the one she shared with the guests.[27] The British Consul goes into great detail about Lion's impressive book collection conveying how Marta's extensive knowledge about Lion's work highlights her talent and skill as tour guide. He writes:

> Your husband's library is indeed superb (…) It is scarcely surprising that they [books] have been translated in practically every language in the world. I was fascinated to see the Chinese-Shanghai pirated edition. It gave me immense pleasure, as British Consul-General, to see the Shakespeare folio and also the Ben Johnson. His edition of the Nuremberg Chronicles of 1493 with their splendid engravings is just one more treasure. The Beaumarchais edition of Voltaire and your delightful anecdote was another source of interest and delight. I had also not known before that Brecht was a protégé of your husband's. But then coming down to more earthly things, we were also both grateful for and charmed by the sherry and the Crabmeat biscuits.[28]

In a letter to Peter Fuerst, Marta grants a glimpse into her famed house tours:

> I show the library to visitors from all over the world but especially to American and German professors and students. I always start with the German classic collection. It consists predominantly of first editions. The room is entirely surrounded by books, you can also see a tea cart where Lion and I used to have our tea while he read from his manuscript. On the one side there is the complete first edition of Goethe which includes the first edition of Faust part II, as well as a Heine first edition and a very rare edition of Heine's last poems that was found in his room in Paris … Then we walk to the biggest room with a view of the ocean: the international collection beginning with Greek and Latin books … Three steps up in the hall is Lion's oeuvre approximately in 30 languages among them Japanese, Chinese and Indian. Then the first editions in German, insofar as they have not been destroyed … From the hall one enters the historical collection. One wall with world history, art history, music history, biographies and philosophies … Then upstairs in the hall the three *Kupferbibeln* from

27   Letter from Werner Montag in University of Southern California Library, Special Collections, Marta Feuchtwanger Papers, Box 7a, Folder 3.

28   University of Southern California Library, Special Collections, Marta Feuchtwanger Papers, Box 7a, Folder 3.

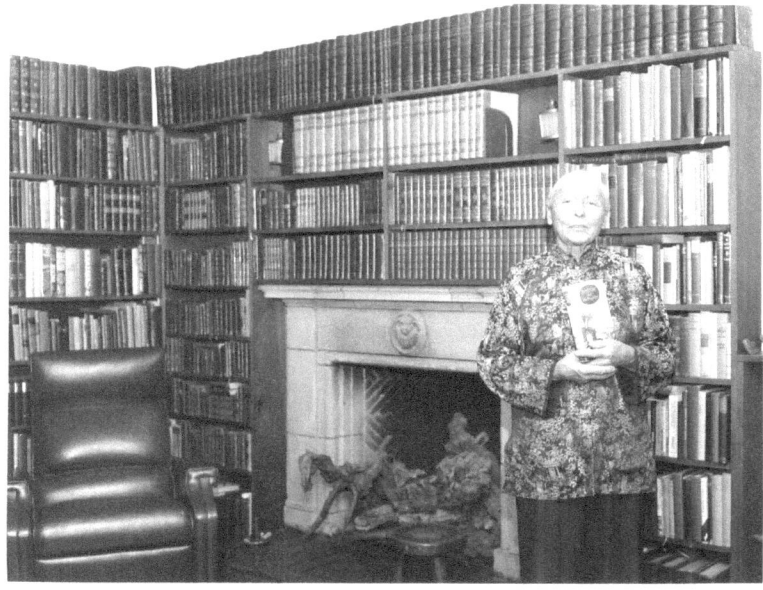

Figure 4. Marta Feuchtwanger in Lion Feuchtwanger's study holding a copy of
Jephthah and His Daughter, Villa Aurora, 1964. Feuchtwanger Papers,
USC Libraries, University of Southern California.

Scheuzer, as well as a two volume luxury edition of Flavius Josephus … On the main
wall books in French about the French Revolution, Napoleon, and ancient regimes.[29]

Social Networking: Marta Shapes Lion's Literary Legacy

House tours were not the only publicity and outreach that Marta organized; she also continued to plan house parties and attended many social events all around Los Angeles. In fact, Marta's social calendar became

---

29   University of Southern California Library, Special Collections, Lion Feuchtwanger
     Papers, Box 7a, Folder 11. Italics added by author.

busier after Lion's death. At times she would attend three different events in an evening. She received invitations to many official functions in Los Angeles and was a guest at consulates of different nations.[30] Lawrence Weschler writes, "... she seemed to appear at every major cultural event—concerts, theaters, films, art openings, consular and university receptions—the living embodiment of a noble tradition, a bridge with the past ... . In short, she had become an institution."[31] Marta more and more shaped and personified Lion's literary legacy. She not only preserved his oeuvre for posterity but also became Lion's devoted agent to the literary world. In this role, Marta was noticed and known for her distinctive personality. Manfred Flügge writes:

> Sie konnte zuweilen recht autoritär sein, sogar rechthaberisch. Doch in der richtigen Gesellschaft zeigten sich ihr Humor und ihr pointensicheres Erzähltalent. Sie hatte immer Anekdoten parat, über Alma Mahler-Werfel, Thomas Mann, Charlie Chaplin. Sie lebte in der realen wie in der imaginären Welt, die Lion zugänglich gemacht hatte, aber ihre letzte Rolle mit ihrer auffälligen und wirksamen Präsenz in Los Angeles hat sie allein geschaffen.[32]

> [At times, she could be rather authoritarian, even opinionated. However, with the right company she revealed her humor and ability to deliver a good punchline. She always had an anecdote ready about Alma Mahler-Werfel, Thomas Mann, Charlie Chaplin. Sie lived in the real as well as imaginary world that Lion had opened for her, but her last role with her flamboyant and effective presence in Los Angeles, is something she created all by herself.]

As time passed, Marta added her own distinctive personal note to the public memory of Lion's work and life. The cause seemed to rejuvenate her. Following his extensive interviews with Marta, Weschler came to admire Marta's social, outgoing, and energetic personality and observed

---

30 Flügge, *Vier Leben*, 365.
31 Lawrence Weschler, Assistant Editor, UCLA, Oral History Program, Los Angeles, CA, 1978, in *An Émigré Life: Munich, Berlin, Sanary, Pacific Palisades: Marta Feuchtwanger*, vol. 1, interviewed by Lawrence M. Weschler, Oral History Program (Los Angeles: University of California, 1976), xxv–xxvi.
32 Flügge, *Vier Leben*, 398.

in her a person who sought to impress with intelligence and wit. Weschler reports:

> During the months of our interviews, she seemed as fresh and sassy as the young woman whose tale she was recounting. Occasionally we had to cut our sessions short because she had to drive off to yet another function: at age eighty-four she was chauffeuring friends a generation younger than she. She disarmed with her dry wit, endeared with her glowing charm, fascinated with her penetrating intellect.[33]

This focus on Lion's work allowed Marta to create a specific memory of Lion's past and to weave her own energy and life story into that of her husband's.

Revitalization of Lion's Legacy through Transatlantic Connections

Beginning in the 1960s, Marta did not only promote Lion's heritage in America but also sought contact with leading public officials in Germany. Due to the early postwar period when both Germanies were foremost preoccupied with rebuilding from the rubble and began to pursue different political directions, exile authors and their publications did not always receive the public attention they might have deserved.[34] In the late 1960s, however, renewed interest in the work of exile authors began to emerge. For example, in 1967, a Sister City Partnership between Berlin and Los Angeles was initiated in which Marta was involved.[35] Marta

---

33   Weschler, *Oral History*, xxvi.
34   In the case of Lion Feuchtwanger and Bertolt Brecht their reception in West Germany was hindered by the anticommunist literary politics of the West. This was different in East Germany where exiles and their work were more recognized and became part of the literary scene. In fact, the Aufbau publishing house was founded as an antifascist publication house with an explicit focus on exile from Nazi Germany.
35   Flügge, *Vier Leben*, 373.

revitalized her contact with Willi Brandt whom she had met in the 1930s.[36] Looking for opportunities to rehabilitate what the Nazis had destroyed, Marta asked Brandt (then Foreign Minister of West Germany) to change the name of her former residential street in Berlin back to Mahlerstraße (Mahler Street), the name it carried before the Nazis came to power. While Brandt could not grant this request, the rekindled relationship reopened a pathway to Germany for Marta. Brandt invited Marta to visit Berlin.[37] When the (West) Berlin Academy of the Arts created a special exhibit for the exile works of Lion Feuchtwanger, Marta accepted Willy Brandt's invitation. As a result, in April 1969 she traveled for the first time—since her forced exile—to postwar Germany. From this time on, Marta began to keep Lion's legacy alive in an international setting.[38] During her stay in Berlin, she visited the exhibit dedicated to Lion at the Academy of the Arts.[39] Her determined engagement on Lion's behalf initiated further public memory projects. Marta was shown plans for a "Lion-Feuchtwanger Weg" in the newly developed section of Berlin Gropiusstadt. During her Berlin visit, she was invited to spend one day in East Berlin. The Aufbau publishing house honored Marta with a banquet. During her day in East Germany, she met with Walter Janka who at the time was working on a film script and adaptation of Lion's *Goya* novel.[40] After her stay in Berlin, Marta cultivated and strengthened these transatlantic ties even further. Together with the Berlin Academy of Arts, she created a Lion Feuchtwanger Prize for historical prose in the 1970s. The prize is presented on July 7 (the anniversary of Lion's birthday) by the Berlin Academy of the Arts. It is worth €7,500 and has been awarded yearly from 1971 to 1992, and a little less regularly subsequently.[41]

---

36   Ibid..
37   Ibid.
38   Ibid., 374.
39   Ibid.
40   Ibid., 375. Janka had just finished his prison term under the Ulbricht government. He supposedly assured Marta that freedom of expression was possible in the GDR.
41   <https://www.adk.de/de/akademie/preise-stiftungen/L_Feuchtwanger_Pr eis.htm>.

Marta's efforts of reaching out to postwar Germany were met with interest and, in turn, sparked new transatlantic connections. In 1981, the journalist Volker Skierka traveled together with the newly elected Berlin mayor, Richard von Weizsäcker, to Los Angeles to personally get to know the 90-year-old Marta and widow of the author who wrote the novel *Erfolg*. Following this visit, Skierka published an article in the *Süddeutsche Zeitung*, in which he describes his encounter with Marta. He presents her as a beautiful-looking woman who recounts Lion's life with much humor and wit.[42] Subsequently, Skierka began to work on a biography of Lion which he published in 1984.[43] Marta gave Skierka her full support, locating photos, documents, and letters that she found throughout the house.[44]

A Feuchtwanger Literary and Cultural Heritage Site: Villa Aurora

When Marta Feuchtwanger died on October 25, 1987, at the age of 94 (she was buried next to Lion in the Woodlawn Cemetery in Santa Monica), the increasingly dilapidated Villa Aurora was going to be sold. It is at this point that Marta's relentless efforts on Lion's behalf, her visits to Germany, her personal connections to influential and public figures in Germany, as well as public appearances (on both continents) spark a major support of Lion's legacy that would last beyond both of their deaths. While Lion's work was known to some in Germany, it was Marta's presence and meetings with key politicians and officials that preserved Villa Aurora in Los Angeles as a cultural site that in time would be known

---

42 Volker Skierka, "Kalifornien: Besuch bei Marta Feuchtwanger: Ein Gesicht, geformt vom Jahrhundert," *Süddeutsche Zeitung* 274 (November 28, 1981): 3.

43 Volker Skierka, *Lion Feuchtwanger: Eine Biographie* (Berlin: Quadriga, 1984).

44 Volker Skierka, "Encounters with Lion and Marta Feuchtwanger", in *Against the Eternal Yesterday: Essays Commemorating the Legacy of Lion Feuchtwanger*, eds, Bill Dotson, Marje Schuetze-Coburn and Michaela Ullmann (Los Angeles: USC Libraries, 2009), 50–3. Here 52. See also, Flügge, Vier Leben, 389–90.

internationally for exile memorialization. Already in September 1987, lifelong friends of the Feuchtwangers (such as USC Professor Harald von Hofe, Ludwig Marcuse, and Professor Stanley Townsend) informed the Feuchtwanger biographer Skierka (who then worked as a correspondent for the *Süddeutsche Zeitung* in Hamburg) about the pending sale of the Villa. Skierka reacted quickly and was able to gain the support of leading German politicians (among them chancellor Willy Brandt),[45] as well as prominent authors, the German PEN-Club, and numerous other well-known celebrities of public life and in the media.[46] Support for Lion's literary heritage was discussed in the German Parliament which reached a wide consensus (involving all political parties) to preserve the Feuchtwanger home as cultural heritage site of exile. This initiative was motivated by a desire to signal to the world that German postwar society had learned its historical lesson and that the exiles driven out by Nazi Germany are recognized as part of the German heritage.[47] In December 1987, the University of Southern California was told that there were efforts in Germany to provide donations to preserve the memory of Lion Feuchtwanger. The German government initiated its intention to preserve Lion's residence as a German literary heritage site in Los Angeles to acknowledge Lion's extraordinary significance for the exile community. This was to benefit Germany as well as the United States. With the help of many public officials from politics and society, as well as institutions, a kind of Villa Massimo was created for the Feuchtwanger's house.[48]

---

45 The interest reached across party lines and attracted the attention of high political officials in West Germany. In addition to Willy Brandt, support was also extended from other top officials such as Hans-Jochen Vogel (chair of the SPD), foreign minister Hans-Dietrich Genscher (FDP), President Richard von Weizsäcker (CDU)—all of whom had met Marta Feuchtwanger in person—as well as the *Kreis der Freunde und Förderer der Villa Aurora e.V.* and several artists. For more information, see Marianne Heuwagen, "Martas Vision," in *10 Jahre Years Villa Aurora 1995–2005*, ed., Villa Aurora (Munich: Dölling und Galitz, 2005), 22–9. Here 23. See also, Skierka, Encounters, 52.

46 Heuwagen, "Martas Vision," 23.

47 Ibid., 24.

48 Flügge, *Vier Leben*, 405.

In order to save the Feuchtwanger's house, foundations were created in 1988: one in Berlin called "Kreis der Freunde und Förderer der Villa Aurora e.V." (Friends and Sponsors of the Villa Aurora) and one in Los Angeles under the name "Foundation for European-American Relations."[49] The German Parliament dedicated public money from the "Stiftung Deutsche Klassenlotterie Berlin" (German Lottery Endowment) and the German Foreign Office. Additional funds were made available later between 1992 and 1994 when expensive and complicated renovations to secure the building had to be undertaken.[50] After the Villa was purchased by the foundation,[51] the library, archive, furniture, and art remained in the possession of the university, while the garden and house became the property of the foundation.[52] Nowadays the house has been placed under historical protection. In this way, Marta's memory work continues beyond her death with the help of the two German-American foundations and is expanded to include a broader spectrum of exile studies and the preservation of the arts.[53] Since 1995 Villa Aurora functions as an international artist retreat. It was officially opened on December 1, 1995, when the first fellows arrived (authors Irina Liebmann and artist Lisa Schmitz).[54]

49 Ibid.
50 In order to use the villa as a professional center, the foundation of the house had to be raised, and new concrete pillars were inserted. Air conditioning, heating, e-lectric wires, and pipes all were done in a way that the outside of the house was not changed. See, Heuwagen, "Martas Vision," 25–6.
51 The German Parliament with the approval of all parties promised to contribute on an annual basis 500,000 DM to organize cultural programs at the Villa Aurora. See, Heuwagen, 10 Jahre, 24. From the money of the Stiftung Deutsche Klassenlotterie in Berlin (DKLB) the German foundation was able to purchase the Villa Aurora. See, Flügge, *Vier Leben*, 406.
52 Marje Schuetze-Coburn, "Die Feuchtwanger Memorial Library an der University of Southern California", in *10 Jahre Years Villa Aurora 1995–2005*, ed. Villa Aurora (Munich: Dölling und Galitz, 2005), 32.
53 Flügge, *Vier Leben*, 405.
54 The initial fellowship holders did not spend the night at the Villa, instead they stayed at the Getty Center. The first to spend the night at the Villa Aurora was the playwright Heiner Müller because he was unhappy at the Getty Center. See, Heuwagen, "Martas Vision," 27.

Starting in 1995 there has been an integrated administrative and program structure between Berlin and Los Angeles. The Berlin office is located
in the Jägerstraße 23 (nearby the DAAD)[55] and manages the finances and
the yearly selection of the fellows. In addition, there are transatlantic
events which promote a lively cultural exchange between Berlin and Los
Angeles, that is, Germany and the United States. Among the events are
film screenings, author readings, lectures, concerts, and musical encounters between European and American composers, symposia, conferences,
film premiers, discussions, and other special programs.[56] The main focus of
Villa Aurora concentrates on the fellow programs for artists in residence.
Each year sixteen artists are selected from the areas of film, music, visual
art, and literature. The fellows are selected in Berlin and invited to stay
at the Villa Aurora in Los Angeles for three months. In addition, there is
also an annual "Feuchtwanger Fellowship" for an author who is forced to
live in exile because of political persecution or whose work is censored in
the home country.[57]

When taking the strong monetary and cultural transatlantic connections into account that were initiated by Marta's enthusiastic efforts to
promote Lion's work, one has to acknowledge that her self-chosen task to
preserve Lion's literary heritage for posterity did succeed. Today the Villa
Aurora is a memorial to Lion Feuchtwanger and exile studies. It has become
a public site that promotes artistic creation and cultural exchange for artists from all over the world. Every once in a while, the terrace providing a
magical view of the ocean turns into a place for Hollywood parties when
a German film is nominated for an Academy Award. Flügge points out
that the name "Villa Aurora" which was used more commonly after 1987
seems fitting as it stands for continuity and new beginnings, for memory

55   The close location to the DAAD was a stroke of luck as it promoted exchanges
     about the structure and organization of the DAAD selection jury. It helped the
     foundation in setting up its own selection process regarding fellowships in the area
     of literature, visual art, music and film. Mechthild Borries-Knopp, "10 Jahre Villa
     Aurora—eine Bilanz," in *10 Jahre Years Villa Aurora 1995–2005*, ed. Villa Aurora
     (Munich: Dölling und Galitz, 2005), 34–41. Here 34.
56   Ibid., 34–5 and 38.
57   <https://www.vatmh.org/en/feuchtwanger-fellowship.html>, Ibid., 36–7.

and collaboration, and for creativity and reassurance.[58] Since Marta's death, the Villa has remained an attraction for researchers and artists alike.[59]

Marta's Ingenuity: Feuchtwanger Research and Exile Studies

By donating Lion's library to the university, Marta secured a place where the extensive book collection would not only be adequately preserved but also made available to a broad spectrum of scholars. In 1995, the University of Southern California established the Feuchtwanger Memorial Library. The most valuable and oldest books (around 8,000 volumes) were placed in the climatized rooms of Doheny Memorial Library's Special Collections which also preserves the papers of other German-speaking emigrants. The remaining 22,000 books remain on permanent loan in the Villa Aurora.[60] This memorialization and institutionalization of Feuchtwanger and exile studies generated the creation of a scholarly society. To enhance the scholarship of Lion Feuchtwanger and other exiles, as well as spark new research directions, in 2001 researchers from the United States and Europe founded the International Feuchtwanger Society (IFS).[61] The Society organizes conferences that convene every two years alternating between Europe and U.S.C. and Villa Aurora in Los Angeles. It encourages scholarship and Feuchtwanger news by circulating the *Feuchtwanger*

---

58   From the time Villa Aurora was instated in 1995 as a culture center and fellowship residence, it has served an unprecedented role promoting German culture in Los Angeles in the cosmopolitan spirit of Lion and Marta Feuchtwanger. Flügge, *Vier Leben*, 407.

59   Ibid., 364.

60   After Lion's death more books were added. Visitors of the Villa showed their appreciation for the tours and hospitality by gifting signed books. Schuetze-Coburn, "Memorial Library," 72.

61   Ian Wallace, "The International Feuchtwanger Society," in *Against the Eternal Yesterday: Essays Commemorating the Legacy of Lion Feuchtwanger*, eds, Bill Dotson, Marje Schuetze-Coburn and Michaela Ullmann (Los Angeles: Figueroa Press, 2009), 80–5.

and Exile Studies Journal and publishes the *Feuchtwanger Studies Series*, an anthology that presents research about Feuchtwanger and other exiles during the Nazi regime.

Conclusion

Beginning with her marriage to Lion Feuchtwanger, Marta proved to be one of his strongest supporters and promoters. She supported her husband's career during his lifetime and actively endorsed his legacy after his death. In the process Marta not only shaped the memory of Lion and his legacy but also fashioned her own image. To the world she portrayed herself as an athletic, fashionable, strong, witty, energetic, and intelligent woman who stood by her husband during good and bad days, during Nazi persecution, exile, countless affairs, physical hardship, and great literary successes. In a conversation with Reinhard Hoffmeister, Marta is asked if she ever had the urge to create something of her own, in her youth or later, something apart from her husband or even something against him.[62] To this Marta responded:

> Ich war immer nur seine Frau und froh, wenn er mich zu Rate zog, wenn ich mitarbeiten konnte. Da war kein Augenblick der Langeweile, es war immer aufregend, mit ihm zu leben … Ich hatte nie den Gedanken, mich selbständig zu machen. Man hat mir oft angeboten, als Schauspielerin zu arbeiten … . Dazu hatte ich nie ein Bedürfnis.[63]

> [I have always been only his wife. I was happy when he asked for my advice and I was allowed to participate. There was never a dull moment, to be with him was always exciting … I never entertained the thought to be on my own. Often I was offered to work as an actress … . I never had a desire to do such a thing.]

---

62   Ingo Hermann, ed., *Marta Feuchtwanger: Leben mit Lion: Gespräch mit Reinhart Hoffmeister in der Reihe "Zeugen des Jahrhunderts"* (Göttingen: Lamuv Verlag, 1991), 38.

63   Hermann, *Marta*, 38–9.

Marta never concealed her enthusiasm for Lion's personality and career. Her marriage was a desired partnership that complemented her own skills and goals. She was an outgoing energetic person who could have carved a public career of her own right, yet Lion allowed her to participate in his career with the freedom to pursue her own ambitions. She knew how to enrich his life with the outcome that even after their deaths both remained at the center of public attention.

Marta chose to make Lion's literary success part of her life story. This is evident from the beginning of their marriage and documented in her conversation with Hoffmeister. When Hoffmeister remarked that she had a major influence on Lion's success as a novelist, Marta explained that when Lion was a young writer, he only wanted to write theater plays and that she made it clear to him that novels would be more profitable. With great confidence Marta asserted, "Ich habe ziemlichen Einfluß auf ihn gehabt." (I had a lot of impact on him.)[64] This reveals that in the dynamic of their relationship, Marta was not merely a supportive wife but also Lion's advocate and counsel who actively advised and guided his work. Having survived Lion by almost thirty years, it is therefore not surprising that Marta is remembered as the dynamic widow who shaped Lion's image and became an exile celebrity in her own right.

After Lion's death, Marta reinvented herself as a person who ingeniously generates institutional memorization of their traumatic past that—due to the widespread international interest in Lion's work—transcends nations. Through her energetic youthful enthusiasm that lasted into her old age, she made a public commitment to the cause of exile and exile studies. In this, the fruits of her vibrant energy seemed to have outlived her. With the help of many personal and public friends, a large amount of public funding and transatlantic support, her relentless advocacy for exile studies flourishes well into the future. In the final analysis one has to acknowledge that Marta was a successful and ingenious executor of Lion's literary estate. Due to her advocacy, Lion's and Marta's legacy is preserved for subsequent generations as can be seen in the effective international exile work of the

---

64   Ibid., 39.

Villa Aurora through its two foundations, the success and public interest in USC's Feuchtwanger Memorial Library, recent press releases,[65] theater productions, as well as the continued scholarship by Feuchtwanger scholars, and the publications and activities of the International Feuchtwanger Society.

65   A recent reissue of Feuchtwanger's novel *The Oppermanns* generated renewed public attention that was captured in the *New York Times*. See, Sean Nye, "Feuchtwanger's Return in America: A Major Reissue of the *Oppermanns* Sparks New Interest," *Feuchtwanger and Exile Studies Journal* 38 (2023): 17–22.

HEIKE SPECHT

2 Women of Valor: The Feuchtwanger Women—An Untold Family History

ABSTRACT

A popular anecdote in the Feuchtwanger family was that Auguste Hahn brought ugliness into the family. The untold story, however, is that without her business connections, know-how, and dowry she brought into her marriage with Jakob Löw Feuchtwanger, the family business would not have flourished in the way it did. This family lore shows how one-sided and underexposed the female side of this family history has been represented throughout the decades. As "Women of Valor," Auguste, Fanny, Rahel, Marta, and numerous other women of the Feuchtwanger family have been influential in more than one way. Women, like Auguste, raised their children to be good Jews, headed large households, did the bookkeeping, were businesswomen, and equal partners in their marriage. Later in the nineteenth and early twentieth century, the Feuchtwanger women became elegant ladies of the house with great ambitions for their husbands and children; they acted as social and professional pioneers. In times of political persecution, as with the example of Marta, the women became true lifesavers. It is clear that in the Feuchtwanger family, there were not only strong patriarchs but also impressive matriarchs.

It is a well-known fact that Lion Feuchtwanger early on broke with the orthodoxy of the "Feuchtwanger Clan," as this was something he liked to point out. Not surprisingly, his remarks about his upbringing and family tend to sound harsh.[1] Yet, despite all of his criticism, he was also proud of the deep ancestral roots that connected his family to Bavaria. In fact, the history of his family goes back well into the eighteenth

---

[1] Lion Feuchtwanger: "Aus meinem Leben," in Colloquium, Nr. 7, 1964, 15–17. Lion Feuchtwanger, "Selbstdarstellung, 1933," in *Ein Buch nur für meine Freunde*, (Frankfurt/Main: Fischer, 1984), originally published under the title: *Centum opuscula. Eine Auswahl* (Rudolstadt: Greifenverlag, 1956), 35–61. Lion Feuchtwanger, "Der Autor über sich selbst," in *Ein Buch nur für meine Freunde*, 365–9.

century. Feuchtwanger's forefathers and foremothers lived in the large and flourishing Jewish community of Fürth in Bavaria. An anecdote from the late seventeenth century illustrates how influential the Jews were in Fürth. It was customary that the local night watchman began his call every evening with "Gute Nacht, Ihr lieben Christen" [Good night, dear Christians].

The Jewish community, however, took offense at this and submitted a request to the city council. Shortly thereafter the call was changed to "Gute Nacht, Ihr Lieben Herren" [Good night, dear gentlemen].[2] This story speaks to the self-confidence and vitality of the Jewish community. Whether the women of Fürth took umbrage at the implied gender bias is not reported. After all, the women, whether Jewish or Christian, were not addressed by the watchmen's call at all.

This exclusion of the women of Fürth leads smoothly into the theme of this *tour de femmes* that sheds light on the other half of the Feuchtwangers which has remained hidden in the shadows of family history. This author wants to demonstrate that the women of the Feuchtwanger family have been influential in more ways than one. Without these women there would be no Feuchtwanger dynasty at all! Without their perspective, their contributions, and their side of the story, one does not really understand what the Feuchtwangers were all about.[3]

2   Gerhard Renda, "Fürth, das 'Bayerische Jerusalem,'" in *Geschichte und Kultur der Juden in Bayern*. Aufsätze, ed. Manfred Treml and Josef Kirmeier (Munich: Haus der Bayrischen Geschichte, 1988), 225–35, 226–34.

3   This essay leans on my previous work *Die Feuchtwangers. Familie, Tradition und jüdisches Selbstverständnis* (Göttingen: Wallstein, 2007) and my forthcoming book *Die Frauen der Familie Feuchtwanger. Eine unerzählte Geschichte* (Munich: Piper, 2024).

Marrying Up

One story told over and over again in the Feuchtwanger family was that of Auguste Feuchtwanger, née Hahn, from Frankfurt, supposedly brought ugliness into the family.[4] Yet, part of the untold story is that Auguste contributed valuable assets. She brought business connections, a sizable dowry, and critical know-how into her marriage with Jakob Löw Feuchtwanger from Fürth in 1850. Without her influence, the family business would never have flourished in such an impressive way. Her dowry_18,000 *Gulden*[5]—made up almost two-thirds of Jakob Löw Feuchtwanger's starting capital when he opened a banking business of his own in Munich, the aspiring royal capital of Bavaria. Regarding the notion that the Feuchtwanger men married up, Auguste is no exception. Without Auguste, Fanny, Johanna, and other women of the family, there would not have been a flourishing private bank or an innovative, successful margarine factory in Munich. The women played a major part in the family's ascent to wealth and public recognition in the late nineteenth century as the family moved from Wirtschafts- to Bildungsbürgertum [economic bourgeoisie to educated upper class].

Contrary to the assumed ugly looks of Auguste, which have been subject to speculation time and time again, her monetary and intellectual contributions to the Feuchtwanger family are strangely overlooked. The fact that several women of the Feuchtwanger family were valuable stakeholders, is gravely underexposed. One reason for this is that women are absent in many historical accounts. For a long period in history married women were not allowed to own or establish a business, they lacked legal authority. They could not hold a public office or become a member in a club, association, or political party. Jewish women were not even allowed to sit on the board of the local Jewish community. As in many other family histories, one tends to get the impression the family history of the Feuchtwangers

---

4   Rahel Straus, *Wir lebten in Deutschland. Erinnerungen einer deutschen Jüdin 1880– 1933*, DVA: Stuttgart 21962, S. 123.

5   Einbürgerungsakte Jakob Löw Feuchtwanger, Stadtarchiv München.

has been written by men and men alone. To find traces of the women one
has to look more closely.

Female Entrepreneurs

The fact is that Fanny, Auguste, Johanna, and several other women who
married into the Feuchtwanger family did not only bring substantial capital that allowed to accrue family wealth and establish two large family
companies in Munich (J. L. Feuchtwanger Bank and the margarine
factory)[6] but also played key roles in making the newly established companies successful. Those matches were not just good catches, they were
full-fledged door openers. In a marketing leaflet to merchants in Munich
Jakob Löw Feuchtwanger announced in the mid-1850s:

> Meine Beziehungen in Frankfurt a/M. zu dem Bankhause meines Schwiegervaters,
> Herrn L. A. Hahn, und zu jenen des Herrn S. M. Schwarzschild, Schwiegervaters
> meines Bruders, erleichtern meine Transactionen mit diesem Handelsplatze, und lasse
> ich meinen Committenten, die sich desselben bedienen wollen, diese Begünstigungen
> gerne zu Statten kommen.[7]
>
> [My connections to the Bank L. A. Hahn in Frankfurt on Main, the bank of my father-
> in-law, and those to Mr. S. M. Schwarzschild, father-in-law of my brother Moritz, will
> advance my transactions with this trade institutions and benefit my clients as well.]

Jakob knew that his clients would profit from his good connections with
the well-known banking houses Hahn and Schwarzschild in Frankfurt
that belonged to his father-in-law and the father-in-law of his brother,
Moritz.

In the next generation of Feuchtwangers, family wealth was maintained through the children, nieces and nephews of Auguste and Jakob

---

6   The J. L. Feuchtwanger Bank was founded 1857 by the two brothers Jakob Löw and
     Moritz Feuchtwanger. The margarine factory opened its doors in 1887 with Elkan
     und David Feuchtwanger as the senior directors.
7   Brief Jakob Löw Feuchtwangers an Abraham Fraenkel, May 1, 1857, Privatarchiv
     Nathan Drori, Tel Aviv.

Löw Feuchtwanger, who used arranged marriages to secure formal relationships. At the time, entrepreneurial families often followed the example
of the famous Habsburg dynasty: "Bella gerant alii, tu felix Austria nube"
[Let others wage war, thou, happy Austria, marry.] Lion Feuchtwanger's
father and uncle, for example, married two sisters, Johanna and Sophie
Bodenheimer, daughters of a wealthy family in Darmstadt that imported
and exported food. This double connection proved to be very convenient as
the Feuchtwangers wanted to revolutionize the innovative *Margarine- and
Kunstbuttersector [margarine and artificial butter market]*. Artificial butter
became popular during these years and proved to be especially practical
for orthodox Jews as it was *parve, neutral*, and could, thus, be eaten with
milk and meat products.[8]

While marriage policy played a major role in the ascent of the family
during the nineteenth century, the women were much more than figures on
a chessboard. Mothers and brides played an active role as can be seen with
Fanny Wassermann. As early as 1818, the patriarch of the family, Seligmann,
born in 1786 in Fürth, made a significant step up the social ladder through
his marriage with Fanny Wassermann. This rise in social status was made
possible because his mother Hanna endowed him with 3,000 *Gulden*, and
also because Fanny received a dowry of 5,000 *Gulden* (according to their
Ketubah [marriage contract]) and brought along a bridal gift of another
500 *Gulden*.[9] In current U.S. dollars was the equivalent of a substantial
five-digit figure. Thus, the money from Seligmann's mother together with
Fanny's dowry formed the couple's starting capital.

Fanny, called Vögele, was the daughter of a drapery dealer and finan-
cier in the Bavarian town of Wallerstein who came to considerable wealth
during the Napoleonic Wars.[10] She knew quite well how important the
connections to her father's businesses were for her husband. She had grown

8   Familienbogen Elkan Feuchtwanger, Stadtarchiv München.See also Pelzer, Birgit
     and Reith, Reinhold, *Margarine. Die Karriere der Kunstbutter* (Berlin: Wagenbach,
     2001), 7–22.
9   Ansässigmachung Seligmann Feuchtwanger, Fach 18a F, Nr. 9, Stadtarchiv Fürth.
10   See Diana-Elisabeth Fitz, *Vom Salzfaktor zum Bankier. Familie Wassermann:
     Spiegelbild eines emanzipatorischen Einbürgerungsprozesses* (Nördlingen: Steinmeier,
     1992).

up in a busy merchant house, she had probably worked in the office herself and had helped her father and brothers with bookkeeping. So, when Fanny moved from Wallerstein to Fürth, she became not just the future wife of Seligmann, but also his future business partner. Fanny and Seligmann traded in gold, silver, and brass. After the death of her husband, Fanny was the sole owner of the business for many years until she named two of her sons as partners.[11] The final analysis: the matriarch was equally important as the patriarch of the family.

Double Burden

Many women of the Feuchtwanger family in the first half of the nine-teenth century came from wealthy entrepreneurial families and had been raised at a time when the gender divide between private and public spaces was less sharply defined than in the late nineteenth century. The line be-tween family and business was quite blurry. And even in the later part of the nineteenth century, one has to question the alleged strict separation between the private sphere and public business. This is especially true in the context of upper-class German-Jewish marriages. The hostile so-ciety that surrounded the Jewish minority in the Middle Ages, the early modern period, and beyond led to strengthening Jewish family and busi-ness ties. One's own brother, son, sister, and mother were in many cases the most trustworthy partners. Another important factor that increased the involvement of the Feuchtwanger women in business affairs is the fre-quent absences of many husbands at least until the mid-1850s. During the extended periods when the men were on business trips, the women were running the businesses at home and in the office.

Regine Feuchtwanger-Ellern, sister-in-law of Auguste Feuchtwanger, for example, kept the books, trained the staff, and dealt with business

---

11   Note written and signed by Fanny Feuchtwanger, 1859, in The Feuchtwanger
      Family, 1786–2009, Tel Aviv 2009, S. LIX.

partners when her husband Hayman was away. The double burden of being a businesswoman and caring for her ever-growing family was challenging for the young woman. In one of her letters to Hayman, she laments:

> Diese Woche, lieber Hayman, sind die Geschäftsbriefe nicht sehr angenehm. Was wird wohl da zu machen sein? Ich versichere Dir, dass mich diese Angelegenheiten ganz missgestimmt machen. Ich zähle nicht nur die Tage, wirklich die Stunden bis wir uns wiedersehen. Es ist doch viel angenehmer, wenn man nur seine Ansichten theilen kann, als alles in sich vergraben lassen (…) ich bitte Dich, lieber Hayman, sehr, schreibe mir doch wie lange Du noch gedenkst dort zu bleiben. Ich lebe da doch (…) so im Traum, bald denke ich Du kommst recht bald, dann umschwebt mich wieder ein trüber Gedanke, der mir zuruft, es dauert noch lange und dabei vergehen Wochen—erfülle mir doch meine Bitte![12]

> [This week, dear Hayman, the business correspondence is not very pleasant. What can we do about it? I can assure you, that these affairs make me quite upset. I count the days, even hours until we see each other again. It is more pleasant to share one's views instead of burying everything inside (…) please, dear Hayman, let me know how long you are planning to stay away. I live in a dreamlike state, at times I think it won't be long until you come back, then again sad thoughts cross my mind and I am convinced that this will go on for much longer and so the weeks go by. Please, do write!]

Regine Ellern-Feuchtwanger's example illustrates the heavy burden that lay on many women who had to face the challenges of the business world on their own. Since inventions such as telephones, fax machines, and emails were many decades in the future, these women had to make decisions on their own without being able to consult their husbands. While this was difficult for them, it also gave them independence. We can assume that women who were used to being the boss in the office met their husbands eye-to-eye in family as well as in business matters. And as previously mentioned, for them the two spheres were often inseparable.

12   Letter from Regine Feuchtwanger-Ellern to Hayman Ellern, Fürth, undatiert, Privatarchiv Margot Ellern, Tel Aviv. Translated by the author.

Women of Valor

Throughout the centuries, Jewish women (like their husbands) were in charge of the prosperity of their families and contributed material as well as spiritual wealth. In the *Tanakh*, the Hebrew Bible, one finds the "Woman of Valor," an image of a woman that is part of the Jewish tradition and carries strong connotations for Auguste, Fanny, and Regine and many other Feuchtwanger women. The *Eshet Chayil*, the "Woman of Valor" mentioned in the Book of Proverbs states:

> A woman of valor who can find?
> For her price is far above rubies.
>
> The heart of her husband doth safely trust her.
> And he hath no lack of gain.
>
> She doeth him good and not evil
> All the days of her life.
> She seeketh wool and flax,
> And worketh willingly with her hands.
>
> She is like the merchant-ships,
> She bringeth her food from afar.
>
> She riseth also while it is yet night,
> And giveth food to her household, And a portion to her maidens.
>
> She considereth a field, and buyeth it;
> With the fruit of her hands she planteth a vineyard.
>
> She girdeth her loins with strength,
> And maketh strong her arms.
>
> She perceiveth that the merchandise is good;
> Her lamp goeth not out by night.
>
> She layeth her hands to the distaff,
> And her hands hold the spindle.

She strecheth out her hand to the poor;
Yea, she reacheth forth her hands to the needy.

She is not afraid of the snow for her household;
For all her household are clothed with scarlet.

She maketh for herself coverlets;
Her clothing is fine linen and purple.

Her husband is known in the gates,
When he sitteth among the elders of the land.

She maketh linen garments and selleth them;
And delivereth girdles unto the merchant.

Strength and dignity are her clothing;
And she laugheth at the time to come.[13]

What a remarkable phrase: "she laugheth at the time to come"! In order to accomplish all of the virtues, this "Woman of Valor" not only has to stand on her own two feet, but also shapes the family business. Interestingly since the late nineteenth century and until today, *Eshet Chayil* has been interpreted as a praise of the Jewish mother and wife. Yet, the "Woman of Valor" described in the Biblical text is not only a well-behaved home-maker, but also a tough businesswoman, one that invests, calculates, buys, and sells, one who tills a field, plans for the future, manages a house—a woman who is clearly a leader.

In this sense, Fanny, Auguste, and Regine were truly "Women of Valor." Of course, over the decades, the roles of the Feuchtwanger women began to change. The bustling businesswomen of the first half of the nine-teenth century, who spent a good part of their day in the office dealing with clients and staff, were gradually replaced by the elegant ladies of the house. The women of the upper class slowly turned from producer to con-sumer. In many entrepreneurial Jewish families, the separation between public and private space was never as strict as in families of civil servants

---

13   JPS Tanakh 1917, Proverbs, 31: 10–25.

or in military families of the upper class. Nevertheless, in the process of "Verbürgerlichung" (embourgeoisement) the Feuchtwanger women stayed home and the husbands left each morning to spend their days in the office. Yet, even as women were increasingly pushed into the private sphere of their homes, many Feuchtwanger women became leaders of distinguished houses at excellent addresses in Munich, while the businesses flourished and the families' wealth increased.

Heading the household in the late nineteenth and early twentieth century became a major enterprise. Each household consisted not only of a considerable number of children—Lion Feuchtwanger had eight siblings— but also a number of servants such as cooks, maids, women who came for laundry day, a seamstress, and the Jewish private tutor who taught the boys the *Alef Bet*, the Hebrew alphabet, *Gemara* and *Mishna*, the two parts of the *Talmud*. Lion's brother, Martin, gives an impressive portrayal of his parental home at St. Anna Platz in Munich. Their mother, Johanna, held a strict regimen not only over the servants, but also over her children and husband. The catholic servants were expected to know every detail of the Jewish religious laws, especially those regarding *Shabbat*, the day of rest, and *Kashrut*, the dietary laws. Johanna Feuchtwanger expected her staff to go to church every Sunday. Piousness and respect for the religion of the house and religion per se was a non-negotiable requirement. And it was Johanna's task to watch over it.[14] At the end of the nineteenth century, the Feuchtwanger women were less involved in the daily activity of the family business (that had been mostly taken over by the men); however, they worked equally hard, so that the family smoothly shifted from *Wirtschafts-* to *Bildungsbürgertum* [economic bourgeoisie to educated upper class]. Education became one of the primary goals for the children. Lion reports that his mother was rather ambitious and strongly encouraged him to work toward an academic career. The sons visited the elite *Wilhelmsgymnasium*. To know Goethe and Schiller were equally important as knowing the *Torah*.[15]

14   Martin Feuchtwanger, *Zukunft ist ein blindes Spiel. Erinnerungen* (Frankfurt/ Main: Ullstein, 1992), 14ff.
15   Lion Feuchtwanger, *Aus meinem Leben*, 15, in Colloquium, Nr. 7, 1964, 15–17.

Women in Exile

In Lion's generation the term *Eshet Chayil* carried yet another meaning. The women born in the 1880s and after not only made sure that their family businesses thrived and that their children grew up in the Jewish faith but also proved to be true lifesavers in times of revolution, counter-revolution, inflation, and the horror that began with the Nazi rise to power in 1933. Oftentimes it was the wives who realized earlier than their husbands that there was no future in Nazi Germany. This might have been due to the fact that men were too caught up in their leadership positions, be it in their business or the Jewish community. Many of the men could not envision themselves in any other position than "*Herr Bankdirektor*" [Mr Bank Director], "*Herr Fabrikdirektor*" [Mr Factory Director], or "*Herr Verleger*" [Mr Publisher]. The women were connected to the daily lives of their children. They experienced their children's misery as they faced discrimination at school and on the streets. They had to comfort a heartbroken son or daughter who was no longer allowed to participate in a sports club or use the local swimming pool. Lion's Zionist sisters, Henny and Medi, for instance, emigrated to Palestine with their families even before 1933.[16] Rahel Straus, the wife of Lion's cousin Eli, was also eager to leave behind the rising antisemitism in Germany.

Rahel was a true pioneer. She studied medicine in Heidelberg and became one of the first female physicians to open a gynecological practice at the beginning of the twentieth century when she moved to Munich. An orthodox Jewish woman, Rahel was an outspoken advocate for sex education, contraception, and safe abortion. She was a strong believer in gender equality and women's suffrage.[17] Spring 1933 was hard for Rahel not only because of political developments, but her husband, Eli, suffered

---

16   For example: Rosa Feuchtwanger, Rahel Straus, Rebekka Feuchtwanger, see Heike Specht, *Die Feuchtwangers*, 328ff., 355.

17   Rahel Straus, *Wir lebten in Deutschland. Erinnerungen einer deutschen Jüdin 1880– 1933* (Stuttgart: Deutsche Verlags-Anstalt, 1962).

from esophageal cancer and died shortly after *Pessach* that year. She alone
faced the hard decision to emigrate to Palestine. In her memoirs she writes:

> Die Tage und Wochen, die folgten, sind mir noch heute wie ein wirrer, schwerer
> Traum. Man tut, fast nachtwandlerisch, was nötig ist, aber man lebt nicht, ja
> man fühlt nicht einmal. Langsam erst spürt man die Leere um sich, die sich nie
> wieder füllt, die große Einsamkeit. Aber das Leben forderte sein Recht, es forderte
> in diesen Tagen Entscheidungen weittragender Bedeutung. Ich hatte nur einen
> Wunsch: München und Deutschland so schnell wie möglich zu verlassen. Es gab nur
> eine Entscheidung: Palästina, Erez Israel für die Kinder und für mich, neue Heimat,
> neue Lebensmöglichkeit.[18]

> [The days and weeks that followed seemed like a confused bad dream. Like a sleep-
> walker one does what is necessary, but you don't actually live, you feel nothing. Slowly
> you start to realize the emptiness around you, that will never be filled again, the lone-
> liness. But life demands to be lived, far-reaching decisions have to be made. I had just
> one wish: to leave Munich and Germany as fast as possible. And there was just one
> possibility: Palestine, Erez Israel for the children and me, a new home, a new chance.]

In summer 1933, the 53-year-old gynecologist and her children embarked
on a ship to Palestine, where started her life over and opened a medical
practice in Jerusalem.

Lion Feuchtwanger's wife, Marta, was ten years younger than Rahel
Straus. Marta also had to make life-changing decisions when Nazi politics posed a threat to the couple's existence. In January 1933, when Marta
was spending her annual skiing vacation in the picturesque Austrian village of St. Anton, the news broke that Hitler had become Chancellor. At
the time Lion was finishing an extensive reading tour across the United
States. Lion did not return to Germany but joined Marta in Austria in
March 1933. With the Nazi regime in power, it would have been dangerous
to return to Berlin. Even parts of Austria were not safe. Marta urged her
husband to leave Tyrol as rumors spread that Nazi agents would kidnap
critics of the new regime even those in Austrian territory.[19] Soon after, the

18   Straus, *Wir lebten in Deutschland*, 293.
19   Marta Feuchtwanger, *Nur eine Frau. Jahre, Tage, Stunden* (Munich: Knaur,
      1983), 238. Lion Feuchtwanger, *Ein möglichst intensives Leben. Die Tagebücher*
      (Berlin: Aufbau, 2020), 16. März 1933.

couple escaped to France and ultimately, they sought refuge in the United States. Throughout this period, Marta's pragmatism, efficiency, and valor are legendary. First in France and later in California, she managed to build a world around them that was inspiring and yet calm enough for Lion to continue to be creative and write. She was an indispensable adviser to Lion and nurtured a home that would become a social meeting place within the emigrant community. Here she became legendary as a marvelous hostess.[20]

More than once, Marta saved Lion's life during their escape to the United States. Unforgettable is the episode in summer 1940 when—after fleeing herself from Camp de Gurs where she had been interned—Marta visited Lion in the internment camp in Nîmes in Southern France. Marta understood that with the German army advancing quickly, Lion had to get out of France immediately. She traveled to Marseilles to meet the American consul. Masses of people queued in front of the building, but Marta just passed them, ignoring their hissing and ranting. It was hard but it had to be done. She remembers:

> Als ich dort ankam, wartete bereits eine große Menschenmenge, viele Straßen entlang. Es herrschte glühende Hitze, und viele wurden ohnmächtig; aber ich konnte mich nicht anstellen. Man sagte, um fünf Uhr würden alle wieder weggeschickt, das war jeden Tag so. Ich musste Lion retten und durfte keine Zeit verlieren.[21]

> [When I arrived, a huge crowd queued alongside many streets. The heat was unbearable, many fainted, but I just couldn't wait in line. I was told that at five o'clock each day they send everyone home. I had to save Lion. I could not lose time.]

And miraculously, she was let in after mentioning her husband's name. Traumatized from the weeks in Gurs, exhausted and filthy from the journey, she broke down in the office of a young consul named Mr. Standish, who promised to help. With Miles Standish, Marta schemed a plan to free her husband. To Lion, she wrote a note stating, "Don't ask, just follow." Mr. Standish drove to Nîmes with his wife, to make it look like a casual excursion. The note somehow found its way to Lion, who

---

20 Lion Feuchtwanger, *Ein möglichst intensives Leben*, 27. Mai 1933, 3. Juni 1933, 3. Mai 1934. Marta Feuchtwanger, *Nur eine Frau*, 245, 248.

21 Marta Feuchtwanger, *Nur eine Frau*, 290. Translated by the author.

read it and followed Marta's written instructions. Standish smuggled Lion into the car, put a coat around him, and wrapped a scarf around his head, so he would look like an old lady. Whenever the car was stopped by the military, Standish claimed the person in the back was his mother-in-law. In this way, Lion was saved. Weeks later the couple managed to cross the Pyrenees, travel to Portugal, and eventually crossed the Atlantic Ocean to safety in America.[22]

Lion Feuchtwanger seemed aware of the contribution women made to the safety of their family in exile. In his book *The Devil in France* (about his experiences in wartime France), Lion Feuchtwanger wrote a "Praise of our Women." Although his words appear somewhat patronizing, one wonders if they are an instantiation of *Eshet Chayil*:

> Ich muss hier ein paar Sätze einschalten zum Lob unserer Frauen. Sie bewährten sich großartig in dieser ganzen bösen Zeit. Wohl schimpften und klagten sie zuweilen, doch Weinkrämpfe, Zusammenbrüche, Hysterie gab es nicht. Die Frauen hielten tapfer zu ihren Männern, die deutschen sowohl wie die französischen, und taten besonnen, was sie konnten.[23]

> [I have to say a few sentences in praise of our women. They proved their worth exceptionally during that horrible time. Even though they scolded and complained at times, there was no sobbing, mental breakdowns or hysteria. The women bravely stood by their men, the German as well as the French, and prudently did what they could.]

It is no secret that Lion Feuchtwanger had rather conventional views on gender roles. Although he and Marta liked to emphasize that they lived like Bohemians,[24] their marital life was in large part bourgeois. The husband's career was given priority over everything else and the wife was expected to shield him from the ugly trivialities of everyday life. In the 1970s when Marta had been widowed many years, she stated in an interview that in Lion's opinion a woman "should be only for luxury." She had to be pretty and take care of the needs of her husband. In return, the

---

22   Marta Feuchtwanger, *Nur eine Frau*, 296ff.

23   Lion Feuchtwanger, *Der Teufel in Frankreich. Tagebuch 1940, Briefe* (Berlin: Aufbau, 2000), 246. Translated by the author.

24   Marta Feuchtwanger, *An Emigrés Life. Munich, Berlin, Sanary, Pacific Palisades*, UCLA Oral History Program (Los Angeles: UCLA, 1976), Part III, 1047.

husband provided a suitable lifestyle.[25] In many respects Marta and Lion lived by those standards. Of course, Lion knew very well that Marta was much more than a beautiful muse and a diligent homemaker. Without her astuteness and talent to deal with moments of crises, he would not have managed to get out of the "Devil's France." However, even Marta maintained this image of a supposedly strict gender divide in their marriage and points out in her memoirs that she took care of daily necessities while Lion concentrated on his writing. When he was working, Marta recalled that Lion would forget everything around him.[26] Josephus' trials and tribulations with the Jews and Romans seemed much more urgent to him than the approaching Germans. The Jewish War of the year sixty-six seemed much closer to him than the war that was raging in Europe just outside his door in the year 1940.

Marta not only saved Lion's life and took care of daily chores but also left a significant footprint on Lion's work. Without her, he would have continued to write plays and reviews and not have become a novelist. After all, it was Marta who planted the idea of writing a novel in Lion's head, after he had written many semi-successful plays and theater reviews.[27] Over the decades of their marriage, Marta was the first to read everything her husband wrote and gave him honest, sometimes brutal feedback.[28] Marta outlived Lion by almost thirty years. During that time, she kept his legacy alive, shaped his memory, and oversaw the reception of his work. She crafted the image of Lion Feuchtwanger from the beginning and managed the Feuchtwanger-brand for decades.

---

25   Marta Feuchtwanger, *An Emigrés Life*, Part II, 741.

26   Marta Feuchtwanger, "Die Flucht, in Der Teufel in Frankreich," in *Der Teufel in Frankreich. Tagebuch 1940, Briefe*, ed. Lion Feuchtwanger (Berlin: Aufbau, 2000), 246. Translated by the author.

27   Marta Feuchtwanger, *An Emigrés Life*, Part I, 107, 109. See also, Birgit Maier-Katkin, "Lion und Marta Feuchtwanger: Ein junges Paar in München," in *Feuchtwanger und München*, ed. Tamara Fröhler and Andreas Heusler (*Feuchtwanger Studies*, Vol. 8) (Oxford: Peter Lang, 2022), 39–41.

28   Marta Feuchtwanger, *An Emigrés Life*, Part IV, 1542f.

Conclusion

The rescue story of Lion and Marta Feuchtwanger certainly is a spectacular one, but in one way or the other, many Women of Valor saved their families during the years of persecution. The Holocaust put an end to the centuries-long history of the Feuchtwangers in Germany. The family members that survived were scattered all over the world: in Palestine/ Israel, England, the United States, and South America. Many of the Feuchtwanger women successfully navigated their husbands and families through times of hardship and crisis. In Jerusalem, Rahel Straus and her children witnessed the creation of the State of Israel in 1948, as did Lion's sisters, Medi and Henny and their families. Their commitment to Zionism helped to cope with the loss of their homes in Germany and to process the devastating news reaching them from Europe. Lion's sister, Bella, was the only sibling who did not manage to flee in time and was trapped in Prague after the German invasion., Tragically, she was deported to Theresienstadt, where she died in 1943. The experience of exile was hard on both men and women, husbands and wives, but often it was the wife and mother that tackled the most pressing challenges. While many men grieved about lost careers and opportunities, their wives proved to be more adaptable and pragmatic. In exile, many worked as receptionists, cleaning ladies, private tutors, or saleswomen to see their families through.[29]

When looking at the Feuchtwanger women throughout the centuries it becomes apparent that they made valuable contributions to the family's rising material wealth and education. Auguste, Fanny, and Rahel showed a great deal of entrepreneurship, courage, and skill as they navigated their families through diverse socio-political times. As political events threatened the survival of the Feuchtwanger family and, ultimately, exile from Nazi Germany, the call for a true *Eshet Chayil*, a true Woman of Valor, can be seen with Marta: times of extreme world crises make it at times difficult to laugh "at the time to come."

---

29   Compare Claudia Koonz, "Courage and Choice among German-Jewish Women and Men," in *Die Juden im nationalsozialistischen Deutschland*, ed. Arnold Paucker (Tübingen: Mohr Siebeck, 1986), 283–94, 287–92.

PART II

Women and Their Influence on Lion Feuchtwanger's Life and Work

ROLAND JAEGER

3 „Liebste Lola"—„Liebster Lion".
Zum Briefwechsel von Lion Feuchtwanger
und Lola Humm-Sernau

ABSTRACT

In addition to his dramatic, literary and essayistic work, Lion Feuchtwanger wrote and left
behind extensive correspondence. Most of it is archived in the Feuchtwanger Memorial
Library, Los Angeles, where it is indexed by correspondent. Quite a number of selected
letters has already been published. However, what has not yet been systematically recorded and evaluated is Feuchtwanger's extensive correspondence of over 500 documents
with Lola Humm-Sernau (1895–1988), his long-time secretary in Berlin (1926–33) and
Sanary-sur-Mer (1933–40). An ongoing editing project is intended to make the scholarly
relevant content of this correspondence, which continued until Feuchtwanger's death, in
an annotated form available to researchers and readers. The focus is not only on additional
information about the writer and his work, but also and especially on the previously little-
known life and complicated personality of Lola Humm-Sernau, who (formally married to a
Swiss citizen) was not granted a visa to follow Feuchtwanger into US exile and henceforth
lived in Ascona, Switzerland. Of particular interest is her own work as a translator of over
50 novels from 1943 onwards and her later role as a "witness of exile."

Neben seinem dramatischen, belletristischen und essayistischen
Werk hat Lion Feuchtwanger eine umfangreiche Korrespondenz ge-
führt und hinterlassen. Sie ist zum größten Teil in der Feuchtwanger
Memorial Library, Los Angeles, archiviert und dort nach Briefpartnern
erschlossen.[1] Die bereits veröffentlichten Briefwechsel sind zudem
in der Feuchtwanger-Bibliographie von Spalek/Hawrylchak (2004)

---

1   <https://archives.usc.edu/repositories/3/archival_objects/31542> (Lion Feuchtwanger
     Papers, Correspondence).

verzeichnet,[2] darunter vor allem die von Harold von Hofe herausge-
gebene Korrespondenz Feuchtwangers mit Arnold Zweig (1984) und
mit Freunden (1991).[3] Hinzu kommen einige weitere, in Aufsatzform
ausgewertete Briefwechsel, etwa mit dem amerikanischen Verleger
Ben Huebsch.[4] Sie alle belegen, dass Feuchtwangers Korrespondenz
ein erheblicher Quellenwert zum Verständnis seiner Persönlichkeit,
seiner Arbeitsweise und seinem Werk sowie seinem Verhältnis zu den
jeweiligen Briefpartnern und seiner Haltung zu den Zeitumständen zu-
kommt. Dies gilt vor allem für die Jahre ab 1933, als der Briefverkehr
aufgrund des Exils und später der geografischen Distanz zu Europa
zu seiner wichtigsten Kommunikationsform wurde. Darüber hinaus
ergänzt die Korrespondenz des Schriftstellers seine eher knappen
Tagebucheintragungen, die mit Unterbrechungen zudem nur bis Mitte
1940 reichen.[5] Die Feuchtwanger-Biographik stützt sich daher neben
anderen Quellen auch und gerade auf Zitate und Informationen aus
seinen Briefen.[6]

2   Sandra H. Hawrylchak and John M. Spalek, *Lion Feuchtwanger: A Bibliographic
     Handbook, vol. 3/Ein bibliographisches Handbook, Bd. 3* (München: Saur, 2004),
     S. 1–28 (Published Letters/Veröffentlichte Briefe).

3   Harold von Hofe, Hrsg., *Lion Feuchtwanger/Arnold Zweig. Briefwechsel 1933–1958*,
     2 Bde (Berlin: Aufbau, 1984).—Ders.; Sigrid Washburn, Hrsg., *Lion Feuchtwanger.
     Briefwechsel mit Freunden 1933–1958*, 2 Bde (Berlin: Aufbau, 1991).

4   Vgl. u. a. Jeffrey B. Berlin, „A Relentless Drive for Meaning: Lion Feuchtwanger's
     Unpublished Correspondence (1948–51) with His American Publisher Ben
     Huebsch Regarding *Goya oder Der arge Weg der Erkenntnis*", in Ian Wallace, Hrsg.,
     Feuchtwanger and Film (Oxford: Peter Lang, 2009) (Feuchtwanger Studies, 1),
     S. 41–124.—Ders.: „A Relentless Drive for Meaning (Part II): Lion Feuchtwanger's
     Unpublished Correspondence with His American Publisher Ben Huebsch (1952–
     1956)", in Ian Wallace, Hrsg., *Feuchtwanger and Remigration* (Feuchtwanger
     Studies, 3) (Oxford: Peter Lang, 2013), S. 93–184.

5   Lion Feuchtwanger, *Ein möglichst intensives Leben. Die Tagebücher*, Nele Holdack,
     Marje Schuetze-Coburn und Michaela Ullmann, Hrsg. (Berlin: Aufbau, 2018).

6   Vgl. u. a. Wilhelm von Sternburg, *Lion Feuchtwanger. Die Biografie* (Berlin: Aufbau,
     2014).—Andreas Heusler, *Lion Feuchtwanger. Münchner-Emigrant-Weltbürger*
     (St. Pölten: Residenz, 2014).—Zuletzt auch Maik Grote, *Bücher schreiben und ver-
     legen im Exil 1933–1939; 1940–1949* (Norderstedt: BoD, 2021/2023).

Zu Feuchtwangers Korrespondenz gehören einige Briefwechsel mit Frauen, darunter mit der Tänzerin Eva van Hoboken (1905–1987) und der Künstlerin Eva Hermann (1901–1978) sowie vor allem mit Lola Humm-Sernau (1895–1988), seiner Sekretärin von 1926 bis 1940.[7] Während Feuchtwangers Briefe an Eva van Hoboken seit 1996 publiziert und kommentiert vorliegen,[8] hat Manfred Flügge die Korrespondenz mit Eva Hermann 2012 für seine Biographie dieser „Muse des Exils" ausgewertet.[9] Auch der Briefwechsel zwischen Feuchtwanger und Lola Humm-Sernau ist schon berücksichtigt worden,[10] doch steht seine systematische Erfassung und Erschließung noch aus.

Aus zwei Gründen erscheint es lohnend, für die biografisch, literaturwissenschaftlich und zeitgeschichtlich relevanten Inhalte dieser Korrespondenz eine geeignete Form der Edition zu finden. Erstens, um weitere Einsichten zu Person und Werk von Lion Feuchtwanger, zur jeweiligen Exilsituation der beiden Briefpartner nach 1940, zu ihren späteren Lebens- und Arbeitsumständen in den USA beziehungsweise in der Schweiz sowie zu den verschiedenen Aspekten ihrer Beziehung zu gewinnen. Zweitens, um Lola Humm-Sernau jenseits ihrer Rolle als Sekretärin und Vertrauter des Schriftstellers als eigenständiger Person gerecht zu werden—mit all ihrer individuellen Problematik sowie emotionalen, kommunikativen und nicht zuletzt finanziellen Abhängigkeit von Feuchtwanger, aber auch hinsichtlich ihrer ab 1943 ausgeübten Tätigkeit als Übersetzerin. Dies gilt umso

7   <https://archives.usc.edu/repositories/3/archival_objects/33521> (Lion Feuchtwanger correspondence with female friends).

8   Nortrud Gomringer, Hrsg., *Lion Feuchtwanger. Briefe an Eva van Hoboken* (Wien: Splitter, 1996).

9   Manfred Flügge, *Muse des Exils. Das Leben der Malerin Eva Herrmann* (Berlin: Insel, 2012).

10   Vgl. u. a. Karl Kröhnke, „Der Weltbürger als Staatenloser. Die Aporien des späten Feuchtwanger", in *Neophilologus*, Bd. 78, 1994, Nr. 2, S. 289–300.—Alexander Klose, „Lion Feuchtwanger an Lola Humm-Sernau (1940)", in Andreas Bernhard und Ulrich Raulff, Hrsg., *Briefe aus dem 20. Jahrhundert* (Frankfurt/Main: Suhrkamp, 2005), S. 120–125.—Vor allem bei von Sternburg 2014 (Anm. 6).

mehr, als der bisher veröffentlichte Kenntnisstand über ihren Lebensweg eher lücken- und teils auch fehlerhaft ist.[11]

Die Bearbeitung der Korrespondenz wurde begonnen, ist aber noch nicht abgeschlossen, weshalb hier nur ein Zwischenstand des Editionsprojekts mitgeteilt werden kann.[12] Zunächst werden Lola Sernau und ihre Tätigkeit für Feuchtwanger in Berlin und Sanary-sur-Mer kurz vorgestellt, sodann die Überlieferungsform und beispielhafte Inhalte ihres Briefwechsels geschildert. Den Abschluss bildet eine Würdigung von Lola Humm-Sernau als Übersetzerin und Zeitzeugin des Exils, im Anhang ergänzt um eine Titelliste der von ihr übersetzten Bücher.

Lola Sernau

Lola Sernau stammte aus einer jüdischen Familie. Sie wurde am 2. Juli 1895 in Berlin als Tochter eines Textilfabrikanten aus Halle an der Saale geboren. Ihr Vater Theodor Sernau leitete die Berliner Zweigniederlassung der Firma Gebr. Sernau, Halle. Er starb bereits 1910 im 61. Lebensjahr. Lola hatte zwei ältere Schwestern, Hertha (1889–1953) und Irma (1892–1965); ihr Bruder James Sernau (geb. 1886) fiel 1915 als Freiwilliger im Ersten Weltkrieg. Sie wuchs in einem literarisch interessierten Elternhaus auf. Ein eigenes Exlibris von 1918 weist sie als Leserin und Büchersammlerin aus. Ihre Schwester Hertha heiratete den Schweizer Textilkaufmann Max Rudolf Howald und lebte in Burgdorf bei Bern, während ihre Schwester Irma in Berlin als Schauspielerin und Modejournalistin tätig war.[13]

---

11   Vgl. u. a. Gudrun Wedel, *Autobiographien von Frauen. Ein Lexikon* (Köln: Böhlau, 2010), S. 367 (Geburts- „1896" und Todesjahr „1990" falsch, recte: 1895 und 1988).

12   Mit Dank an Michaela Ullmann für ihre Unterstützung bei der Zugänglichmachung der in der Feuchtwanger Memorial Library verwahrten Korrespondenz.

13   Irma Sernau spielte u. a. in dem Stummfilm *Aus eines Mannes Mädchenjahren* (1919).

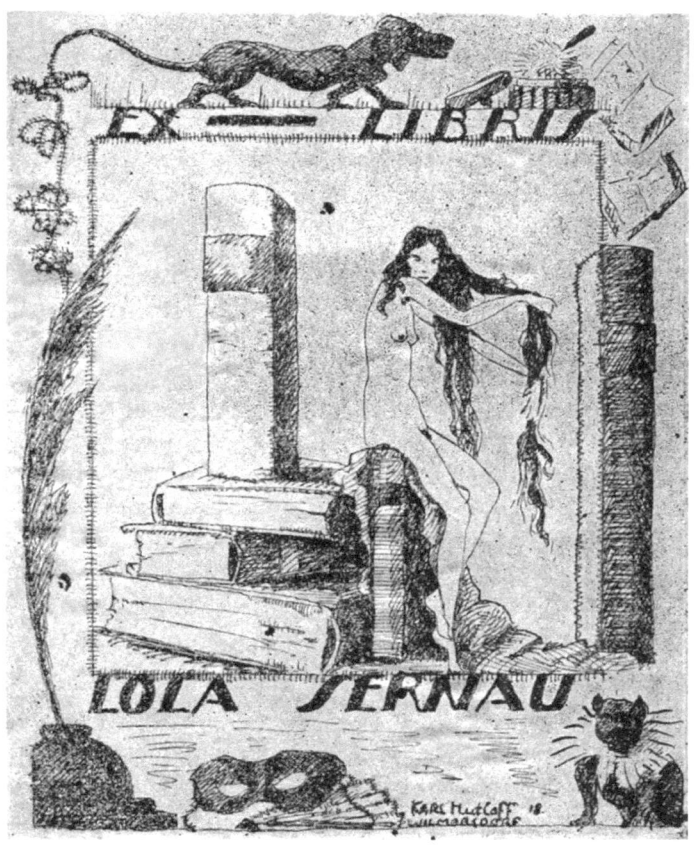

Figure 5. ExLibris Lola Sernau von Karl Hutloff, 1918. Archiv Roland Jaeger.

Lola Sernau führte in Berlin ein Leben zwischen Bourgeoisie und Boheme. Sie wohnte zusammen mit ihrer Schwester Irma in Charlottenburg und hatte regen Umgang mit Künstlern und Literaten. Im Sommer 1920 beispielsweise bestand eine nähere Bekanntschaft mit dem Schriftsteller Rudolf Leonhard (1889–1953), der ihr ein Exemplar seines Romans *Beate und der große Pan* (1918) mit einem handschriftlichen Gedicht widmete. Von einer beruflichen Ausbildung hingegen ist nichts bekannt, das Schreibmaschineschreiben brachte sie sich selbst bei.

Feuchtwangers Roman *Jud Süss* (1925) hatte Lola Sernau bereits mit Begeisterung gelesen. Zur persönlichen Begegnung mit dem Schriftsteller, der 11 Jahre älter war als sie, kam es 1926 in Berlin bei einem literarischen Salon des Augenarztes Alfred Rosenberg am Kurfürstendamm. Zu der Zeit war die Dreissigjährige im Büro des Malik-Verlags tätig, einem Zentrum der damaligen literarischen und politischen Avantgarde. Wenig später bot Feuchtwanger ihr an, seine Sekretärin zu werden. Lola Sernau war zunächst entsetzt und erwiderte: „Um Gottes Willen, nein, dazu bin ich doch viel zu dumm". Feuchtwanger antwortete vergnügt: „Dumm? Ich weiß nicht, töricht vielleicht; aber klug bin ja ich, und das genügt. Kommen Sie morgen früh um zehn Uhr her, wir wollen es miteinander versuchen".[14] Dies war der Beginn einer beruflichen und persönlichen Verbindung, die über 30 Jahre andauern sollte.

Besonderen Anteil hatte Lola Sernau an der Entstehung von Feuchtwangers Roman *Erfolg*. Sie kümmerte sich um die Material- und Informationsbeschaffung, führte die begleitende Korrespondenz und erstellte die verschiedenen Manuskriptfassungen. Diese Phase der Zusammenarbeit ist leider nicht in Feuchtwangers Tagebüchern dokumentiert, die 1921 unterbrechen und erst 1931 wieder einsetzen. Um so wichtiger ist daher ein Artikel, den Lola Sernau im März 1929 im *Berliner Tageblatt* unter dem Titel *An Lion Feuchtwangers Schreibmaschine. Intimitäten des Diktats* veröffentlicht hat.[15] Darin erläutert sie sein Diktieren von Texten und die farbigen Papierstufen der Manuskripterstellung, das Verhältnis des Schriftstellers zu historischer Faktizität, seinen Umgang mit Kritik und seine Förderung anderer Autoren. Dabei ist bemerkenswert, dass sie von ihrer Tätigkeit als „wir" schreibt, sich also als Teil von Feuchtwangers literarischem Produktionsbetrieb begriff.

---

14   L.[ola] S.[ernau], „Wie Lion Feuchtwanger aus Deutschland vertrieben wurde. Erinnerungen seiner Sekretärin", *Das Magazin*, Nr. 7 (Juli 1959), S. 32–34, zit. S. 32 f.

15   Lola Sernau, „An Lion Feuchtwangers Schreibmaschine. Intimitäten des Diktats", *Berliner Tageblatt*, Jg. 58, Nr. 148 (Morgenausgabe), 28. März 1929, 1. Beiblatt.— Wiederabgedruckt u. a. bei Reinhard G. Wittmann, Hrsg., *Erfolg. Lion Feuchtwangers Bayern* (München: Literaturhaus, 2014), S. 12 f.

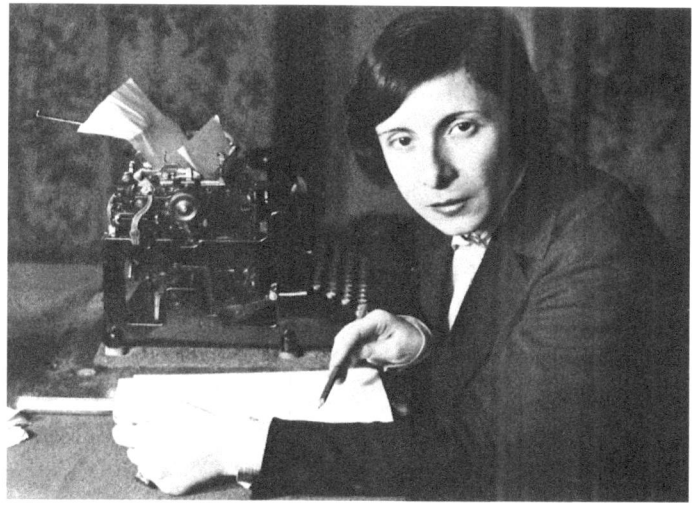

Figure 6. Lola Sernau an der Schreibmaschine, um 1929. Archiv Roland Jaeger.

Schriftsteller und Sekretärin verband zunächst ein vertrauensvolles Arbeitsverhältnis. In seinem Tagebuch spricht Feuchtwanger anfangs von „die Sernau", ab Mitte 1933 dann von „Lola". Im Zuge der gemeinsamen Arbeit am *Josephus*-Roman verliebte sie sich in ihn, woraufhin es bis Mitte der 1930er Jahre auch zu intimen Begegnungen kam.

Sanary-sur-Mer 1933 bis 1940

Aufgrund der Machtübernahme der Nationalsozialisten in Deutschland und seiner damit verbundenen Gefährdung kehrte Feuchtwanger von einer im November 1932 über London angetretenen Vortragsreise in die Vereinigten Staaten nicht nach Deutschland, sondern Anfang März 1933 über Paris nach Österreich zurück, wo sich seine Frau Marta, mit der er seit 1912 verheiratet war, zu einem Skiurlaub aufhielt. Fortan verbrachten sie ihr Leben gemeinsam im Exil, zunächst kurz in der Schweiz. Als Jüdin und Feuchtwangers Sekretärin ebenfalls eine Bedrohung spürend und um ihm näher zu sein, floh auch Lola Sernau Mitte März 1933 von Berlin in die Schweiz. Es sollte 18 Jahre dauern, bevor sie ihre Heimatstadt wiedersah. Aus Zürich berichtete sie dem Schriftsteller von der Besetzung seines Berliner Hauses durch S.A.-Truppen sowie der Entwendung von Akten und Manuskripten. Wenig später trafen sich Feuchtwanger und Lola Sernau in Bern. Anschließend folgte sie ihm nach Südfrankreich, wohin Lion und Marta Feuchtwanger im April emigriert waren und wo sie wieder als seine Sekretärin tätig wurde. Am 20. Mai 1933 notierte er in Bandol in sein Tagebuch: „Den Roman *Familie Oppermann* begonnen. Lola gevögelt".[16]

In den folgenden, arbeitsintensiven Jahren entstanden ferner Feuchtwangers Romane *Der falsche Nero, Exil, Die Söhne* und *Der Tag wird kommen*, außerdem der Reisebericht *Moskau 1937*. Alle Texte wurden in mehreren Fassungen von Lola Sernau getippt; außerdem legte sie bibliografische Listen von Feuchtwangers Veröffentlichungen an. Einige ihrer Eigenschaften sind in die Figur der Anna Trautwein des Romans *Exil* eingeflossen. Ihre Zusammenarbeit mit dem Schriftsteller wurde allerdings durch andauernde Reibereien mit dessen Ehefrau belastet. Dazu trug nicht nur ihr enges Verhältnis zu Feuchtwanger bei, sondern auch ihre Lebensuntüchtigkeit und labile Stimmungslage, die einer lebenspraktischen Frau wie Marta Feuchtwanger wesensfremd waren.[17] Dieser waren die Affären ihres Mannes zwar duldend bekannt, doch blieb sie davon nicht unberührt. Um die Situation zu entspannen, ließ Feuchtwanger seine Sekretärin nicht im gemeinsamen Haus wohnen und schickte sie 1934 vorübergehend nach Paris.

Lola Sernau war häufig launisch, außerdem oft kränkelnd. Dies bekam regelmäßig auch Feuchtwanger zu spüren, der gleichwohl an ihr festhielt, weil er die gut eingespielte Arbeitsverbindung mit ihr schätzte. Marta Feuchtwanger schrieb am 5. Juni 1934 an Arnold Zweig, Lola sei „heuer dauernd mit Lion beleidigt, doch da sie fleißig und gewissenhaft arbeite,

---

16   *Feuchtwanger Tagebücher* 2018 (Anm. 5), S. 327.
17   Vgl. Karin Feuerstein-Praßer, *Die Frauen der Dichter. Leben und Lieben an der Seite der Genies. 12 Porträts* (München: Piper, 2015), S. 195 f.

läßt er sich nicht anfechten".[18] Am 22. April 1935 vermerkte Feuchtwanger in seinem Tagebuch „Lola macht mir eine Szene, weil sie so einsam und freudlos hier lebt und ich mich viel zu wenig um sie kümmere".[19] Lola Sernau fühlte sich in Sanary tatsächlich unglücklich, weil sie dort kaum ein eigenes Leben führte und sich lieber in einer Großstadt wie Paris aufgehalten hätte. Außerdem war sie vollständig von Feuchtwangers Arbeitsplänen und ihrer Anstellung bei ihm abhängig.

Allerdings hatte sie durchaus regen Umgang in der Emigrantenkolonie von Sanary, wo sie früheren Bekanntschaften aus Berlin wiederbegegnete und neue Freundschaften schloss, etwa zu Rudolf Leonhard oder mit Ludwig und Sascha Marcuse. Ein Foto zeigt sie neben Feuchtwanger im Freundeskreis am Strand, ein weiteres an der Seite des Schriftstellers, als 1935 die ersten Exemplare von dessen Roman *Die Söhne* in Sanary eintrafen. Anwesend war dabei auch der 1933 nach Frankreich geflohene Mathematiker und Publizist Emil Julius Gumbel (1891–1966), mit dem sie ebenfalls eine engere Freundschaft verband.

Auf Feuchtwangers Initiative hin veröffentlichte Lola Sernau 1937 in der von ihm mitherausgegebenen Moskauer Literaturzeitschrift *Das Wort* eine Besprechung von Arnold Zweigs Roman *Erziehung vor Verdun*.[20] Im Sommer 1938 heiratete sie den Schweizer Staatsbürger Fritz Humm, einen Gärtner, der gelegentlich mit dem Schweizer Übersetzer Rudolf Jakob Humm (1895–1977) verwechselt wird.[21] Die lediglich formell bestehende Ehe verschaffte ihr einen Schweizer Pass und sollte so ihren Aufenthalts- und Reisestatus sichern. Marta Feuchtwanger berichtete darüber Arnold Zweig am 27. Juli 1938: „Lola hat heut einen Schweizer geheiratet, für sie bestehen keine Paßschwierigkeiten mehr […]. Sie ist nach wie vor die Modedame von Sanary, und es ist erstaunlich, wie sie Bummeln und Arbeiten unter einen Hut bringt. Die Heirat hat auch viel Arbeit und Unkosten verursacht, aber jetzt haben wir's geschafft, und sie heißt von heut ab Frau Humm".[22]

---

18   *Feuchtwanger/Zweig Briefe* 1984 (Anm. 3), Bd. 1, S. 52.

19   *Feuchtwanger Tagebücher* 2018 (Anm. 5), S. 368.

20   Lola Sernau, „Erziehung vor Verdun". *Das Wort*, Jg. 2 (1937), H. 6, S. 93 f.

21   U. a. Manfred Flügge, *Die vier Leben der Marta Feuchtwanger. Biographie* (Berlin: Aufbau, 2008), S. 253.

22   *Feuchtwanger/Zweig Briefe* 1984 (Anm. 3), Bd. 1, S. 196.

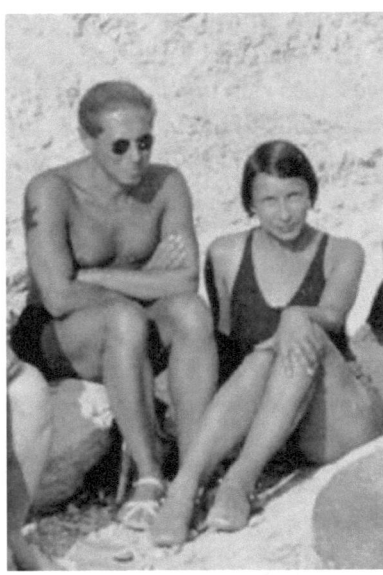

Figure 7. Lion Feuchtwanger und Lola Sernau am Strand von Sanary-sur-Mer
(Ausschnitt), um 1934. Feuchtwanger Memorial Library, USC Libraries, University of
Southern California.

Ihre Schweizer Staatsbürgerschaft bewahrte Lola Humm-Sernau
jedoch nicht davor, von den Franzosen als Deutsche angesehen und im
Juni 1940 im Lager Gurs interniert zu werden, ebenso wie ihre Schwester
Irma, die inzwischen pro forma einen Engländer namens White geheiratet
hatte. Vorher hatte sie allerdings noch Feuchtwangers gerade abgeschlosse-
nen Roman *Der Tag wird kommen* ins Reine getippt und die Typoskripte
an Verleger in Holland, der Schweiz und den USA geschickt, wodurch das
Erscheinen dieses Buches gesichert war. Nach Interventionen der Schweizer
Behörden wurde sie Mitte Juli 1940 wieder freigelassen und konnte nach
Sanary zurückkehren.

Lola Humm-Sernau und Lion Feuchtwanger, dem am 21. Juli die
Flucht aus dem Lager Les Milles gelungen war, sahen sich zuletzt im
September 1940 in Marseille im Haus des amerikanischen Konsuls, wo
sich der Schriftsteller versteckt hielt. Sie erinnerte sich später: „Als wir uns

[…] verabschiedeten, glaubten wir in längstens drei oder vier Monaten in Amerika wieder zusammenzutreffen, um, wie seit so vielen Jahren in Berlin und Sanary, zusammenzuarbeiten. Es sollten aber siebzehn Jahre vergehen, ehe wir uns wiedersahen".[23]

Um der unsicheren Lage in Südfrankreich zu entgehen, übersiedelte Lola Humm-Sernau in die Schweiz, zunächst zu ihrer Schwester nach Burgdorf und anschließend dauerhaft nach Ascona im Tessin. Zuvor sorgte sie noch dafür, dass Feuchtwangers Bibliothek und Arbeitsmaterial aus Sanary verpackt wurden und schließlich über Marseille und Lissabon in die USA gelangten. Ohne diese verdienstvolle Aktion gäbe es die Feuchtwanger Memorial Library in ihrer heutigen Form nicht. Da ihre eigene, von Feuchtwanger intensiv betriebene Emigration in die USA nicht gelang, hielt Lola Humm-Sernau fortan mit dem Schriftsteller brieflich Kontakt. Erst Anfang 1957 kam es zu einer kurzen Wiederbegegnung in Pacific Palisades.

Zeitraum, Umfang und Art der Korrespondenz

Weil in Berlin nahezu täglich ein persönlicher Austausch zwischen Feuchtwanger und seiner Sekretärin bestand, liegen aus dieser Zeit keine Briefe vor. Die erhaltene Korrespondenz setzt vielmehr im Frühjahr 1933 ein, als der Schriftsteller sein neues Leben im Exil organisierte. Weil aber auch Lola Sernau alsbald nach Südfrankreich kam und die Zusammenarbeit mit ihm fortsetzte, wurde in den weiteren 1930er Jahren einander nur dann geschrieben, wenn einer der beiden Partner auf Reisen war. Der Hauptteil der Korrespondenz beginnt daher erst 1940 mit der zweiten Internierung Feuchtwangers und seiner anschließend erfolgten Emigration in die

---

23   Lola Humm-Sernau, „Erinnerungen an Lion Feuchtwanger", in Karl Dietz, Hrsg., *Der Greifen-Almanach 1960* (Rudolstadt: Greifenverlag, 1959), S. 38–41, zit. S. 38. Sie datiert ihre letzte Begegnung mit Feuchtwanger in Marseille irrtümlich auf „Oktober 1940", recte: September, denn bereits am 23.9.1940 schrieb er ihr aus Lissabon.

USA. Während des Krieges war der Postverkehr vorübergehend unter-
brochen, einzelne Sendungen gingen verloren und Verzögerungen bei
der Zustellung führten auch später noch zur Überkreuzung von Briefen.
Nach 1945 entwickelte sich wieder ein recht regelmäßiger Austausch, der
bis zum Tod des Schriftstellers im Dezember 1958 reicht.

Die Korrespondenz zwischen Lion Feuchtwanger und Lola Humm-
Sernau ist sehr umfangreich, aber nicht komplett überliefert, da in
wechselseitigen Schreiben dankend auf Briefe verwiesen wird, die—aus
welchen Gründen auch immer—nicht erhalten sind. Mit insgesamt nahezu
500 Schriftstücken handelt es sich gleichwohl um den zumindest quantitativ
bedeutendsten Briefwechsel des Schriftstellers. Er wird in der Feuchtwanger
Memorial Library (FML), Los Angeles, und im Deutschen Literaturarchiv
(DLA), Marbach, in den jeweiligen Originalen sowie teils in Durchschriften
und Kopien aufbewahrt.[24]

Bis auf während jeweiliger Reisen von Hotels aus mit der Hand ge-
schriebene Mitteilungen liegen die Briefe getippt vor, zuweilen ergänzt
um handschriftliche Anmerkungen. Dies ermöglicht eine Roh-Erfassung
der Texte mit OCR, wofür sich die anderthalbzeilig getippten Briefe von
Feuchtwanger allerdings besser eignen als die aus Gründen der Luftpost-
Portoersparnis eng beschriebenen Blätter von Lola Humm-Sernau. Die
Briefe von Feuchtwanger aus Pacific Palisades wurden zunächst von ihm
selbst getippt, was an der generellen Kleinschreibung erkennbar ist. Später
hat er die Schreiben seiner Sekretärin Hilde Waldo (1906–1994) diktiert,
sofern sie nicht allzu privater Natur waren.

Feuchtwangers Briefe sind überwiegend knapp und sachlich gehalten,
wenngleich es von ihm auch mehrseitige, gehaltvolle Berichte über seine
Lebens- und Arbeitsverhältnisse gibt. Er beklagte sich selbst darüber, dass
er als Briefeschreiber kein großer Stilist sei. Die Briefe von Lola Humm-
Sernau hingegen sind durchweg sehr ausführlich. Sie enthalten zwar auch
faktische Mitteilungen, die jedoch stark von Befindlichkeitsschilderungen
und Alltäglichkeiten durchsetzt sind. Ihre Briefe an Feuchtwanger beginnen

---

24   Feuchtwanger Memorial Library (FML), Lion Feuchtwanger Papers, Box C 13
     und weitere; Deutsches Literaturarchiv (DLA), Handschriftensammlung, Bestand
     „Feuchtwanger, Lion".

mit der Anrede „Sehr lieber Wetcheek" oder „Liebster Lion", seine wiederum mit „Liebste Lola" oder ganz kurz „l l". Gleichwohl wird von beiden
durchgängig das förmliche „Sie" beibehalten (im Unterschied etwa zu Eva
van Hoboken, die Feuchtwanger in seinen Briefen duzte). Zudem sind
die Schreiben des Schriftstellers frei von den Erotizismen seiner früheren
Tagebucheinträge. Allerdings schließen viele Briefe mit dem Wunsch, seitens Lola Humm-Sernau der Sehnsucht, nach einem baldigen Wiedersehen.
Am 29. August 1942 etwa schrieb Feuchtwanger: „ach, Lola, wann endlich? es wird zeit".

Inhalte der Korrespondenz

Im Briefwechsel von Lion Feuchtwanger und Lola Humm-Sernau kommt
eine Fülle von Themen und Personen zur Sprache, die hier nur exemplarisch angedeutet werden kann—und soll, um einer späteren Edition
nicht vorzugreifen. So gab Feuchtwanger im April 1933 von Marseille aus
schriftlich Anweisungen an Lola Sernau, die sich noch in der Schweiz
aufhielt, welche Bestände aus seinem Haus in Berlin-Grunewald zu retten
seien. Die Ausführung sollte durch Werner Cahn-Bieker (1903–1983),
seinen noch in Berlin gebliebenen Assistenten, erfolgen: „es liegt mir
daran, vor allem auch unsere manuskripte, aufsätze usw. zu bekommen
und dann die schwarzen ziemlich grossen leinwandhefte, die im sekretär
im untersten fach rechts liegen, es sind etwa 6 hefte, alte tagebücher, die
ich für die allenfallsige autobiografie brauche". Feuchtwangers Angabe,
es handle sich um „etwa 6 Hefte", entspricht genau jener Anzahl, die in
der Feuchtwanger Memorial Library als Textgrundlage für die Edition
der Tagebücher zur Verfügung stand (das siebte Tagebuch hatte er damals
bei sich, denn es reicht bis zum 16. August 1933). Da die Tagebuchhefte
für 1921 bis 1931 eine Lücke aufweisen, hat es für diesen Zeitraum offenkundig keine Aufzeichnungen gegeben, denn sonst hätte Feuchtwanger
diese ebenfalls aufgezählt. Dank der Kommunikation von Lola Sernau
mit Werner Cahn-Bieker gelangten Bücher und Materialien aus

Feuchtwangers Berliner Haus anschließend über die Schweiz zu ihm nach Südfrankreich.

Einen erheblichen Umfang der Korrespondenz nehmen von 1940 bis 1942 Feuchtwangers Bemühungen ein, für Lola Humm-Sernau ein Visum zur Übersiedelung in die USA zu erwirken. Am 23. September 1940 hatte er ihr bereits aus Lissabon geschrieben: „Betonen Sie überall, daß Sie meine Mitarbeiterin und Sekretärin sind. [...] betonen Sie die Gefahr, in der Sie schweben, und die Wichtigkeit Ihrer Mitarbeit für mein Werk". In der Folgezeit wandte der Schriftsteller viel Zeit und Geld auf, um die Ausreise seiner bewährten Sekretärin in die USA zu ermöglichen. Die amerikanischen Behörden verweigerten Lola Humm-Sernau jedoch ein Visum, weil sie (aufgrund ihrer Heirat) Schweizer Staatsbürgerin und in der Schweiz nicht von Verfolgung bedroht war. Als sich abzeichnete, dass sie ihm nicht nach Los Angeles würde folgen können, stellte Feuchtwanger im Frühjahr 1941 die ebenfalls aus einer Berliner jüdischen Familie stammende Hilde Waldo als seine neue Sekretärin ein. Noch am 27. März 1945 tröstete er Lola Humm-Sernau jedoch mit der Bemerkung: „Das bedeutet aber keineswegs, daß ich Sie, Liebste, nicht außerordentlich vermisse".

Jener Brief enthält auch einen ausführlichen Bericht des Schriftstellers über seine gegenwärtigen Lebensumstände und seine Arbeit: „Gesundheitlich geht es sehr gut. Alterserscheinungen, wie ich sie schon in Sanary hatte, bleiben nicht aus [...]. Ich lebe hier sehr ruhig, außerhalb der Stadt, in einer Landschaft ähnlich wie in Sanary, in wunderbarem Klima, ich mache täglich mein Turnen und Laufen, Marta hält darauf, daß ich sehr vernünftig esse [...]. Ich arbeite viel und noch regelmäßiger als in Sanary. [...] Es sind so unzählige Bekannte hier und alte Freunde von überallher aus Europa und Amerika, und im Lauf der Jahre kommen beinahe alle Leute hier durch, die man irgendwo getroffen hat. [...] In den ersten Jahren habe ich es wirtschaftlich hier nicht leicht gehabt. [...] Wenigstens konnte ich mir jetzt ein Haus kaufen, in dem ich die Bücher bequem unterbringen kann, die ich für die Romane brauche, die ich noch schreiben will".

Lola Humm-Sernau erhielt von Feuchtwanger regelmäßig Mitteilungen über den Fortgang seiner Arbeit, seine Verhandlungen mit Verlegern, seinen Unmut über schlechte Übersetzungen, seine Verkaufserfolge und seine

Zukunftspläne. Anhand seiner Briefe lässt sich daher die Entstehung seiner Romane gut nachvollziehen—von *Waffen für Amerika* über *Goya* und die *Jüdin von Toledo* bis hin zu dem unvollendeten Essay über den historischen Roman (*Das Haus der Desdemona*) und das kurz vor seinem Tod aufgegebene Filmdrehbuch *Bolívar. Das Leben eines Helden.* Allerdings beklagte sich Feuchtwanger stets darüber, wegen des täglichen „Kleinzeugs", allfälliger Posterledigungen und anderer Inanspruchnahmen seiner Person kaum zu seiner eigentlichen Arbeit zu kommen. Lola Humm-Sernau wiederum nahm an seiner schriftstellerischen Produktion regen Anteil und erbat sich Exemplare seiner Neuerscheinungen, die er ihr über die Verlage jeweils großzügig zukommen ließ.

Aus gutem Grund, denn sie lebte in Ascona in finanziell schwierigsten Verhältnissen. Ihre Wohnsituation war oft unzureichend und während eigener Reisen, bei denen sie zumeist bei Freunden oder Bekannten übernachtete, musste sie ihre Zimmer untervermieten, um Geld zu sparen. Feuchtwanger versorgte sie nicht nur mit aufbauenden Worten und guten Ratschlägen, sondern auch mit einer monatlichen Schecksendung von 50 Dollar, die jeweils sehnlich erwartet wurde. Beide betrachteten dies offenbar als „Rente" aufgrund ihrer langjährigen Anstellung bei ihm. Außerdem ließ er Lola Humm-Sernau wiederholt ihm in Europa zustehende Guthaben zukommen. Ohne seine Loyalität und fortdauernde Unterstützung hätte sie nicht existieren können. In ihren Briefen berichtete sie ihm aber auch von ihren psychischen und gesundheitlichen Problemen sowie ihren schwierigen Beziehungen zu Männern, die sie gegenüber Feuchtwanger meist schamhaft als „amants" anonymisierte.

Doch wie in Sanary pflegte Lola Humm-Sernau auch in Ascona einen durchaus lebendigen Umgang mit dort lebenden oder durchreisenden Künstlern, Autoren und Bekannten aus alten Zeiten. Ein enger Kontakt bestand zu Eva van Hoboken, einer weiteren früheren Affäre Feuchtwangers, die nun ebenfalls in Ascona wohnte. Mit ihr tauschte Lola Humm-Sernau jeweils erhaltene Briefe Feuchtwangers aus und unterstützte sie mit Tipparbeiten bei ihren literarischen Ambitionen. Häufig berichtete sie Feuchtwanger über Begegnungen mit ehemaligen Weggefährten und Berufskollegen, gelegentlich mit einer Neigung zum „Klatsch". So schrieb sie ihm am 18. Oktober 1949: „Remarque war hier aufgetaucht, hatte heftiges

Leben entwickelt. Ich [...] war vorige Woche zur grossen Abschiedsparty in seinem wunderschönen Haus, leider mit von Feuchtigkeit völlig lädierten Wänden, eingeladen. Ich glaube für das Geld, das er hier versoffen hat, hätte er sein Haus in Ordnung bringen lassen können. Ich finde es schade um ihn. Er sieht, wenn er nicht völlig versoffen ist, sehr gut aus, ist, finde ich wenigstens, sehr gescheit, sehr amüsant, etwas boshaft und ungeheuer charmant. Er flirtete heftig mit mir, was aber nichts sagen will, da er das anscheinend sozusagen berufsmässig betreibt, und wohl überhaupt nicht anders kann. Er sprach auch viel von Ihnen: freundschaftlich und boshaft".

Zu den ernsthaften Themen der Korrespondenz gehörten Erwägungen über Feuchtwangers etwaige Rückkehr, besuchsweise oder gar dauerhaft, nach Europa. Diese wurde von Lola Humm-Sernau immer wieder angesprochen, auch weil sie ihr ein Wiedersehen mit dem Schriftsteller ermöglicht hätte. Am 10. März 1953 erläuterte Feuchtwanger ihr jedoch seine Bedenken: „Ich brauche Ihnen nicht zu sagen, wie furchtbar gern ich nach Europa käme, wenn nicht für immer, dann doch auf längere Zeit. Aber ich mache mir nichts darüber vor, daß ich damit mir Amerika in jeder Hinsicht für immer versperrte. Nicht nur könnte ich nicht zurückkehren, ich müßte wohl auch mein Haus und meine Bücher im Stich lassen [...]. Außerdem ist es ganz gewiß, daß kein amerikanischer Verleger mehr wagen würde, ein Buch von mir zu veröffentlichen, da die Aussicht, es regulär vertreiben zu können, dann minimal wäre. Von Buchklubs ganz zu schweigen. Zudem müßte ich, wenn ich in Europa bin, ganz sicher mich zu vielen Dingen äußern, und das bedeutete, daß die westdeutschen Buchhändler, die schon jetzt nur mit Mühe dazu gebracht werden können, meine Bücher auszustellen, mich vollends boykottieren würden, und das heißt, ich könnte nicht in der Schweiz oder in Italien oder in Frankreich leben, sondern würde unweigerlich zuletzt nach Ostdeutschland getrieben werden. Das ist an sich nicht schlimm, nur fürchte ich eben, daß ich dort die vierzehn Bücher, die ich noch schreiben möchte [...] nicht würde schreiben können [...]. Bitte, betrachten Sie diesen ganzen Brief als vertraulich und sagen Sie Leuten, die es wissen wollen, immer nur, ich trüge mich mit der Absicht, bald nach Europa zu kommen".

Feuchtwanger hielt auch deshalb den Kontakt zu Lola Humm-Sernau aufrecht, weil er in ihr eine vertrauensvolle Vertreterin seiner Interessen und Angelegenheiten in Europa wusste. So ist sie verschiedentlich mit seiner Vollmacht für ihn tätig geworden—ob sie dafür immer geeignet war, steht dahin. Die Initiative zur Betreibung einer „Wiedergutmachung" für sein in Deutschland verlorenes Eigentum ging sogar vor ihr aus. So schrieb sie ihm bereits am 25. August 1949: „Was ist eigentlich mit Ihrem Haus und Ihrem Geld in Deutschland? Sollte man da nicht jetzt etwas unternehmen?". Feuchtwanger hat dieses Thema eher widerwillig behandelt, weil er sich davon wenig versprach und vor allem zutreffend befürchtete, dafür eine endlose, ihn von seiner Arbeit abhaltende Korrespondenz mit Anwälten und Behörden führen zu müssen. Auf Lola Humm-Sernaus nicht ganz uneigennütziges Nachhaken und ihre Empfehlung der Beauftragung eines Berliner Anwalts antwortete er am 5. September 1951: „Wenn ein Anwalt die Sache übernehmen will, bin ich natuerlich gern bereit, ihm die zehn Prozent zu geben; aber Geld moechte ich von hier aus keines hineinstecken. […] Wenn Sie, Lola, es fuer der Muehe wert halten, dem Geld nachzujagen, dann tun Sie es und Sie sollen dann selbstverständlich auch Ihre zehn Prozent haben. Ich lege Ihnen eine Vollmacht bei". Lola Humm-Sernau beauftragte daraufhin einen Berliner Anwalt, wurde aber auch selbst tätig.

Darüber hinaus bemühte sie sich um Feuchtwangers deutsche Verlagskontakte, verhandelte mit dem Aufbau-Verlag in Berlin und dem Greifenverlag in Rudolstadt über die Veröffentlichung seiner Romane in der DDR und nahm Honorare für ihn entgegen, die er zum Teil ihr überließ. Ferner versorgte sie den Schriftsteller mit Informationen und Einschätzungen über die für ihn aus der Ferne schwer zu beurteilenden kulturpolitischen Vorgänge in der DDR, ebenso mit Eindrücken von ihren Begegnungen mit Arnold Zweig, Bertolt Brecht und anderen in Berlin.

Nach 17 Jahren Trennung sahen sich Lola Humm-Sernau, inzwischen 62 Jahre alt, und Feuchtwanger schließlich wieder. Von November 1956 bis Ende Februar 1957 unternahm sie eine Reise in die USA, die ihr der Schriftsteller finanzierte. Zunächst verbrachte sie einige Zeit in New York mit Emil Julius Gumbel, den sie von Sanary her kannte (und der sie heiraten wollte). Im Januar 1957 folgte ein vierzehntätiger Aufenthalt in Los Angeles, während dessen Lola Humm-Sernau bei Hilde Waldo wohnte. Es kam zu mehreren Begegnungen mit Feuchtwanger und der unvermeidlichen

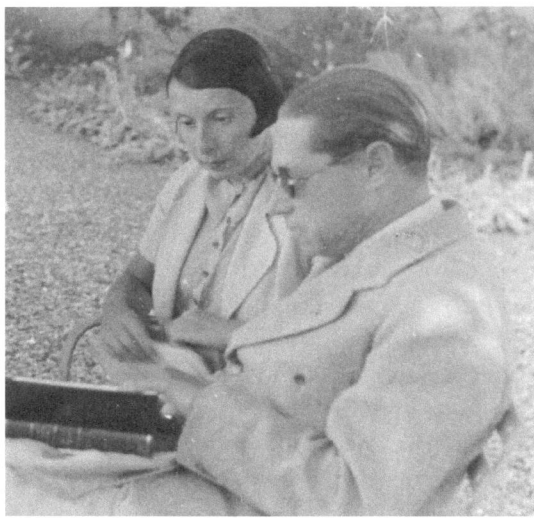

Figure 8. Lola Sernau und Lion Feuchtwanger in Sanary-sur-Mer (Ausschnitt), 1935.
Feuchtwanger Memorial Library, USC Libraries, University of Southern California.

Führung durch seine Bibliothek sowie Gesprächen über gemeinsame
Bekannte und Freunde.

Insgesamt verlief das Wiedersehen jedoch nicht wie erhofft. Einerseits
waren Feuchtwanger und Humm-Sernau durch die kontinuierliche
Korrespondenz übereinander auf dem Laufenden, andererseits hatten sich
ihre Lebenswege naturgemäß völlig auseinanderentwickelt. Anschließend
brachten daher beide in Briefen ihre Enttäuschung über den Verlauf der
Wiederbegegnung zum Ausdruck. Feuchtwanger schrieb: „Ich habe darauf
gerechnet, mit Ihnen nicht nur über meine äußerlichen Dinge reden zu
können, sondern vor allem auch über Probleme, die mich jetzt mehr beschäftigen, über historisch-politische Fragen, über literarische Prinzipien,
über Stilistisches, viele der Bücher, die ich noch schreiben möchte in den
wenigen Jahren, die mir noch bleiben. Es gibt sehr wenige Menschen, mit
denen ich darüber reden kann. Deshalb hatte ich mich doppelt auf Sie
gefreut. Dann sah ich gleich, dass Sie mir zwar die alte Treue—und ich
schreibe es etwas platt und altmodisch hin—Liebe bewahrt haben, aber
geistig waren Sie mir nicht mehr nah und ich konnte mit Ihnen nicht reden".

Der vermutlich letzte Brief von Feuchtwanger an Lola Humm-Sernau, in dem er ihr am 8. Dezember 1958 über seine Erkrankung, eine überstandene Operation und anschließende Untersuchungen berichtete, endete mit einer Formulierung, die für seine auch in schwierigen Lebenslagen optimistische Grundhaltung typisch war: „Es geht mir [...] im ganzen recht gut, viel besser jedenfalls als seit langem". Er starb am 21. Dezember 1958. 1959 veröffentlichte Lola Humm-Sernau in der DDR Erinnerungen an den Schriftsteller, die allerdings im Wesentlichen wiederholten, was sie schon 1929 veröffentlicht hatte.[25]

Der Tod von Feuchtwanger bedeutete aber nicht nur einen menschlichen Verlust, sondern stellte Lola Humm-Sernau auch finanziell vor Probleme, da nun die monatlichen Schecksendungen an sie in Frage standen. Außerdem vermisste sie die Kommunikation mit Los Angeles, die sie daher einige Zeit mit Feuchtwangers Sekretärin Hilde Waldo fortsetzte. Auch zu Marta Feuchtwanger bestand noch ein gelegentlicher Kontakt, der jedoch zwischen 1961 und 1965 eine ungute Wendung nahm, als es zum Streit um Lola Humm-Sernaus Anteil an der inzwischen erfolgten „Wiedergutmachung" für Feuchtwangers Haus in Berlin kam.[26] Marta Feuchtwanger legte eine entsprechende Formulierung ihres Mannes von 1951 so aus, dass im Erfolgsfalle der betreuende Anwalt *oder* Lola Humm-Sernau mit 10 % des Erstattungsbetrags zu beteiligen seien. Letztere beharrte jedoch darauf, dass Feuchtwanger es so gemeint habe, dass sie aufgrund ihrer eigenen Bemühungen *ebenso* wie der Anwalt mit 10 % zu honorieren sei.

In der Folge wurden böse Briefe gewechselt, auch unter Hinzuziehung von Anwälten, und gegenseitige Vorwürfe ausgesprochen, bei denen wohl auch alte Animositäten eine Rolle spielten. Wenngleich Lola Humm-Sernau hier aus existenzieller Not handelte, weil sie lange Krankenhausaufenthalte zu bezahlen hatte, erscheint der gesamte Vorgang doch dem Erbe Feuchtwangers unwürdig. Der Auseinandersetzung überdrüssig hat Marta Feuchtwanger schließlich den geforderten Anteil nach Abzug inzwischen

---

25   L.[ola] S.[ernau], „Wie Lion Feuchtwanger aus Deutschland vertrieben wurde. Erinnerungen seiner Sekretärin", *Das Magazin*, Nr. 7 (Juli 1959), S. 32–34.— Humm-Sernau [1959] (Anm. 23), S. 38–41.

26   FML, Lion Feuchtwanger Papers (Anm. 24), Box C13, File 33.

entstandener Kosten ausgezahlt. Von ihrem im Verlauf angedeuteten
Vorhaben, in ihren Lebenserinnerungen unvorteilhafte Wahrheiten über
ihre Kontrahentin auszusprechen, sah sie jedoch ab. Vielmehr hat sie Lola
Humm-Sernau in ihren Memoiren mit keinem Wort erwähnt, was im
Hinblick auf den über 30jährigen Kontakt zwischen ihrem Mann und
dessen Sekretärin Einiges über ihre anhaltende Abneigung gegenüber Lola
und ihrem Anspruch auf die Deutungshoheit über ihren Mann aussagt.[27]

Tätigkeit als Übersetzerin

Aufschlussreich ist Lola Humm-Sernaus Korrespondenz mit Feuchtwanger nicht zuletzt hinsichtlich ihrer 1943 in Ascona aufgenomme-
nen Tätigkeit als freie Übersetzerin. Denn dabei handelte es sich um
eine klassische Erwerbsmöglichkeit von Frauen im Exil.[28] In ihren
Briefen an den Schriftsteller schilderte sie anschaulich ihre Mühen der
Auftragsbeschaffung bei Schweizer Verlagen, das oft niedrige Niveau der
Originaltexte, die chronisch unzureichende Honorierung, den zu Lasten
der Qualität gehenden Zeitdruck, die ermüdende bis erschöpfende
Tipparbeit und die Unregelmäßigkeit der damit zum Lebensunterhalt
erzielbaren Einkünfte. Am 6. Februar 1946 beispielsweise beklagte sie
sich darüber, „dass mein Leben nur daraus besteht, dass ich wie eine Irre
tippe".

Neben einigen französischen Titeln übersetzte Lola Humm-Sernau
vor allem Texte aus dem Englischen und Amerikanischen, obgleich sie nach
eigener Aussage nicht einmal gut Englisch sprach. Anfangs war sie für die
Exilverlage Oprecht und Europa in Zürich tätig, dann aber vor allem für

27   Marta Feuchtwanger, *Nur eine Frau. Jahre, Tage Stunden* (München: Langen
      Müller, 1983).
28   Ernst Fischer, *Geschichte des deutschen Buchhandels im 19. und 20. Jahrhundert.*
      Drittes Reich und Exil. T. 3: Der Buchhandel im deutschsprachigen Exil 1933–
      1945, Teilbd. 2 (Berlin: de Gruyter, 2021), S. 787–816, hier S. 811 kurz zu Lola
      Humm-Sernau.

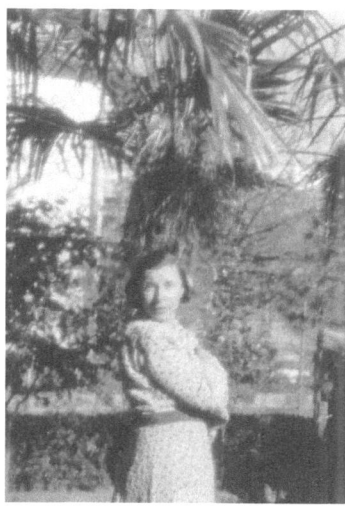

Figure 9. Lola Humm-Sernau in Ascona (Ausschnitt), 1947. Akademie
der Künste Berlin, Leonard Steckel Archiv.

die in Bern ansässigen Belletristik-Verlage Hallwag und Scherz. Dabei handelte es sich überwiegend nicht um literarisch besonders anspruchsvolle
Titel, sondern zumeist um Unterhaltungs- und vor allem Kriminalromane,
darunter auch Titel von Agatha Christie.

Lola Humm-Sernau berichtete Feuchtwanger nicht nur über ihre
jeweiligen Übersetzungsaufträge, sondern bat ihn wiederholt auch um
Empfehlungen von amerikanischen Romanen, um diese wiederum
Schweizer Verlagen als aussichtsreiche Titel für eine Übertragung ins
Deutsche vorschlagen zu können. Der Schriftsteller erwies sich dabei als
über amerikanische Neuerscheinungen erstaunlich gut informiert. Am
24. Januar 1949 beispielsweise schrieb er ihr: „Von Buechern, die fuer
Uebersetzungen in Frage kommen, scheinen mir die wichtigsten: Norman
Mailer: THE NAKED AND THE DEAD. [...] Das ist ohne Frage bei
weitem der beste Roman, der in den letzten Jahren hier erschienen ist; aber
er ist sehr lang und sehr schwer zu uebersetzen".

Insgesamt hat Lola Humm-Sernau bis Mitte der 1960er Jahre über
50 Romane übersetzt (vgl. die Liste im Anhang). Hinzu kommen noch

einige unter dem Namen ihres ebenfalls in Ascona lebenden Kollegen und Lebensgefährten Carl Bach (1898–1968) veröffentlichte Übersetzungen, an denen sie mitgewirkt hat. In Zusammenarbeit mit Bach entstand auch die Übersetzung von Henry Millers griechischen Reiseerinnerungen *Der Koloss von Maroussi* (1955), von deren deutschsprachiger Ausgabe bis heute über eine Viertelmillion Exemplare verkauft wurden. Die wohl bekannteste eigene Übersetzung von Lola Humm-Sernau ist der Kriminalroman *007 James Bond und sein gefährlichster Auftrag* (1964) von Ian Fleming, die erste deutsche Fassung von *On Her Majesty's Secret Service*.

Neben ihrer Übersetzungstätigkeit schrieb sie gelegentlich Artikel für Schweizer Zeitungen, darunter 1946 für den *Berner Bund* über die ersten Filmfestspiele in Cannes.[29] 1971 veröffentlichte sie in der Zürcher Tageszeitung *Die Tat* eine Erinnerung an das Zustandekommen der Publikation des Romans *Stepan Varesku* (1942) von Jo Mihaly, bei der auch Feuchtwanger eine Rolle spielte.[30] Sie war Mitglied im P.E.N. Basel und im ISDS (Internationaler Schutzverband deutschsprachiger Schriftsteller). 1968 verstarb ihr langjähriger Freund Carl Bach in Ascona. Die Traueranzeige in der *Neuen Zürcher Zeitung* wurde „Im Namen seiner Freunde" von Lola Humm-Sernau unterzeichnet.[31] *Kürschners Deutscher Literatur-Kalender* verzeichnete sie letztmalig 1978 mit einer Auswahlliste ihrer Übersetzungen.[32] Einige dieser Titel sind bis heute in Neuausgaben lieferbar, teils auch als e-book.

Die finanzielle Bedrängnis von Lola Humm-Sernau hielt offenkundig im Alter an. Denn Anfang der 1970er Jahre lieferte sie bei ihren Berlin-Besuchen einzelne Briefe aus ihrer Korrespondenz mit Feuchtwanger beim dortigen Auktionshaus Bassenge ein. Diese wurden von dem Stuttgarter Antiquar Herbert Blank (1929–2023) ersteigert, der sie 1975 in einem seiner Kataloge mit ausführlicher Zitierung als Autographen

---

29   L.[ola] H.[umm], „Internationale Filmwoche in Cannes", *Der Bund*, Bd. 97, Nr. 473 (11.10.1946), S. 7.

30   Lola Humm-Sernau, „Die Preisverleihung fand nicht statt", *Die Tat* [Zürich] Nr. 260 (November 5, 1971), S. 5.

31   *Neue Zürcher Zeitung*, Nr. 353, 12.6.1968, S. 18.

32   Werner Schuder, Hrsg., *Kürschners Deutscher Literatur-Kalender 1978. 57. Jg* (Berlin: De Gruyter, 1978), S. 433 f. (mit falschem Geburtsjahr „1896", recte: 1895).

anbot.[33] Der Antiquar Carl-Ernst Kohlhauer (1929–2020) erwarb die Briefe und bestückte damit 1976 zusammen mit Büchern und Bildern in Feuchtwangen eine kleine Ausstellung zu Feuchtwanger.[34] Ebenfalls aus finanziellen Gründen, aber wohl auch im Sinne einer Lebensregelung und im Bewusstsein um die Bedeutung der Korrespondenz hat Lola Humm-Sernau schließlich 1975 den Großteil ihres Briefwechsels mit Feuchtwanger an das Deutsche Literaturarchiv in Marbach verkauft. Auf ihren Wunsch hin blieben die Briefe dort allerdings bis zu ihrem Tod für eine Benutzung gesperrt.

Zeitzeugin des Exils

Als Zeitzeugin des Exils in Sanary-sur-Mer und vor allem aufgrund ihrer Zusammenarbeit mit Feuchtwanger wurde Lola Humm-Sernau in den 1980er Jahren in Ascona von einigen Publizist(inn)en und Wissenschaftler(inne)n besucht und befragt. Bereits 1980 führte die Autorin Gabriele Kreis Gespräche mit ihr für ihre 1984 veröffentlichte Studie über die Rolle von *Frauen im Exil*.[35] 1982 entstand ein Dokumentarfilm des Senders Freies Berlin über *Die Jahre mit Feuchtwanger. Erinnerungen von Lola Humm-Sernau* mit Interviews an deren Lebensstationen Berlin, Sanary und Ascona.[36] Dabei präsentierte sie sich als recht selbstbewusste ältere Dame, geradezu als Grande Dame des Exils, was nicht ihrer damaligen Lebenssituation und Rolle entsprach.

---

33 Antiquariat Herbert Blank, *Katalog 18. Literatur und Kunst des 20. Jahrhunderts* (Stuttgart: 1975), S. 11–13.

34 Carl-Ernst Kohlhauer, *Ausstellung Lion Feuchtwanger. Bücher, Briefe, Bilder* (Feuchtwangen: Kreuzgangspiele, 1976), Nrn. 34–45.

35 Gabriele Kreis, *Frauen im Exil. Dichtung und Wirklichkeit* (Düsseldorf: Claasen, 1984; Darmstadt: Luchterhand, 1988), S. 46–54 und 230.

36 *Die Jahre mit Feuchtwanger. Erinnerungen von Lola Humm-Sernau.* Ein Dokumentarfilm von Bettina Arnoldi, Annette Dietrich und Jürgen Stahf. SFB: Berlin 1982.

Während sie ihren Umgang mit namhaften Zeitgenossen und ihre
Tätigkeit für Feuchtwanger anschaulich schilderte, kam ihre langjährige
Abhängigkeit von dessen finanzieller Unterstützung nicht zur Sprache.
Die Feuchtwanger-Biographen Wilhelm von Sternburg und Volker
Skierka haben Lola Humm-Sernau für ihre dann 1984 erschienenen
Bücher zum 100. Geburtstag des Schriftstellers ebenfalls aufgesucht.[37] Zu
ihrem 90. Geburtstag 1985 hat Skierka zudem einen Artikel über sie in der
Süddeutschen Zeitung veröffentlicht.[38]

In der Anzeige zum Tod von Lola Humm-Sernau, die am 26. September
1988 in Locarno im 94. Lebensjahr verstorben war, heißt es: „Ihre Freunde in
Ascona, in der Schweiz, in Europa und in Übersee empfinden ihren Tod als
einen unersetzlichen Verlust".[39] In Deutschland wurde davon hingegen keine
Notiz genommen, auch nicht seitens der akademischen Exilforschung.[40] Weder
der Verbleib ihres Nachlasses, noch die Rechtsnachfolge am Urheberrecht
ihrer Übersetzungen konnten bisher geklärt werden.[41] Auch Bücher, Briefe
und Fotos sowie autobiographische Notizen, die sich noch in ihrem Besitz
befanden, müssen daher wohl als verloren gelten.

Etwas mehr Beachtung erfuhr Lola Humm-Sernau durch die zu-
nehmende Beschäftigung mit Sanary-sur-Mer als Exilort deutschsprachiger Schriftsteller. In den entsprechenden Veröffentlichungen findet sie
zumindest Erwähnung, wenngleich meist nur im Zusammenhang ihrer
Tätigkeit für Feuchtwanger.[42] Ferner wird auf einer im Stadtbild von Sanary

---

37   Wilhelm von Sternburg, *Lion Feuchtwanger. Ein deutsches Schriftstellerleben*
     (Königstein/Ts.: Athenäum, 1984).—Volker Skierka (Autor) und Stefan Jaeger,
     Hrsg., *Lion Feuchtwanger. Eine Biographie* (Berlin: Quadriga, 1984).
38   Volker Skierka, „Eine Dame voller Erinnerungen. Zum 90. Geburtstag von Lola
     Sernau", *Süddeutsche Zeitung*, Nr. 147 (29./30.6.1985), S. 146.
39   *Neue Zürcher Zeitung*, Nr. 227 (29.9.1988), S. 56.
40   Im *Nachrichtenbrief der Gesellschaft für Exilforschung e.V.* war ihr 90. Geburtstag
     noch vermerkt worden (1986, Nr. 5–6, S. 131); ihr Tod jedoch nicht mehr.
41   Freundl. Auskünfte des S. Fischer Verlags, Frankfurt am Main, vom 3.1.2022 und
     des Rowohlt Verlags, Hamburg, vom 6.1.2022.
42   Vgl. u. a. Manfred Flügge, *Wider Willen im Paradies. Deutsche Schriftsteller im Exil
     in Sanary-sur-Mer* (Berlin: Aufbau-Taschenbuch, 1996).—Ville de Sanary-sur-Mer,
     Hrsg., *Sur le pas des Allemands et des Autrichiens en exil à Sanary, 1933–1945* (Sanary-
     sur-Mer: 2004), S. 79–81 (falsches Todesjahr „1990", recte: 1988, und falsches

angebrachten Gedenktafel an sie erinnert, allerdings mit einem etwas feh-
lerhaften Text[43] und einem Porträtfoto aus der Feuchtwanger Memorial
Library,[44] bei dem es sich wohl um eine Verwechslung handelt, denn es hat
mit der Sekretärin des Schriftstellers keine Ähnlichkeit.[45]

Ausblick

Die Tatsache, dass Lola Humm-Sernau ihre von Feuchtwanger erhalte-
nen Briefe aufbewahrt und zu Lebzeiten an das Deutsche Literaturarchiv
gegeben hat, unterstreicht ihre Einschätzung, dass es sich bei dieser
Korrespondenz nicht bloß um sentimentale Erinnerungsstücke, sondern auch um Dokumente von literatur- und exilgeschichtlichem
Quellenwert handelt. Daraus resultiert eine gewisse Verpflichtung für die
Feuchtwanger-Forschung, diesen Briefwechsel zu erschließen und einer
interessierten Leserschaft zugänglich zu machen.

Allerdings ergibt bereits eine kursorische Durchsicht der
Korrespondenz, dass eine Volltext-Dokumentation dafür nicht in Betracht

---

Foto).—Ulrike Voswinckel und Frank Berninger, Hrsg., *Exil am Mittelmeer.
Deutsche Schriftsteller in Südfrankreich 1933–1941* (München: Buch&Media,
2005).—Magali Laure Nieradka, *„Die Hauptstadt der deutschen Literatur". Sanary-
sur-Mer als Ort des Exils deutschsprachiger Schriftsteller* (Göttingen: V & R Unipress,
2010).—Magali Nieradka-Steiner, *Exil unter Palmen. Deutsche Emigranten in
Sanary-sur-Mer.* (Darmstadt: wbg Theiss, 2018).—Andrea Schultz und Guenter
Schmidt, *Sie emigrierten nicht, fliehen mussten sie. Die Gedenktafel in Sanary-sur-
Mer. So könnte es gewesen sein* (Berlin: SDL, 2022) (3. Aufl.), S. 109–114 (falsches
Todesjahr „1990", recte: 1988).

43 Falsches Todesjahr „1990", recte: 1988. Die Heirat mit dem Schweizer Fritz Humm
erfolgte 1938, nicht „1939". Die Formulierung „übersetzte die Romane von Ian
Fleming" ist übertrieben, tatsächlich war es ein Roman von ihm.

44 FML, Lion Feuchtwanger Papers (Anm. 24), Box C13, Folder 16.

45 Ebenso bei von Sternburg 2014 (Anm. 6), n. S. 272, Abb. 9 (S. 93 zudem falsches Todesjahr „1990", recte: 1988) und in den *Feuchtwanger-Tagebüchern* 2018
(Anm. 5), n. S. 400, Abb. 30.

kommt, da zahlreiche Briefe, insbesondere jene von Lola Humm-Sernau, zu viele Mitteilungen über Alltäglichkeiten (Wetter) und Befindlichkeit (Gesundheit, Stimmungslage), Wohnsituation und Finanznöte sowie Wiederholungen von Freundlichkeiten etwa zu Geburtstagen enthalten, die wenig Erkenntniswert bieten. Andererseits sind auch Feuchtwangers Briefinhalte nicht durchgängig exklusiv, sondern decken sich zum Teil mit bereits bekannten Äußerungen gegenüber anderen Briefpartnern.

Für die Briefedition soll daher eine Auswahl getroffen werden, die sich auf relevante und spezifische Abschnitte dieser Korrespondenz konzentriert. Ob sich dafür eine erläuternde Kommentierung als wissenschaftlicher Anhang oder der besseren Lesbarkeit halber im unmittelbaren Zusammenhang mit den Briefstellen empfiehlt, wird die weitere Bearbeitung ergeben. Zu Detailaspekten und einigen der in der Korrespondenz erwähnten Personen besteht zudem noch Forschungsbedarf.[46] Als Orientierung und Ermutigung helfen dabei zwei charakteristische Eigenschaften von Lion Feuchtwanger: Geduld und Zuversicht.

Anhang: Übersetzungen von Lola Humm-Sernau

Die Datierung bezieht sich auf die Erstveröffentlichung, während die Übersetzung oft bereits im Jahr zuvor erfolgte. Zahlreiche Titel sind später auch in Lizenzausgaben, Folgeauflagen und Neuausgaben erschienen.

Moore, John: Das gleiche Ziel. Roman eines Staffelführers aus Englands dunkelsten Tagen. Oprecht: Zürich/New York 1943.—Prokopovicz, S. N.: Die natürlichen Hilfsquellen der UdSSR. Europa: Zürich/New York 1944.—Daniel, Laurent: Die Liebenden von Avignon. Roman. Oprecht: Zürich/New York 1944.—Kelly, Judith: Das Leben

---

46   Zur Rolle von Lola Humm-Sernau bei der Rettung von Feuchtwangers Bibliothek vgl. zuletzt Julia Schneidawind, Schicksale und ihre Bücher. Deutsch-jüdische Privatbibliotheken zwischen Jerusalem, Tunis und Los Angeles (Göttingen: Vandenhoeck & Ruprecht, 2023), S. 75–113 (Rekonstruiertes zwischen München, Sanary-sur-Mer und Los Angeles – Die Bibliothek von Lion Feuchtwanger).

ist nicht traurig. Hallwag: Bern 1944.—Payne, Robert: David und Anna. Hallwag: Bern 1945.—Fedorova, Nina: Die Familie. Hallwag: Bern 1945.—Abramson, Alexandre: Die Curzon-Linie. Das Grenzproblem Sowjetunion-Polen. Europa: Zürich/New York 1945.—Street, James: Verheissenes Land. Hallwag: Bern 1946.—Wagner, Friedelind; Cooper, Page: Nacht über Bayreuth. Die Geschichte der Enkelin Richard Wagners. Hallwag: Bern 1946.—O'Neill, Eugene: Der Zar ist weit, 1946 (Veröffentlichung nicht nachweisbar).—Fedorova, Nina: Die Kinder. Hallwag: Bern 1947.—Deeping, Warwick: Die Gnadenfrist. Scherz: Bern 1947.—Henderson, Nevile: Wasser unter den Brücken. Episoden einer diplomatischen Laufbahn. Rentsch: Erlenbach-Zürich 1949.—Yeh [Ye Junjian], Chun-Chan: Dorf in den Bergen. Hallwag: Bern 1949.— Feiner, Ruth: Bist du bereit, Caroline? Hallwag: Bern 1949.—Deeping, Warwick: Zwei Leben. Scherz: Bern 1950.—McNeilly, Mildred: Der Himmel ist zu hoch. Hallwag: Bern 1951.—Deeping, Warwick: Das Haus der Abenteuer. Scherz: Bern 1951.—Deeping, Warwick: Licht im Dunkel. Scherz: Bern 1952.—Deeping, Warwick: Kitty. Scherz: Bern 1952.— Rinehart, Mary Roberts: Das gelbe Zimmer. Scherz: Bern 1952.—Queen, Ellery: Wer ist der Nächste? Scherz: Bern 1953.—Deeping, Warwick: Sybilla. Scherz: Bern 1953.—Spring, Howard: Rachel Rosing. Scherz: Bern 1953.— Bromfield, Louis: Ein Held unserer Zeit. Scherz: Bern 1953.—Queen, Ellery: Vom Teufel gehetzt. Scherz: Bern 1954.—Christie, Agatha: Mord in Mesopotamien. Scherz: Bern 1954.—Sayers, Dorothy L.: Lord Peters schwerster Fall. Scherz: Bern 1954.—Gann, Ernest K.: Im Spiel der Gewalten. Scherz: Bern 1954.—Decrest, Jacques: Hasard. Scherz: Bern 1954.—Christie, Agatha: Der Wachsblumenstrauß. Scherz: Bern 1954.— Bromfield, Louis: Das Leben der Lily Shane. Scherz: Bern 1954.—Gann, Ernest K.: Niemandsland der Liebe. Scherz: Bern 1955.—Deeping, Warwick: Liebe in Fesseln. Scherz: Bern 1955.—Decrest, Jacques: Drei Mädchen aus Wien. Scherz: Bern 1955.—Queen, Ellery: Detektive entführt! Scherz: Bern 1955.—Houston, Margaret Bell: Yonder. Roman einer Leidenschaft. A. Müller: Rüschlikon bei Zürich 1956.—Queen, Ellery: Der zehnte Tag. Scherz: Bern 1956.—Miller, Henry: Der Koloss von Maroussi. Eine Reise nach Griechenland. Rowohlt: Hamburg 1956 *(zusammen mit Carl Bach)*.—Deeping, Warwick: Geheimnis um Isabella. Scherz: Bern

1957.—Marsh, Ngaio: Ein Schuss im Theater. Scherz: Bern 1957.—
Queen, Ellery: Zwei blutige Buchstaben. Scherz: Bern 1957.—Queen,
Ellery: Die Drachenzähne. Scherz: Bern/Stuttgart/Wien 1958.—Queen,
Ellery: Trauung in der Luft. Scherz: Bern/Stuttgart/Wien 1959.—Gann,
Ernest K.: Es wird immer wieder Tag. Deutscher Bücherbund: Stuttgart
1959.—Kaye, Mary Margaret: Es geschah auf Zypern. Kriminalroman.
Desch: München/Wien/Basel 1960.—Gillian, Michael: Schatten der
Schuld. Scherz: Bern/Stuttgart/Wien 1960.—Catto, Max: Fähre nach
Hongkong. Scherz: Bern/Stuttgart/Wien 1960.—Deeping, Warwick: In
den Fängen der Nacht. Scherz: Bern/Stuttgart/Wien 1961.—Dickson,
Carter: Hinter den Kulissen. Scherz: Bern/Stuttgart/Wien 1961.—Durrell,
Lawrence (Hrsg.): Ein Henry-Miller-Lesebuch. Rowohlt: Reinbek bei
Hamburg 1961 *(zusammen mit Carl Bach und anderen)*.—Fleming,
Ian: 007 James Bond und sein gefährlichster Auftrag. Scherz: Bern/
München 1964 (spätere Auflagen unter dem Titel „007 James Bond im
Dienst Ihrer Majestät").—Wallace, Irving: Die sieben sündigen Tage.
Droemer/Knaur: München/Zürich 1969 *(zusammen mit Carl Bach)*.

WILLIAM KATIN

4   Two Women Behind-the-Scenes in Lion Feuchtwanger's Escape: Ingrid Warburg and Eleanor Roosevelt

ABSTRACT

Varian Fry's role in Lion Feuchtwanger's elusion of the Gestapo is well known and Fry's recognition as a Righteous Among The Nations is well deserved. Nevertheless, there are several other participants, whose activities are less well known. This chapter acknowledges Eleanor Roosevelt's and Ingrid Warburg's roles in rescuing persecuted European intellectuals.

Lion Feuchtwanger's Escape to the United States

Thanks to Lion Feuchtwanger's autobiographical work *Der Teufel in Frankreich* [The Devil in France] many of the heroic details regarding Lion's internment along with Adolf Lekisch and numerous others in San Nicola and his escape from the French internment camp are well known. The daredevil aspects include U.S. Vice-Consul Miles Standish handing Lion an overcoat and scarf and whisking him away from the internment camp Les Milles in his car, claiming at checkpoints that the person in the back seat was his mother-in-law. Since Feuchtwanger was at the top of Hitler's list of most wanted men, Consul Hiram Bingham suggested Lion use a pseudonym on his American visa. So, an English translation of his surname was used: "James Wetcheek". The Unitarian humanitarian Martha Sharp rented a room in the hotel adjacent to the train station and enabled the Feuchtwangers to safely board the train departing from Marseilles. They climbed over the Pyrenees and at the Spanish customs booth, Marta Feuchtwanger boldly threw a mound of Camel cigarettes on the table, distracting the border officials so they wouldn't notice the famous Feuchtwanger name on her papers. Varian Fry took the baggage ahead to Portugal. Franz Werfel and Heinrich Mann sailed from Spain aboard the *Nea Hellas*, arriving in New York on October 13, 1940, and Feuchtwanger aboard the *Excalibur*.[1]

Varian Fry deserves fame for rescuing thousands of Jewish intellectuals, both before and after the Feuchtwangers' escape. But there are several women, who have never been recognized for their efforts which enabled the Emergency Rescue Committee's success. I would like to bring attention to two of them: Ingrid Warburg and Eleanor Roosevelt. My research is based on Ingrid's many prior years of engagement with the antifascist movement as well as the unpublished correspondence between Ingrid and Eleanor after the Feuchtwangers' flight, which is archived in the FDR Presidential Library and Museum. Lion's enigmatic book dedication "… for Ingrid Warburg and Harold Oram, who made it possible" will be explicated.[2]

Ingrid Warburg

Early in the twentieth century, the Warburg brothers further expanded the Hamburg banking dynasty by marriage and operating abroad. Their mother was Charlotte Oppenheim of the Salomon Oppenheim Bank, headquartered in Cologne. Felix Warburg not only married Frieda Schiff, but also became a partner with Kuhn, Loeb & Company in New York. Similarly, Paul Warburg served as the Second Vice Chair of

---

1   Lion Feuchtwanger, *Der Teufel in Frankreich; Erlebnisse 1940* (Berlin: Aufbau Verlag), 344–50. Varian Fry, *Surrender on Demand* (Scranton: Random House, 1945), 57–65. Also see Varian Fry Papers 1940–67, Columbia University Libraries, Series II: Arranged Correspondence Box 3 for Lion Feuchtwanger. Sheila Isenberg, *A Hero of Our Own* (New York: Random House, 2001), 90.

2   Varian Fry Papers 1940–67, Columbia University Libraries, Series I: Catalogued Correspondence Box 1 for Eleanor Roosevelt; Series II: Arranged Correspondence Box 5 for both Eleanor Roosevelt and Ingrid Warburg.

the Federal Reserve Bank and lived in New York. In contrast with his two brothers, who sought new banking careers in the United States, Fritz Moritz Warburg remained in Hamburg directing M. M. Warburg, one of Germany's largest privately owned banks. Fritz married Anna Beata Josephson and had three children, the eldest of whom was Ingrid, born in 1910.

In the Summer Semester of 1932, Ingrid began studying at Oxford, where she started a friendship with Adam von Trott, which lasted until his 1944 execution as part of the Kreisau Circle in the aftermath of the failed assassination attempt against Hitler. During their first conversation, she presciently said to him that they were living in the last moment of peace in which it was still possible to freely exchange opinions.[3]

Returning to a Ph.D. program in Hamburg during the winter of 1932, she witnessed daily street fighting between Nazis and Communists. She was already using her organizational and financial problem-solving skills to assist Jewish youth to learn agriculture before emigration to the kibbutzim of Palestine in the HeHalutz program.[4] Ingrid was rewarded for passing her doctoral exams with a six-week visit with her uncle Felix in New York. Before her departure she took the Zionist Pioneers sightseeing through Munich, Füssen, and Freiburg. On June 22, 1935, she wrote to von Trott how distraught she was in seeing signs warning Jews not to enter villages in Bavaria and Franconia.[5]

Jewish members of M. M. Warburg's Supervisory Board had been forced to relinquish their seats since 1933 and Felix and Paul Warburg were encouraging their brothers Max and Fritz to emigrate from Germany, so it was unsurprising that Ingrid's stay in the United States became permanent. Adam's work for the Institute for Pacific Relations allowed stopovers in New York to visit Ingrid on his way to China. In his 1937 and 1939 U.S. layovers, he impressed Ingrid's friends Eleanor Roosevelt and Trude

---

3   Ingrid Warburg Spinelli, *Erinnerungen 1910–1989. Die Dringlichkeit des Mitleids und die Einsamkeit nein zu sagen* (Hamburg: Dölling und Galitz Verlag, 1990), 83–6.
4   Spinelli, *Ibid.*, 95–7.
5   Spinelli, *Ibid.*, 104.

Pratt. Also in 1939, von Trott wrote a letter to President Roosevelt, unsuccessfully attempting to persuade him to oppose Hitler.[6]

Emerging Friendship between Ingrid Warburg and Eleanor Roosevelt

Ingrid's Uncle Felix in New York became a role model for Ingrid by financially supporting the Joint Distribution Committee and helping violinists Jehudi Menuhin, Jasha Heifetz, and many other artists to come to America. In shaping Ingrid's future, Felix relied upon past cooperation between Warburg bankers and aid for the Jewish community by cooperating with the Joint.[7] Ingrid had emotional support from the male descendants of the Warburg banking empire in sharp contrast to Eleanor's isolation by the Roosevelt clan. Over a dinner during the winter of 1937, Rabbi Philip Bernstein asked Felix to come to Rochester, New York, and represent the Joint. Instead, Felix proposed that Ingrid speak, since she had more up-to-date experiences of Germany. In antithesis, it was Associated Press reporter Lorena "Hick" Hickok, who encouraged Eleanor Roosevelt to begin writing *My Day*, the six-day-per-week syndicated column for United Features in January 1936. The newspaper articles became the fount for "a new source of confidence" and "a regular forum to express her most heartfelt concerns."[8]

6   Spinelli, *Ibid.*, 116, 126–7.
7   For example, the *Zentralausschuss der deutschen Juden für Hilfe und Ausbau* (Central Relief Committee) was established on April 13, 1933, two weeks after the Nazi boycott of Jewish businesses. The *Zentralausschuss* was under the direction of Leo Baeck, who was assisted by Heinrich Stahl and Dr. Karl Melchoir, a Partner in the M. M. Warburg Bank in Hamburg. The *Zentralausschuss* was an umbrella organization which provided counseling centers for all occupations as well as granting of loans. Friedrich Brodnitz, "Zentralausschuss der deutschen Juden für Hilfe und Aufbau," *Der Morgen*, Band 9 Heft 4 (October 1933), 276–9.
8   Blanche Wiesen Cook, *Eleanor Roosevelt: Vol. 2, the Defining Years 1933–1938* (New York: Penguin Books, 1999), 290, 302.

During her 1937 speech for the Joint, Ingrid mentioned the signs upon entering villages in Bavaria and Franconia warning Jews to enter at their own risk. Several hundred in the hotel donated money, leading the Joint to offer Ingrid a position raising funds in 220 cities across America. While on tour, Ingrid stayed at the homes of leading figures and thus met famous individuals such as the novelist Thomas Mann, his children Klaus and Erika as well as screen star Douglas Fairbanks and the Austrian actress and screenwriter Salka Viertel. In addition, the Joint supplied her with useful fundraising information about wealthy individuals in the Jewish community.[9] A crucial friendship with Eleanor Roosevelt formed during Ingrid's extensive speaking tour.[10] During the same time period, Eleanor also developed a working association with the Joint Distribution Committee. From her syndicated column, Eleanor wrote shortly after the close of the war:

> Of the 7,000,000 Jews who lived in Europe when Hitler first came to power, nearly 6,000,000 were put to death in the most brutal manner possible. The methods used frequently included deliberate starvation and torture. Among those murdered were 2,000,000 Jewish children. Just the other day, I talked to a man and his wife who had finally managed to come to this country from a concentration camp near Frankfurt. They are educated, scholarly people—he is a poet … . This committee in New York is helping these people in 51 countries through a joint distribution committee, which does the work of providing food, clothing, shelter and medical supplies.[11]

Accounts of Nazi Violence by Warburg, Fry, and Roosevelt

Coincidentally both Ingrid Warburg's accounts of violence by the Nazis and the two articles on National Socialist mayhem from Berlin penned by Varian Fry for *The New York Times* were all composed in the summer

---

9   Spinelli, *Erinnerungen*, 137–40.

10   Ron Chernow, *The Warburgs: The Twentieth-Century Odyssey of a Remarkable Jewish Family* (New York: Random House, 2016), 493–6.

11   Eleanor Roosevelt, *My Day* June 11, 1946, Eleanor Roosevelt Papers Digital Edition, George Washington University.

of 1935. To her winter 1932 observation of street fighting between Nazis and Communists in Hamburg, Ingrid added the signs warning Jews not to enter villages in Bavaria and Franconia. Before accepting the position of Editor at *The Living Age*, Fry stayed at the Pension Stern on the Kurfürstendamm from May through July, in order to have personal exposure to everyday life in Nazi Germany. Varian reported a violent incident on the eastern end of the Kurfürstendamm with cars being stopped so that the SA could look for occupants with supposed Jewish facial features. More ominous was the onlooking mob's pleasure in watching Jewish men and women receiving beatings. Although police were present, they did not attempt to protect the Jewish motorists.

Because Fry and Ernst Hanfstaengl were both Harvard alumni, Hitler's friend Hanfstaengl granted Fry an interview "explaining the causes of the anti-Semitic outburst." Hanfstaengl claimed that there had been hissing by Jews at a Swedish movie shown in the Ufa Palast on the Kurfürstendamm, which the SA could not tolerate. Several hundred Brown Shirts directed 500 youths to drag Jewish patrons out of cafes neighboring the theater. Police involvement seemed confined to arresting Fry for taking Nazi propaganda off the walls as a souvenir.[12] Regrettably, Eleanor Roosevelt's *My Day* column was silent with regard to the Nazi persecution of the Jewish people for five years. Belatedly, she did decry the developing genocide:

> But good or bad, they [the Jewish people] have suffered in Europe as has no other group. The percentage killed among them in the past few years far exceeds the losses among any of the United Nations in the battles which have been fought throughout the war.[13]

12   "Editor Describes Rioting in Berlin," *The New York Times*, July 17, 1935, and "Editor holds Riots Inspired by Nazis," *The New York Times*, July 26, 1935. Also see Andy Marino, *A Quiet American: The Secret War of Varian Fry* (New York: St. Martin's Press, 2000).

13   Eleanor Roosevelt, *My Day* August 13, 1943, Eleanor Roosevelt Papers Digital Edition, George Washington University.

Ingrid Warburg's and Eleanor Roosevelt's Support for Jewish Refugees

The urgent need to assist Jewish refugees increased in 1940 as France capitulated and asylum seekers in France were suddenly in mortal danger. In response, the American Friends hosted a banquet in New York's Commodore Hotel on June 25, 1940, in which more than $3,400 were raised. A few days later, the Emergency Rescue Committee (ERC) under the direction of Karl Frank was formed in Ingrid's apartment. Ingrid's official capacity was to locate new donors, a task for which the prior years of securing contributions for the Joint had admirably prepared her.[14]

Fry's involvement on the Kurfürstendamm matched the engagement of the ERC's Chair Frank Kingdon, who expressed his opposition to America's isolationism, "Americans cannot hold themselves aloof from the miseries of mankind."[15] Frank Kingdon was a Methodist pastor before accepting the responsibility for directing the ERC. Other rescuers of Europeans threatened by the Nazis, who represented Protestant denominations included the previously mentioned Unitarians Waitstill and Marsha Sharp as well as the Quaker Clarence Pickett. Eleanor Roosevelt promoted the same goals of liberating the trapped refugees but was far more direct in private engagement than in her public expression. Thus, her mention of Frank Kingdon appeared in a "folksy" manner:

> I went first to the lunch of the Women's Division of the National Citizens' Committee for Political Action. I was sorry that I had to leave before I had finished hearing Dr. Frank Kingdon, who is always an interesting speaker, and Quentin Reynolds,

14   Spinelli, *Erinnerungen*, 165–75.

15   Kingdon later added, "I cannot stay on the sidelines and say that this is not my struggle. It must be fought through so that the institutions of tomorrow shall be molded by those who believe in freedom rather than in tyranny," in "War's Basis Social, Dr. Kingdon Holds," *The New York Times*, January 16, 1940 and "Liberals' Outlook seen as Handicap," *The New York Times*, February 3, 1941.

who is one of my favorite speakers. I did have the pleasure, however, of hearing two charming ladies as presiding officers, Mrs. Edward Warburg and Dorothy Parker.[16]

One could have wished that the casual manner in the newspaper column would have been replaced by a more informative journalism, providing details of how civilians being persecuted during the war were being aided by the ERC. Towards the conclusion of World War II, Eleanor referred to Clarence Pickett's remark that the American Friends had been confronted by the crisis in which 50% of the liberated French children had tuberculosis.[17] Similar to the vague remarks she had published regarding Frank Kingdon, a pre-war article about Clarence Pickett is enigmatic:

> Mr. Clarence Pickett (…) is leaving for Europe in about a week. He, his wife and daughter will have a three weeks vacation in England and then will travel to all the various places on the Continent where the American Friends are trying to contribute something to the health and well-being of under-privileged people, primarily the children. The list of places took my breath away but increased my admiration for the unostentatious service rendered.[18]

This syndicated column appeared after the September 15, 1935, Nuremberg Laws stripped citizenship from German Jews as well as after the July 14, 1938, Annexation of Austria, which subjected Austrian Jews to the same fate as the German Jews. Although the article did appear before the September 30, 1938, Munich Agreement annexing the industrial heartland of Czechoslovakia, one wonders whether Eleanor was begging her readers to read between-the-lines or whether the President and the State Department were coercing her to limit her foreign affairs statements.

Eleanor's biographer, Blanche Wiesen Cook was perplexed by her public silence with regard to the violence perpetrated by the Nazis against European Jews:

---

16   Eleanor Roosevelt, *My Day* October 11, 1944, Eleanor Roosevelt Papers Digital Edition, George Washington University.
17   Eleanor Roosevelt, *My Day* February 3, 1945, Eleanor Roosevelt Papers Digital Edition, George Washington University.
18   Eleanor Roosevelt, *My Day* July 14, 1938, Eleanor Roosevelt Papers Digital Edition, George Washington University.

How does one understand ER's failure to interpret the Picketts' message to her readers? How did she decide to neglect their presentation of fascist violence and repression, omit entirely the situation confronting Jews and refugees, ignore indeed the gravamen and substance of their observations? ER's silence, despite all the information sent to her, remains in retrospect thunderous. She was frequently advised by her husband or State Department officials to remain discreet and uninvolved .... [19]

Eleanor made approximately 300 radio broadcasts for which she received up to $3,000 from advertisers. Almost all of the funds were donated to the American Friends project to help displaced coal miners in West Virginia.[20] Thus it appears impossible that she had not understood the gravity of reports from Clarence and Lilly Pickett. A better interpretation appears to be that in private, great results were achieved. But in public, Eleanor's freedom of speech and actions were strictly limited by the President and his similarly minded State Department.

Ingrid contrasted earlier abstract political discussions in Heidelberg and Oxford with the later exciting active participation in initiatives and organizations during the first two terms of Roosevelt's Presidency (1933– 41), in which ideas were transformed into deeds. One example occurred in 1939 when Anna and Karl Frank (aka Paul Hagen) of the American Friends of German Freedom went to Ingrid's apartment, persuading her to raise funds so that Hitler's opponents could get out of prison or concentration camps and flee to America.

Ingrid Warburg's Fundraising Success

Ingrid's fundraising contributed enormous dividends to Varian Fry's rescues in September 1940. Fry and Dick Ball escorted Heinrich and Nelly Mann, Thomas Mann's son Golo, Franz Werfel, and his wife Alma Mahler Werfel as well as Egon and Bertha Maria Adler to Cerebère,

---

19   Cook, *Eleanor*, 312.
20   Stephen Smith, "Eleanor Roosevelt: The First Lady of Radio," *American Public Media Reports*, November 10, 2014.

the French train station at the border with Portbou, Spain. The French Police Commissaire would not allow the Manns, Werfels, and Adlers to board the train without French exit visas, but advised Dick Ball to guide the refugees over the Pyrenees on what proved to be a very lucky Friday September 13, 1940. As Fry took their seventeen pieces of luggage across the border via the train, he was concerned about the corpulent Franz and the 70-year-old Heinrich. On the same evening, Varian telegraphed Lena Fishman in Marseille telling her to send the Feuchtwangers over the same trail. The Manns and the Werfels flew from Barcelona to Lisbon on Monday, September 16, while a representative from the Unitarian Service Committee escorted the Feuchtwangers.[21]

Not only did donations raised by Ingrid Warburg pay off, but so, too, did the mere mention of the name Eleanor Roosevelt. When Rudolf Breitscheid, Rudolf Hilferding, and Arthur Wolff were arrested in Marseille, Fry's staff member Miriam Davenport was able to scare off six French policemen by claiming that Eleanor Roosevelt was personally intervening for the poet Walter Mehring.[22]

21   Others rescued in the first few weeks of September included the Nobel prize win-
      ning physiologist Otto Meyerhof, the economist Heinrich Ehrmann, the Austrian
      journalist Herta Pauli and Hitler's unflattering biographer Konrad Heiden.
      Varian Fry, *Surrender on Demand* (New York: Random House, 1945), 55–85. Also
      see Bernadette Costa-Prades, *La Liste de Varian Fry; août 1940–septembre 1941*
      (Paris: Albin Michel, 2020), 58.
22   Sheila Isenberg, *A Hero of Our Own* (New York: Random House, 2001), 76–83. In
      his September 10, 1940, appeal for $300 to transport one refugee, Frank Kingdon
      of the ERC mentioned that a first group of refugees had arrived. Presumably his
      abbreviated telegram meant their September 6 arrival in Portugal, since Lion
      Feuchtwanger and a group of exiles aboard the American ship *Excalibur* did not
      arrive in Hoboken until October 5, 1940. These immigrants must have disclosed
      to reporters the route from France to Spain and ultimately to Portugal, because
      the American press had endangered future escapes by publicizing the path to
      freedom. Thus, the second group of fifteen aboard the Greek liner *Nea Hellas*,
      which included Franz Werfel and his wife Anna Mahler Werfel, Heinrich and
      Nelly Mann along with their nephew Golo Mann, Alfred Polgar, Walther Victor,
      Hermann Budzislawski, and Konrad Heiden were unwilling to disclose any de-
      tails of their rescue. Compare Postal Telegram, September 10, 1949, Oram Group
      Box 10 Folder 21 Item 2, Ruth Lilly Special Collections and Archives, Indiana

Escorting refugees from Marseille to Lisbon became more difficult on October 1, 1940, when the Portuguese consuls ceased providing transit visas. This intensification provoked a series of four reports by Varian Fry to the ERC during the period from October 27, 1940, to November 15, 1940. Ingrid Warburg mailed the reports to Eleanor Roosevelt in her plea for assistance. Varian's accounts detail the worsening condition of those fleeing Nazi-occupied Europe. One fate itemized by Fry was internment, "Paul Wertheim, the well-known art historian; Prof. Pringsheim, a celebrated physicist, the brother-in-law of Thomas Mann; and Ernst Busch, a famous German tenor; are being held in detention camps unfit for dogs."[23]

One of Ingrid's major responsibilities was to locate donors for basic necessities of the refugees as well as travel funds.[24] Varian had come to France in August 1940 with $25,000 to begin the rescue of Jewish intellectuals, but by the end of October 1940, these funds had been mostly expended. In New York, Frank Kingdon regularly requested donations of $350 from supporters, but by the end of October 1940, Varian Fry pleaded with the ERC for a monthly budget of $10,000. Despite luminaries such as the Feuchtwangers, Manns and Werfels being safe in the United States, Ingrid Warburg needed to accelerate and expand her search for charitable donations.

University—Purdue University Indianapolis Library with "Writers Fleeing Nazis Here by Underground," *New York Herald Tribune*, October 14, 1940.

23　A condition making the French camps so untenable was the diseases of typhoid, dysentery, and malaria. Another death-inducing circumstance was suicide, undertaken by three of the authors and clients under the ERC's care. FDR Presidential Library & Museum, Series 100, October 27, 1940, Report from Varian Fry in the correspondence between Ingrid Warburg and Eleanor Roosevelt, Document 6. Note that in the October 31, 1940, Report, Fry had added that Andre Breton and Victor Serge were living with him half a mile outside Marseille.

24　Fry listed some of the beneficiaries of these donations, "There is Franz Hessel, the man who translated Proust into German, and his wife, son, and daughter-in-law. There is Andre Breton, wife and child. There is Walter Mehring, one of the best German poets living. There is Hans Sahl, a really bright playwright and Hans Jacoby the producer; Ernst Aufricht; Joseph Bernstein; and Victor Serge." FDR Presidential Library & Museum, Series 100, October 27, 1940; Document 6.

Loans also needed to be made available for prominent Jewish personalities, because their bank accounts had been blocked. As an example
of the necessity of Ingrid's endeavor, Fry mentioned Theodor Wolff, the
former editor of the *Berliner Tageblatt*. He was facing pauperization, although he had funds in London. Transferring money via American Express
or the Guaranty Trust was also required by other refugees, whose assets
were in Paris or New York.[25] The passage of time merely underscored
the urgency of Ingrid's fundraising. Varian Fry began sending the ERC
lists of impoverished intellectuals, whom he financially supported every
week.[26] The audited financial statement from July 1, 1940, through June
30, 1941, indicated that the ERC had collected donations totaling nearly
$216,000. From this sum, the bulk of nearly $128,500 went to the refugees
(59.5%), with other major expenditures of $22,426 (10.3%) for fundraising
expenses. One example of such an expenditure was a March 1941 benefit
concert. Those publicly recognized for supporting the gala event included
Thomas and Katia Mann, Bruno Walter, Friderike Maria von Winternitz
(Stefan Zweig's former wife), Ingrid Warburg, and her cousin Gerald Felix
Warburg.[27] Surprisingly, the largest ERC expense for FY 1941 was for about

25   FDR Presidential Library & Museum, Series 100, October 31, 1940, Report from
      Varian Fry in the correspondence between Ingrid Warburg and Eleanor Roosevelt,
      Document 7. Feuchtwanger had experienced this financial difficulty as early as June
      13, 1940 according to *Teufel in Frankreich*, 273–328.
26   A prominent example was Siegfried Kracauer, who applied for a French exit visa
      in August 1940, but was still waiting in November. Fry could not have known it at
      the time, but Siegfried and his wife Lili Ehrenreich would continue being in need
      of funds until March 1941 when the French Ambassador Henri Hoppenot person-
      ally intervened allowing the Kracauers to emigrate to the U.S. FDR Presidential
      Library & Museum, Series 100, November 3, 1940, Report from Varian Fry in the
      correspondence between Ingrid Warburg and Eleanor Roosevelt, Document 5.
27   Another large expense of approximately $18,000 (8.3%) paid for Varian Fry's
      rented house outside Marseille and his downtown office. In Emergency Rescue
      Committee, Inc. Statement of Receipts and Disbursements for the Year Ended
      June 30, 1941, July 23, 1941. Oram Group Box 10 Folder 21 Item 1, Ruth Lilly Special
      Collections and Archives, Indiana University—Purdue University Indianapolis
      Library. Also See "Musicians Guests at Cocktail Party," *The New York Times*, March
      4, 1941.

$34,000 (15.9%) for supporting other refugee organizations. A glimpse of this effort is depicted in a December 2, 1940, letter from John Dos Passos. Although most famous for having penned the *U.S.A.* trilogy, Dos Passos was heavily engaged in politics and as treasurer for the Campaign for Political Refugees, he sent an appeal to Ingrid Warburg. This inter-agency rescue effort was also documented by Frank Kingdon's testimony before the Dies Committee[28] as he represented not only his own ERC but also the following four other relief organizations: Reinhold Niebuhr's American Friends of German, Charles A. Beard's International Relief Association, Oswald Garrison Villard's New World Resettlement Fund, and Bishop Francis J. McConnell's Spanish Refugee Relief Campaign.[29]

Ingrid Warburg and Eleanor Roosevelt Tried to Offset U.S. Immigration Policy

Another urgent problem was securing immediate entry visas to the United States, a task in which Eleanor Roosevelt was extolled by Ingrid as "of decisive significance." In October 1940 Fry had raised the question: "Is America interested in doing something to rescue what is left of European culture before it is too late?"[30] Varian's query may have prompted a discussion between Karl Frank and Joseph Buttinger in Eleanor's New York apartment. Eleanor telephoned her husband and after twenty minutes of being unable to convince Franklin, Eleanor threatened him that antifascist German and Austrian leaders would lease a ship which would cruise along the East Coast until the shamed and annoyed American people would coerce the President and Congress to allow these victims of political persecution to land in America. In addition, Eleanor personally sent

---

28 Martin Dies served as the Chair of the House of Representatives' Committee on Un-American Activities.

29 Campaign for Political Refugees, December 2, 1940. Also see "Denies Refugees are Gestapo Aides," *The New York Times*, June 1, 1941.

30 FDR Presidential Library & Museum. Series 100, November 3, 1940, Document 5.

the list of refugee names from the Committee to the State Department and exerted pressure on Sumner Welles. She asked for an immediate explanation why the U.S. Consul in Marseille could not help a few of these people.[31]

At the end of October 1940, Fry threatened to lodge a protest with Senator Robert F. Wagner of New York and mused about overcoming the U.S. Consul in Marseille's reluctance to issue American visas to Jewish intellectuals.[32] Instead of assisting, the New York Headquarters of the ERC put pressure on Varian to return to the United States, causing him to lament the availability of a replacement, who would be conversant in both German and French as well as having "the most cordial personal relations with the Prefect, the Bishop, the Sûreté Nationale, etc."[33] Fry's November 3, 1940, Report to Mildred Adams, the Secretary of the ERC, recounted the June flight of hundreds of intellectuals to Marseilles. The urgency prevented the refugees from withdrawing funds from bank accounts or packing suitcases. Consequently, they had neither winter clothing nor any sources of income, necessitating Ingrid Warburg's fundraising efforts to avoid the non-French refugees from internment. Although Fry acknowledged that his assigned mission was to enable the escape of men of letters, he was dependent on donations raised by Ingrid to keep these prominent people alive. Financial support from Ingrid Warburg's contacts had startling effects with some internees being released and packages of cigarettes and fruit or money being brought into the French camps. An unnamed

31   Spinelli, *Erinnerungen*, 175f.
32   FDR Presidential Library & Museum, Series 100, October 31, 1940, Report from Varian Fry in the correspondence between Ingrid Warburg and Eleanor Roosevelt, Document 7. The desire for publicity to attract donations conflicted with Varian's need to conceal his illegal smuggling of refugees out of southern France. Frank Kingdon's reception of the Manns, Werfels, Adlers and the Kaufmans disembarking from the Greek liner *Nea Hellas* provoked American Consul Hugh Fullerton's ouster of Varian Fry from Marseille as well as the demotion of Hiram Bingham to a less important State Department post. "Writers Fleeing Nazis Here by Underground," *The New York Times*, October 14, 1940. Also see Isenberg, *Hero*, 86, 103.
33   FDR Presidential Library & Museum, Series 100, November 3, 1940, Document 7.

American volunteer was in charge of this aspect of Fry's rescue operation, presumably Mary Jayne Gold.

The years of friendship between Ingrid Warburg and Eleanor Roosevelt, occasioned by Warburg's 1937 speaking tour for the Joint, were about to pay handsome dividends. Ingrid forwarded Fry's report along with three others to the President's wife on December 4, 1940, with a critical statement on ERC letterhead, "The State Department, in turn, promises to cable visas to Europe, but delays them."[34] Within a week, Eleanor contacted both her husband and Sumner Welles. Since the President's and the State Department's policy was to restrict German and Jewish immigration, the concern expressed by Eleanor was already well known to Under Secretary of State Sumner Welles as expressed in his December 11th response to Eleanor Roosevelt. As a rejoinder to Eleanor's attempt to influence the State Department to expedite American visas to Jewish refugees, Welles had slyly retorted that Fry's superiors had directed him to return to New York because he had upset the French police.[35] Although Captain Dubois of the Sûreté Nationale in Marseille was aware of the ERC's smuggling people out of France as well as its trading in foreign currency, Varian was told that the U.S. Consul-General's attitude towards Fry "was a joke."[36] Dr. Frank Bohn of the German-American Congress for Democracy yielded to the pressure to leave Marseille at the end of the first week in October 1940.[37] In contrast Fry's report to the ERC at the beginning of November rejected the notion offered by Ingrid Warburg and Karl B. Frank (aka Paul Hagen) that the rescue of hundreds of intellectuals could soon be "wound up."[38]

34   FDR Presidential Library & Museum, Series 70, December 11, 1940, Letter from Welles to Eleanor, Document 8.

35   FDR Presidential Library & Museum, Series 70, December 11, 1940, Letter from Welles to Eleanor, Document 8.

36   Fry, *Surrender*, 90.

37   Fry, Ibid., 92.

38   FDR Presidential Library & Museum, Series 100, November 3, 1940, Document 7. For example, Siegfried Kracauer and his wife Lili Ehrenreich were unable to leave France until March 1941. A few of the other world-renowned personalities unable to depart until the Spring were artists Max Ernst and Marc Chagall; the physicist Peter Pringsheim; and the writer Hans Sahl. Fry, Ibid., 197.

Eleanor was equally unsuccessful in her struggles with Breckinridge Long and the State Department with regard to their practice of delaying entry visas in order to limit Jewish immigration. As the President's curt memo to Eleanor on December 18, 1940, indicated, he would not intervene with the Consulate in Marseille in order to assist the ERC's attempt to quickly rescue Jewish intellectuals. The nine-word memo immediately nullified any hope that the President would fulfill any political agenda from his own wife: "I suggest you take up with the State Department.—F.D.R."[39] The new year brought no relief in the State Department's resistance to issue visas to potential political and Jewish immigrants. Welles wrote Eleanor again on January 2, 1941, returning her list of ten members of the Internationaler Sozialistischer Kampfbund (ISK), who had broken away from the Sozialdemokratische Partei Deutschlands (SPD) in 1925. Welles marked in blue pencil those individuals who had not been approved by James McDonald's "President's Advisory Committee on Political Refugees." The ISK's July 1932 *Urgent Call for Unity* had been supported by Albert Einstein, Heinrich Mann, and Arnold Zweig, but Sumner Welles rejected endangered socialist refugees in 1941.[40] Ironically, this list was typed by Eva Lewinsky, who fled from Marseilles over the Pyrenees and sailed aboard the Greek liner *Nea Hellas* on October 3, 1940. This was the same ship and the same day as the Werfels, and the Manns departed.

Conclusion: Eleanor Roosevelt's and Ingrid Warburg's Roles in Rescuing Jews

The restrictive posture regarding granting visas to Jews and those politically persecuted could lead one to wonder whether the anti-immigration posture of President Roosevelt and his State Department was shared by

39   FDR Presidential Library & Museum, Series 100, Memo from Franklin to Eleanor December 18, 1940, Document 1.
40   FDR Presidential Library & Museum, Series 70, January 2, 1941, Letter from Welles to Eleanor, Document 9.

Eleanor. Yet, to the contrary her September 17, 1940, column *"My Day"*, affirms her differing position from her husband. The column praised the merits of Irmgard Litten's book *Beyond Tears*, in which the mother lamented the murder of her son in Dachau.[41] Roosevelt's State Department privately voiced their restrictions about allowing Jewish refugees to enter the country, while publicly expressing concern that immigrants could not be allowed to take scarce jobs away from Americans as the Roosevelt administration attempted to overcome the Great Depression. This left Eleanor's role to assist the rescue mission from backstage in order not to interfere with her husband's politics.

In time, Ingrid Warburg's involvement grew from soliciting and securing funds for relief agencies to assisting with transit visas and travel arrangements.[42] Due to her native knowledge of German, Kingdon directed his November 7, 1940, letter to Ingrid, pleading on behalf of Wilhelm Herzog, Emil Alfons Rheinhardt,[43] and Ludwig Ullmann to arrange an escort over the Spanish border.[44] One month later, Alma Mahler Werfel also sought to enlist Ingrid's non-financial expertise for the refugees.[45] As a final analysis one has to say, that without the power and influence of Congress,[46]

41   Two factors contributed to the friendship between the First Lady and the recent immigrant Eva Lewinsky. First, the publishing arm of Eva Lewinsky's political party produced the book. Second Eleanor's friend Dorothy Hill endorsed Eva. Barbara McDonald Stewart, *Refugees and Rescue: The Diaries and Papers of James G. McDonald* (Bloomington: Indiana University Press, 2009).

42   Ingrid's German skills were involved when Franz Werfel attempted a telephone conversation with ERC Founder Frank Kingdon.

43   Feuchtwanger had been interned with Emil Alfons Rheinhardt during a first Les Milles' detainment in September 17–27, 1939.

44   In the case of Annemarie Meier Graefe, neither Ingrid's finesse with regard to financial support nor her influence in securing travel papers were requested. Instead, her aid in obtaining an escort over the Spanish border was sought.

45   Spinelli, *Erinnerungen*, 435, 465–6.

46   The magnitude of the behind-the-scenes activities of Ingrid Warburg and Eleanor Roosevelt in the August 1940—September 1941 rescue of one to two thousand intellectuals from Marseille becomes evident in comparison with the attempt by Senator Robert F. Wagner and Congresswoman Edith Rogers. Their bill proposed that 20,000 German-Jewish children be allowed into the United States apart from the immigration quota system. The Wagner-Rogers bill had the encouragement

Ingrid Warburg and Eleanor Roosevelt enabled Varian Fry to rescue perhaps as many as two thousand refugees. With the invaluable background
help of these two ingenuous and socially engaged women, Fry's organization overcame the State Department's prejudices. American women's role
in rescuing Jewish victims of Hitler's aggression has not been sufficiently
noted by historians. This chapter is a small contribution to acknowledging
the combined efforts of Ingrid Warburg and Eleanor Roosevelt, whose
multi-faceted involvement included diplomacy, negotiation, fundraising,
translation, and inspiring teamwork.[47]

---

of former President Herbert Hoover, who sent a supportive telegram to Clarence
Pickett of the American Friends Service Committee. The text was read to the Senate
Immigration Committee along with helpful testimony by Rabbi Stephen S. Wise
and Canon Anson Phelps Stokes of the Washington Episcopal Cathedral. Canon
Stokes affirmed that the immigration of 20,000 children had the endorsement of
the American Federation of Labor and the Congress of Industrial Organizations.
Furthermore 5,000 American families had already offered to adopt one or more
children. Nevertheless, the resistance was so great in Congress that the bill was
amended to read that the children would be included within the German quota.
"Bill to Shut Out Aliens is Reported," *The New York Times*, July 1, 1939. In comparison with Ingrid and Eleanor's success, the Wagner-Rogers bill was never reported
out of either the Senate or the House Committee and was thus never voted on.
Another failed attempt began as the Nazis bombed London. It was hoped that
thousands of British children could be brought to safety in the U.S. "U.S. Studies
Haven for Young Britons," *The New York Times*, June 19, 1940. An American
sponsor wrote a letter to the editor in exasperation regarding the numerous hurdles
that the State Department erected in order to prevent British children from being
allowed entry. The American citizen would need to be willing and able to purchase
a $500 bond. In addition, the donor needed to provide in triplicate proof of em-
ployment, the amount of his wages, the sum in bank accounts, property in possession, mortgages, insurance and the total of owned stocks and bonds. The potential
philanthropist gave up under the bureaucratic demands of the State Department.
Harold A. Littledale, Letter to the Editor, *The New York Times*, July 13, 1940.

47   Rafael Medoff, "American Responses to the Holocaust: New Research, New
     Controversies," *American Jewish History*, 100, no. 3 (July 2016), 379–409. Also
     note Bat-Ami Zucker, *Cecilia Razosky and the American-Jewish Women's Rescue
     Operations in the Second World War* (Portland: Vallentine Mitchell, 2008).

PART III

Female Protagonists and Gender Dynamics in Lion Feuchtwanger's Work

FRANZISKA WOLF

5 Poe's Death-of-a-Beautiful-Woman-Motif in Feuchtwanger's *Wartesaal*

ABSTRACT

Building on a critical exploration of the role of female deaths in literature and visual arts, this chapter investigates the deaths of female characters in Feuchtwanger's *Wartesaal* and argues that these primarily function as plot devices: they appear necessary—in a narrative sense—to move the plot forward, but they are only marginally concerned with the female character herself. Thereby, the deaths of the female characters Anna Elisabeth Haider and Amalia Sandhuber in *Success* [*Erfolg*] and Anna Trautwein in *Paris Gazette* [*Exil*] resemble Edgar Allan Poe's death-of-a-beautiful-woman-motif which claims that the death of a beautiful woman is "the most poetical topic in the world." Their deaths appear as gendered when compared to the deaths of male characters in the trilogy, particularly that of Berthold Oppermann and Harry Meisel. In contrast to their female counterparts, who die to drive the plot forward or fulfill a need of a male character, the young men's deaths establish their political and artistic legacies.

Poe's Death-of-a-Beautiful-Woman-Motif

In his essay "Philosophy of Composition" of 1846, Edgar Allan Poe claims that "the death, then, of a beautiful woman is, unquestionably, the most poetical topic in the world—and equally is it beyond doubt that the lips best suited for such topic are those of a bereaved lover."[1] Following his own poetics, Poe's texts feature a multitude of beautiful women suffering an untimely death, which has sparked interest in this

---

1   Edgar Allan Poe, "The Philosophy of Composition," *Graham's American Monthly Magazine of Literature and Art*, 28, no. 4 (1846), 163–7, 165.

death-of-a-beautiful-woman-motif.[2] In her analysis of Poe's feminine
ideal, Karen Weekes discusses the purpose of the dying woman in Poe's
writing and concludes: "The most significant trait of his ideal [...] is her
role as emotional catalyst for her partner. The romanticized woman is
much more significant in her impact on Poe's narrators than in her own
right."[3] According to Weekes, the dead woman in Poe's texts is therefore
not more than "a *tabula rasa* on which the lover inscribes his own needs"
and "a placeholder [...] for some need in the narrator himself."[4]

Building on a critical exploration of the role of female deaths in literature and visual arts, this chapter investigates the deaths of female characters in Feuchtwanger's *Wartesaal*[5] and argues that death itself appears as a
gendered concept in Feuchtwanger's texts, insofar as the deaths of female
characters primarily function as plot devices: they appear necessary—in a
narrative sense—to move the plot forward, but they are only marginally
concerned with the female character herself. This is contrasted with the
prominent death of a male character in the trilogy, Berthold Oppermann,
whose suicide confirms his moral integrity and political resistance against
Nazism. Berthold's death in *Die Geschwister Oppermann* thereby also bears
resemblance to the killing of Harry Meisel in *Exil*, who posthumously
becomes a famous writer whose talent even attracts the jealousy of Nazi
sympathizers.

As in Poe's writings, there is no shortage of dead women in
Feuchtwanger's trilogy. In *Erfolg*, the trilogy's first novel which narrates the
political turmoil in Bavaria in the years 1921–3, the painter Anna Elisabeth

---

2   See Eleftheria Tsirakoglou, "Aesthetic Desire: Edgar Allan Poe, Nikolaos
     Episkopopoulos and the Death-of-a-Beautiful-Woman Motif," *Cultural Intertexts*
     2, no. 3 (2015), 137–46.

3   Karen Weekes, "Poe's Feminine Ideal," in *The Cambridge Companion to Edgar
     Allan Poe*, ed. Kevin J. Hayes (Cambridge: Cambridge University Press, 2006),
     148–62, 148.

4   Ibid., 150.

5   Lion Feuchtwanger, *Success: Three Years in the Life of a Province*, trans. Willa
     and Edwin Muir (London: Martin Secker, 1930); *The Oppermanns*, trans. James
     Cleugh (London: Martin Secker, 1933); *Paris Gazette*, trans. Willa and Edwin Muir
     (New York: Viking Press, 1940).

Haider commits suicide when her alleged love affair with the museum director Martin Krüger becomes the object of a judicial smear campaign. A second plot-driving dead woman in the novel is Amalia Sandhuber, who falls victim to a *Fememord*, a brutal assassination by a right-wing gang.[6] The motif of the dead woman is picked up again in *Exil*, the trilogy's last novel, that centers on the German exile community in Paris in 1935. In the novel, Anna Trautwein commits suicide after her last financial securities melt away and she is confronted with her husband's infidelity.

While none of the main female characters die in the trilogy's second novel, *Die Geschwister Oppermann*, an untimely death occurs there, too. In the book, Berthold Oppermann commits suicide after his Nazi teacher Bernd Vogelsang fabricates a scandal when Berthold gives a presentation on the Cheruscan Arminius and his legacy.[7] Berthold, being pressured to revoke his statement, chooses to end his life rather than comply with his teacher's politically motivated demands. Berthold's death thereby symbolizes an act of political resistance, which stands in contrast to the already mentioned deaths of female characters that emerge out of despair or violence. While Berthold's suicide makes him appear extraordinarily committed and upright towards his political beliefs, the death of Harry Meisel in *Exil* establishes the young poet's literary fame and liberates him from a world in which he no longer wanted to live.

---

6   "Fememord" is a collective term for "extrajudicial murders by bands technically illegal, but winked at by the national government. [...] At the foundation of institutionalized *Feme*-justice is a rejection of law as the supreme normative force in society." Robert D. Rachlin, "Roland Freisler and the Volksgerichtshof: The Court as an Instrument of Terror," in *The Law in Nazi Germany: Ideology, Opportunism, and the Perversion of Justice*, ed. Alan E. Steinweis and Robert D. Rachlin (New York: Berghahn Books, 2013), 63–88, 81–2.

7   Arminius (18/17 BC–AD 21) was a leader of the Germanic tribe of the Cheruski. Defeating the Romans in the Battle of the Teutoburg Forest ("Varusschlacht") in AD 9, he became the key figure in the foundation myth of the Germans. For a detailed study of the historical Arminius and his role in German national mythology, see Tillmann Bendikowski, *Der Tag, an dem Deutschland entstand: Die Geschichte der Varusschlacht* (Munich: Bertelsmann, 2008).

The Death of a Maid(en): Amalia Sandhuber

Poe's death-of-a-beautiful-woman-motif oscillates between life and death, beauty and horror, attraction and repulsion. In *Erfolg*, this can be studied exemplarily through the murder of the 35-year-old domestic worker Amalia Sandhuber who is employed by the Army General Klöckner, a friend of General Vesemann who later leads a fascist putsch attempt. Amalia Sandhuber is introduced to the reader as:

> a daughter of a crofter. In her teens she fled from her sorry home and engaged herself as a servant-maid in the town. While still very young she had relations with men. She was inquisitive, good-natured, credulous and sentimental. Once she brought a dead child into the world, and a second child died soon after birth. Her experiences made her more worldly-wise, and she began to keep a diary with the names of the men whom she had been with. […] She was very proud of this piece of cunning. […] [S]he was buxom, smart and very willing.[8]

Amalia Sandhuber's promiscuity mentioned in the above passage becomes her death warrant. Naively thinking that she is charmed by a gentleman, she agrees to accompany Ludwig Ratzenberger, her stalker and member of the fascist movement *Wahrhaft Deutsche*, on a drive to Starnberg. But instead of going to Starnberg, he kidnaps her to the Forstenrieder Park, where the boxer Alois Kutzner kills her by first hitting her with a horse-shoe, and then choking her to death.[9]

Amalia Sandhuber becomes the target of the fascists through her love affair with a communist butcher. She is being sentenced to death by the fascists' *Femegericht* as a "traitress," as information about the whereabouts of the family Klöckner, for which she works as a maid, enters left-wing circles through her communist lover. The butcher warns her of her new suitor Ludwig but Amalia Sandhuber is unable to recognize the danger to herself and instead feels pride over her supposed popularity, which is

8   Feuchtwanger, *Success*, 578.
9   See ibid., 584.

expressed most clearly when she is sitting in the car that takes her to the park: "Amalia was proud of her Ludwig and of her drive."[10]

Amalia Sandhuber's death may be read as an allegory of the proximity between lust and death and an adaptation of the death-of-a-maiden-motif, which itself is placed "in the tradition of the 'dance of death.' "[11] In pictorial representations of the death-of-a-maiden-motif,

> the female figure is eroticized and, at the same time, punished for her sexuality, which is conflated with vanity, pride, and folly, not least by association with the female figure *voluptas*. Significantly, the woman is exposed to the gaze of the (male) artist and viewer. Her revealing garments, in some cases even her nudity, render her exciting, while her powerlessness in the face of death—which, if gendered, appears as male—harnesses her sexuality and makes it safe.[12]

Stefanie Knöll elaborates that "nakedness and the beauty of death's victim have always been part of the motif," alongside the association of women "with vanity, pride, and infidelity."[13] In a similar analysis of artistic representations on the dance-of-death-motif, ranging from the Middle Ages to the twentieth century, Ulrike Wohler also sees a connection between the topic of death and the depiction of a young woman, arguing that the image of a deceased woman or girl symbolizes a contrast between life and death.[14] The death of a young woman thereby represents key elements of the dance-of-death-motif:

> The dance of death contains three elements: *memento mori* (remember you must die), *vanitas* (remember that everything is ephemeral and vain, which is hence a warning

---

10   Ibid., 581.
11   Stefanie Knöll, "Death and the Maiden: A German Topic?," in *Women & Death: Representations of Female Victims and Perpetrators in German Culture 1500– 2000*, ed. Helen Fronius and Anna Linton (Rochester: Camden House, 2008), 9– 27, 11.
12   Helen Fronius and Anna Linton, "Introduction," in *Women & Death: Representations of Female Victims and Perpetrators in German Culture 1500–2000*, ed. Helen Fronius and Anna Linton (Rochester: Camden House, 2008), 1–8, 5.
13   Knöll, "Death and the Maiden," 21.
14   Ulrike Wohler, "Totentanz," in *Gesellschaftsepochen und ihre Kunstwelten*, ed. Lutz Hieber (Wiesbaden: Springer, 2018), 221–47, 230.

against vanity), and, consequently, *ars moriendi* (the art of dying [...]). These three aspects command to lead a good life and hence to refrain from vice and deadly sins, as when faced with death, everything becomes *vain*.[15]

This relationship between death, (sexual) temptation, and arousal (captured in the gaze of the male observer) can also be traced in the killing of Amalia Sandhuber. She complies with the death-of-a-maiden-motif in multiple ways. Her vanity and pride are fueled by Ludwig Ratzenberger's interest in her, and she perceives his hesitancy in approaching her as "the height of chivalry"[16] and mistakes this behavior as lack of sexual experience. Her communist lover explicitly warns her of Ludwig: "[T]his fellow had a hang-dog [...] look about him."[17] Yet, Amalia's vanity leads her to brush all doubts aside, "Amalia puts down the words of the butcher to jealousy, she was glad that she could still attract young gentlemen."[18] Her naivety and vanity make her an "ideal" victim, unaware of her fate, and her death appears to be a punishment for her frivolous behavior.

The description of Amalia Sandhuber confirms the motif of the death of a maiden not only by being characterized by "vanity, pride, and folly" but also due to her powerlessness in the face of her own death and the sexualization of her motionless body. When Sandhuber is lying on the ground dead, the narration continues with sexual innuendos, describing her exposed body:

> There she lay in the mud and the melting snow. She had put on her Sunday best for the excursion, and wore a very short skirt, as was the mode then. Her skirt had been disarranged: above the knee a small strip of skin was visible and a coarse white pair of knickers. Her stout legs ended in a pair of shoes too dainty for her.[19]

Being surrounded by her murderer Alois Kutzner and his two accomplices Ludwig Ratzenberger and Erich Bornhaak, the narrative perspective mimics the three men's inspection of the dead female body. This male

15   Ibid., 222.
16   Feuchtwanger, *Success*, 580.
17   Ibid., 580.
18   Ibid., 581.
19   Ibid., 584.

gaze is characterized by the mentioning of her uncovered body parts, specifically her knees and thighs. Her skin and undergarments are exposed
due to her "very short" skirt, which carries an eroticized connotation that
reinforces her characterization as sexually available.

Her executioner Alois Kutzner, on the other hand, is described as
"uncouth."[20] When being informed about the murderous plans, he "had
agreed at once":

> It was good that something was going to be done at last, that they could find some
> use for Alois Kutzner, for his strength, his hands. To strangle someone, to squeeze
> the red life out of someone: that would do him good, that would be a relief.[21]

Amalia Sandhuber's death thereby is an outlet for Kutzner's aggression
and a tool to quench his thirst for action. The importance of the murder
for the rest of the plot lies in its cruelty and arbitrary character as well
as in the lack of prosecution of the criminals: even after Alois Kutzner
confesses to the police, he is not punished for the crime.[22] The narration
of the murder itself under the chapter title "Caliban"[23] gives further significance to the nature of this female character's death, as this allusion
elucidates "the barbaric, animalistic nature of the murder and of the
movement [*Wahrhaft Deutsche*]."[24] This effect is also achieved through
the way in which Alois Kutzner ends Amalia's life, namely, through the
strength of his bare hands: "Then he knelt down beside her, made a rapid
prayer that God might grant him the strength to kill her utterly, and
strangled her."[25]

20 Ibid., 581.
21 Ibid., 581–2.
22 Ibid., 715.
23 Caliban is the name of a key figure in Shakespeare's *The Tempest* (1611). Half-human
    and half-monster, he lives under the rule of Prospero, whose daughter Miranda he
    attempted to rape. Being persuaded by Stefano, Caliban conspires against Prospero,
    but the coup fails. Caliban is characterized as beastlike and seducible.
24 Synnöve Clason, *Die Welt erklären: Geschichte und Fiktion in Lion Feuchtwangers
    Roman "Erfolg"* (Stockholm: Almqvist & Wiksell International, 1975), 154.
25 Feuchtwanger, *Success*, 584.

From a narrative standpoint, Amalia Sandhuber's death complies with the motif of the death of a maiden as it features a promiscuous female character who enters a frivolous dance of death while her sexuality, vanity, and naivety become her death warrant. Subsequently, her dead body is sexualized through the gaze of her male executioner and spectators. Moreover, her death sits in line with Poe's motif of the death of a beautiful woman as it serves the author to emphasize the "barbarism" of the fascists as well as the injustice of the Bavarian judiciary.[26]

Transgression and the "New Woman": Anna Elisabeth Haider

A second female character in *Erfolg* through which Poe's death-of-a-beautiful-woman-motif can be examined is the painter Anna Elisabeth Haider, who is introduced to the reader only when she is already dead. Having painted a nude portrait of herself, that was later bought by Martin Krüger for the Bavarian art gallery, a disciplinary procedure is opened against her, and she is put on trial for causing public indignation. Sentenced guilty and being let down by Krüger, who is later accused of having entertained an affair with the painter and having committed perjury to protect the woman, she commits suicide by inhaling gas.

Described by witnesses in court as "a very slatternly creature," Haider transgresses societal norms and expectations in many ways.[27] She is being characterized by her landlady as "slovenly and dirty, came in at all hours, […] was very unpunctual in her payments, and received questionable and rowdy visitors."[28] The narrator describes her as "terribly estranged from

---

26   This is further supported by the comment of the uninvolved narrator: "Traitors shall be dealt with by the Feme." (579). This comment is likely to be an allusion to the title of a nonfiction book from 1929, in which Emil Julius Gumbel reveals the machinations of far-right secret organizations, including their political murders. Emil Julius Gumbel, *Verräter verfallen der Feme: Opfer/Mörder/Richter 1919–1929* (Berlin: Malik, 1929).

27   Feuchtwanger, *Success*, 34.

28   Ibid., 33.

life, absolutely indifferent to externals so long as she could keep going on, and slovenly to such an extent that her neglected appearance was compromising."[29] Like Amalia Sandhuber, Anna Elisabeth Haider is understood as frivolous due to the self-portrait which she painted of her naked body as well as through the alleged affair with Martin Krüger. Through her actions Haider becomes a threat to normative behavioral expectations, thereby aligning with the tradition of the so-called "New Woman" of the 1920s. As Ingrid Sharp writes, "[T]he New Woman came to be seen as the symbol of the age. While the New Woman is associated with the 1890s in America and England, in Germany, as in Ireland, she is very much a phenomenon of the 1920s."[30] Sharp points out the relationship between this idea of the "New Woman" and the crisis of German national identity:

> The position of women became a visible symbol of the underlying state of the nation [...]; in an intensification of the traditional Madonna/Whore dichotomy, women appeared to hold the key to the salvation or destruction of Germany. [...] The New Woman of conservative nightmares was selfish and predatory, a degenerate who preyed on men's sexual weakness and threatened bourgeois marriage. The uncontained sexual woman was dangerous, a source of fascination and temptation but also of disease and destruction.[31]

Sharp's exploration of the "New Woman" offers insights into Anna Elisabeth Haider's characterization. In many respects, the painter can be regarded as a contrast to the bourgeois female ideal as her behavior infringes on the moral values of the conservative Bavarian society depicted, earning her the reputation of a "Bohemian."[32] Her transgressive behavior can be seen not only in her naked self-portrayal but also in her relationships: "[S]he had taken up with a pretty numerous collection of lovers."[33]

---

29   Ibid., 40.
30   Ingrid Sharp, "Riding the Tiger: Ambivalent Images of the New Woman in the Popular Press of the Weimar Republic," in *New Woman Hybridities: Femininity, Feminism and International Consumer Culture, 1880–1930*, ed. Ann Heilmann and Margaret Beetham (London: Routledge, 2004), 118–41, 118.
31   Ibid., 120–1.
32   Feuchtwanger, *Success*, 40.
33   Ibid., 40.

Although she does not comply with normative ideas of female beauty either—"she skipped too much for a woman so heavily built—her face broad and round, really the face of a peasant girl, with thick, fair hair never properly cared for; her eyes were gray, with a profound and absent expression which disturbed one in a face otherwise so naive"—she appears attractive to Krüger due to "the determination with which she followed her art. [...] [T]his woman he considered one of the rare born artists of the age."[34] For Krüger, his attraction towards Anna Elisabeth Haider extends to a feeling of regret and desperation in the final moments of his life, in which he calls himself "an idiot, [...] a cast-iron, eight-cornered donkey [...] not to have had her."[35]

Although Anna Elisabeth Haider is not a representation of "classical" beauty, her sexual allure is hinted at repeatedly and affects Martin Krüger until the moment of his own death. While little information about her is offered to the reader, her nude portrait as well as her relationship to Krüger are central drivers of the plot, as they form the precondition for the trial against him, which itself is merely a tool to criticize the flawed justice system. Taken a step further, this critique of the Bavarian judiciary offers a narrative discussion of a "predisposition of the gradually emerging fascism."[36] Hence, it can be said that Feuchtwanger's novel is primarily concerned with providing a critical examination of the genesis of fascism in Bavaria, for which the deaths of both Haider and Krüger are effective tools, as they offer societal and political criticism, while also pointing out specificities of a Bavarian *Spießermoral*, "*Success* can be understood equally as an accusation against the justice system of the Weimar Republic and as a literary negotiation of the origins of German fascism."[37]

Anna Elisabeth's uncontained sexuality, liberal attitude towards her own body and nudity, and her avant-gardist sense of art turn her into an enemy figure of German nationhood. Despite (or, rather, because of) her

34   Ibid., 40.
35   Ibid., 626.
36   Wolfgang Müller-Funk, *Literatur als geschichtliches Argument: Zur ästhetischen Konzeption und Geschichtsverarbeitung in Lion Feuchtwangers Romantrilogie "Der Wartesaal"* (Frankfurt/Main: Peter Lang, 1981), 164.
37   Ibid., 196.

transgressive behavior, she appears alluring to Martin Krüger, and the public interest in her persona is significant, as evidenced in the depictions of the trial against her. Her dead body is subject to the male gaze through its e-ternal representation in the nude she painted and which is purchased first by Martin Krüger and, subsequently, by Paul Hessreiter. Hessreiter, himself a member of the jury in the trial against Krüger, acquires the painting as a political statement, "a demonstration."[38] When he reveals the artwork at a dinner party, the spectator's gaze is met by the painting and the roles of observer and observed are inverted:

> With a forlorn and yet strained expression the dead girl looked out into the discreetly-lit room, her eyes on the picture that hung opposite, a stark, gloomy painting of an Upper Bavarian farmhouse.[39]

Here, the dead holds the living accountable, and the permeating gaze that emerges through the painting represents an accusation of moral corruption to which the Bavarian people—symbolized by the farmhouse—have subjected themselves. This inversion of who is observing and who is being observed is repeated towards the end of the novel when the painting is auctioned after Hessreiter had to sell his house: "and the dead girl looked out at the crowd with a helpless and touching expression."[40] This time, not only the woman's powerlessness is mentioned but also her uncanny allure:

> Strongly tempted, but uneasy, the buyers gazed at the notorious canvas. It had been the cause of much trouble. Bad luck and scandal. Its painter had come to a bad end; Krüger […] had come to a bad end; Hessreiter too, as was now evident, hadn't had much luck with it.[41]

This passage hints at the significance of Anna Elisabeth Haider, her painting, and her death for the wider plot. In the sense of a leitmotif, the portrait connects various plot elements and characters with one another,

---

38   Feuchtwanger, *Success*, 32.
39   Ibid., 154.
40   Ibid., 700.
41   Ibid., 700.

thereby reinforcing the overall social criticism that stands at the center of the novel. Furthermore, the narrative depiction of the nude resembles Poe's conception of the death of a beautiful woman as the most poetic topic, insofar as Haider is Krüger's unattained lover and object of metaphorical and literal observation, enabled through the alluring self-portrait that serves as a backdrop from where the entire plot evolves. The motif of the painting—and with it of the transgressively alluring dead female painter—keeps reappearing to criticize not only the hypocrisy among certain parts of the Bavarian public, but also the corrupted judicial system, and connects otherwise isolated plot strands. Anna Elisabeth Haider's death thereby confirms Weekes' claim that the death-of-a-beautiful-woman-motif primarily serves to fulfill a need in the (male) character, such as Hessreiter, who uses the painting to demonstrate his political beliefs, or with the narrator in its use as a plot device.

Self-Sacrifice, Decline, and the *Wartesaal*-Motif:
Anna Trautwein

Aside from Anna Elisabeth Haider there is another character in the trilogy who resembles the "New Woman." She seems to have more in common with the socialist conceptualization of the ideal proclaimed by the Russian revolutionary Alexandra Kollontai. "Her vision of the New Woman was of an independent, strong woman who was working her way through life without the protection of a man," and who further experienced a feeling of comradeship with her husband and economic independence for herself.[42] Working for Dr. Wohlgemuth, Anna Trautwein is the provider for her exiled Bavarian family in Paris, and a dedicated and pragmatic facilitator of her husband Sepp's music career. He, however, fails to recognize her efforts and sabotages a move to London, which was offered to Anna by her employer. Already suffering from the social

42   Sharp, "Riding the Tiger," 123.

decline that she experiences in Paris, the hardships of life in exile, and her family's inability to appreciate her efforts, while suddenly being faced with even greater pauperization and her husband's infidelity, the 38-year-old Anna Trautwein commits suicide like her namesake Anna Elisabeth Haider by inhaling gas.[43] Her death thereby also serves an allegorical function: "Anna Trautwein allows Feuchtwanger to show exemplarily the misery of exile."[44]

Anna Trautwein's suicide relates to Poe's death-of-a-beautiful-woman-motif in various ways. At the beginning of the chapter, Anna comes home on a sweltering summer evening, pulling off her dress before she "lay naked on the bed."[45] Having devoted all her energy in exile for the well-being of her family, Anna can no longer carry on when she finds out that her husband Sepp had lost his job on the editorial board of the newspaper *Pariser Nachrichten* and kept the news from her. She turns into "a helpless woman, weeping a storm of tears, incapable of any further effort."[46] The chapter repeatedly addresses her feelings of powerlessness and despair, for instance, when she thinks to herself: " 'The sick man dies, and the strong man fights.' How lovely that she was not a strong man,"[47] or when the narration continues with a bitter comment: "Poor Anna, handsome Anna, stupid Anna, brave Anna, all your bravery was foolishness, all your struggling was in vain; only now, at thirty-eight, have you learnt wisdom."[48]

As is indicated in the above passages, Anna Trautwein's suicide signifies that she succumbs to feelings of utter despair and powerlessness over her situation. This is in part brought upon by her husband and in part due to the lack of perspective of life in exile. Even in the moment of approaching death, Anna is still concerned about Sepp and their son Hanns, as she tidies up the flat before she places herself in the bathtub—still naked—a

43   See Feuchtwanger, *Paris Gazette*, 587.

44   Jan Hans and Lutz Winckler, "Von der Selbstverständigung des Künstlers in Krisenzeiten: Lion Feuchtwangers 'Wartesaal-Trilogie'," *Text + Kritik* 79/80 (1983): 28–48, 39.

45   Feuchtwanger, *Paris Gazette*, 569.

46   Ibid., 575.

47   Ibid., 577.

48   Ibid., 577.

tube in her mouth through which she inhales the deadly gas. In accordance with the death-of-a-beautiful-woman-motif, her suicide combines beauty and terror as it combines life and decay: "She had once read that people who committed suicide by inhaling coal gas had a bloom on their faces and looked incredibly lifelike. It would be fine if Hanns had a presentable picture of her to keep in his memory."[49] When Sepp finds her, he indeed first assumes she is still alive: "[S]he looked fresh, her cheeks were blooming, her lips red. Thank God, she was alive."[50] Only when he carries her dead body from the bathtub onto the bed, the formerly beautiful face of the beloved reveals her decay: "[H]er jaw had fallen, and her mouth with the fine white teeth gaped grotesquely and horribly."[51] Spending the rest of the night with Hanns sitting next to the bed, Sepp is reminded of Anna's lost beauty, "he described her with a loving particularity[52] which in other circumstances he would have avoided in speaking to his son. It was simply his duty to explain how beautiful she had been in the time of her bloom."[53] In a moment of catharsis, he realizes how much he has benefited from Anna's support:

> Sepp was suddenly overwhelmed. In a flash he knew that to the very end she had been concerned only for his welfare. [...] And all at once he saw, almost corporeally, the figure of Anna doing things for him, endless little daily attentions performed with love, and putting up with hardships for his sake, sacrificing herself completely.[54]

Sepp's grief about his dead wife is characterized primarily by thoughts that concern himself, that *he* was the last thing on her mind before she died—and "only" he—and that Anna made sacrifices for *him* specifically. This introspection illustrates how Anna Trautwein's suicide encapsulates the death-of-a-beautiful-woman-motif as "the most poetical topic":

---

49   Ibid., 580.
50   Ibid., 587.
51   Ibid., 588.
52   In the German original, the physical dimension of Sepp's description is more obvious. There, it reads: "er schilderte ihren Körper mit Einzelheiten." Lion Feuchtwanger, *Exil*, 4th edn (Berlin: Aufbau, 2008), 596.
53   Ibid., 593.
54   Ibid., 592.

What makes the death of a beautiful woman "the most poetical" of topics is the fact that it is related to the element of desire: irresistible loveliness and the impossibility of its recovery. In designating the death of a woman in such terms, Poe makes reference to the poet and to the state he finds himself in when he loses a lover. The death of a woman certainly generates grief but it also makes the poet experience a supreme sense of self-awareness.[55]

Sepp Trautwein—although not a poet but a composer—consequently draws inspiration and new strength from the events and produces his opus magnum, the "Wartesaal" in which his artistic genius and his political activism merge together. Hanns, on the other hand, pities Anna as she "had belonged to an unfortunate generation, a generation doomed to destruction," and solidifies his plans to emigrate to Moscow.[56] Anna's death is thereby depicted as the tragic surrender of a beautiful and self-sacrificing, but essentially weak mother and wife, incapable of surviving through the hardship that exile brings. For her two male observers and family members, her death prompts a new self-awareness as politicized individuals: Hanns believes to be able to change the course of history by devoting himself to communism in Moscow, and Sepp finishes his masterpiece and transforms into a politically engaged artist. Among all the female characters discussed so far, Anna Trautwein and her suicide therefore capture most evidently that at the center of the death-of-a-beautiful-woman-motif stands the surviving male figure.

Conclusion: Gendered Deaths in the *Wartesaal* Trilogy

The analysis of the deaths of three female characters in Feuchtwanger's *Wartesaal* trilogy demonstrates that Poe's death-of-a-beautiful-woman-motif can be traced in Feuchtwanger's novels—with similar effects. The *Fememord* to which the maid Amalia Sandhuber falls victim in *Erfolg*

---

55   Tsirakoglou, "Aesthetic Desire," 141.
56   Feuchtwanger, *Paris Gazette*, 593.

serves to demonstrate the brutality of the fascist movement *Wahrhaft Deutsche* and, subsequently, the corrupted legal system in Bavaria of the time of "White Terror."[57] Amalia Sandhuber's death further complies with the motif of the death of the maiden, as her naivety, promiscuity, and pride make her an ideal victim. Once dead, her body is being observed through the male gaze of her murderer Alois Kutzner and his accomplices.

Anna Elisabeth Haider as another dead female character in *Erfolg* illustrates how the death-of-a-beautiful-woman-motif can be read in relation to the "New Woman" of the 1920s and the alleged threat she posed to German national identity. Haider's transgressive behavior turned her into an enemy figure for conservative Bavarians, which is expressed most clearly in the eventful provenance of her nude self-portrait that inverts the male gaze but also serves a narrative function as it works as the backdrop from where the entire plot evolves and through which independent plot strands are connected into a coherent whole.

Anna Trautwein in *Exil*, who gives up hope when faced with her husband's betrayal and impending poverty, is also depicted as a dead woman. In her death, the motif of the beautiful woman reappears, as the description of the dying scene alludes to both beauty and decay. Anna Trautwein's death illustrates that at the heart of the motif stands the surviving male figure: successively, her husband Sepp who composes his opus magnum and her son Hanns who commits to his political project and emigrates to Moscow.

While no central female character dies in *Die Geschwister Oppermann*, Berthold Oppermann's suicide in the second *Wartesaal*-novel illustrates the extent to which death itself appears as a gendered concept in Feuchtwanger's texts. The school boy Berthold takes an overdose of sleeping pills after being pressured to revoke a statement about Arminius and his legacy for

---

57 The term "White Terror" refers to assaults committed by counterrevolutionary forces in Munich after the end of the Bavarian Soviet Republic in 1919. Violence committed as part of "White Terror" was used by military and paramilitary troops to intimidate political opponents. See Bruno Thoß, "Weißer Terror, 1919," in *Historisches Lexikon Bayerns* (11 September 2012), available online: <https://www.historisches-lexikonbayerns.de/Lexikon/Weißer_Terror,_1919>.

German nationhood. His decision to end his life appears spontaneous, but he acts in determination, inspired by his reading of Heinrich von Kleist's *Michael Kohlhaas* (1810), in particular the passage in which Kohlhaas proclaims: "Better to be a dog, if I am to be trampled on, than a man," which Berthold writes down as a suicide note and puts on top of his manuscript on Arminius.[58] Berthold's death is thereby framed not as a surrender but instead symbolizes resistance and unyieldingness. Rather than live a lie, Berthold sticks to his principles so that his death can be regarded as an act of opposition to Nazism.

Similar to Berthold's suicide, the death of 19-year-old Harry Meisel in *Exil* establishes the poet's literary fame and legacy.[59] Having secured a job in Akron, Ohio, the impoverished young man wants to celebrate his last night in Paris in a rundown establishment, where he is stabbed by a "Clubfoot" who envies Harry's success with the women present.[60] Earlier in the novel, Harry quotes from Rilke's *Stunden-Buch* [*Book of Hours*] (1905), which has the poor masses as its subject matter and famously proclaims that "[t]hey will persist further than any end,/outlive the rich, whose meaning seeps away,/and at last raise themselves like rested hands/when those of other lands,/peoples and classes weary."[61] As the narration of *Exil* reveals, Harry fulfills this message by becoming posthumously famous and even inspiring the son of a prominent Nazi propagandist in Paris to follow into his literary footsteps, albeit to no avail. Harry Meisel's killing is narrated in the chapter "Sonnet LXVI" as an intertextual reference to Shakespeare's eponymous sonnet. The sonnet is quoted as a peritext at the beginning of *Exil*'s second book. Its first line reads: "Tired with all these, for restful death I cry."[62] This line could also be read as coming from Harry Meisel himself,

---

58   Feuchtwanger, *The Oppermanns*, 270.

59   For a detailed analysis of the character Harry Meisel, see Franziska Wolf, "The Figure of the Exiled Writer in Comparison: Intertextuality in Lion Feuchtwanger's *Exil* (1940) and Abbas Khider's *Der falsche Inder* (2008)," *TRANSIT* 13, no. 1 (2021): 34–51.

60   Feuchtwanger, *Paris Gazette*, 410.

61   Rainer Maria Rilke, *Das Stunden-Buch/The Book of Hours*, ed. Ben Hutchinson, trans. Susan Ranson (Rochester: Camden House, 2008), 188–9.

62   Feuchtwanger, *Paris Gazette*, 270.

who quotes Shakespeare during the night of his death, and about whom
his close companion and admirer Oskar Tschernigg notes:

> The essential truth was that Harry Meisel had longed to be out of this vulgar world,
> he had wanted to go further than America, he had yearned for death. "Tired with
> all thee, for restful death I cry." It had been his own wish to perish; he had himself
> wrought his destruction, and he had done right to refuse to live any longer in a
> soulless world.[63]

Harry Meisel's death can therefore also be seen as an act of self-liberation
which, simultaneously, establishes his literary legacy and fame. His death,
alongside that of Berthold Oppermann, thereby becomes a political act
of resurrection and resistance: these two young men bring death upon
themselves not to live on in a world with which they fundamentally dis-
agree. Their deaths manifest their perception as politically committed
(in Berthold Oppermann's case) or artistically gifted (in Harry Meisel's
case). By contrast, when the female characters Anna Trautwein and Anna
Elisabeth Haider end their lives, it is depicted as an emotional reaction
out of despair that is orchestrated to reflect the importance of the male
characters surrounding them.[64]

The analysis of deaths in Feuchtwanger's *Wartesaal* demonstrates
how these deaths are gendered and how they reproduce gender-specific
stereotypes. The deaths of female characters serve primarily as plot devices
through which the entire plot is set up and driven forward. The death-of-a-
beautiful-woman-motif, that Poe considered to be the most poetical topic
of all, thereby also finds application in Feuchtwanger's *Wartesaal* so that
Weekes' observation that female characters die to fulfill a need in the male
observer or narrator largely holds true for Feuchtwanger's texts.

---

63   Ibid., 411.
64   Martin Krüger's death in *Erfolg* only partly fits this gender binary. Although he
     becomes immortalized in Joanna Krain's film "Martin Krüger," his death primarily
     serves as a narrative foil to expose a corrupt Bavarian justice system. His oscillating
     position may also be a result of the repeated allusions to his potential Jewishness,
     rendering him effeminate, for instance by the antisemitic prison physician Dr. Gsell
     who believes to detect "a light infusion of a Semitic strain" in Krüger. Feuchtwanger,
     Success, 557.

HELGA SCHRECKENBERGER

6 The Heroic and the Mundane: Gender Dynamics in Lion Feuchtwanger's *Exil*

ABSTRACT

Lion Feuchtwanger's novel *Exil* focuses on the situation of the German exiles from Nazi Germany in Paris. In the novel's often-anthologized chapter "Trübe Gäste," the narrator points to two old German terms associated with exiles, "Elend" (misery) for those banned from their land and "Recke" (warrior) meaning outlaw. According to the narrator, succeeding in exile demands a "Recke" whose nomadic spirit makes him resilient and able to meet new challenges. "Elend" represents those who break under the pressure of exile. In the novel, these two concepts of exile are connected to gender. "Recke" is embodied by the male protagonist, Sepp Trautwein, a free-spirited artist who cares little for status, financial, and domestic stability. His wife, Anna, who cannot let go of her pre-exile existence and commits suicide, is identified with "Elend." I argue that the gender dynamics in Feuchtwanger's novel are tied to the notion of the exile as a solitary artist, which has its roots in Romanticism but still surfaces in the writings of postmodern thinkers like Edward Said.

Two Poles of Exile

Comprised of the novels *Erfolg* (1930), *Die Geschwister Oppermann* (1933), and *Exil* (1940), Lion Feuchtwanger's *Wartesaal-Trilogie* represents the author's literary examination of the political developments in Germany from 1914 to 1939.[1] While the first two novels of the cycle focus on the National Socialists' rise to power in Germany, the third novel, *Exil*, portrays the consequences of the Nazi terror for the regime's opponents and victims by exploring the precarious situation of the German

---

1   Cf. Lion Feuchtwanger, "Nachwort des Autors 1939," in *Exil* (Frankfurt/Main: Fischer, 1979), 787.

exile community in 1935 Paris. Two major plotlines emerge in *Exil*: the depiction of the existential difficulties and hardships of everyday life in exile, and the political and artistic development of the main protagonist, the composer Sepp Trautwein.

Both plotlines refer to two different aspects of exile, which the novel's narrator defines in the often-anthologized chapter "Trübe Gäste" ("Unwelcome Guests"). The chapter starts off with the narrator listing the many different reasons that drove Germans to leave their home country, ranging from fear of persecution to political opposition. He also names the numerous hardships and indignities resulting from the condition of exile, which for the narrator constitute a character touchstone for the exiles: "Den wenigsten bekamen die Leiden, die sie durchzumachen hatten. Denn es ist so, daß die Leiden nur den Starken stärker, den Schwachen aber schwächer machen."[2] ["Very few benefited from the sufferings which they had to endure. For it is only the strong who are strengthened by suffering."][3] Following this observation, the narrator differentiates between two types of refugees represented by two old German terms for the experience of exile:

> Das alte Deutsch kennt für den Vertriebenen, für den Exilanten, zwei Worte: Das Wort "Recke", das nichts anderes bedeutet als eben Vertriebener, Geächteter, und das Wort "Elend", das wiederum den Mann ohne Land, den aus dem Land Gestoßenen bedeutet.[4]

> [In the old German language there are two words for the exile: the word "Recke," which meant simply an outlaw, and the word "Elend," which meant a man without country, someone driven from his land.]

The exact meaning of this distinction between "Recke" and "Elend" becomes clear when the narrator elaborates a couple of pages later:

2   Feuchtwanger, *Exil*, 123.
3   Although *Exil* has been translated under the title *Paris Gazette* by Willa and Edwin Muir (New York: The Viking Press, 1940), I am providing my own translations that keep closer to the original text.
4   Ibid., 123–4. *The Deutsches Wörterbuch von Jacob und Wilhelm Grimm* (Munich: Deutscher Taschenbuch Verlag, 1984) confirms both meanings for exile. "Exilium" is given as a synonym for "Elend" (v. 3, 406) and "aus der Heimat vertriebener Held" is listed as one of the meanings for "Recke" (v. 14, 443).

Ja, Exil zerrieb, machte klein und elend: aber Exil härtete auch und machte groß
und reckenhaft. Das Leben des Bodenständigen, des Seßhaften verlangt und verleiht
andere Tugenden als das Dasein des Nomaden, des Freizügigen. Im Zeitalter der
Maschine aber, im Zeitalter, da die Maschine den größeren Teil der Bauern über-
flüssig macht, sind die Tugenden des Freizügigen für die Gesellschaft zumindest
ebenso wichtig wie die des Seßhaften und geeigneter für den, der sich sein Leben
täglich neu erkämpfen muß.[5]

[Yes, exile was exhausting, it made small and miserable: but exile also hardened and
made great and mighty. The life of the settled and sedentary demands and produces
other virtues than the existence of the nomad, of the free-spirited. But in the age of
the machine, in the age in which the machine makes the greater part of the peasants
superfluous, the virtues of the free-spirited are at least as important for society as
those of the sedentary and more suitable for those who have to fight for their lives
anew every day.]

According to the narrator, succeeding in exile demands a nomadic spirit
that is not rooted in a particular geographic place, as well as resilience
and the willingness to meet new challenges. Yet the terminology of the
narrator is also confusing. While the noun "Recke," which also has the
meaning of "warrior," stands for a person, "Elend" ("misery") connotes
a condition. It seems that rather than referring to two different types of
refugees, the narrator's terminology identifies the figure of the exile with
"Recke" and the condition of exile, the enduring aftermath of displacement and its impact on identity and mobility, with "Elend."

In *Exil*, this dual manifestation of exile—the misery of the exile condition and the resilient nomad—is not only connected to the two main plotlines of the novel but also to gender. The mundane reality of exile fraught
with poverty, drudgery, humiliation, and dependence on the good will of
others is mainly the domain of the female protagonist, Sepp Trautwein's wife
Anna. Sepp Trautwein, on the other hand, is little affected by this aspect
of exile so long as he is able to freely pursue his art and his political fight.
Consequently Anna, who breaks under the pressures of exile and commits
suicide, is identified with "Elend," while Sepp embodies the "Recke," who
becomes stronger and more heroic with each new challenge.

5   Feuchtwanger, *Exil*, 125.

Representing "Elend": Anna Trautwein

Anna Trautwein is at the center of the plotline that focuses on the difficulties of daily life in exile: living in cramped, shabby hotel rooms, financial worries, working menial jobs, and dealing with an unsympathetic, often hostile bureaucracy. Initially, Anna Trautwein appears more than capable of dealing with the new situation. She is the main breadwinner of the family, allowing her son, Hanns, to continue his education and her husband to concentrate on his music. She fights the legal battles over i-dentification cards and residency permits for her family. Even other members of the exile community turn to her for help in finding employment. Furthermore, she uses her considerable charm to lobby for her husband's career, attempting to secure a radio production of Sepp's latest composition. Thus, she represents the resilient, practical-minded wives of German exiles that exiled sociologist Ernst Bornemann praised:

> Diese Frauen stammten meist aus dem bürgerlichen Mittelstand. Sie waren oft Intellektuelle. Sie waren nicht sehr praktisch. Nun mußten sie lernen, ihren schreibenden Mann irgendwie durchzubringen. Sie verdingten sich in Berufen, die sie nicht gelernt hatten. Sie mußten lernen, auf Gasfeuer im möbilierten Zimmer zu kochen. Sie mußten den verzweifelten Mann mit Trost und Hoffnung versorgen—mit einer Hoffnung, die sie selbst keineswegs verspürten. Die meisten unserer großen Autoren wären im Exil verreckt, wenn die Frauen sie nicht irgendwie durchgefüttert hätten. Deshalb nach all diesen Jahren nochmals all diesen Frauen ein Wort des Dankes.[6]

> [These women mostly came from the middle class. They were often intellectuals. They weren't very practical. Now they had to learn how to support their writer-husband somehow. They worked in jobs they had not learned. They had to learn to cook on a gas fire in a furnished room. They had to provide the desperate man with comfort and hope—a hope they did not feel themselves. Most of our great authors would

---

6   Ernst Bornemann, "Vom freiwilligen Exil," in *Literatur des Exils. Eine Dokumentation über die P.E.N.-Jahrestagung in Bremen vom 18.–20 Sept, 1980*, ed. Bernd Engelmann (Munich: Goldmann, 1981), 54. Bornemann's perspective on the significance of women's contribution in securing their families' survival in exile is shared by exile scholars, i.e., Heike Klapor, "Das Exil der Frauen. Thesen zu einer überlesenen Geschichte," in *Sammlung 5: Jahrbuch für antifaschistische Literatur und Kunst*, ed. Uwe Naumann (Frankfurt/Main: Röderberg, 1982),

have died in exile if women hadn't pulled them through somehow. Therefore, after all these years, once again a word of thanks to all these women.]

The gender dynamics revealed in Bornemann's remarks also show that in exile, the domestic sphere and the fight for the economic survival of their husbands and families became largely the domain of women. In sacrificing their own ambitions as intellectuals, they thus experience both displacement and marginalization. Although Bornemann recognizes this sacrifice and praises women for it, Feuchtwanger's Anna Trautwein receives little thanks for her efforts. While Sepp feels sorry for her having to carry all the financial worries, he himself is hardly bothered by them nor does he take them very seriously: "[…] so verwickelt die kleinen Dinge ausschauen, am Ende, wenn man lange genug wartet, erledigen sie sich von selber."[7] ["… as complicated as these little things appear, if you wait long enough, they'll take care of themselves."] It also becomes clear that Anna's efforts regarding the radio broadcast of Sepp's oratory "Die Perser" ["The Persians"] are more important to her than him. In addition to the much-needed honorarium, she hopes that the broadcast of Sepp's music would help them regain some of their prior social status and recognition, the loss of which Anna is painfully aware of.

By focusing primarily on the mundane, Anna becomes more and more alienated from her former self. In Germany she was her husband's main sounding board: he discussed every detail of his music with her and repeatedly called her his "musical conscience." Sepp expects his wife to reassume this role in exile: "seinen besten, teilnahmsvollsten Hörer hat er mitnehmen können: Anna,"[8] ["… he had been able to take his best, most engaged listener with him: Anna."] Yet because of her worries about the family's economic survival, Anna is no longer able to devote attention to her husband's music:

115–22 and Susanne Mittag, "Im Fremden ungewollt zuhaus," Frauen im Exil, in *Exil. Forschung, Erkenntnisse Ergebnisse* 1 (1981): 49–56.

7   Feuchtwanger, *Exil*, 11.
8   Ibid.

Aber sie hat einfach keine Zeit, mit ihm über Dinge zu sprechen, die ihr im Inneren ebenso wesentlich sind wie ihm. Die ganzen Sorgen des kleinen Alltags liegen auf ihr; es ist kein Wunder, wenn ihr davon der Mund übergeht. Dabei bleibt es ein Monolog, er versteht nichts von diesen Sachen.[9]

[But she just doesn't have time to talk to him about things that are as important to her as they are to him. All the worries of everyday life weigh on her; it's no wonder she needs to talk about them. However, it remains a monologue, he understands nothing about these things.]

It is important to point out that rather than presenting them as his own point of view, the novel's omniscient narrator relates Anna's thoughts in the form of an inner monologue. This creates the impression that Anna reproaches herself for failing to live up to Sepp's expectations while excusing her husband's shortcomings. Since Anna does not have the time to concern herself with Sepp's music and Sepp has little interest in Anna's worries, the bond between the couple weakens more and more over time. Moreover, because of her hard work and their strained finances, Anna loses the second attribute that not only made her useful to her husband but was also the source of her self-confidence—her beauty:

Alt werden wir alle, aber daß es gerade jetzt mit ihrer Blüte zu Ende geht, kommt sehr zur Unzeit. In München, in Berlin hat sie, die schöne Frau, manches wiedergut-machen können, was er versiebt hat, einfach durch ein freundliches Lächeln oder durch ein bißchen Flirt mit einem Maßgebenden. […] Hier in Paris hätte sie es noch ganz anders nötig zu strahlen, zu bezaubern, wenn sie für ihn etwas erreichen soll. Aber die zwei Jahre Emigration haben sie nicht schöner gemacht.[10]

[We are all getting old, but it is just the wrong time for her bloom to begin to fade. In Munich, in Berlin, she, the beautiful woman, had been able to make up for his blunders, simply with a friendly smile or a little flirtation with someone influential. […] Here in Paris she would have needed to shine and to charm far more if she were to achieve something for him. But the two years of emigration had not improved her looks.]

9   Ibid., 10.
10   Ibid., 14.

Being the sole breadwinner of the family, Anna has neither the money nor the time to color her graying hair or get sufficient rest. Consequently, she sacrifices both her beauty and her position as Sepp's "musical conscience" to keep the dreadful consequences of exile at bay. Anna fulfills the stereotype of the self-sacrificing woman who lives her life through her husband. When Sepp gets involved in politics instead of pursuing his music,[11] and she realizes how little Sepp appreciates what she has done, Anna's downward spiral begins. She becomes quarrelsome and malicious, attitudes that the narrator in the chapter "Trübe Gäste" attributes to those who crumble under the burden of exile: "Aus sicheren Verhältnissen ins Unsichere gestoßen, verzappelten sie sich, wurden [...] streitsüchtig, anspruchsvoll, besserwisserisch. Sie wurden wie Früchte, die man zu früh vom Baum gerissen hat, nicht reif, sondern trocken und holzig."[12] ["Torn from security and pushed into uncertainty, they floundered, became [...] quarrelsome, demanding, know-it-alls. They did not ripen, like fruit that was torn from the tree too early, but dry and tasteless."] This also applies to Anna, who grows more embittered and resentful under the daily pressures of exile. Moreover, her vicious attack of the music critic Sahling, a fellow exile who had criticized Sepp's music back in Germany, demonstrates her inability to let go of her old life and adapt to her new situation. In contrast, Sepp harbors no ill feelings towards his former detractor: "Im Grunde tat der Mensch ihm leid. Für Trautwein war das Vergangene wirklich tot, für ihn existierte nur der Sahling von heute, und der war ein Emigrant, wie er selber einer war."[13] ["He basically felt sorry for the men.

---

11 Sepp Trautwein freelances for the exile newspaper *Pariser Nachrichten*. When the Nazis kidnap the paper's journalist Friedrich Benjamin in Switzerland, he decides to work fulltime for the paper and fight for Benjamin's release. With this, Feuchtwanger adapts the case of the journalist Berthold Jacob who was abducted to Germany in 1935 and released after six months due to vehement public protests. For more information see Wolfgang Müller-Funk, *Literatur als geschichtliches Argument. Zur ästhetischen Konzeption und Geschichtsverarbeitung in Lion Feuchtwangers Romantrilogie Der Wartesaal* (Frankfurt/Main: Peter Lang, 1982), 226–34.

12 Ibid., 124.

13 Ibid., 266.

The past was really dead for Trautwein, only the Sahling of today existed for him, and that Sahling was an emigrant like himself."] Sepp's generosity towards Sahling contrasts with Anna's pettiness and shows that he is able to leave the past behind and respond to the demands of the moment. These are characteristics that in the chapter "Trübe Gäste," the narrator attributes to the "Recke": "Viele engte das Exil ein, aber den Besseren gab es mehr Weite, Elastizität, es gab ihnen Blick für das Große, Wesentliche und lehrte sie, nicht am Unwesentlichen zu haften."[14] [Exile restricted many, but to the better ones it gave more breadth and flexibility, it gave them an eye for the big picture, the essential and taught them not to cling to the unessential.]While Anna holds on to old grudges, Sepp, recognizing their insignificance in the context of the looming threat of fascism, has moved on. However, by associating Sepp with the "Besseren," the text clearly ranks Anna among the weak and morally inferior.

Anna loses more ground when Sepp turns to Erna Redlich, the administrative assistant the exile newspaper *Pariser Nachrichten* (*Paris News*). Erna Redlich replaces Anna as Sepp's confidante as she takes as much interest in his political work as Anna used to in his music. The final straw comes when Anna learns that Sepp has been fired from his job with the newspaper at the very moment when she is about to lose her own job as a dentist's assistant. Feeling both useless and hopeless, she commits suicide. Yet, she does not reproach her husband either for the difficulties in their relationship or for her suicide; rather she blames it all on exile:

> Sie will nicht selbstgerecht sein, sie will ihm nicht unrecht tun. Es sind die Verhältnisse, an denen ihre Beziehungen kaputtgegangen sind. [...] Kunst geben braucht Zeit, und Kunst nehmen braucht Zeit, Zeit und einen freien Kopf. In Deutschland haben sie Zeit und einen freien Kopf gehabt, darum ist alles zwischen ihnen gut gegangen. Jetzt, im Exil, haben sie weder Zeit noch den freien Kopf. Es ist das Exil, das ihre Liebe kaputtgeschlagen hat. [...] Ihr Betrieb, ihr blöder kleiner Betrieb hat sie aufgefressen, auch innerlich. In Deutschland sind ihr die Sorgen des Alltags so erschienen, wie sie waren, in ihrer ganzen Winzigkeit und Erbärmlichkeit: im Exil haben sie sich ihr vergrößert und ihr schließlich keinen Raum mehr gelassen für anderes.[15]

---

14   Ibid., 123.
15   Ibid., 533.

[She doesn't want to be self-righteous, she doesn't want to be unfair to him. It's their circumstances that destroyed their relationship. […] Creating art takes time, and appreciating art takes time, time and a mind free of worry. In Germany they had had time and a mind free of worry, so everything had gone well between them. Now, in exile, they have neither time nor the freedom from worry. It is exile that destroyed their love. […] Her business, her stupid little business, had consumed her, had hollowed her out. In Germany, she had seen the worries of everyday life as they were, small and trivial: in exile, they appeared bigger to her and ultimately left no room for anything else.]

Anna blames herself for having lost perspective and letting insignificant daily worries overwhelm her, not taking into account that in exile these daily worries are a matter of survival. Anna's self-recriminations, which are again presented in the form of an inner monologue, not only confirm the narrator's assertion of the negative impact of exile on the "weak," but they also exonerate her husband from any responsibility for her suicide. Sepp's thoughts express the same sentiments. While he reproaches himself for not having shown interest in her problems, he still concludes that ultimately it was the misery of exile that wore Anna down:

Das alles war nicht recht von ihm, aber das sind natürlich auch nicht die wahren Gründe gewesen dessen, was sie getan hat. Die lagen tiefer, die lagen nicht bei ihm, und kann er dafür, daß alles in der Emigration so klein, elend und kümmerlich geworden ist? […] Und weil dieser ständige kleine Dreck Anna ganz anders hergenommen hat als ihn selber, hat sie jetzt den Mut und Glauben verloren.[16]

[That all had been very wrong of him, but of course those weren't the real reasons why she had done what she did. They lay deeper, they had nothing to do with him, and is it his fault that everything in emigration has become so small, wretched, and miserable? […] And because these constant little trivialities had affected Anna more than him, she had lost courage and faith.]

With Sepp echoing the words of the narrator in "Trübe Gäste" "Ja, das Exil zerrieb, es machte klein und elend"[17] ["Yes, exile was exhausting, it made you small and miserable"], the text identifies Anna with "Elend." While blaming Anna's suicide on the grueling exile situation suggests that

16   Ibid., 546.
17   Ibid., 125.

both Anna and Sepp are blameless, it also points to a difference between
the two of them. In "Trübe Gäste," the narrator distinguishes between the
strong who only get stronger under pressure and the weak who get weaker.
Sepp's reaction to Anna's suicide confirms this assessment: the misery of
exile has diminished Anna and taken away her courage, while Sepp was
affected differently and has grown with the challenges. However, the
moral judgment that the narrator attaches to the different reactions to
exile—strength and weakness—suggests that Anna herself is at fault. Her
inability to withstand the misery of exile means that she was weak from
the beginning. Sepp, however, embodies the "Recke" who only becomes
stronger and more heroic in exile.

Sepp Trautwein as the Heroic Exile

Sepp Trautwein's successful negotiation of exile results from the fact that
he is not bound by success, position, or even place like Anna was: "Ihn
schiert es nicht, daß er für die Welt niemand mehr ist, er ist innerlich der
gleiche geblieben. Sepp hat seine Musik, er schreibt sie für sich selber und
für sie [Anna], im übrigen arbeitet man und schlägt sich durch."[18] ["It
doesn't bother him that he's nobody to the world anymore, inwardly he's
remained the same. Sepp has his music, he writes it for himself and for
her [Anna], otherwise you work and make ends meet."] This suggests that
while Anna's self-worth and well-being are dependent on her social environment and her husband, Sepp draws his strength from inside and from
his music. Moreover, he is open to the challenges of exile and grows with
them: "Er hat seine Politik, seine Musik, der Tag hat für ihn ausgefüllte

18   Ibid., 18. Sepp Trautwein taking refuge in his music recalls Theodor Adorno's
      proposition to find a home in writing as a solution to exile: "For a man who no
      longer has a homeland, writing becomes a place to live." (Theodor Adorno, *Minima
      Moralia: Reflections from a Damaged Life*, trans. E. F. N. Jephcott (London: New
      Left Books, 1974), 87.

sechzehn Stunden, eine reicher als die andere."[19] ["He has his politics,
his music, his day has sixteen full hours, each one richer than the next."]
This independence reflects the nomadic spirit that the narrator in "Trübe
Gäste" attributes to the "Recke." It also marks Sepp as a cosmopolitan
and puts him in opposition to the nationalistic ideology of the Nazis.
However, it does not mean that Sepp is indifferent to his environment.
He left Nazi Germany because he saw the political developments as det-
rimental to his art:

> Gute Musik und schlechte Politik vertragen sich nicht, das ist für ihn nicht mehr eine
> Meinung, das ist für ihn Teil seines Wesens geworden. [...] Man kann sich vor der
> Politik nicht drücken, wenn die eigene Kunst nicht leiden soll. Seine Musik jedenfalls,
> wenn sie klingen soll, dann muß reine Luft da sein. Und wenn reine Luft nicht da ist,
> dann muß man sie schaffen.[20]

> [Good music and bad politics are not compatible, that's no longer a matter of opinion
> for him, it's become part of his being. [...] You can't ignore politics if you don't want
> your art to suffer. In any case, for his music, if it is to sound good, the environment
> needed to be right. And if the environment was not right, then you create one that was].

In Sepp's case, emigration is both an act of political opposition as well
as an essential prerequisite for the integrity of his art. Moreover, while
he considered himself apolitical and nothing but an artist before his emigration, he becomes politically active in exile. Following the Gestapo's
abduction of the journalist Friedrich Benjamin, Sepp puts off working on
his oratory, accepts a position with the exile journal *Pariser Nachrichten*
[*Paris News*], and successfully mounts a journalistic campaign to free
Benjamin. This campaign also demonstrates Sepp's ability to adapt to
the demands of the situation. He changes his nuanced writing style for
an aggressive but more effective way to attack the Nazi regime.[21] The

---

19   Feuchtwanger, *Exil*, 187.
20   Ibid., 11–12.
21   This development is connected to Sepp's discussion with his son Hanns if the use
      of force is justified in the fight against the Nazis. Initially opposed to the idea, Sepp
      eventually concedes "Eine gerechte Ordnung auf der Welt läßt sich ohne Gewalt
      nicht herstellen. Diejenigen, die Interesse haben an der ungerechten Ordnung,
      geben nicht klein bei, wenn man sie nicht mit Gewalt dazu zwingt" (Ibid., 698).

"praktisch-politische Handlungsfähigkeit"[22] ["practical-political capacity to act"] that he acquires through his political work adds to the dimensions of his character. No longer "nichts als ein Musiker"[23] ["nothing but a musician"], in exile Sepp Trautwein emerges as a formidable fighter against Nazism and thus a "Recke."

The Exile as Artist

Sepp's political engagement also has consequences for his music, which in exile evolves from "Nur-Kunst" to an art that adequately responds to the political situation. This is demonstrated through the three works that Sepp composes in exile, each marking an important step in his artistic development. His first work, the oratory "Die Perser," is considered "anständige, wagemutige Musik"[24] ["honest, courageous music"] mainly because it would be banned in Germany. Sepp, however, is dissatisfied with its "aestheticism."[25] His second composition, the "Walther-Lieder," is closely related to Sepp's political activities and resembles the articles he wrote for the *Pariser Nachrichten*. Artistically less refined, they are characterized by their "derber Humor" ["ribald humor"] and "Volkstümlichkeit" ["folklore"] but they are also "kämpferisch" ["combative"] and "revolutionär"

["A just order in the world cannot be established without violence. Those who are invested in the unjust order will not back down unless they are compelled to do so by force."]

22   Stephan Dreyer, *Schriftstellerrollen und Schreibmodelle im Exil: zur Periodisierung von Lion Feuchtwangers Romanwerk 1933–1945* (Frankfurt/Main: Peter Lang, 1988), 212. For Lutz Winckler, Sepp's development represents a "weltanschauliche[n] Positionsgewinn bürgerlicher Antifaschisten im Exil" (Winckler, "Ein Künstlerroman. Lion Feuchtwangers *Exil*," in *Faschismuskritik und Deutschlandbild im Exilroman*, ed. Christian Fritsch and Lutz Winckler (Berlin: Argument, 1981), 161 ["a gain of ideological position of bourgeois anti-fascists in exile"].

23   Feuchtwanger, *Exil*, 11.

24   Ibid., 368.

25   Ibid., 561.

["revolutionary"].[26] For Sepp, they capture the defiant, resilient spirit of emigration:

> Ja, das ist die richtige Musik, das ist der Siegesjubel, der durch den Untergang durch-klingt, das ist jenes "Stirb und werde," das ist das, was sie heute in Moskau "tragischen Optimismus" nennen, das ist der Sinn der Emigration.[27]

> [Yes, that is the right music, that's the jubilation of victory that penetrates through the destruction, that's that "die and become," that's what they call "tragic optimism" in Moscow today, that's the meaning of emigration.]

As much as his political evolution, Sepp's artistic development also connects him to the concept of "Recke." In "Trübe Gäste" the narrator states: "Viele von diesen Emigranten wurden innerlich reifer, erneuer-ten sich, wurden jünger. Jenes 'Stirb und werde,' dass den Menschen aus einem trüben zu einem frohen Gast dieser Erde macht, wurde ihnen Erlebnis und Besitz."[28] ["Many of these emigrants matured emotionally, renewed themselves, became younger. This 'die and become' that turns people from a weary to a happy guest on this earth became their expe-rience and their gain."] Both his music and his political work transform Sepp Trautwein from the tragic emigrant—the "trübe Gast" ["weary guest"]—to the heroic exile, the "Recke."

Sepp's last composition, a symphony with the title "Der Wartesaal" ["The Waiting-Room"], transcends both the aestheticism of his earlier music and the mere political dimension of the "Walther-Lieder." While the image of the "Wartesaal" stands for the experience of exile and the con-comitant uncertainty, despair, and—despite everything—undying hope, it takes on symbolic meaning as a representation of the modern condition: "Es war aber dieser Saal erfüllt von einem Gewimmel von Menschen; nicht nur

---

26   Ibid. Stefan Dreyer considers the political dimension of the Walther-Lieder as ar-tistically limiting, as "ein Kunstwerk, das zwar 'Rebellion' und Wut transportiert, aber auf der Eben der Anklage stehen bleibt, ohne Perspektiven zu entwickeln" (Dreyer, *Schriftstellerrollen*, 216) ["a work of art that transmits 'rebellion' and anger, but remains on the level of accusation without developing perspectives"].

27   Feuchtwanger, *Exil*, 164.

28   Ibid., 125–6.

die Menschen unserer kümmerlichen deutschen Emigration waren darin, sondern alle Zeitgenossen Sepp Trautweins."[29] ["But this room was filled with a swarm of people; not only the people of our miserable German emigration were there, but all of Sepp Trautwein's contemporaries."] With this symphony, Sepp frees himself of the "künstlichen und kalten Humanismus" ["artificial and cold humanism"] of his earlier music but also achieves artistic authenticity and autonomy: "Er brauchte für seine Kunst nicht mehr den Umweg über die Kunst anderer, er hatte in die Wirklichkeit hineingefunden."[30] ["He no longer needed to take a detour via the art of others for his own art, he had found his way into reality."] Moreover, Sepp's artistic development is accompanied by personal growth and maturation. At the end of the novel when he sits alone, listening to the performance of his symphony, he concludes:

> Es waren böse Jahre gewesen, es waren gute Jahre gewesen, und wie er so saß, ganz still, dachte er, ihm sein sie zum Heil gewesen, ihn hätten sie nach oben gerissen. Früher hatte er's nur mit dem Verstande gewußt, daß es nicht möglich war, die scheußlich geordnete Gesellschaft auf sich beruhen zu lassen und dabei gute Musik zu machen: jetzt wußte er's mit dem Herzen. Jetzt hätte er's auch Anna beibringen können.[31]

> [They had been bad years, they had been good years, and as he sat there, very still, he thought, they had been good for him, they had made him soar. Previously he had only known rationally that it was not possible to accept the hideous state of society and make good music at the same time: now he knew with his heart. Now he could have taught Anna that too.]

Although it tested him, Sepp feels ultimately uplifted and transformed by the exile experience, Anna on the other hand, had been unable to change and grow in exile and would have to be "taught" by her husband why it was important to fight for a just society. Missing from Sepp's reflections is the realization that his growth happened at the expense of his wife who had assumed the responsibility for their financial survival and had kept the family's problems and worries from him. He sees Anna's efforts

---

29   Ibid., 586.
30   Ibid., 588.
31   Ibid., 784.

as trivial not meriting the energy she puts into them.[32] In fact, he turns to another woman because he feels that Anna neglected him. It would be a mistake to see in Anna and Sepp two equal partners representing two different aspects of exile that carry equal weight. By aligning the two protagonists with "Elend" and "Recke" the text passes a moral judgment. Despite all his faults and egoism, Sepp occupies the position of the hero in Feuchtwanger's novel. Anna, on the other hand, becomes the collateral damage of exile due to her innate weakness and inability to let go of her old life.

Sepp Trautwein's positive equation with the itinerant nomad who is better suited for exile, and by extension modern life, reflects a metaphoric notion of exile that has its roots in Romanticism when artists conceived themselves as separate from society and thus even in exile in their home countries.[33] The equation of exile and creativity became the norm in the modern period. In this interpretation, the meaning of exile was conceptually bound with creativity, a widening perspectival horizon, and self-transcendence through intellectual or aesthetic effort. Moreover, it is a conception of exile that is defined by maleness and class privilege.[34]

The persistence of the modernist notion of exile is underscored by the fact that it still surfaces in the writing of a postmodern thinker like Edward Said who has emerged as one of the most influential voices of modern

---

32   As Gabriele Kreis shows, this is not an unusual position. In her book, *Frauen im Exil. Dichtung und Wirklichkeit,* she juxtaposes statements by women exiles like Marta Feuchtwanger, Salka Viertel, Karola Bloch and depictions of women in exile novels by Lion Feuchtwanger, Klaus Mann, and Bruno Frank. Mittag concludes that male authors have quite a different perception of women's exile experiences than women themselves. Cf. Kreis, *Frauen im Exil. Dichtung und Wirklichkeit* (Düsseldorf: Classen, 1984).

33   Cf. Caren Kaplan, "The Poetics of Displacement: Exile, Immigration and Travel in Autobiographical Writing." Ph.D. diss. (Santa Cruz, CA: University of California, Santa Cruz, 1987), 13f.

34   For a detailed discussion of modernist discourses of exile, see Caren Kaplan, *Questions of Travel: Postmodern Discourses of Displacement* (Durham: Duke University Press, 1996), 27–40.

exile.[35] In his essay "Movements and Migrations," he links the exile with
the intellectual and the artist:

> Yet it is no exaggeration to say that liberation as an intellectual mission, born in the re-
> sistance and opposition of the confinements and ravages of imperialism, has now shifted
> from the settled, established, and domesticated dynamics of culture to its unhoused,
> decentered, and exilic energies, energies whose incarnation today is the migrant, and
> whose consciousness is that of the intellectual and artist in exile, the political figure be-
> tween domains, between forms, between homes, and between languages.[36]

Said's exile or migrant has the same qualities as Feuchtwanger's "Recke"
and protagonist, Sepp Trautwein. Both seek liberation from oppressive
political systems, they are nomadic, reterritorialized, and creative. Like
Feuchtwanger, Said differentiates between the figure of the exile and the
condition of exile, which he identifies with the refugee experience. While
the refugee experience is defined by the "compounded misery of 'undo-
cumented' people, suddenly lost,"[37] the "exiled poets and writers lend
dignity to a condition legislated to deny dignity—to deny identity to
people."[38] While Said warns against romanticizing the experience of exile
and refers to the refugee phenomenon as the new form of exile,[39] he himself seems to valorize the notion of solitary exile. In "Reflections on Exile"
he states: "The word 'refugee' has become a political one, suggesting large
herds of innocent and bewildered people requiring urgent national assistance, whereas 'exile' carries with it, I think a touch of spirituality."[40]

---

35   However, Caren Kaplan warns of reducing Said's writings on exile to a singular
      position as he draws on both modernist and postmodernist positions: "At its most
      historically specific moments, when the discussion focuses on contemporary his-
      tory, it converges with postmodernism, enacting a powerful critique of modernist
      aesthetics and politics. At other moments his concerns remain intimately linked
      with modernist traditions and cultures" (Kaplan, *Questions*, 112–13).

36   Edward W. Said, "Movements and Migrations," in *Culture and Imperialism*
      (New York: Alfred A. Knopf Publishers, 1993), 332.

37   Said, "Reflections on Exile," in *Reflections on Exile and Other Essays* (Cambridge,
      MA: Harvard University Press, 2000), 176.

38   Ibid., 175.

39   Cf. Ibid., 174.

40   Ibid., 181.

Caren Kaplan criticizes Said's differentiation between singular and mass experience categories as it reduces refugees to hapless victims of displacement and marginalization while elevating the achievements—artistic or intellectual—of the modernist exile: "In this representation, the refugee is a faceless political construct outside the sphere of literature and aesthetics. The exile, on the other hand, is a romantic figure that can be readily identified and positioned in an aestheticized world of creativity and loss."[41]

Conclusion

Kaplan's critique of the privileged position of the solitary exile can be extended to Feuchtwanger's novel *Exil*. Sepp Trautwein is not only the central protagonist but also his political and artistic development overshadows and diminishes the existential and materialist concerns of the exile condition represented by Anna Trautwein. Consequently, the scholarly reception of *Exil* primarily focuses on the Sepp Trautwein plot and understands the novel as a representation of Feuchtwanger's own political and artistic development. For example, Stefan Dreyer summarizes his discussion of *Exil* as follows: "Im dritten Band der *Wartesaal*-Trilogie spiegelt Feuchtwanger sein eigenes Schaffen seit Beginn der dreißiger Jahre. *Exil* markiert das vorläufige Ende einer Schriftstellerrolle, die den Anforderungen des antifaschistischen Kampfes genügen will, ohne das literarische Werk vollständig der Politik auszuliefern."[42] The challenges and concerns of the German exile community in France and the plotline focusing on Anna Trautwein are relegated to "Nebenhandlungen" of

---

41   Kaplan, *Questions*, 120. However, Kaplan points out that in the same article and in the body of his later work, Said does imagine the possibility of a poetics of "mass politics" (121).

42   Dreyer, *Schriftstellerrollen*, 274.

little critical interest.[43] Lutz Winckler, one of the few critics addressing
the Anna Trautwein plot, assesses her suicide as follows:

> [A]ls Ausdruck der alltäglichen Schwierigkeiten des Exilalltags "wirklicher Menschen"
> […] erscheint der Selbstmord Annas fast unvermeidlich; vermeidbar erscheint er
> nur unter dem historischen Aspekt eines moralischen, politisch-gesellschaftlichen
> Neuanfangs im Exil. Dieser Neuanfang–und das ist in der ästhetischen Motivation
> des Romans schließlich der weiterführende Aspekt der Exilthematik—ist nur einer
> Minorität der Exilierten möglich.[44]

> [(A)s representation of the daily difficulties of the everyday life in exile of "real
> people" […] Anna's suicide seems almost inevitable; it only seems avoidable under
> the historical aspect of a moral, socio-political new beginning in exile. This new
> beginning—and in the aesthetic motivation of the novel this is ultimately the con-
> tinuing aspect of exile theme—is only possible for a minority of the exiles.]

On the one hand, Winckler blames Anna's suicide on the exile condition;
on the other hand, on her inability to achieve a "moralischen, politisch-
gesellschaftlichen Neuanfang im Exil" ["a moral, socio-political new
beginning in exile"]. Moreover, he identifies the ability to achieve this
new beginning, which can only be achieved by a minority, with the aesthetic aspect of the novel. The focus on this minority, "tätige und kräf-
tige Menschen"[45] ["active and strong people"] deflects attention from
Feuchtwanger's moralizing hierarchy that he establishes with the concepts of "Elend" and "Recke." Not only does it reduce the very real existential worries and hardships of life in exile to insignificant trivialities,
but it also positions those who break under the pressures of the exile condition as "weak," and their failure as self-induced. Lastly, by representing

---

43 Cf. Joseph Pischel, "Zeitgeschichtenroman und Epochendarstellung. Lion
     Feuchtwanger: *Exil*," in *Erfahrung Exil. Antifaschistische Romane 1933–1945*, ed.
     Sigrid Bock and Manfred Hahn (Berlin: Aufbau, 1981), 224, or Roland Weinert,
     *Feuchtwangers "Wartesaal-Trilogie." Zur Konzeption des Zeitromans vom "Typ
     Feuchtwanger"* (Cologne: Pahl-Rugenstein, 1988), 96–8. Both see the plotline of
     Sepp Trautwein's development as "Kernstück" of *Exil*.
44 Winckler, "Ein Künstlerroman," 155.
45 Ibid.

"strength" ("Recke") with the male protagonist and "weakness" ("Elend") with the female protagonist, Feuchtwanger not only perpetuates gender stereotypes but also continues the tradition of excluding women from participating in the artistic and intellectual practice of exile.

TANJA KINKEL

7 "To Know a Woman"—The (Im)Possibility of Communication between the Sexes in the *Josephus Trilogy*

ABSTRACT

Titus and Berenice, Joseph and Dorion, Joseph and Mara, and Domitian and Lucia, this chapter seeks to analyze how Lion Feuchtwanger uses gender relations in his *Josephus Trilogy* written in the 1930s. By connecting the couples to questions of acculturation, identity, changing relationships of power, and different experiences of home and exile, Feuchtwanger portrays the eventual inability to fully understand and communicate with each other that exists between the sexes in these novels.

"We wanted to be Greeks, you and I, and yet to be Jews, too, and it can't be done. Jehova won't allow it. We wanted too much, we were insolent."[1] With these words, Berenice, one of the major characters in Lion Feuchtwanger's *Josephus Trilogy* summarizes her life in the second volume of said trilogy and foreshadows the overall conclusion of Feuchtwanger's narration that he draws about the trilogy's main character. Berenice is one of several female characters through whom Feuchtwanger explores the main themes of his trilogy. In this work, women are often placed as parallel characters or in contrast to male protagonists. This article explores the way in which the narrative does or does not engage with the women's perspective, and how it uses them as symbols or treats them as characters with their own agenda. It examines how the emphasis on their own experience of home and homelessness

---

1   Lion Feuchtwanger, *The Jew of Rome*, trans. Willa and Edwin Muir (London: Hutchinson, 1935), 178.

shifts in regard to national or cosmopolitan identity, powerlessness, or influence with actual power, and portrays the way they are perceived as women.

Berenice's statement comes in the middle of a discussion with her brother about her relationship with her lover, the Roman Emperor Titus, the impending failure of which she can sense, but she's referring to more than her failing romance. She also addresses the cross-cultural ideal confronted with its reality as experienced by her not solely as a Jewess but as a woman. Feuchtwanger devotes considerable narrative space to gender relations between the main couples of the *Josephus Trilogy* and connects those relationships between the sexes to the overall themes of the novels, namely, nationalism and world citizenship, the experience of home and exile, the flow of power, the attempts at communication and their eventual overwhelming breakdown. Along with the narrative choices, Feuchtwanger bases his fictionalized characters on historical sources.

The writer Joseph Ben Matthias, known as Flavius Josephus states, "He had sought the world, but he had found only his land; for he had sought the world too soon."[2] Feuchtwanger published the first volume of his novels about the ancient writer Josephus in 1932, in the twilight of the Weimar Republic and the impending rise of the Nazis. At this point, he was only planning a two-volume series. In the afterword of the second volume, Feuchtwanger writes that he, "learned a great deal more about the theme of 'Josephus,'"[3] and subsequently, set out to write a third volume. This belated change is noticeable in the depictions of the relationships as well as the novels' themes. Conclusions about world citizenship, the role of a Jewish writer in a time of catastrophe, and changing cultural identity become complicated or at times negated.

Feuchtwanger's main character, Joseph Ben Matthias, a young Jewish priest of the first rank starts out in the first volume as ambitious. He is a little conceited, his motives contain a mixture of idealism and shadiness (which isn't that clear to himself), and like most of Feuchtwanger's

2   Lion Feuchtwanger, *Josephus and The Emperor,* trans. Caroline Oram (New York: Viking Press, 1942), 445.
3   Feuchtwanger, *The Jew of Rome,* 601.

main characters, he has no trouble attracting women, though he seems far less skilled at understanding them. Young Joseph is in Rome to achieve a pardon for three Jewish prisoners, due to both genuine pity for the men and a wish to make a name for himself. He manages to get an audience with the Empress Poppea. Here the novel foreshadows how male/female relationships (especially between Jews and Gentiles) are based on miscommunication. Poppea orders Joseph to present his petition in the original Aramaic instead of using a Greek translation, despite not speaking a word of Aramaic. She judges the petition on aesthetic merits alone based on the sound and the demeanor of the petitioner. Feuchtwanger does not present this as hostility on Poppea's part, but as privileged playfulness. It leads to Joseph's first case of hubris. The narrative points to the difference between his perception of events and what actually occurs. Joseph is convinced that Poppea is attracted to him and agrees to his petition for that reason. Yet, she does not become genuinely interested until he quotes a statement by his archrival Justus of how "God is now in Italy."[4] Eventually, Poppea secures the freedom of the three prisoners not because of Joseph's attractiveness but for completely different reasons. The release of the prisoners is contingent on the condition that the actor Demetrius Liban performs as the "Jew Apella" (a stereotypical Jew based on Roman folklore); this condition comes with a hefty price that is detrimental to the Jewish cause. The antisemitic cabinet minister Talaß uses the opportunity to push through an edict that changes voting rights for the city of Caesarea to negatively affect the Jewish population, judging correctly that Poppea's intervention on behalf of the three Jewish prisoners will have created the impression that Jews were being favored over the Greek and Roman populations in Judea. The Poppea episode, however, is only a prelude. *Der Jüdische Krieg*, published in English under the title *Josephus*, introduces all but one of the main couples and female characters of the trilogy. Here it's worth pointing out that Feuchtwanger departs from what little is known about the historical Joseph's marital history, eliminating the first and fourth wife of Flavius Josephus altogether. Instead, Feuchtwanger uses the backgrounds of wives

---

4   Feuchtwanger, *Josephus*, trans. Willa and Edwin Muir (London: Martin Secker, 1932), 24.

number two and three as the basis for the characters of Mara and Dorion, Joseph's only wives in the novels.

Joseph and Mara

In the novel, Mara starts out as a 14-year-old captive who is first raped by Vespasian, and then by his orders married to Joseph. This order is given despite the fact that Joseph, as a member of the priest caste, is forbidden to marry a captive of war. Vespasian has one of the trilogy's more balanced and functional male/female relationships with his long-term mistress, Caenis. Despite having started out as his social inferior (former slave, now freedwoman), Caenis is treated by Vespasian as a spouse and equal partner. Conversely, Caenis shows loyalty, affection, and respect but not awe towards Vespasian, and is aware of his flaws. The narrative does not dwell on her looks but brings up her status as a successful business-woman. Caenis is a Roman woman, who not only lacks the experience of belonging to more than one culture or living in exile but also is unin-terested in non-Roman people and repeatedly hostile towards them. For his part, Vespasian cannot relate to Jewish characters other than by force, power abuse or taunts, and his treatment of Mara is characteristic of this.

Vespasian does not know Aramaic and insists that Mara speak to him in Latin. But Mara would not learn and he spent much of his time keeping her from stabbing herself.[5] Joseph, who is attracted to Mara and resents her for this, sees the order to marry her mainly as a humiliation. When Vespasian a few months into Joseph's marriage decides to have sex one more time with Mara to celebrate his pending ascendancy to the throne, Joseph shows himself completely incapable of seeing this as anything but another humiliation and a slight against himself. The complete lack of compassion towards the raped Mara makes for one of the novel's most chilling passages:

5   Feuchtwanger, *Josephus*, 247.

The night was a short one, and morning had not yet come when Mara returned to Joseph. She walked heavily, as if she were weighed down by the separate weight of all her limbs; her face was stupid and expressionless, and as if it were made of some damp and heavy stuff. She took off her dress. Slowly and painfully, she tugged at it, tugged at it until the cloth parted, tore it into little pieces, laboriously and ceremoniously. Then she seized the beloved perfumed sandals, tore at them with her nails and her teeth, slowly and soundlessly as before. Joseph hated her for not complaining, for not reviling him. There was only one thought in his mind: I must get away from her, far away from her. I shall never rise from my shame as long as I breathe the same air as her.[6]

Mara as a reminder of their shared status as powerless slaves, and Mara as a symbol of the raped population of Judea is unbearable to Joseph. He ends the marriage despite her being pregnant by him, which fits with the trajectory of his rise from war captive to freedman to Roman citizen as well. The first volume of the trilogy still postulates that Joseph's successful integration of both his Jewish background and his cosmopolitan ideal is possible, though difficult; the reality of Mara, a teenaged girl who was brutalized and raped by Joseph's patron Vespasian, must be left behind. Significantly, while the novel shares inner monologues of various female characters throughout the trilogy, Mara's is never one of them, despite her continued presence as a supporting character in all three novels. Denying this character, a knowable inner voice puts an emphasis on how both Joseph and the reader perceive her.

The second novel sees a far more confident Mara return to Joseph's life while his marriage to the Greek-Egyptian Dorion is failing. At first, he grants Mara's presence in Rome with their shared son due to selfish motives: it's ego-boosting, as she admires him while Dorion increasingly despises him, it serves to help his standing in the Jewish exile community as their son Simeon is raised Jewish while his son by Dorion, Paulus, is raised Roman. As time goes on, he finds he can communicate with Mara in a way he cannot with Dorion and ends up marrying her again—under her conditions. This plot twist is purely an invention of Feuchtwanger, as the historical Josephus never remarried his war captive wife.[7] Feuchtwanger's

---

6   Feuchtwanger, *Josephus*, 292–3.
7   "I also received from Vespasian no small quantity of land, as a free gift, in Judea; about which time I divorced my wife also, as not pleased with her behavior, though

choice to omit Josephus' third marriage to a Jewish woman from Crete
and let him remarry the war captive Mara maintains an ambiguity about
this particular female character. On the one hand, it allows him to de-
velop Mara beyond the traumatized and powerless teenage girl in the first
volume. On the other hand, the reader only sees her through Joseph's eyes.
This is in sharp contrast to Joseph's second wife, Dorion, whose perspective is shared with the reader. While Mara becomes a stronger character,
the narrative emphasis remains on what she symbolizes to Joseph, rather
than on Mara as a character with her own story. Joseph's reconnecting
with Mara is paralleled with his reconnecting to the Jewish community.
As with their original marriage, a violent act precedes their union, in this
case the death of their son for which Joseph blames himself, and which
causes Mara's return to Palestine. When Joseph returns to his country for
the first time since the war against the Romans, he seeks out Mara, and
finds the balance of power between them has shifted:

> "Greetings, Mara," he said giving her the customary Aramaic salutation, and she
> replied to it with the prescribed: "Peace be with you, my master."

> But then she asked like Dorion: "What have we left to say to each other?" And as
> he did not reply she added: "I'm kept very busy here. The vineyards have run wild,
> and the olives are going to ruin. And the cream-coloured Babylonian she-ass is with
> foal, too. She needs much looking after just now, and she cost a great deal of money."

> "Let me just sit here and look at you," he said pleadingly. And he sat quite still and
> looked at her. He had come back to the land of Israel to gain clarity, but his sojourn
> in Caesarea and Galilee, in Samaria and Emmaus, in Lydda and Jabne had only

---

not till she had been the mother of three children, two of whom are dead, and one
whom I named Hyrcanus, is alive. After this I married a wife who had lived at Crete,
but a Jewess by birth: a woman she was of eminent parents, and such as were the
most illustrious in all the country, and whose character was beyond that of most
other women, as her future life did demonstrate. By her I had two sons; the elder's
name was Justus, and the next Simonides, who was also named Agrippa. And these
were the circumstances of my domestic affairs." Flavius Josephus, *The Life of Flavius
Josephus*, Chapter 76, translated by William Whiston, Project Gutenberg Ebook,
Posting Date: December 23, 2008, EBook #2846, URL: <https://www.gutenberg.
org'/files/2846.txt>

brought him deeper confusion. The peace, the strength to work that he needed, he could only find here on his own estate.[8]

The second marriage between Joseph and Mara is described as one where they actually communicate with each other; by the time the second novel ends, he's even asking her for advice on what to do about the newly crowned Domitian's first humiliation exercise and finds himself shamed by her honesty, since he's still holding something back. As opposed to what Joseph tells Mara, one of the reasons why he feels so torn about following Domitian's orders is that he knows it will destroy any chance he has of a relationship with his Roman son Paulus (by Dorion). For Joseph, Mara has gone from symbolizing powerlessness, degradation, and defeat to representing a truthfulness and wisdom he aspires to but does not see himself as possessing. The novels of the *Josephus Trilogy* only portray how Joseph sees Mara. Unlike other female characters, her point of view, impressions of Rome, of exile situations (she shares with Joseph while there), her changing perspective on her husband are never given. Though the second volume of the trilogy presents the two characters as close as they will ever get to be.

This almost, but not complete, state of knowing each other breaks down entirely in the third novel after Joseph insists on keeping their second son Matthias, with Empress Lucia, despite Mara's pleas and advice against it. With his insistence, Joseph intends to follow his dream of ambition and of uniting Jewish and Roman culture. Unfortunately, this results directly in the killing of Matthias at Domitian's orders. After this, Mara does not even bother to curse Joseph, she just treats him like a complete stranger when they see each other again, and he is too broken to reach out to her. The relationship between Mara and Joseph is both the longest he has been with a woman and the one most filled with failure: it ends three times. Joseph divorces Mara in the first novel, befriends her again in the second until their first son dies, then loses and wins her again after they have both returned to Judea, ultimately losing her for good after the death of their

8   Feuchtwanger, *Josephus*, 462.

second son. The reader never learns her thoughts about this; Mara is simultaneously the most present and elusive of the trilogy's female characters.

Joseph and Dorion

While Joseph's two marriages to Mara fail, his marriage to Dorion (one of three narratively important relationships between a Jew and a Gentile) fails for a variety of reasons, chief among them a lack of cultural connection. Dorion, who is partly Egyptian and partly Greek and a citizen of multicultural Alexandria, initially symbolizes all the attractions of the Gentile world without the drawbacks: she is not Roman, and thus, she is not a part of the occupying power. From the start, Dorion and Joseph are sexually attracted and become mutually obsessed. Each makes considerable sacrifices to engineer their marriage, as a union between a Greek and a Jew is frowned upon in Alexandria by both communities; however, given the equal citizen status of the Jewish Alexandrians, the objections on the gentile side are social, not legal in nature.[9] As the novel points out, the last pogrom against Jews in Alexandria predates Joseph's first visit by only three years.[10] On the Jewish side, Dorion's religious conversion is an indispensable requirement for her marriage to Joseph, a demand

---

9   The historical Flavius Josephus about the legal status of the Alexandrian Jews: "Alexander permitted them the same rights as the Greeks. This privilege they preserved under the successors of Alexander, who permitted them to call themselves Macedonians. Nay, when the Romans took possession of Egypt neither the first Caesar nor his successors suffered the rights, which had been bestowed upon the Jews by Alexander, to be diminished." Josephus quoted by Schürer, Emil: Alexandria-Egypt, Ancient: <https://www.jewishencyclopedia.com/artic les/1171-alexandria-egypt-ancient#anchor3>.

10   "Their religious isolation, their riches and their insolence had again and again led to savage pogroms. Only three years before, when the revolt broke out in the province of Judea, fifty thousand Jews had lost their lives in a savage butchery in Alexandria." Feuchtwanger, *Josephus*, 300.

that she first regards as madness, yet eventually agrees to as legal fabrication.[11] In an intriguing contrast to Feuchtwanger's treatment of Mara, the novel provides its readers with Dorion's own point of view in addition to Joseph's. While Dorion might occasionally be a mystery to Joseph, the narrative always tells the readers exactly what she is thinking and feeling. This reveals the rift between them before he even acknowledges it.

From the beginning, Dorion has no interest in Jewish customs or history even at their most enamored stage of the relationship. Joseph, in turn, dislikes the Greek art of her father the painter Fabullus and feels instinctive revulsion towards her Egyptian cat. He becomes a Roman citizen for her sake and she converts to Judaism for him. Yet, she makes no attempt to understand the Jewish religion and sheds it as soon as the marriage becomes troubled. The scene in which their marriage first ruptures starts with Dorion attempting to speak in Hebrew (which she will never attempt again) and ends with her cursing Joseph in Egyptian, Greek, and Latin for his decision to return with Titus to Israel.

Before the first novel is over, there is a second rupture after the end of the Jewish War, a traumatized Joseph feels unable to reconnect to Dorion and her Graeco-Roman world:

> Joseph stood alone in the reception hall; his face became overcast. The place was cluttered with pictures, statues and mosaics, all probably by that man Fabullus. What was he doing here? He could not live here. And then Dorion entered. […] This was the golden brown girl that he loved. Her skin was sweet and smooth, but oh, how cold it was, and that was because she loved him. […] He can only think of his book, the waste landscape and the ravine filled with corpses, the Temple mount fiercely glowing from its root to its summit. What was the meaning of these silly mosaics round him, these stupid idyllic pictures of peaceful household scenes? What was he doing here? What did the woman want?
>
> He felt like a stranger.
>
> "You feel like a stranger here," she said; it was the first words that she had spoken to him for a year.[12]

11   "After much hesitation Joseph finally agreed that Dorion's conversion to the Jewish religion should be reduced to a formal declaration before the competent official of the community that she had taken that step." Feuchtwanger, *Josephus*, 343.

12   Feuchtwanger, *Josephus*, 499.

Feuchtwanger provides Dorion's own perspective on this encounter and shows that she is not bothered by the alienation that Joseph feels.[13] If the relationship between Joseph and Dorion by the end of the first novel has started to fail due to their mutual inability to relate to each other's experiences and cultural backgrounds, it is still presented as a mutually affectionate and respectful connection. Yet, it becomes toxic in the second novel, as they compete over their son Paulus, who is taught contempt for his father's Jewish identity by both his mother and his Greek teacher Phineas. The point of no return arrives when Dorion's father, the painter Fabullus, dies after she has argued with him and defended Joseph. Dorion, the narrator argues, may have loved Joseph more, but she understood her father and he understood her, whereas there is no understanding between her and Joseph. From this point onwards, she becomes obsessed with destroying Joseph, something that occupies her for the remaining one and a half novels of the trilogy and contributes to the death of his son Matthias. In a narrative irony, it also ensures that her son Paulus, whom she wanted to become a Greek scholar or artist, ends up shedding his cultural influences from her, and becomes fully Roman, thus as estranged from her as he is from his father. Paulus chooses to define himself entirely as a Roman soldier, thus rejecting the heritage of both his parents, and Joseph ends up dying at the hands of Roman soldiers under his son's command. As failures of intercultural romances and male/female relationships go, it can hardly get worse.

However, the Joseph/Dorion romance and marriage is not the only example of a failed cross-cultural experience. In the first volume of Feuchtwanger's trilogy, one of the most famous romances of the era, the union between Vespasian's son, Titus, and the Judean princess Berenice is developed in direct parallel. As with Joseph's marriages, it's instructive to look at the narrative choices Feuchtwanger makes vis-à-vis his historical material in order to analyze how he uses the relationship between the sexes as a metaphor. For the repeated attempts—and failures—at cross-cultural coexistence and understanding.

13   Feuchtwanger, *Josephus*, 500.

Titus and Berenice

Titus Flavius Vespasianus, Emperor for barely two years, played an important part in his father Vespasian's government in the previous decade and is treated rather well by Roman historians[14] He is seen as one of the "good" Emperors with emphasis put on his effective organization of relief efforts regarding the three natural catastrophes plaguing his short reign: the eruption of Mount Vesuvius destroying Pompei and Herculaneum, a fire in Rome (which burned three days and three nights and destroyed large parts of the city, including the original Pantheon), and a plague among the now homeless refugees. Furthermore, his career in the army and at his father's side marks him as a trusted and trustworthy supporter of

---

14   Suetonius, *The Lives of the Caesars: The Life of Titus*, 1.1, English translation published in the Loeb Classical Library, 1914, online at: <https://droitromain. univ-grenoble-alpes.fr/Anglica/Suetonius11_engl.gr.htm>

"Titus, of the same surname as his father, was the delight and darling of the human race; such surpassing ability had he, by nature, art, or good fortune, to win the affections of all men, and that, too, which is no easy task, while he was emperor."

Cassius Dio, Roman History, Book LXVI, 18. English translation published in volume VIII of the Loeb Classical Library Edition, 1925, online: <http://www.brainfly.net/html/books/diocas66.htm>

"Titus after becoming ruler committed no act of murder or of amatory passion, but showed himself upright, though plotted against, and self-controlled … (H)is satisfactory record may also have been due to the fact that he survived his accession but a very short time (short, that is, for a ruler), for he was thus given no opportunity p. 299 for wrongdoing. For he lived after this only two years, two months and twenty days—in addition to the thirty-nine years, five months and twenty-five days he had already lived at that time. In this respect, indeed, he is regarded as having equaled the long reign of Augustus, since it is maintained that Augustus would never have been loved had he lived a shorter time, nor Titus had he lived longer. For Augustus, though at the outset he showed himself rather harsh because of the wars and the factional strife, was later able, in the course of time, to achieve a brilliant reputation for his kindly deeds; Titus, on the other hand, ruled with mildness and died at the height of his glory, whereas, if he had lived a long time, it might have been shown that he owes his present fame more to good fortune than to merit."

Vespasian, with his key commanding role in the Jewish War seen as contributing to the glory of the Empire. By contrast, Titus in the Talmud is the cursed destroyer of Jerusalem and the Temple, an unredeemable villain, with his early death straightforward divine punishment. The Talmud does not mention his relationship with Berenice. Instead, "wicked Titus" is described as engaging in sex with a prostitute on a Torah scroll during the destruction of the Temple.[15] By depicting the relationship between Titus and Berenice, Feuchtwanger had to choose from two different historical narratives. For Roman and Greek historians, the relationship ended with Titus sending Berenice away "against her will and against his own,"[16] as Suetonius puts it, because a Jewish Empress would never have been accepted by the Roman population in Roman eyes. This differentiates him favorably from Mark Antony. Meanwhile, the sole historian who was both Jewish and Roman, Flavius Josephus—the historical figure for Feuchtwanger's main character—has a positive opinion of Titus, his patron, though his works also contain evidence of Titus' brutal tactics. For example, when he did not let civilians escape the siege of Jerusalem. Josephus is also Feuchtwanger's main source for Berenice's life, outside her romance with Titus. To Roman historians, she was not of interest beyond her relationship with him. Josephus' attitude towards the granddaughter of Herod the Great and daughter of Herod Agrippa is an ambiguous one. Josephus presents her as a client ruler nearly as powerful as

---

15 Babylonian Talmud (Gittin 56b): "Vespasian went back to Rome and sent Titus in his place. The Gemara cites a verse that was expounded as referring to Titus: "And he shall say: Where is their God, their rock in whom they trusted?" (Deuteronomy 32:37). This is the wicked Titus, who insulted and blasphemed God on High. What did Titus do when he conquered the Temple? He took a prostitute with his hand and entered the Holy of Holies with her. He then spread out a Torah scroll underneath him and committed a sin, i.e., engaged in sexual intercourse, on it." Aramaic from The William Davidson digital edition of the Koren Noé Talmud, with commentary by Rabbi Adin Even-Israel Steinsaltz Nikud (vocalization) by Dicta—the Israel Center for Text Analysis. Punctuation: Rabbi Shimon Maryles. Online: <https://www.sefaria.org/Gittin.56b.9?lang=bi&with=About&lang2=en>.

16 Suetonius, *The Lives of the Caesars: The Life of Titus*, 7,2. English translation published in the Loeb Classical Library, 1914, <https://droitromain.univ-grenoble-alpes.fr/Anglica/Suetonius11_engl.gr.htm>.

her brother who repeatedly pleads for the Jewish people with a variety of incompetent Roman governors in the prelude to the war,[17] and insinuates that she may have had an incestuous relationship with her brother. Neither Josephus nor any other historian records what happened to Berenice after she left Rome. Feuchtwanger thus chose the only named historical female character of the era with a similarly ambiguous image for his subplot: like Flavius Josephus himself, Berenice is seen as both a traitor—because of her relationship with Titus—and a Jewess expressing solidarity with her people.

Feuchtwanger depicts Berenice parallel not to Mara or Dorion but to Joseph himself, both in terms of being a Jewish character who tries to live in two worlds and in terms of how she starts out as the partner with the emotional power and how this changes. None of the other female characters in the trilogy are given this type of inner conflict mirroring the male heroes, and the moral ambiguity of being driven by ego as much as by ideals that is the attribute of not solely Joseph but many a Feuchtwanger (male) main character.[18] Dorion is repeatedly described throughout the

17 Berenice's appeal to Gessius Florus on the eve of Jewish War is a good example of how closely Feuchtwanger's characterization of her draws on Flavius Josephus as a source. "In thanksgiving for her recovery from sickness she had made a vow, and now appeared without ornament and with her hair cut short. [...] Now this great lady appeared barefoot in the guise of a suppliant, wearing a black robe fastened only by a cord around her waist, and bowed her shorn head" (Feuchtwanger, *Josephus*, p. 103). "Now she dwelt then at Jerusalem, in order to perform a vow which she had made to God; for it is usual with those that had been either afflicted with a distemper, or with any other distresses, to make vows; and for thirty days before they are to offer their sacrifices, to abstain from wine, and to shave the hair of their head. Which things Berenice was now performing, and stood barefoot before Florus's tribunal, and besought him [to spare the Jews]. Yet could she neither have any reverence paid to her, nor could she escape without some danger of being slain herself." (Flavius Josephus, *The Jewish War*, 2.15.1, translation by William Whiston, *Release Date: January 10, 2009 [EBook #2850, Project Gutenberg:* <https://m. gutenberg.org/files/2850/2850-h/2850-h.htm#link22HCH0015>.

18 Looking at other female Jewish characters in Feuchtwanger's works, Rahel, the heroine of *The Jewess of Toledo*, does see herself as belonging not solely to Jewish but also to Muslim culture by virtue of her upbringing in one of the Muslim ruled Spanish states. She sees and experiences no conflict between these identities. She

trilogy as having a "childish" high voice,[19] and Mara a "child."[20] Both are years younger than Joseph and far less experienced.[21] All of which is not to say that Berenice is ever described as less than feminine, just that the traditional gender roles appear complicated in how she relates to the world and how she is perceived.

Like Joseph, whose attachment to the Flavians starts as a survival tactic and then is justified by him as a means to teach the Roman world about Jewish philosophy and history, Berenice's seeking out Flavians begins as a political necessity. When she notices Titus' attraction, the emotional leverage this offers appears to her as a way to gain influence and prevent the destruction of the Temple. Like Joseph, she has other motives which only later she is ready to acknowledge. It is characteristic for the Titus and Berenice relationship as interpreted by Feuchtwanger that during their first conversation, he demonstrates his ability to imitate any handwriting. At first, his father's handwriting and then sentences written on a wax tablet culminating in Berenice writing "The Temple of Jerusalem must not be destroyed," with Titus replying, "The Temple of Jerusalem shall not be destroyed."[22]

It is a promise, a pledge, a communication between them. It is also doomed to be broken since the Temple of Jerusalem was destroyed. Of the three Flavian Emperors and of all the Roman characters, Titus as written by Feuchtwanger is both the one with the greatest potential to actually accomplish the creation of a genuine cosmopolitan world and the greatest

---

also does nothing morally ambiguous. It is her father Jehuda who gets the mixture of ego and ideal driven motives as well as the cultural conflict. Naomi, the secret daughter of Joseph Süss Oppenheimer in *Power*, and Ja'ala, Jephtah's daughter in *Jephthah and His Daughter*, Feuchtwanger's last novel, contain even more innocent daughter figures indirectly or directly doomed through their fathers. The difference to Berenice's characterization in the *Josephus Trilogy* is startling.

19   Feuchtwanger, *Josephus*, 309.

20   Ibid., 248.

21   Berenice is just 11 years older than Titus and described as having a husky, low voice, for other women there "childish" features are mentioned. Titus gets assigned adjectives such as "boyish" or "childish" repeatedly (Feuchtwanger, *Josephus*, 278), not just in volume 1 when he is still in his 20s but also when he is 40 years old.

22   Feuchtwanger, *Josephus*, 278.

failure. Both his father Vespasian and his younger brother Domitian feel comfortable in their Roman-ness. They do not feel drawn to other cultures; they find them occasionally useful but relate to the Jewish characters in the trilogy solely by using their power over them, often brutally so. They are described as decisive and energetic whereas Titus, who is genuinely fascinated with the Eastern world beyond his love for Berenice, is described as eternally torn, hesitant, caught between conflicting impulses, then later passive, and depressed. He is self-sabotaging, able to sense that there is more to the union of man and woman than sex or simple victory. Yet, he is unable to achieve the understanding he craves because he keeps either resorting to force or refusing to accept responsibility when he does not get what he wants. In one of the key passages of the second novel, *The Jew of Rome,* he muses about Berenice:

> "I must tell you, my Joseph," (Titus) added, standing close to Joseph, his arm round his friend's shoulders, smiling and shy like a boy. "I always feel like a youngster before her. She is remote and high above me, even when I take her. I want her to be one with me, I want to be fused with her. But she is shut off from me even when she gives herself to me. You Jews have an infernally clever word for the sexual act: you say a man 'knows' a woman. I have never known Berenice. But if she comes to Rome now, I am certain that she will open her heart to me at last. For I've discovered why I've never been able to come near her. I've been caged in stupid conventionality, my Roman pride was like a shield between us. But I've learned sense in these last weeks. I know now that the Empire is more than a glorified Italy."[23]

Feuchtwanger lets the Titus/Berenice relationship fail twice, possibly because his concept for the Josephus novels changed from a two-part to a three-volume saga. At the end of the first volume, Berenice failed to a-chieve the salvation of the Temple in Jerusalem and thus has no longer the pretext of a noble mission regarding her relationship with Titus. To her surprise, she has fallen in love with him despite seeing all his flaws. She is willing to come to Rome for no other reason than her love for him. However, when Titus demands that she should attend his triumph, it is one request too many. Refusing to attend a Roman triumph over her

---

23   Feuchtwanger, *The Jew of Rome*, 142.

people at his side, Berenice leaves him, and as far as this novel is concerned, he loses her then and there. She realized:

> She had swallowed every insult because she had been unable to tear herself away from this man, from his broad peasant face, his brutality, his childish cruel whims. She had breathed the smell of blood, the smell of burning; she had renounced her days in the wilderness and the voice of her God. And now this man invited her to stand in the Imperial box and witness his triumph over Jehova. Really he was acting quite logically, and for the Romans it would no doubt be a piquant adjunct to this triumph if she, a Maccabean princess, where to look on. But to sit of one's own free will in the victor's box, and provide the sauce to his banquet, no. [...][24]

It is exactly the same challenge presented to Joseph, who as opposed to Berenice does attend the triumph. Had there been no further sequel to this novel, the conclusion that Berenice is treated as a female character with her own agenda, and the same type of cultural and ethical conflicts as the male main character would have been justified.

By the time Feuchtwanger published the second volume, however, his plans for the Josephus saga had expanded into a trilogy.[25] In the novel *The Jew of Rome*, Titus and Berenice are back in love as if the fallout at the end of the previous novel did not happen. Titus is now Emperor. Berenice hesitates to come to Rome. She has lost part of her physical attraction due to an accident.[26] When Titus finally sees her again, her fears come true: the

---

24   Feuchtwanger, *Josephus*, 512.

25   Feuchtwanger, *The Jew of Rome*, 601: "The novel *Josephus* was originally intended to contain only two parts. The second, final volume was sketched out to the end and a great part of it was written in 1932, when the first was published. But when the National Socialists looted my house in Berlin in March 1933, they destroyed the manuscript of that final volume, as well as the historical material that was also there. To restore the lost part in its original form proved to be impossible. I had learned a great deal more about the theme of 'Josephus'—Nationalism and world-citizenship—the material bursts its earlier mould, and I was compelled to divide it into three volumes."

26   Feuchtwanger, *The Jew of Rome*, 178: "Do tell me, tell me a hundred times over, that it isn't because of the way I walk that Titus loves me. All the same, and you ought to know it, isn't it always some absurdly trivial attribute that attracts a man to a woman, and when she loses it, even if he doesn't notice that she's lost it, isn't the magic gone forever?"

passion between them has been lost. Their encounter is a shift in motivation and narrative treatment. No longer is she described as conflicted about Titus, only he is conflicted about her. She leaves in acknowledgment of this. At her departure, Titus makes a token protest while basking in the new popularity this end of his relationship with the Jewish princess gives him among the Romans. To sustain this new popularity, he agrees to a few new anti-Jewish laws and organizes the longest series of games Rome has seen, but at the same time rewrites the ending of his relationship with Berenice in his head so that she left him, and while outwardly content sinks into increasing depression. The Roman crowd observes his occasional unexplained outbursts of tears.

Feuchtwanger is quite sharp about Titus and his occasional fits of ineffectual, inconsequential humanity in the middle of Roman barbarism, as in his description of the brutal games taking place in the new Flavian Theatre, the Colosseum:

> The human birds had their flights arranged in such a way that they had the Imperial box in full view all the time. Perhaps it was a consolation to one or the other of them, before he crashed to his death, that the man who had taken him prisoner and who was now watching him die had tears in his eyes.[27]

The self-inflicted loss of Berenice goes hand in hand with the repressed but increasing guilt Titus feels about the destruction of the Temple and the sacking of Jerusalem. His failure to create a multicultural Empire and fallback to remain a Roman among Romans instead becomes glaringly obvious once Joseph returns from his trip to Judea.[28] Feuchtwanger uses one of the most famous anecdotes about the historical Titus. When Titus was dying, he had one true regret that he destroyed the Temple which brings the theme of the impossibility of true understanding between cultures and genders to a climax:

> "Why was Jerusalem destroyed?" [...] The Emperor went on to implore: [...] I was never your enemy, my Jew, and I never made you pay for what *she* did to me. I stood

---

27   Feuchtwanger, *The Jew of Rome*, 267.
28   Ibid., 516–7.

by you even as *she* deserted me. [...] The man was dying and yet he was striving to delude both of them, pretending that Berenice, whom he had abandoned, had abandoned him of her own accord, and he was maintaining this delusion simply to extort an answer to the question of why Jerusalem had been destroyed, the city which he himself had destroyed. [...]. He knew well enough that the problem was the fusion of East and West, but he had turned back half-way and destroyed the East instead of conciliating it, and became again the Roman that he had always been, [...] Now he had his reward. There he lay, and his face was the face of an old peasant, [...] The Master of the World, the Emperor, the Roman, the world-citizen gone wrong, the handful of dust and ashes, the man that dies even as a beast dies.[29]

If the relationship between Titus and Berenice in the *Josephus Trilogy* stands for a "world citizen gone wrong," the last prominent female character in the *Josephus Trilogy*, his sister-in-law Lucia, represents a more successful cosmopolitanism. She is the wife of the third and last Flavian Emperor, Domitian. Lucia is the sole prominent character in the trilogy who manages to be both completely Roman and interested in other cultures, without the distrust or insecurity or aggressive destructiveness associated with the other prominent Roman characters, who also happen to be overwhelmingly male.

Lucia, Domitian, and Joseph

Lucia, like Berenice, is described as a woman, not a girl, she is experienced, and secure in her sexuality.[30] She has the energy and decisiveness coded as Roman in the trilogy but without the cruelty. Lucia is the sole person not afraid of her husband, Domitian. Once he is Emperor, she is not faced by temporary exile and while enjoying both sex and conversations with men, she remains resolutely unimpressed by them. For most of the two novels she appears in, she has the emotional upper hand with

29   Feuchtwanger, *The Jew of Rome*, 565.
30   The historical wife of Domitian was named Domitia Longina; Feuchtwanger changed the name in his novels.

Domitian, laughing at any attempt to terrify her and setting the conditions for their relationship. She is by far the most independent and self-contained female character in the trilogy and the only one to experience exile. While Mara is introduced as a war captive and spends the second volume with Joseph in Rome, Dorion leaves her native Alexandria for Rome, and Berenice moves through the Mediterranean world (without being able to return to Judea after the fall of the Temple). Lucia, by contrast, gets briefly exiled by Domitian in the third novel, but the readers learn about this fact only after her return; she is only shown in her native Roman environment, and the narrative makes a point of letting her infuriate her husband by treating her brief banishment as a vacation.[31] Lucia's fearlessness does eventually reach its limit, for while she can't be intimidated on her own account, she cares for other characters. Including, for a good while, Domitian himself.

As Domitian grows ever more paranoid as a dictator, increasingly incapable of relating to anyone whom he doesn't completely control, he cannot resist attempting to hurt Lucia by arranging for the death of Joseph's son, Matthias, whom she has grown attached to. Both she and Joseph see Matthias as uniting Roman and Jewish qualities. While the murderous action of Domitian devastates Joseph and destroys any hope Joseph has for world citizenship, the incident does not break Lucia. It does, however, cure her of any remaining affection she has for Domitian, and ultimately proves to be his doom.

In a trilogy where the loss of a child usually serves to doom relationships and makes the survivors incapable of feeling for anyone else, Lucia finds her salvation in the continued affection for her two nephews, Matthias' friends, and her ability to break them out of the masculine mold of behavior:

> Finally Lucia could stand it no longer. "Come here," she said, "don't be men. You be Constans and you be Petronius, and weep for Matthias and for your mother." And she embraced them and they no longer heeded Quintilian's presence but let themselves go in sweet and sad memories of Matthias and in dark words of anger.[32]

---

31   Feuchtwanger, *Josephus and the Emperor*, 59.
32   Feuchtwanger, *Josephus and the Emperor*, 388.

Discovering Domitian's list of soon-to-be-executed enemies and Lucia's name on it, the boys are able to warn her, which in turn enables Lucia to quickly, efficiently, and without regret organize Domitian's assassination. Here Feuchtwanger indulges himself in an intertextual joke. In both *Josephus* and *The Jew of Rome*, characters are comparing Berenice to Esther in their hopes and fears for her relationship with Titus, and she herself in her final acknowledgment of its failure perceives herself as a failed Esther. In the third novel, *Josephus and the Emperor*, Joseph and his rival and friend Justus debate the Book of Judith, presented in this novel as newly and anonymously written text, and not yet part of the Torah. Joseph finds himself moved and impressed by the story of Judith, whereas Justus points out its logistical flaws and pours scorn on the idea that a successful leader would act as foolishly as Holofernes towards a female enemy like Judith, or that someone like Judith could carry the plan out. By the end of the novel, Lucia stages Domitian's death almost exactly like Judith's assassination of Holofernes. Lucia professes repentance for having defied Domitian and invites him to spend the night with her. Despite already having condemned her to death, Domitian sleeps with her, and thus is helpless, disarmed, and without bodyguards when his assassins show up. As the novel has it, this is the last time a falling out between one of the main couples reaches its fatal conclusion:

> The Emperor defended himself, struggled with the man, went on screaming. "Lucia, you bitch, why don't you help me?" he cried in a breaking voice, and turned his head towards the bed. Lucia was kneeling on the bed, half naked, and with a heavy and expectant gaze she looked at the man struggling for his life. "It's for Matthias," she said, and her voice sounded strangely calm and objective. At that he understood that this was the God Jehova with whom he had to deal, and he defended himself no longer.[33]

Lucia's other important relationship with a man in the last of the Josephus novels is with the titular hero himself: Josephus. Like all of the other prominent female characters in the trilogy, she finds him attractive. However, their relationship remains flirtatious despite gaining emotional importance for both of them. It's the trilogy's last version of a male/

---

33   Feuchtwanger, *Josephus and the Emperor*, 400.

female relationship attempting to cross the barriers between cultures and sexes, though Lucia rejects the symbolism both Joseph and Feuchtwanger as the narrator attributes to her:

> Her robustness, her merrily bold frankness, the Roman brightness and vitality which emanated from her, her mature, womanly beauty—all that made a much deeper impression on (Joseph) than ever before. […] He read all kinds of symbolic meanings into their relationship. […] Was it not an image of the mysterious relation between victor and vanquished? Once he could not resist hinting something of this nature to Lucia. But she simply laughed outright and said: "You just want to sleep with me, my dear fellow; and that you look for such deep meanings behind it is proof that you yourself are aware how impudent you actually are." […] He was now seeing Lucia daily; they understood each other better and better, forgave each other's weaknesses, and enjoyed each other's virtues.[34]

Could this then be the one relationship between a man and a woman, between a Jew and a Gentile, which actually manages to succeed? Alas, no. The loss of Matthias separates them as surely as it does Joseph and Mara, or Lucia and Domitian, because Joseph, like all the adult men in this novel, is incapable of reaching out to a woman in his grief, and like every Jewish main character in a Feuchtwanger novel who goes through such a tragedy,[35] the loss of a child for which he is in part to blame makes him reject his previous efforts at acculturation and fall back on an exclusively Jewish identity.

> Lucia was not offended that in his misfortune, which after all was hers as well, Joseph had not turned to her, that he had not allowed her to share it, that he had not even had a word for her. […] What had been between them might still have had a long growth and blossoming; now he had broken it off by the way he had left for Judea. He was a doomed man doomed by his own violence; he attracted misfortune by his wildness and by his ideas of sin. She was almost glad that he had broken off their relationship.[36]

34   Feuchtwanger, *Josephus and the Emperor*, 278.
35   See also: Joseph Süss Oppenheimer in *Power* (*Jud Süß*), or Dr. Geyer in *Success* (*Erfolg*); Jehuda from *The Jewess of Toledo* dies with his daughter, while Jephthah from *Jephthah and His Daughter* kills his daughter and loses his humanity altogether.
36   Feuchtwanger, *Josephus and the Emperor*, 379.

In the end, Joseph grieves and dies alone, in Judea, and Lucia accomplishes her revenge and lives alone in Rome. Like the other couples in the trilogy, they sought to know each other: they failed. Maybe they, too, had sought understanding between the sexes too early.

FRANK STERN

8 Die Tochter: Der Roman *Jefta und seine Tochter* als moderner Midrasch[1]

ABSTRACT

Feuchtwanger's last novel deals with one of the central narratives in the "Book of Judges/ Schoftim" and focuses on the troubled relationship between Jefta and his daughter in ancient Israel. The essay proposes to read the novel as a modern Midrash, a critical interpretation and investigation into the role of women in a period of historical, cultural, and spiritual transition. The analysis follows Feuchtwanger's remark that it is *not a biblical novel*.

Der Roman *Jefta und seine Tochter* erschien 1957 im Aufbau Verlag Berlin, die englischsprachige Ausgabe folgte 1958. Das *Buch der Richter/ Schoftim* mit der Erzählung über Jefta und seine Tochter gehört zweifelsohne zu den systematischen literarischen Erkundungen des Jüdischen durch den jungen Lion. Es ist der letzte publizierte Roman von Lion Feuchtwanger und rundet seine epische Darstellung jüdischer Frauen, weiblicher Legenden und Mythologien seit der jüdischen Antike ab.[2]

---

1   Für die hilfreiche Recherche in Primärquellen, Übersetzungen der Thora und Sekundärliteratur möchte ich hier Bianca Plattner danken. Ohne ihre Mitwirkung und Diskussion der Übersetzungen von Schoftim / Buch der Richter hätte der Essay in der gegenwärtigen Form nicht entstehen können. Zugleich gehen Recherche und Diskussion der Bedeutung der Tochter von Jefta und ihrer kulturellen und visuellen Rezeption am Institut für Judaistik der Universität Wien weiter. Vor allem die Untersuchung der visuellen, literarischen und performativen Präsentationen durch die Jahrhunderte ist ein offenes Projekt.

2   Der vorliegende Text, außer in Zitaten, folgt Feuchtwangers Schreibweise des Namens Jefta, der im Buch der Richter Jefta, in anderen Quellen Jephta geschrieben wird.

Von der Zeit an, da ich als Knabe das Buch der Richter mühevoll aus dem Hebräischen
ins Deutsche übersetzen mußte, ließ mich die merkwürdige Erzählung von Jeftas
Gelübde nicht mehr los.[3]

Die, wie eine faktische Chronik erzählte, Geschichte der hebräischen
Frühzeit zwischen 13. und 10. Jahrhundert vor der Zeitwende handelt
in der Periode der Landnahme durch die Stämme, der wechselnden
Regierungen durch Richter und Richterinnen vor der Zeit der Könige und
überschaubarer Herrschaftsgebiete, vor der Zeit „der Einigung Israels",
wie Feuchtwanger den Erzpriester Abijam des Stammes Gilead denken
läßt.[4] Kriege mit umliegenden Völkern und auch unter den Stämmen
waren an der Tagesordnung, die Landnahme oder die Entwicklung einer
von allen Stämmen akzeptierten Autorität waren noch lange nicht abgeschlossen. Es ist zugleich eine Zeit starker Frauen wie Debora, Jael,
Dahlia, deren Taten im Buch der Richter erzählt werden. In einer Zeit der
Not und von den Ammonitern bedroht wird der eigentlich verstoßene,
missachtete und seines Erbes beraubte Jefta aufgrund seiner kriegerischen
Erfahrungen zum Richter gewählt und schwört vor der entscheidenden
Schlacht gegen die Ammoniter, dass er bei einem Sieg das Erste, das
ihm bei der Rückkehr entgegentritt, opfern wird. Die epische Tragödie
ist vorgezeichnet. Feuchtwanger weist im Nachwort daraufhin, dass die
Geschichten „von der Opferung geliebter Menschen", etwa Iphigenie
oder die Geschichte von Idomeneus um die gleiche Zeit in Griechenland
entstanden sind wie in Israel die Erzählung von der Opferung Isaaks oder
der Tochter Jeftas, und bereits als unmenschlich empfunden wurden.[5]
Die Geschichte von Jefta und seiner Tochter ist eine Geschichte wi-
dersprüchlicher Wandlungen, deren Katalysatoren ein väterlicher Schwur
und die Liebe einer Tochter sind.

Das Erste, was Jefta entgegentritt, ist das einzige Kind, seine Tochter,
geboren von Ketura, seiner ammonitischen Frau. Eingebettet ist die Tochter-
Vater-Beziehung in Glaubens-, Macht- und Geschlechterfragen. Es geht

---

3   Lion Feuchtwanger, Nachwort (1957) zu: *Jefta und seine Tochter* (Berlin: Aufbau,
     1957), 284.
4   Lion Feuchtwanger, *Jefta und seine Tochter* (Berlin: Aufbau, 1957), 131.
5   Nachwort, 283. Folgend in Fußnoten: Nachwort.

um den Konflikt eines Gottesverständnisses zwischen jüdischer und am-
monitischer Tradition, zwischen Monotheismus und Vielgötterverehrung.
Aber auch der Monotheismus, etwa bei Jefta ist durch ammonitische Götter
beeinflusst. Jeftas Vater war zwar der Richter Gilead seines Stammes, die
Mutter Lewana aber eine weibliche Kriegsbeute, eine Zweitfrau. Jefta
wächst gleichzeitig mit der monotheistischen Gottesvorstellung der israelitischen Stämme durch den Vater und einer durch Idole, Götterminiaturen
und Amulette gekennzeichneten Göttervielfalt seiner ammonitischen
Mutter auf, was durch seine Ehe mit Ketura, ebenfalls eine Ammoniterin,
noch verstärkt wird. Doch hier setzt Feuchtwanger ein Motiv, das in der
Erzählung bis zum offenen Schluss eine große Bedeutung hat. Jefta gibt
nach dem Sieg seiner Gier, der fliehenden Ammoniterin Ketura sofort
Gewalt anzutun, nicht nach.

> Ich will sie ganz haben, diese Hassende, ich will mehr haben als ihre Scham, ich will
> sie „erkennen" ganz und gar, ich will sie haben mit ihrem fremden Gott und mit
> ihrem Haß, ich will sie brechen.[6]

Er hätte nach dem Sieg Ketura einfach vergewaltigen können, und sie
wäre dann nach gültigem Brauch mit den anderen Gefangenen erschlagen
worden. Er bringt sie zurück „als Jungfrau", wie Feuchtwanger schreibt.
So kann sie seine rechtmäßige Beute nach „Brauch und Recht" werden.[7]
Aber sie bringt auch ihren fremden Gott mit. Die gemeinsame Tochter
ist Vaterskind, ersetzt ihm den Sohn—auch im Glauben. Aber was ist sein
Glaube? Feuchtwanger schreibt im Nachwort, worum es im Roman unter
anderem geht—„… den Gott des Jefta sehen, den andern der Ja'ala …"[8]
Aber erkennt Jefta in seiner Tochter auch den Gott Abrahams, auch die
weibliche Seite Gottes oder nur einen fürchterlichen Feuergott? Das
Buch der Richter diskutiert solche Fragen nicht, schweigt über die namen-
lose Tochter und die Tatsache, dass ihre Opferung im Widerspruch zur
Thora steht.[9] Feuchtwanger verweist bereits beim Schreiben des Romans

---

6   Feuchtwanger, *Jefta*, 51.
7   Feuchtwanger, *Jefta*, 51–52.
8   Nachwort, 288.
9   *Fünftes Buch Moses* 18:9–10, vgl. FN. 41.

in einem Brief an Arnold Zweig im November 1955 daraufhin, dass es „natürlich kein ‚biblischer Roman' " sei.[10]

Buch der Richter: Jüdische Überlieferung und der Roman als Midrasch

Die vorhandene Erzählung Feuchtwangers kann nur intertextuell gelesen
werden, intertextuell mit Bezug auf andere Passagen in der Thora, intertextuell in Bezug zur jüdischen Tradition der Interpretation der Thora
in Talmud und Midraschim seit der Antike, aber auch selbst-referentiell
und intertextuell mit Bezug auf die direkte und indirekte Gegenwart des
Jüdischen in seiner Entwicklung, seinem Milieu und seiner Person, wie
sie in seinem Werk zum Ausdruck kommen.[11] So klingt zum Beispiel
sein literarisches Exposé zu Jael in *Jefta und seine Tochter* auf, wenn Jefta
unter dem Einfluß eines laut gesungenen Liedes zum Ruhm der Richterin
Deborah, in dem Jael den feindlichen Heerführer Sissera erschlägt, über
die Namen der beiden jungen Frauen denkt:

---

10   Lion Feuchtwanger, Arnold Zweig, *Briefwechsel 1933–1958*, Bd. II (Berlin: Aufbau,
      1984), 302.
11   Vgl. Klaas Spronk, „Jephta and Saul: An Intertextual Reading of Judges 11:29–40
      in Comparison with Rabbinic Exegesis", in *Hebrew Texts in Jewish, Christian and
      Muslim Surroundings*, Hrsg. Klaas Spronk and Eveline van Staalduine-Sulman
      (Leiden: Brill, 2018), 23–35. Zu Judentum und jüdischen Figuren im Werk
      Feuchtwangers vgl. Tanja Kinkel, *Naemi, Ester, Raquel und Ja'ala. Väter, Töchter,
      Machtmenschen und Judentum bei Lion Feuchtwanger* (Bonn: Bouvier, 1998); Paul
      Lerner und Frank Stern, Hrsg., *Feuchtwanger and Judaism. History, Imagination,
      Exile* (Feuchtwanger Studies, 6) (Oxford: Peter Lang, 2019); Wolfgang Müller-
      Funk und Lion Feuchtwanger, „Jefta und seine Tochter", in *Feuchtwanger und
      Exil. Glaube und Kultur 1933–1945. „Der Tag wird Kommen"*, Hrsg. Frank Stern
      (Feuchtwanger Studies, 2) (Oxford: Peter Lang, 2011), 41–55.

Ja'el und Ja'ala, die Wildziege und die Gazelle, waren nahe verwandt. Ja'ala war sanfter, lieblicher von Klang, aber die Art war die gleiche. Jefta spürte, wie ihm die klare Vernunft verschmolz, verwirrende Bilder glimmerten auf. Waren Ja'ala und Ja'el *eines*?[12]

Die historische Gegenwart der Vergangenheit ist jüdisches Allgemeinwissen, die Erfahrungen der Figuren aus der Thora sind nicht abgehobene Metaphern, Gleichnisse sondern Menschen aus Fleisch und Blut, denen man eigentlich auf den Wegen, in der Stadt oder auf dem Land begegnen kann. Sie werden als in den Schriften aufgehobene Erfahrungen weiter gegeben und in der Kultur der Stämme durch Legenden, Namensgebungen, Gesang und Tanz Teil des gelebten Alltags. Die mündliche Überlieferung wird zum Teil in den Midraschim späterer Jahrhunderte festgehalten.

In den folgenden Überlegungen wird Feuchtwangers Roman als Midrasch interpretiert. Midrasch bedeutet Fragen zu stellen, zu suchen, zu interpretieren, Widersprüche zu benennen und bezieht sich traditionell auf die Gesamtheit der *Heilige Schrift, Hebräische Bibel* oder *Mikrah* genannten Bücher. Ein Midrasch impliziert, dass ein Text, ein Vers, eine Geschichte sich in der ursprünglichen Quelle nicht vollständig erschließen lassen, sondern eher durch eine oder mehrere weitere Quellen. Ein Vers, ein Satz in den hebräischen Büchern der jüdischen Antike kann immer mehr als eine Bedeutung haben. Wenn wir ein Gedicht interpretieren, fragen wir auch nie nur nach dem *Was* sondern danach, *Wie* es etwas bedeutet, was können wir zwischen den Zeilen sehen, was ist der mögliche Inhalt von Leerstellen. Die hebräische Bibel ist daher eine Schrift, die durch Zeit und Raum getragen wird, ständig den eigenen kulturellen und historischen Kontext, Wortbedeutungen und Ungesagtes betont. Sie ist voller Interpretationen, Wiederholungen, Veränderungen, Erweiterungen, Infragestellungen, Rätseln, Metaphern, Gleichnissen, Beispielen, die sich durchaus widersprechen können. Deren Interpretationen können Veränderungen, Adaptionen erfahren. Das wird noch erweitert durch zwei Jahrtausende Übersetzungen, die in sich bereits Interpretationen ihrer Zeit sind. Jüdischdeutsche Übersetzungen vor allem seit dem 19. Jahrhundert und seit dem

---

12 Feuchtwanger, *Jefta*, 179.

Wirken der Wissenschaft des Judentums existieren in einer Vergleiche
fordernden Vielfalt, haben zum Teil Illustrationen und entsprechen dem
Bedürfnis jeder jüdischen Generation nach linguistischen Anpassungen,
Variationen und Modernisierungen. Wahrscheinlich kann man von 500
bis 1.000 textlichen und visuellen Präsentationen der Tochter Jeftas und
Keturas ausgehen, mit einer heute wachsenden Zahl von Midraschim.

In der deutsch-jüdischen Unterhaltungsliteratur im 19. Jahrhundert
war das Thema *Jephtas Tochter* Gegenstand einer Kurzgeschichte des damaligen Bestseller-Autors S. H. v. Mosenthal, dessen *Tante Guttraud Bilder aus
dem jüdischen Familienleben* zahlreiche Auflagen erlebte. Die Holzstiche
sind nach Zeichnungen von Moritz Daniel Oppenheim eingefügt. Die
Kurzgeschichte spielt unter der armen jüdischen Landbevölkerung in
Hessen und konzentriert sich auf eine ebenfalls namenlose Tochter, deren
Vater in einer Notsituation geschworen hat, sie einem reichen alten Mann,
zur Frau zu geben. So wie bei Feuchtwanger haben auch hier die Frauen das
Sagen, und es gibt ein kurzweiliges Happyend, in dem der Schwur gelöst
wird. In diese literarische deutsch-jüdische Tradition ist auch Feuchtwanger
einzuordnen.[13] Jefta war so wie andere Gestalten der Thora ein Bezugspunkt
der deutsch-jüdischen literarischen und visuellen Kultur.

Auf der Internetseite *Jewish Women Archive* finden sich unter anderem
nicht nur eine Diskussion der Passagen im Buch der Richter, sondern auch
ganz konkrete Anleitungen, möglichst neue Midraschim zu Jeftas Tochter
zu entwickeln. Unter dem Titel *Girls in Trouble. Stories of Women in Torah
Reflect the Complexity of Our Own Lives* schreibt die Autorin bereits zu
Beginn des vielschichtigen Materials:

> But what draws me to this story most profoundly is neither tragedy nor violence nor
> God, but the complexity of Yiftach's daughter herself. (…) In my reading, Yiftach's
> daughter is a cautionary tale: not about the dangers of vowing carelessly, but of in-
> terpreting texts and traditions literally. Not about Yiftach's lack of faith, but of his

---

13   Salomon Hermann Mosenthal, *Tante Guttraud. Bilder aus dem jüdischen
      Familienleben.* Jüdischer Novellenschatz II (Berlin: Verlag von Hermann Seemann
      Nachfolger, 1876), darin: Jephthas Tochter, 153–222: <https://www.projekt-gu-
      tenberg.org/mosenthl/juedfam/juedf41.html>, abgerufen am 7.6.2023.

daughter's excess. To remind us that faith, like all human traits, is a double edged sword.[14]

Die analytischen und in jüdischer Tradition auf gemeinsames Studium ausgerichteten Materialien sind begleitet von einem poetischen Lied *Mountain/When My Father Came Back*, das im Volkslied-Stil oder als Rock-Song gehört werden kann.

> I could have run from him
> I almost thought he wished it
> but I could not run from God[15]

Dieser Midrasch geht davon aus, dass die Stimme der Tochter hörbar gemacht werden kann. Derartige Entwicklungen weisen über die jahrhundertealten Midraschim hinaus und belegen, dass die Tochter in der heutigen jüdischen Populärkultur zu hören ist, dass sie aus der Namenlosigkeit im Buch der Richter tritt. Feuchtwanger hat genau dies für das deutsch-jüdische Schreiben erreicht.

Die Stimme der Namenlosen hörbar machen

Da es traditionell seit der Antike nur männliche Schreiber der Schriftrollen gab, ist es kein Wunder, dass die meisten Midraschim oder Talmudpassagen sich mit dem Mann Jefta beschäftigen. Mit der bewussten Betonung der Rolle von Frauen im jüdischen Leben und dem verstärkten Interesse an den Frauengestalten in der Thora erfolgten Neuinterpretationen, die tiefgehender nach den Stimmen jener Frauen und der weiblichen Seite Gottes fragten. In den Künsten, der Malerei,

---

14 <https://jwa.org/teach/girlsintrouble/yiftachs-daughter-at-stake>, abgerufen am 7.6.2023.

15 Ebenda. Für den Hinweis auf das im Internet abrufbare Lied möchte ich Bianca Plattner danken.

der Lyrik, dem Gesang, dem Theater, Ballett und der Literatur finden sich immer wieder Präsentationen der Tochter von Jefta.

1909 bis 1917 war sie Gegenstand in sehr kurzen Stummfilmen der entstehenden Filmindustrie in den USA und Frankreich.[16] Als neuere und sehenswerte Produktion ist der israelische Kurzfilm *Bat Yiftach*, 1997, Regie Einat Kapach zu nennen, in dem sich eine äthiopisch-jüdische Tochter in den 1980er Jahren auf dem Weg in die Freiheit von Wegelagerern ent-führen lässt, wenn diese zusagen, den Vater nicht zu töten. Dramatisch gekonnt ist das Tanzduett *Jephta's Daughter*, USA 1998 von Ze'eva Cohen, das zweigeteilt *Das Kollektiv der Töchter Israel* und *Die namenlose Tochter* als Modern Dance Performance darstellt. Umfangreicher sind bildliche Darstellungen seit den illuminierten Handschriften des Mittelalters und neuere Gemälde. Mit der an Umfang wachsenden und feministisch orien-tierten künstlerischen Präsentation der Tochter rückt sie aus einer inter-pretativen Marginalisierung in den Kreis jener Frauen in der Thora, die ihre Geschichten und Stimmen hörbar machen wollen—im Fall der Tochter mit Musik, Gesang und einem modernen Lesen der Schrift. Anders gesagt, wir können die Tochter immer klarer sehen, die Passagen im Buch der Richter neu lesen und damit auch Feuchtwangers Roman.

Ein Essay aus dem Jahr 1989 hat den Titel *Marginalization, Ambiguity, Silencing. The Story of Jephthah's Daughter* und fasst rückblickend die zwei wichtigen Ansätze der rabbinischen Diskussion seit der Antike zusam-men: Jene, die den Text als Opferung der jungen Frau interpretieren und jene, die davon ausgehen, dass Jefta die Tochter am Leben lässt.[17] Die Autorin erweitert diese überlieferten Sichtweisen, die der junge Feuchtwanger mit seinem Rabbiner diskutierte und legt den Fokus auf die Tochter entgegen den Marginalisierungen durch die Betonung von Jefta und seiner viel aus-führlicheren Geschichte:

---

16   1909 *Jephtah's Daughter: A Biblical Tragedy* und weitere Kurzfilme in den USA und Frankreich in den folgenden Jahren, was insgesamt dem damaligen Interesse an biblischen Geschichten in christlicher Perspektive entsprach.

17   Esther Fuchs, „Marginalization, Ambiguity, Silencing: The Story of Jephthah's Daughter", *Journal of Feminist Studies in Religion* 5, no. 1 (Spring 1989): 35–45. Hier auch eine übersichtliche Zusammenfassung der verschiedenen Midraschim.

If the stuttering description of the daughter is a manifestation of the Bible's sexual politics, if the ambiguity puts a better light on Jephthah, then critique and resistance rather than mourning should inform a feminist reading of the biblical narrative.[18]

In einer am hebräischen Text des *Buches der Richter* orientierten Analyse zeigt die Autorin, dass die viermalige Betonung der Jungfräulichkeit der Tochter, die keinen Mann gekannt habe und damit Jeftas Genealogie zerstöre sowie die völlige Unterordnung unter ihren Vater der empathischen Orientierung auf patriarchale Verhältnisse auf Kosten der Tochter diene.

Das von der Tochter Ungesagte, die Leerstellen, die eine andere Interpretation ermöglichen, der unpräzise allgemein gehaltene Verweis auf die Durchführung des Schwurs und das elende Ende von Jefta und des Priesters bilden sowohl Ausgangspunkte bereits im ersten Jahrhundert, für die Debatten der Rabbiner, Midraschim seit dem 11. Jahrhundert und den Roman von Feuchtwanger. Indem er die Tochter der Namenslosigkeit entreißt, was bereits seit dem ersten Jahrhundert eine jüdischen Tradition ist, knüpft er an die Texte in Midraschim an, die die Tochter zu einem lebendigen eigenständigen Wesen machen, ihr Stimme und Charakter geben.[19] Ist das nur fiktional? Natürlich nicht, da es bis hin zu Dialogpartien an die überlieferten mündlichen und schriftlichen Quellen anknüpft. Feuchtwangers Roman ist ein Midrasch im doppelten Sinne. Er interpretiert die Quellen in der Thora und bezieht auf klassische Weise jüdischen Lesens und Lernens die überlieferten Interpretationen ein und fügt eine weibliche Stimme hinzu, die sich nicht auf Traditionen männlicher religiöser Rituale beschränken lässt. Feuchtwanger schafft für die Tochter narrative weibliche Räume, in denen von ihr das allgemeine Geschehen und ihre Beziehung zum Vater reflektiert werden. Die Mutter spielt hier keine Rolle, ihre Götter und

---

18 Fuchs, 36.
19 Pseudo-Philo (*Liber Antiquitatum Biblicarum*, 1. Jahrhundert) ausführlich mit Dialog der She'ila genannten Tochter; ebenso Flavius Josephus, *Jüdische Altertümer*, 5. Buch, 10. Kapitel mit Betonung der *Jungfräulickeit*. Thematisch bezogene Textstellen: <https://www.sefaria.org>. Auf den christlichen Rezeptionen, die die Tochter zu einer Vorläuferin von Nonnen oder der Jungfrau Maria machen, wird hier nicht weiter eingegangen. Die feine Differenz entgeht dabei oft vereinfachenden Vergleichen: Jeftas Tochter beweint ihre Jungfräulichkeit während Nonnen diese ja gerade preisen.

Schutzgeister sind die der anderen, der Ammoniter. Diese femininen Räume sind stets im Freien, in der Natur, im Wald, auf Bergen und in Tälern. Sie spiegeln das Aufwachsen des Kindes und Mädchens in den Zelten und Gebieten jenseits des Jordan, außerhalb der Stammessiedlungen wider.

> Das Mädchen Ja'ala spürte an der Wildnis die gleiche innige Freude wie die Mutter. (...) Ihr dachten die Bäume und Tiere, jedem Felsen ersann sie seine Geschichte. Sie erfand sich Lieder, die sie mit ihrer dunklen Stimme bewegt vor sich sang.[20]

Sie ist wild, aber sucht nicht die Gottheiten der Mutter, sondern folgt ihrer inneren Stimme. Es sind aber auch die Naturräume, in denen sich die ersten sexuellen Neigungen der jungen Frau zeigen. Das wiederholt sich in den Diskussionen der Rabbiner in den Midraschim, in denen nicht vom Opfertod der Tochter ausgegangen wird, sondern davon, dass sie nie einen Mann *erkennen* und in Abgeschiedenheit leben wird. Textlich wird diese Interpretation damit verdeutlicht, dass sie bereits im Buch der Richter nicht ihren Tod beweint, sondern ihre Jungfräulichkeit. Und das ist die entscheidende Differenz, wenn es um die Interpretation des Schlusses der Erzählung aus dem *Buch der Richter* geht. So wie Ketura, die Ammoniterin, Jefta nur gehört, indem er ihre Jungfräulichkeit bis zum *Mischpat*—dem rechtmäßigen Zuspruch der Frau als Beute—bewahrt, so kann die Tochter am Leben bleiben, solange sie mit keinem Mann *eine Matte teilt*. Sigmund Freud könnte hier seine Freude haben; denn der *kleine Tod* wird wie der *große* der Tochter versagt. Der Vater besitzt sie, sie besitzt ihn, sieht Gott in ihm. Feuchtwanger lässt sehr wohl die beiderseitig fast inzestuöse Beziehung in den Roman fließen, aber nicht die Leben bewahrende Interpretation des Schwurs durch die Schriftgelehrten und Ja'ala. Lange Passagen beziehen sich auf den Schwur und die Möglichkeit seiner Auflösung, allerdings nicht als Austausch zwischen Tochter und Vater, sondern als Streitgespräche zwischen Erzpriester und Vater.

20   Feuchtwanger, *Jefta*, 74.

Vom Lied der Debora zu den Liedern der Ja'ala

Nach alter jüdischer Tradition werden Überlieferungen nicht nur einfach erzählt, sondern gesungen, die Lieder der Debora im Buch der Richter und von Ja'ala im Roman ergänzen sich, beziehen sich auch auf die Rolle wandernder Sänger in der Kommunikation und der Vermittlung des gemeinsamen Erbes unter den disparaten israelitischen Stämmen. Feuchtwanger beschreibt dies ausführlich und geht auch immer wieder ein auf Ja'ala, die mit Trommel und Leier singend zugleich in Gedanken Lieder verfasst. Ein Lied über Debora begeistert sie: „Das Lied trieb, riß, jagte sie. Sie sang, schrie, tanzte, stampfte, wütete."[21]

Die Erzählung über die siegreiche Richterin Debora des Stammes Ephraim ist motivgebend. Zum einen hat sie es mit dem Heerführer Barak und Jael geschafft, die Feinde zu besiegen und Jefta müsste dieses Beispiel des verfeindeten Stammes Ephraim für seine Entscheidung, in den Krieg gegen die Ammoniter zu ziehen oder nicht, berücksichtigen, vor allem, nachdem es seine Tochter so begeistert hat. Zugleich spielt die Erinnerung an Deborah auch eine Rolle in der Hoffnung von Silpa, der Mutter der rechtmäßigen Söhne von Gilead, sie selbst würde einst wie Deborah neben ihrem Sohn als Richterin herrschen und nicht der Bastard Jefta mit seiner Ammoniterin Ketura.[22] Doch als Silpa hört, wie Ja'ala öffentlich mit einem Lied auf den neuen Richter Jefta, auf Gott alle begeistert, erschrickt sie „(…) vielleicht war es nicht ihr, sondern dieser Tochter Jeftas bestimmt, dem Volke Gileads zur Debora zu werden."[23]

Feuchtwanger lässt immer wieder die Frauen die Machtverhältnisse reflektieren und geschickt mit ihren Männern diskutieren oder durch Ungesagtes kommentieren. Anders als im Buch der Richter, haben die männlichen Hauptfiguren hör- und sichtbare Frauen an ihrer Seite. Lewana die Mutter von Jefta, die Erstfrau seines Vaters Silpa, Jeftas Schwester Kasja, seine kriegserbeutete Frau Ketura, seine Tochter Ja'ala. Sie leben

---

21 Feuchtwanger, *Jefta*, 178.
22 Ibid., 156.
23 Feuchtwanger, *Jefta*, 159.

und handeln in einem Geflecht aus Götzen, Idolen, mächtigen Göttern und dem einen unsichtbaren Gott, die alle Machtansprüche zu stellen scheinen und die doch nur in den Köpfen der Menschen existieren.

Zu Beginn der Novelle wird der Richter Gilead in einer Höhle der Toten beigesetzt. Doch dieser faktische Ausgangspunkt wird bereits auf der zweiten Seite in einen Bewusstseinsstrom seiner Witwe Silpa eingeordnet, ihre Gedanken und Erinnerungen resümieren die Narration im Buch der Richter und verdeutlichen, dass Gilead zwar ein großer Krieger war, dass sie aber die ganze Arbeit dieses Richters versah und eine ziemliche Wut auf Gileads Zweitfrau Lewana hatte, die er nach dem Sieg über die Ammoniter zu sich genommen hatte. Das eigentliche Problem lag darin, dass Lewana mit Gilead eine Tochter und einen Sohn hatte, bevor Silpa Söhne gebar. Was sollte nun nach dem Tod Gileads mit dem Bastard Jefta geschehen, vor allem weil Lewana den Sohn von ihren religiösen Traditionen nicht ferngehalten hatte. Die Frage religiöser Identität wird hier von Anbeginn auch als eine Angelegenheit weiblicher Erziehung im Wettstreit mit den Vätern und als Machtfrage verhandelt. Jefta wird in die Wüste verbannt zu den Gesetzlosen in einer Art Niemandsland, wo er seine kriegerischen Fähigkeiten entwickelt und Ja'ala geboren wird.

Die Geschichte von Jefta wird im Roman umfassend erzählt, aber es gibt in jeder Episode eine Perspektive, die durch Frauen bestimmt ist und sich durch den ganzen Roman zieht. Immer wieder hören wir die Stimmen von Silpa, von Ketura. Die weibliche Sicht ist nicht als ein Chor zu sehen, sondern als individualisiertes Eingreifen und eigenständige Motivation. Chor sind die Stämme und ihre Meinungsschwankungen.

Die Tochter wird von Feuchtwanger als Naturkind, wild, als durch den Vater im Geiste seiner Gottesvorstellungen erzogenes Kind, als leidenschaftliches, nachdenkliches und auch ungestümes Mädchen gezeigt; eine junge Frau, die viele Musikinstrumente beherrscht, sprachgewaltig und thoragelehrt ist, an der Seite ihres Vaters aber nur ihn sieht—sozusagen „anhimmelt." Sie wird von allen als etwas Besonderes, zunehmend auch durch ihre Lieder als eine Seherin ausgestattet mit prophetischer Gabe wahrgenommen. Diese Passagen des Romans lesen sich wie Bindeglieder, erinnerte Leerstellen der kargen Erzählung über Jefta und seine Tochter im „Buch der Richter." Sie bereiten implizit die Dialoge zwischen Tochter und Vater und ihre nicht ausgesprochenen Gedanken über den Schwur und seine möglichen Folgen vor. Sie verbinden Feuchtwangers Roman mit überlieferten Midraschim, stellen diese wiederum in Frage und kehren immer wieder zur Erzählung im Buch der Richter zurück.[24]

Ein kaufbarer Feuergott oder ... Feuchtwangers Nachwort kann wie ein Kommentar zum Roman gelesen werden, sozusagen als Randbemerkungen zum Narrativ.

> „Mein Lehrer, der übrigens Jeftas Gelübde höchlich mißbilligte, ergänzte den bibli-
> schen Bericht durch Geschichten, mit denen nachbiblische Erklärer, die Autoren der
> Targumim und Midraschim, die ursprüngliche Erzählung umsponnen hatten: wie
> Jeftas Tochter Sche'ila bei den Rabbinen herumgeht, um diese zu bewegen, das
> Gelübde gemäß der Schrift für ungültig zu erklären; wie Gott empört über das sünd-
> hafte Gelübde, die Rabbinen mit Blindheit schlägt; wie der Hohepriester, der um
> die Nichtigkeit des Schwures weiß, zu stolz ist, zu Jefta zu gehen, und dieser seines-
> teils zu hochmütig, den Hohepriester aufzusuchen; und wie zur Strafe der Priester
> seines Amtes entsetzt wird, dem Jefta aber die Glieder einzeln abfaulen, so daß sein
> Leichnam zerstückelt an vielen Orten begraben liegt.“[25]

In den autobiografischen Erinnerungen nehmen die Thora, die Lehr- und Lernstunden des Schülers Lion mit seinem Rabbiner in München einigen Raum ein. Feuchtwanger ergänzt, dass dies über die Jahre durch methodisches und wissenschaftliches Studium ergänzt wurde. Als Historiker in der Tradition der *Wissenschaft des Judentums* verbindet er die „Gestalten der Bibel (...) mit den Menschen, welche die Forschung mir erschloß.“[26]

„Die unverbundenen, widerspruchsvollen Geschichten, welche die Bibel von Jefta zu erzählen weiß, fügten sich ineinander (...)“[27]

Nach der Einreichung des Buchmanuskripts beim Aufbau-Verlag wird durch die Lektoren des Verlages ein ausführliches Gutachten verfasst, das vor allem darauf hinweist, dass die Betonung des modernen entpersonalisierten Gottes eine Ent-Barbarisierung des frühen hebräischen

---

24 Auf die zahllosen literarischen und visuellen Ausformungen der Geschichte seit
    dem Mittelalter kann hier nicht weiter eingegangen werden.
25 Nachwort, 284.
26 Ibid.
27 Ibid.

Monotheismus bedeute.[28] Wer ist also der Gott der Tochter, die im Roman Ja'ala, in Midraschim Sche'ila genannt wird, im Buch der Richter aber keinen Namen hat. Zu wem hat Jefta geschworen? Zwei Erzpriester lässt der Roman zu Worte kommen, beide Gottesvorstellungen sind nuanciert, doch nur der Erzpriester Elead des Stammes Ephraim weist in die Zukunft, da er die Erfahrungen verschriftlichen wird, während Abijam, der Erzpriester des Stammes Gilead, seine eigenen erfolgreichen Manipulationen nicht überlebt. Zu wem schwört Jephta?

Einem durch Abraham und Moses geprägten Gottverständnis nähert sich Jefta sehr langsam erst nach dem Mord an der Tochter, als ihm dessen Sinnlosigkeit dämmert. Feuchtwanger läßt Abijam, den Erzpriester seines Stammes, Jefta daran erinnern, dass Gott derartige Opfer nicht benötige. Jefta schwört dem Gott Abrahams, aber in ihm denkt es anders. Jeftas Gott ist hier eine Art Super-Warlord, „ein Feuergott", ein menschenähnliches Wesen, dass der Vergangenheit seiner Mutter angehörte und für den immer wieder Kinder als Opfer getötet wurden.[29] Jefta schwankt, denkt an den Gott Abrahams, fürchtet ihn, handelt aber oft unbewußt nach den Göttervorstellungen der Mutter, schließt die Figürchen und Amulette seiner Frau nicht aus. In den theater- und filmreifen Dialogen im „Buch der Richter" und in Midraschim zwischen Tochter und Vater, wird kein Zweifel daran gelassen, wer von beiden eigentlich thoragelehrt ist, Gebote und vor allem Verbote kennt und deren spirituellen und faktischen Sinn erfasst hat. Feuchtwanger lässt uns dies ahnen, verzichtet aber auf solche Dialoge. Ja'ala ist ganz Vatertochter, geht in ihrer Liebe und im blinden Glauben zu ihm auf. Doch Ja'ala liebt es auch, zu Zither und Trommel zu singen, die alten Geschichten zu erzählen, ihre eigenen und die des Vaters.

„Er hatte immer nur wenige Worte: sie fand Worte für alles, was einem Menschen durch die Brust ging."[30]

---

28   *Gutachten, Lion Feuchtwanger Jephta und seine Tochter*, Lektoren: Abramowitz, Slupianek, 26.3.1957, Staatsbibliothek zu Berlin, SBB IIIA, Dep38, 1153 0013 r.
29   Feuchtwanger, *Jefta*, 72.
30   Feuchtwanger, *Jefta*, 77.

Feuchtwanger summiert hier, was die Tochter in Midraschim wort-reich sagt und läßt sie nach der Ernennung des Vaters zum Richter stolz im Geiste des Liedes der Debora singen:

> Alle Kraft dem Jefta. Dem neuen Richter!
> Jahwes Gnade ist mit uns:
> Er hat einen jungen Mann erhöht über die alten.
> Das Feuer Jahwes zürnt von Jeftahs Brauen, wenn er zürnt.
> Der Segen Jahwes leuchtet von Jeftas Antlitz, wenn er segnet.
> Jefta hebt die Faust, und die Feinde stürzen,
> als wären sie Bilder aus Ton. (…)[31]

Sie sang, stampfte, tanzte und begeisterte alle, und die Männer hörten es, sangen, stampften im Glauben, Gott sei in Jeftas Feldzeichen, sei in Jefta selber; denn „dieses Mädchen hatte es gesehen."[32] Und Jefta denkt, dass sein Gott in seiner Tochter mächtiger lebe als in ihm selber und hört nicht, dass ihr Lied sich auf Abraham und den Sturz der Götzen bezieht. Der verhängnisvolle Schwur „erregte im Lande Gilead Bewunderung und Scheu;" denn „seit langem nicht mehr hatten sie Abkömmlinge des eigenen Stammes geopfert:" „Jefta opferte das einzige Kind, er zerriß die Kette seines Geschlechtes."[33] Silpa betrachtet dies voll Genugtuung als einen Sieg über die Ammoniterin Ketura, die nun zuschauen müsse, wie ihr Kind „auf den Steinen des Gottes, den sie haßte (…) zu Rauch und Asche verbrannt wurde."[34] Gleichzeitig verspürte Silpa ein „erhabenes" Gefühl, dass es Ja'ala sei, die das Band zwischen dem Stamm und Gott fester knüpfe.

> Im Grunde war es also nicht Jefta, es war diese Ja'ala, es war eine Frau, die den Sieg am Nachal-Gad errungen hatte. Silpa fühlte einen kleinen trauervollen Neid auf Ja'ala und ein betrachtsames Mitgefühl mit der Feindin, die so furchtbar gestürzt war.[35]

---

31   Ibid., 158.
32   Ibid., 159.
33   Feuchtwanger, *Jefta*, 248.
34   Ibid.
35   Ibid., 249. Die Schlacht mit den Ammonitern bei Nachal-Gad war die entschei-dende, vor der Jefta den Schwur getätigt hatte.

Feuchtwanger läßt Silpa als einzige hier ahnen, was von späteren
Rabbinern und feministischen Midraschim diskutiert wird. Nur durch
den Schwur und das fürchterliche Opfer, so scheint es den Menschen
seiner Zeit, konnte der Sieg errungen und die Macht des Richters Jefta
für sieben Jahre gesichert werden. Und das ist natürlich ein grauenerre-
gender Widerspruch. Die Missachtung der Thora führt scheinbar zum
Sieg, aber es ist eine Missachtung, die dem narzisstischen Selbst- und
Gottesverständnis Jeftas entspricht und die vom Erzpriester im Roman
missbilligt wird, der durch seine Mahnungen und Warnungen eigentlich ebenfalls die späteren kritischen Midraschim vorwegnimmt. Ja'ala
sieht nur den Sieg, richtet Sinn und Glaube auf ihr kommendes Opfer.
Sie singt und preist den Mann und Vater Jefta und ist bereit *die Kette
seines Geschlechts* zu zerreißen. Feuchtwanger lässt die Interpretation,
das Opfer könnte darin liegen, dass es nie Nachkommen für Jefta geben
werde, durchschimmern, betont dann jedoch ausführlich das physische
Opfer, den Tod von Ja'ala, den sie jedoch nicht beklagt—und das ist
entscheidend—sondern ihre unerfüllte Jungfräulichkeit. Jeftas scho-
nungslose sexuelle Gier nach Ketura, als er sie zum ersten Mal sieht und
sein brutales gedachtes Wort, er wolle sie brechen, wiederholt sich viele
Jahre später, als er genauso rücksichtslos nichts anderes zu tun weiss, als
seine Tochter und die Kette seines Geschlechts zu brechen. Im Buch der
Richter ist er einer der fürchterlichsten Antihelden, der sich im Moment
der Opferung seines Gottes gewiss zu sein scheint und daran zugrunde
geht, bis ihm die Glieder verfaulen und abfallen. Gott kann schweigen.

… ein moderner entpersonalisierter Gott

In einer Überblicksanalyse zitiert und interpretiert Shulamit Valler
den Midrasch *Tanhuma*, der sich ausführlich mit dem Konflikt, den
Reaktionen der Tochter und dem Macho-Gehabe des Hohepriesters und
Jeftas befasst. Beide halten den anderen für unwürdig, um aufeinander
zuzugehen. Herrschaftsdünkel, Machtanspruch ignorieren die lebens-
rettende Deutung der Thora und der Halacha. Feuchtwanger übersetzt

dies in Begegnungen und Dialoge zwischen den Erzpriestern und Jefta. Midrasch und Feuchtwanger lassen keinen Zweifel, dass Jefta hier mit allen Konsequenzen seine Herrscherfunktion über das Wohl seiner Tochter setzt. Er maßt sich an, so wie in Verteidigungs- und mörderischen Bruderkriegen gegen den Stamm Ephraim nun auch im Frieden über Leben und Tod zu entscheiden, hält dies für gottesgemäß. Seit der *Akeda*, der nicht vollzogenen Opferung von Isaak durch Abraham gehört es eindeutig zur festgeschriebenen hebräischen Tradition, dass Menschenopfer verboten sind und auch, dass Schwüre durch den Hohepriester oder ein Gericht von Rabbinern ungültig gemacht und aufgehoben werden können. Die Tochter weist im Midrasch eindringlich daraufhin, doch der Vater bleibt halsstarrig, denkt noch nicht einmal darüber nach, dass nach alter Erfahrung tanzende und singende Frauen, darunter die Nächsten, einen Sieger begrüßen, ihm entgegen eilen. Würde er die Geschichten der Thora kennen, hätte er ahnen können, dass die Tochter nach alter Tradition ihm entgegen kommen wird. Zahlreiche Episoden in der Thora erzählen, wie Helden, z.B. David, von tanzenden und singenden Frauen bei ihrer Ankunft begrüßt werden. Überdies beweist die Tochter durch ihre Kenntnisse, dass ein Schwur aufgehoben werden kann. Und sie verlangt von ihm, dass sie *hinunter auf den Berg geht*. Dieses schöne Bild wird von vielen Malern, so Gustave Doré in illustrierten Ausgaben der Heiligen Schriften von Ludwig Philippson als Aufstieg mit ihren Freundinnen, Musik und Tanz dargestellt. Das gibt es in der Erzählung auch, aber *hinunter auf den Berg* meint etwas ganz anderes, sie will ihr Anliegen, dem Höchsten Gericht, dem „Berg" vortragen. Doch diese Weisen erweisen sich als unfähig, die patriarchale Auslegung der Thora verstummt vor ihren Worten.[36] Der Vater, der Hohepriester, die Rabbiner sind unfähig, sich auf die Halacha, die Tradition, die eindeutigen Verbote zu besinnen, auf die sie eine junge Frau hinweist, die offensichtlich die einzige Thoragelehrte in dieser Quelle ist, d.h. interpretieren kann. Feuchtwanger überträgt diese Fähigkeit in seiner Erzählung

---

36 Feuchtwanger läßt Bezüge zum Obersten Gericht, dem Sanhedrin aus, da dieser zur Zeit von Jefta noch gar nicht existierte. Insofern orientiert sich Feuchtwanger stärker am Buch der Richter und frühen Quellen als manch mittelalterlicher Midrasch.

auf die Erzpriester. In beiden Varianten ist Jefta ein ignoranter Gläubiger, doch Glaube allein reicht im Judentum nicht, es bedarf des Wissens, um die komplexen Zusammenhänge in der Thora in aktuellen Situationen zu verstehen. Ein wiederkehrender Satz in den Überlieferungen ist, dass Jefta *die Thora verloren* habe. Die Tochter bleibt allein, die hebräische Welt der Männer versagt sich ihr. Im Midrasch weist sie eloquent mit zahlreichen textlichen und historischen Beispielen Jefta nach, dass es nicht darum geht, historische Fakten zu kennen, sondern sie zu interpretieren und so seinen Schwur ungültig zu machen.[37] Für seine fanatische Halsstarrigkeit, die er für rechten Glauben hält, ist Jefta bereit, die Tochter zu opfern. Feuchtwanger lässt Ja'alas ammonitische Mutter darüber nachdenken, dass sie ihre Tochter „nicht in ihrem bedingungslosen Glauben an den Gott Gileads", also des Großvaters, störe.[38] Doch es ist eine andere Bedingungslosigkeit als die des Vaters. Mit der Vielgötterei hat die Tochter nichts im Sinn, die Enkelin von Gilead, also dritte Generation, ist auch die spirituelle Erbin. Allerdings ist ihr Zugang zu Gott so auf den Vater fixiert, dass ihre Liebe zu Gott mit der fast schon inzestuösen Liebe für ihren Vater verschmilzt, in dessen Gesicht sie meint, Gott wahrnehmen zu können. Angst vor dem Gott Abrahams ließ Ja'ala folglich nicht spüren, während Jefta diesen als „Gott der Götter" sah, der „in Wolken, Wetter und Feuer" einherfuhr und dem man häufig opfern musste.[39] Ein alter Gott, ein vergangener Gott war dieser Gott des Jefta. Jefta war ein Kind seiner Mutter und ihres Irrglaubens. Er ließ sich im Roman nach zahlreichen Siegen im Norden und Osten von einem Künstler ein Feldzeichen für künftige Feldzüge herstellen. Er bezahlte gutes Geld … Jefta hielt:

---

37 Shulamit Valler, Strong Women Confront Helpless Men: Deborah and Jephtah's Daughter in the Midrash, in Athalya Brenner und Frank H. Polak, Hrsg., *Words, Idea, Worlds: Biblical Essays in Honour of Yairah Amit* (Sheffield: Sheffield Academic Press, 2012), 236 ff. Vgl. Athalya Brenner, Hrsg., *A Feminist Companion to Judges* (Sheffield: Sheffield Academic Press, 1999).

38 Feuchtwanger, *Jefta*, 75.

39 Ibid., 76.

(…) das kupferne Bild in Händen. Da flammte aus der Wolke der Blitz Jahwes, grell, herrlich, Schrecken einflößend. Das Herz Jeftas aber füllte er mit mächtiger Freude. Lang und lustvoll, kleine grüne Lichter in den Augen, beschaute er das Bildwerk. Nun war in Wahrheit Jahwe *sein* Gott, und wie er selber dem Gott gehörte, so gehörte der Gott jetzt ihm. Er hatte ihn in nächster Nähe, er hatte ihn erworben durch Opfer, durch gutes Geld.[40]

Nur ist dieser Gott nicht der Gott Abrahams, der ja gerade die Idole zerstört hatte. Gott ist kein zu erwerbender Besitz wie die ammonitischen Gute-Geister-Figürchen von Jeftas Frau Ketura. Doch dieses kupferne Bild und die Gedanken von Jefta summieren sehr gut, was Feuchtwanger intendiert, wenn er vom Gott des Jefta und vom Gott der Tochter spricht. Und dennoch liebt Ja'ala ihren Vater so sehr, dass alles, was er verlangt, wohl von Gott kommen müsse. Feuchtwanger will ein „unmißverständliches Bild des Gottes Jahwe geben", als Gott des Jefta, „eines bestimmten Zeitalters und eines bestimmten Mannes", als Abbild des Gesichtes eines Mannes, als eines geschichtlichen Überganges, den die Tochter ahnt.[41]

Zwei Monate nach dem Gutachten liegt dem Aufbau-Verlag das Nachwort vor. Auf die Rolle der Frauen, das episch-dramatische und selbstbewußt handlungs- und glaubens- und vor allem wissensorientierte Verhalten der Tochter geht das Gutachten von 1957 nicht ein.

Der „rechte Geist" der „israelischen Weiber"

Mit wenigen Ausnahmen gingen die meisten KünstlerInnen seit dem Mittelalter von den traditionellen Interpretationen und nicht-jüdischen Übersetzungen vom „Buch der Richter" aus. Mit den ersten weiblichen Rabbinern, Kantorinnen und Wissenschaftlerinnen einer modernen

---

40 Feuchtwanger, *Jefta*, 122. Feuchtwanger benutzt hier den im Judentum üblicherweise nicht ausgesprochenen, aber in der Thora geschriebenen Gottesnamen. Dass dies dem Autor bewusst war, ist natürlich anzunehmen und verstärkt die Textbedeutung als Midrasch.

41 Nachwort, 287.

zeitgemäßen und egalitären Wissenschaft des Judentums erfolgten Veränderungen und neue Midraschim entstanden in der Form spiritueller Texte, Gedichte, Lieder und performativer Präsentationen und Gemälde, die die Frauen des Tennach ins Zentrum stellen—und darunter die Tochter Jefta, wobei deren Opfer weniger zentral ist als die Kritik männlicher Hybris. In Feuchtwangers Roman erlangen Frauen, Weiblichkeit und vor allem die Tochter eine Bedeutung, die den Roman auch anders lesen lässt als mit einer ausschließlichen Perspektive auf Jefta. Feuchtwanger deutet ziemlich zu Beginn in Silpas Gedankenfluss diese Perspektive an.

„Immer waren es die israelischen Weiber gewesen, die den rechten Geist gehabt hatten in Zeiten der Härte. Israel hätte das Land nicht gewonnen ohne die Begeisterung der Mirjam und der Debora."[42] Die Frauen aus dem Buch der Richter, auch Silpa und die Tochter wissen und erinnern an die Erzählungen der Thora mit aller Geschlechterdifferenz. Die Männer fixieren sich auf ihre patriarchalen Gottesvorstellungen, die sie mit ihren ammonitischen Frauen teilen können. Ketura, Jeftas Frau, denkt genauso wie er in Machtkategorien, allerdings denen der ammonitischen Götter. Der Unterschied ist nicht vereinfachend eine Geschlechterdifferenz, sondern bezieht den Kontext, die Herkunft, die Gottesvorstellungen mit ein. Für Ketura ist Silpa die Feindin, ihre eigene Tochter versteht sie nicht; denn deren Glaube geht weit über den Jeftas hinaus. In den überlieferten Diskussionen der Rabbiner wird immer wieder betont, dass ein Mann wie Jefta zu den Gerechten gehören kann, aber dass dies bedeutungslos sei, wenn er die Thora nicht als Handlungsanweisung nutze. Jefta kann nicht lesen, ist ungebildet und ahnt nur vage, dass ein bloßer militärischer Sieg noch kein Sieg ist. Vor allem ignoriert er den Sinn der Gebote, dass das menschliche Leben als höchster Wert zu gelten habe. Feuchtwanger baut diesen Kontext so wie die Interpretationen der überlieferten Texte vielfach in die Handlung ein und relativiert damit auch narrativ Jeftas militärische Siege, etwa das sinnlose Erschlagen von tausenden Männern des Stammes Ephraim.

---

42 Feuchtwanger, *Jefta*, 35.

Das narrative Element, scheinbar eine Kriegserzählung, ist ein moralisches Gleichnis für sein Versagen, im Großen den Geboten der Thora zu folgen und im Privaten den Schwur annullieren zu lassen und die Tochter zu retten.

Alle Israeliter (wie Feuchtwanger schreibt) in der Erzählung und im Roman kennen das Opferverbot, wie es die eindeutige Aussage im Fünften Buch Moses 18:9–10, bestimmt:

> Wenn du in das Land kommst, das der Ewige, dein Gott, dir gibt, so lerne nicht zu tun gleich den Greueln jener Völker. Es soll unter dir keiner gefunden werden, der seinen Sohn oder seine Tochter durchs Feuer führt.[43]

Unmissverständlicher als die explizite Nennung einer Tochter kann ein Verbot kaum ausgesprochen werden. Hier liegt auch die konsequente Härte von Jeftas Ende; denn kein Grab in Gilead wird jemals von ihm kündigen. Jefta hatte durch den Opfermord an seiner Tochter die Generationenkette zerschlagen, war nur Richter für verbleibende sieben Jahre.

„Während Ja'ala den Männern und Frauen Israels deutlicher wurde, verdämmerte sie dem Jefta. Nebel legte sich um ihr Bild, er sah sie selten und undeutlich."[44]

Die wachsende Zahl von Gedichten, Romanen, Erzählungen, Liedern mit der Tochter im Zentrum zeigen, dass Feuchtwanger nicht irrte. Ihr Bild wird immer deutlicher, wenn wir es bei der Lektüre des Romans verstehen, den Frauen zu folgen.

„Jefta und seine Tochter" als Midrasch zu lesen, bedeutet auch, unsere Kenntnis von Feuchtwangers Judentum und Jüdischkeit besser zu verstehen. Seine unmissverständliche Absage an jeglichen Fundamentalismus, die Betonung der Rolle von Glaube in einer Umwelt, die die Menschen

---

43   Zitiert nach: *Mikrah VeTirgumo. Die Heilige Schrift. Erster Band: Tora,* neu ins Deutsche übertragen von N. H. Tur-Sinai, Jerusalem 1954, S. 637. In einem Brief vom 8.12.1955 schlägt Arnold Zweig vor, Feuchtwanger das *Buch der Richter* in der Buberschen Übersetzung zu schicken, vgl. Lion Feuchtwanger, Arnold Zweig, *Briefwechsel 1933–1958,* Bd. II (Berlin: Aufbau, 1984), 306.

44   Feuchtwanger, *Jefta,* 280.

spirituell vergiften kann, die entscheidende Bedeutung der Stimmen der Frauen in historischen Prozessen und vor allem eine immer wieder neue Lektüre der überlieferten Erzählungen bleiben aktuell. Vielleicht geht ja die Tochter immer noch begleitet von ihren Freundinnen *hinunter auf den Berg.*

PART IV

Women in Exile: Oeuvre, Life, Escape, and Exile of German-Speaking Emigrants

JACQUELINE VANSANT

9   Minna Lachs' Livesaving Networks

ABSTRACT

After March 11, 1938, Jews in Austria faced possible arrest, loss of job and property, physical abuse, social isolation, public humiliation, and even death. Membership in or contact with social networks was often vital for survival within the new National Socialist territory. Moreover, being connected to networks outside Austria could facilitate an escape from Nazi brutality. Once in a safe haven (re)establishing networks eased adjustment to and integration into the new surroundings. Although she does not describe them in terms of social networks, Minna Lachs pays tribute to those people who helped her and her husband in Vienna after the Anschluss and on their journey into exile in her memoir *Warum schaust du zurück* (Why look back, 1986). Drawing on sociologists' work on network theory, I consider how Lachs interacted with a variety of saving networks and examine the ways in which her ethnicity, gender, marital and social status, professional position, and her political convictions intersected with and impacted on the shape of the helping networks.

Introduction

On March 11, 1938, Minna Lachs and her husband Ernst were in Vienna listening intently to the radio, expecting the worst but hoping for a miracle that never came.[1] A little after 7:46 p.m. Chancellor Kurt Schnuschnigg addressed the Austrian people, announcing his resignation under pressure

---

1   Minna Lachs, *Warum schaust du zurück* (Vienna: Europa Verlag, 1986), 186. Lachs devotes the last 85 pages of her 269-page memoir to the time shortly before the annexation of Austria to her escape to the United States in 1941. All the information on her life included in this article is found in these last eighty-five pages. While the page numbers of the quotations will be referenced, I simply point here to the memoir for reference.

from Hitler and asking Austrian civilians and military not to resist the German troops should they invade. As Jewish-Austrian Socialists, the Lachs had to cope with possible arrest, loss of job and property, physical abuse, social isolation, and public humiliation almost overnight.[2] Had they not left Vienna in September 1938, Ernst Lachs faced possible arrest and, along with his wife and infant son, an unknown fate. In her memoir *Warum schaust du zurück* (1986, Why look back) Minna Lachs provides an example of how much one woman's fate was tied up with her personal, professional, and political connections when she pays tribute to those who aided her and her husband in Vienna after the Anschluss and on their journey into exile, first to Switzerland in September 1938 and then to the United States in summer 1941.

Drawing on the work of sociologists on network theory, I examine the networks that Minna Lachs interacted with in Vienna after the Anschluss and in Switzerland after fleeing Austria. Although Lachs never writes of those who helped in terms of social networks, the assistance the former pedagogue and vice-president of the Austrian UNESCO commission received easily fits the definition sociologists attribute to social networks. For example, the sociologist Charles Kadushin notes, "[s]ocial networks evolve from individuals interacting with one another ..." and the "[i]ndividual interaction takes place within the context of social statuses, positions, and social institutions, and so social networks are constrained by these factors"[3] In considering the interactions Lachs had, we must also add historical circumstances and Lachs' multiple identities to this list of factors.

2   Dieter J. Hecht, Eleonore Lappin-Eppel, and Michaela Raggam-Blesch, *Topographie der Shoah. Gedächtnisorte des zerstörten jüdischen Wien* (Vienna: Mandelbaum Verlag, 2017). The first three chapters focus on both the immediate unofficial persecution of the Jewish population as well as the official antisemitic measures in the early months of the new regime.

3   Charles Kadushin, *Understanding Social Networks: Theories, Concepts, and Findings* (Oxford: Oxford University Press, 2012), 11.

Networks in and from Vienna after the Anschluss

Minna Lachs' ethnic identity, gender, marital status, professional position, and her political convictions play varying roles in her interactions
with helping social networks in Vienna. In the days following the arrival
of German troops in March 1938, the unofficial harassment and official
persecution of the Jewish population began.[4] If Lachs' ethnic identity
turned her into a persona non grata at that time, her political affiliation
placed her in further danger. As a Jewish socialist married to a prominent civil servant, she would have been an easy target for the new regime.
Moreover, being pregnant, her gender placed her in a very vulnerable position. The medical care and support she needed during her pregnancy
and after giving birth to her son Thomas in July 1938 posed additional
challenges for her as a Jew.

   As we will see, the social networks with which Lachs interacted varied
"in strength, type and duration," and were based at times on either "reciprocal exchanges or shared goals."[5] This variety points to the ways in which
Lachs' multiple identities shaped her interactions with the helping networks. It also underscores the possibility as well as the limitations of Minna
Lachs' agency in the new regime with its threatening and restrictive laws.

Non-Jewish Networks

Because of the unofficial harassment and the antisemitic laws instituted
by the new National Socialist regime, interaction between the Jewish and
the non-Jewish population was discouraged when not legally prohibited.

---

4   Hecht et al., *Topographie der Shoah*. See particularly 32–3 and 53–4.
5   Monica Boyd and Joanne Nowak, "Social Networks and International Migration,"
     in *An Introduction to International Migration Studies*, ed. Marco Martiniello and Jan
     Rath (Amsterdam: University of Amsterdam Press, 2012). According to Boyd and
     Nowak social networks, are "[t]ies or connections between individuals that vary in
     strength, type and duration" and "[t]hey are often based on reciprocal exchanges or
     shared goals, which can vary over time depending on circumstances" (79).

Lachs recalls how her relationship with many fellow non-Jewish Austrians changed overnight. "Wir lernten in der Nazizeit Charakterstärke und Bekenntnismut nach neuen Maßstäben zu messen. [...] Wir wußten bald, mit Enttäuschung aber auch mit Dankbarkeit, auf wen man sich als Freund verlassen und wen man als Freund vergessen konnte." [During the Nazi period we learned to measure strength of character and courage of convictions according to new standards. [...] We soon knew with disappointment but also with thankfulness whom we could rely on as a friend and whom we could forget as a friend.][6] When Lachs and her family received both non-solicited and solicited help from non-Jews, her professional engagement as a teacher, her gender, and her marital and professional status play varying roles in the nature of the networks. Depending on her needs and shared goals or reciprocal expectations of the networks, they also varied in duration and modus operandi.

Lachs' reputation as a devoted and outstanding pedagogue and her pregnancy played roles in the help two groups of (former) non-Jewish students offered her. Moreover, the ways the networks navigated around the state-sanctioned antisemitic laws adhere to traditional gender roles and expectations. After Lachs announced to her male students at the private *Matura* school in March that she would be leaving since she did not possess the required "Aryan" pass, they were upset that their teacher was being taken away from them. In order to "right" this situation they and perhaps the director of the school circumvented the antisemitic laws by using her pregnancy. The newly appointed director in charge of the "aryanized" school telephoned her with a proposal that would benefit her as well as her students. "Eine Delegation Ihres Kurses sprach bei mir vor und teilte mir mit, daß Sie in nächster Zeit ein Kind erwarten und es Ihnen gewiß schwerfallen würde, bis zur Matura den Unterricht weiterzuführen. Wir haben vereinbart, daß die Herren Ihren Kurs bei Ihnen zu Hause weiter besuchen werden, um Ihnen Weg und Stiegensteigen zu ersparen."[7] [A delegation from your course spoke to me and shared with me that you are expecting a child in the near future and that it would be difficult for

6   Lachs, *Warum schaust du zurück*, 194. Translations throughout are mine.
7   Lachs, Ibid., 196.

you to continue teaching until the *Matura*. We've arranged for the men to
continue to visit the course at your house in order to save you the way and
having to climb stairs.] By focusing on Lachs' pregnant state and not openly
acknowledging her ethnicity, the director ignores the new laws. Using the
impending birth of her child as the pretense for moving the class to her
apartment also allows the director and the school to maintain the appearance of having gotten rid of the Jewish staff. Moreover, the new director
further attends to the dangers of continuing this professional relationship
with a Jew by having one of the students deliver Lachs' honorarium to her
in an envelope. The students as well as the director would have been aware
of her ethnic identity and the director, and no doubt some of the young
men, must have identified with the Nazi ideology. Yet, the students' motivation to help is a reflection both of Lachs' effectiveness as a teacher and
their interest in their own personal success. Her pregnancy may have also
elicited compassion and male "protective instincts."

Not only did the students find a way to have Lachs continue as their
teacher, but they chose a stereotypically male approach in order to guarantee her personal safety—at least until their final exam. From among their
ranks, they delegated one of their colleagues who was unemployed and a
uniform-wearing member of the SA to accompany her around town. "Er
begleitete mich tagtäglich auf meinen Gängen zu den Botschaften, zu den
Ämtern um das Steuerunbedenklichkeitszeugnis, um den Pass und zu der
Speditionsfirma Knauer, die mir ein Bekannter, der im Export arbeitete,
empfohlen hatte."[8] [He accompanied me every single day on my rounds
to the embassies, to the offices for the Certificate of Tax Clearance, the
passport and to the shipping firm, which a friend recommended to me,
who worked in Import-Export.] Being accompanied in public by a man in
an SA uniform opened doors for Lachs and allowed her to move "freely."
The performance appeared so convincing that the rumor that she had been
captured by the SA circulated. In any case, the action points to the power
of a male in a uniform. Although the help ended after the classmates had
taken and all passed the *Matura*, it proved mutually beneficial. Their protest
permitted Lachs to continue to receive compensation, and their actions

8   Lachs, Ibid., 197.

allowed Lachs to prepare to leave Vienna without fear of bodily harm as she ran her errands.

The aid that came from a group of former non-Jewish female students is a further testimony to her effectiveness as a teacher. When she recalls their help, Lachs expresses surprise and joy stemming both from the fact the women are not Jewish and that several years had passed since she had taught them:

> Zu meiner größten freudigen Überraschung stellten sich einige Maturantinnen aus dem Schwarzwald-Gymnasium, denen ich vier Jahre vorher durch die Matura in Französisch geholfen hatte, als Besucherinnen bei mir ein. Sie animierten noch andere aus dieser "verflossenen 8. Klasse" und richteten einen Turnus ein. Jeden Tag kam eine von diesen jungen 'arischen' Frauen zu mir, um mir im Haushalt und bei der Pflege des Kindes behilflich zu sein. [9]

> [To my great joyful surprise some of the women from the graduating class from the Schwarzwald-High School, whom I had helped to get through the *Matura* in French four years previous to this, set themselves up to visit me. They roused still others from the "dissolved 8th class" and organized a rotation. One of these young "Aryan" women came by everyday to help me with household chores and the care of my child.]

Gender is a determining factor in the network's strength, its type, and its duration. Just as the actions of the male students can be viewed as stereotypical, so, too, were the efforts of these former female students from the progressive all-girls school founded by the Jewish Eugenie Schwarzwald.[10] In comparison to the actions of the male students, the impromptu endeavors of the women were far less public and involved much more effort on their part. Moreover, they offered invaluable domestic help in exchange for no apparent rewards.

Another example of unexpected help from a non-Jewish network grew out of Lachs' interaction with the group of male students. Although the network disbanded after the men passed the *Matura*, one of the students remained in contact with Lachs. Tapping into his own family network, her former student Ferry told his mother about the impending birth of Minna's

---

9   Lachs, Ibid., 207.
10   For an in-depth study of Eugenie Schwarzwald see Deborah Holmes, *Langeweile ist Gift. Das Leben der Eugenie Schwarzwald* (St. Pölten: Residenz Verlag, 2012).

baby. Moved by the injustice of the system and personal compassion, mother and son became a part of Lachs' support network. Lachs recalls the generosity of both. "Ferrys Mutter kam täglich zu mir. Sie half mir, wo sie nur konnte, und sprach mir immer wieder Mut zu." [Ferry's mother visited me daily. She helped me wherever she could and fortified my courage.] Their help did not stop there. "Als wir dann im September mit dem zwei Monate und einen Tag alten Baby Wien fluchtartig verlassern mußten, hätte ich es ohne Ferrys Hilfe und die Hilfe seiner Mutter kaum zustande gebracht."[11] [When we had to leave Vienna hastily in September with a 2-month and 1-day-old baby, I would have hardly been able to manage it without Ferry's help and the help of his mother.] This reveals how networks are in constant flux and can spawn other networks. Here, what sociologists term a "weak tie" becomes "a strong tie," that is, acquaintances become valued friends.[12] Also, the fact that Ferry remained in contact with Minna Lachs and drew his mother into the personal network points to the strength of Lachs' personality as well as his sense of justice and his mother's compassion and perhaps her identification as a mother.

Minna Lachs' marital and political status as well as her professional acumen played a role in the help a long-time non-Jewish friend was able to give them. Dr. Hans (Johann) Dostal,[13] a friend of Ernst Lachs from their student days in Graz, a lawyer like Ernst and a fellow Social Democrat, drew on his international professional and political connections to help the Lachs attain the necessary documents to flee Vienna. Knowing of his

---

11 Lachs, *Warum*, 198.

12 See Kadushin, *Understanding Social Networks*, 30–1. Here, he quotes Mark Granovetter's discussion of weak ties (our acquaintances) versus strong ties (our close friends).

13 Dostal also hired Ernst Lachs, who also had a law degree, after he was fired from his municipal job. Lachs worked with Dostal's Jewish clients. I have only been able to find out limited information on Johann Dostal. See for example Manfred Mugrauer, "Hella Altmann-Postranecky (1903–1995) Funktionärin der ArbeiterInnenbewegung und erste Frau in einer österreichischen Regierung," in *Jahrbuch 2018. Forschungen zu Vertreibung und Holocaust*, Dokumentationsarchiv des österreichischen Widerstandes, Hrsg. (Vienna: DÖW, 2018), 267–306. In reference to Dostal see 276–8 and 284. <https://www.doew.at/cms/download/cdhjs/jahrbuch2018_mugrauer.pdf>.

professional-political connections abroad, the Lachs had already sought
his help before the Anschluss when they were first considering emigration.
Dostal drew on familiar international networks to obtain the necessary
papers for the Lachs to flee the *Ostmark*. Aware of Minna's linguistic abilities in French, their friend saw an opportunity to help both the Lachs
and a client living in France who in turn had important French political connections. Lachs explains: "Hans vertrat einen alten sozialistischen
Klienten, der sein großes Unternehmen nach Hitlers Machtübernahme
in Deutschland nach Frankreich überführt hatte."[14] [Hans represented a
long-time socialist client, who had transferred his large company to France
after Hitler's seizure of power in Germany.] This client, a Herr Ram, needed
someone fluent in French to translate business papers, but not necessarily
versed in the subject. Minna Lachs was an ideal candidate, and this job
opportunity would allow her and her husband to emigrate legally. Ram,
part of a larger socialist network, turned to this group to ensure the Lachs
obtained the proper documents. As their friend Dostal related to her: "Herr
Ram ist seit Jahren mit dem einflußreichen sozialistischen Politiker Edgar
Faure befreundet, der seine Hilfe zugesagt hat—und er hat noch immer
Wort gehalten."[15] [Herr Ram has been friends for years with the influential socialist politician Edgar Faure, who promised his help and he's always
kept his word.] Faure did indeed agree to obtain visas for the Lachs and
a work permit for Minna Lachs in France. Herr Ram also saw the danger
of their remaining in Austria to wait for the papers. "Herr Ram schrieb
uns persönlich, er würde uns raten, die Papiere, die zuverlässig kommen
würden, in der Schweiz abzuwarten."[16] [Herr Ram wrote us directly, suggesting we wait for the papers in Switzerland, which were guaranteed to
come.] Consequently, Ram passed on two names of contacts to the socialist
network in Switzerland in order to assure the Lachs' safe exit from Vienna.
Dr. Werner Stocker from the Swiss Social Democratic Party responded
promptly and told them if the situation got desperate to telegraph him or
Dr. Farbstein, another fellow member of the party, with the short, but clear

14   Lachs, *Warum*, 189.
15   Lachs, Ibid., 189.
16   Lachs, Ibid..

message: "Lebensgefahr, müssen sofort abreisen!"[17] [Mortal danger, must leave immediately!]. Minna Lachs' and her husband's linguistic abilities, and their engagement as socialists along Dostal's political-professional international connections and his access to men in positions of economic and political power proved lifesaving. His actions point to the importance of a link between an Austrian personal network and an international political network in obtaining the required documents needed to leave Vienna and enter another country.

Familial and Professional Jewish Networks

In contrast to the ways non-Jewish networks were able to negotiate the antisemitic laws, Lachs' interactions with Jewish networks point to the severe limitations placed on them after March 1938. If in "normal" times of trouble, one could rely on help from family members, the National Socialist regime severely restricted the efficacy of this Jewish network in the new Austria. Despite or perhaps because of the state-sanctioned antisemitism, the help the familial network offered was limited largely to moral support and advice.

The organization of a short-lived Jewish professional network which aided the pregnant Lachs also points to the limits placed upon Jewish Austrians as well as their ingenuity in a desperate situation. Aware of the danger they were in and concerned with the safety of their own family and Jewish patients, a group of doctors devised a plan within their professional network:

> Im Briefumschlag fand ich einen Kassiber von Bianka. Sie sei schon vor zwei Tagen von der Polizei verhaftet worden. Ihre Ordination wurde versiegelt und ihr Konto gesperrt. Ihre Mutter stehe vis-à-vis de rien. Sie habe eine Abmachung mit dem bekannten Gynäkologen Dr. Magulies getroffen, daß im Falle einer Verhaftung einer die Patienten des anderen übernehmen und das Honorar an die Mutter beziehungsweise an Frau Magulies überweisen werde.[18]

17   Lachs, Ibid., 190.
18   Lachs, Ibid., 202.

[I found a secret message from Bianka in the envelope. According to her, she had been
arrested two days ago by the police. Her practice had been sealed and her account
locked. Her mother was facing disaster. In case of the arrest of one or the other, she had
made an agreement with the well-known gynecologist Dr. Magulies. One or the other
of them would take over the others' patients and then would transfer the payment to
her mother or to Frau Magulies.]

Although Lachs was only introduced to the plan after her gynecologist
Bianka Steinhard had been arrested and Dr. Magulies' ability to work was
short-lived, the network extended beyond him. After his arrest, he passed
his patients on to Dr. Karl Kautsky, Jr., who upon his arrest passed them
on to a Czech non-Jewish colleague living in Vienna. The brief existence of
the doctors' network points to the limited possibility of those persecuted
to act and the consequential brutality of the regime. Despite its limitations,
the network of Jewish doctors and their connections to a non-Jewish doctor
played a vital role in Lachs' well-being, the birth of her child, and the health
of the mother and infant son.

Jewish and Non-Jewish Networks Working Together

As a Jewess and woman, Lachs' own ability to activate helping networks
after March 11 was limited. However, she turned to strong ties from both
Jewish and non-Jewish male and female friends for advice and help planning a strategy for leaving Vienna safely after receiving an anonymous
phone call on Monday, September 18, 1938. An unidentified caller deliv-
ered a brief warning, which may have been lifesaving. "Hier gut Freund,
Ihr Mann muß noch vor dem Wochenende Österreich verlassen."[19]
[Greetings friend, your husband must leave Austria before the weekend.]
Because Lachs did not recognize the voice of the caller, how he was linked
to her or her husband remains unknown. However, the caller's short message allows for speculation as to his identity and his link to Lachs. The
Duden defines "gut Freund" as the response to "Halt! Wer da?" [Halt!

19   Lachs, Ibid., 207.

Who goes there].[20] Moreover, the youngest group of scouts greets other scouts with "Hier gut Freund".[21] It is possible that someone from her scout days, who was also in an official position and knew of Ernst Lachs' impending arrest, called. Possibly simply to protect his identity and convey the message, he used as few words as possible.

At this juncture Minna Lachs took a leading role in building a temporary network after she refused her husband's offer to leave without them. The urgency of the call prompted Lachs to turn to strong ties from both Jewish and non-Jewish male and female friends. "Am Abend bat ich auch Hans und Käthe [Dostal], zu uns zu kommen. Ich verständigte Steffi [Feldschuh, who was waiting for her visa to Chile] und Ferry und seine Mutter, und wir hielten einen Kriegsrat ab."[22] [In the evening I also asked Hans and Käthe to come by. I got in touch with Steffi and Ferry and his mother and we put our heads together.] After the group discussion Lachs sent a telegram to Dr. Stocker in Switzerland. In his response a day later he told them when to leave Vienna and informed them that the pertinent papers would be waiting for them at the border.

The help of the mixed Viennese network did not end with the evening consultation. The preparation for the departure from Vienna as well as the trip to the train station were well-orchestrated operations carried out by this group.

> Ferry und Steffi übernahmen die Auflösung der Wohnung. Wir würden nur mit einem Koffer reisen, um nicht noch vorher die Aufmerksamkeit der Nazis zu erregen. Die Wertsachen übernahm Frau Goldschmid—sie war trotz des jüdisch klingenden Namens eine 'lupenreine' Arierin—in Verwahrung. Ferry würde eine Hängematte und eine faltbare Gummibadewanne für das Baby besorgen.[23]

> [Ferry and Steffi took care of closing up the apartment. We would travel with only one suitcase in order not to arouse the attention of the Nazis. Frau Goldschmid, who despite her Jewish-sounding name was a "pure blooded" Aryan, took the valuables

---

20 <https://www.duden.de/rechtschreibung/gut_Freund_>
21 See Gruss "Gruß" at: <https://pbw-fuechse.de/horst-fuechse-abc/>
22 Lachs, Ibid., 207.
23 Lachs, Ibid., 208.

into safe keeping. Ferry was to procure a hammock and a foldable plastic bathtub for the baby.]

This collective effort continued the morning of the Lachs' departure. Lachs passed on a letter she wrote to her parents and siblings via Steffi. Frau Goldschmid waited in the taxi, after which Ferry accompanied them from their apartment to the taxi and on to the train station. He then installed them in an empty compartment on the train, promising to visit them in Zürich. The network's direction resembled both a chain and spokes on a wheel.

Conclusion—Networks in and from Vienna

Although Minna Lachs was cut off from some former networks after the Anschluss, her personal-political ties, her outstanding work as a pedagogue, and her identity as a wife and mother shaped the social networks vital for the survival of Lachs, her husband, and son. From goals, which ranged from helping her continue working and receiving compensation to helping with her new baby and the household, to obtaining the proper documents for leaving Vienna and entering another country, the networks naturally varied in type and duration. The strength of the personal-political networks which extended to ties with networks outside Austria facilitated an escape from Nazi brutality.

"Networking" to and in Switzerland

When Minna Lachs fled to Switzerland with her husband and infant son, their status as refugees in a country reluctantly harboring those fleeing highlights the importance of their ties to personal, political, and ethnic networks. On and after their arrival in Switzerland Lachs and her husband were helped by members of a variety of social networks, including political, professional, ethnic, religious, and personal contacts. The reputation of Lachs and her husband as Austrian socialists was a decisive factor in securing the help they received. As Jewish refugees they found support from the Jewish community in Switzerland and non-Jews sympathetic to their plight. The presence of other Austrian refugees, political and/or Jewish, provided an additional help network. Although faced with fewer legal constraints, the temporary safe haven Switzerland brought with it multiple challenges for Lachs. At the same time, she encountered fewer dangers and constraints in seeking contact to helping networks.

Political Networks

The very first hurdle the Lachs faced was entry into the country. Although the members of the Swiss networks rarely had to bend or break the law or use subterfuge in their actions, this was not the case when the Lachs reached the border and found that their visas had not yet arrived. Anticipating this problem, their Social Democratic Party official contact had informed the Swiss border guard that it would be there the next day. In turn, the Swiss border guard lied to the Nazi official and told him that the family's documents were indeed waiting for them. To Lachs and her husband, he conveyed: "Sie sind mir avisiert, aber das Visum ist leider noch nicht gekommen. Aber ich habe natürlich dem Nazi gesagt, daß es da ist."[24] [I've been advised of your arrival, but the visa is unfortunately not yet here. But of course, I told the Nazi that it was.] He instructed them to get out at the border station and check into the hotel vis-à-vis. Already on edge, Minna broke down and replied that they had no money for a hotel, and she had no protection from the rain for her baby. After Ernst Lachs and the train employee conferred, he called Dr. Stocker, their official contact, and shared Stocker's instructions with the Lachs. In order to avoid possible arrest in Zürich, they had to engage in a bit of playacting. Once in Zürich, they would be greeted by Dr. Stocker and the head of the socialist women's organization in Switzerland as relatives and swept away. As promised, Dr. Stocker immediately took care of the

24 Lachs, Ibid., 211.

necessary paperwork allowing them to stay legally. He continued to be concerned about the Lachs' situation and stepped in at several junctures to offer advice and help. Lachs was particularly thankful for Dr. Stocker's lifesaving help. Had he not alerted the border official, they would most likely not have been allowed to leave National Socialist territory.

Personal, Political, and Charitable Jewish Networks

Once in a relatively safe haven, Lachs drew on a variety of networks, which eased the family's adjustment to the new surroundings. Contact with acquaintances and friends in their personal Austrian refugee and migrant networks proved valuable in both tangible and less tangible ways. They served as social outlets and offered moral support. Able to move freely without fear of arrest, they babysat and even promised to send affidavits once they were established in the United States.

A combination of personal, political, and ethnic networks helped the Lachs when they found themselves faced with the usual refugee financial challenges. They had arrived in Switzerland with only the allowed 20 RM and a piece of jewelry Minna Lachs had smuggled out. As the Swiss did not allow them to be gainfully employed, they drew on various contacts and networks to help pay for expenses. Before Czechoslovakia was invaded an uncle had been able to cable them their portion of the inheritance from Ernst's grandmother. Ferry, from their Austrian network, kept his promise and brought them some of their jewelry they had been unable to take with them. Registered as refugees from Nazism, they were eligible to receive support in the form of an "allowance" from the Joint Distribution Committee:

> Dr. Farbstein telefonierte, um uns über die nächsten Schritte für Flüchtlinge zu informieren. Die Unterstützung für die 'Nazi-Flüchtlinge' komme von dem amerikanischen 'Joint Distribution Committee' und werde von den schweizerischen Kultusgemeinden nur verwaltet und verteilt. Es handle sich um einen Anspruch und nicht um ein Almosen.[25]

25   Lachs, Ibid., 214.

[Dr. Farbstein telephoned in order to inform us of the next steps for refugees. According to him, the support for the refugees from National Socialism comes from the American Joint Distribution Committee and was only administered and distributed by the Swiss Jewish Religious Community. He stated that it was not a hand-out, but something we were entitled to.]

Through the help of friends and these organizations, Ernst and Minna Lachs were able to work around the employment prohibition and received non-monetary payment for their efforts, such as books for Minna Lachs' book reviews and coupons from the Joint for groceries in return for "donated" work. When they unexpectedly received the necessary papers to flee to the United States, Minna turned to a Viennese acquaintance, a jeweler, who had also fled to Zürich, to help her sell her last pieces of jewelry. With his help they attained needed funds for the transatlantic journey.

Quaker Network

When it became clear that their first living arrangement did not meet their needs, Lachs undertook actions of her own, which would not be the first or last time she showed her resourcefulness. Reaching out to what sociologists term an open-system network, Lachs put a detailed advertisement in a newspaper in search of a more suitable apartment. In defining open-system networks, Charles Kadushin admits that the "boundaries are not necessarily clear" as they can be as broad as "the elite of the United States" or "connections between corporations."[26] In this case, Lachs reached out to the open-system of newspaper subscribers. Three days after their advertisement had been posted, a woman appeared. "Und zum ersten Mal trafen wir Schwester Anni Pflüger, die unser Schutzengel wurde. Sie hatte unser Inserat in der Zeitung gelesen und war gekommen, um uns bei der Zimmersuche zu helfen." [And we met Sister Anni Pflüger, who became our guardian angel, for the first time. She had read the ad in the newspaper and came to help us with our search for a room.] Pflüger explained

26 Kadushin, *Understanding Social Networks*, 17.

her willingness to help. "Sie sei Quäkerin und erfülle nur ihre Pflicht."[27] [She was a Quaker and was only doing her duty]. Lachs' initiative resulted in much more than an apartment. Not only did she help them find an apartment, but Pflüger also connected them with Quakers in Portugal who worked to alleviate their suffering on the ship *Navemar*. Once Lachs was in the United States Pflüger provided contacts among the Quaker network, who helped Lachs find work and friendship.

International Socialist Network

If Lachs received help by reaching out to an open network via a newspaper ad, unsolicited aid came from an anonymous member of another open-system network of which Lachs and her husband could also be considered members—the Socialist network. With the beginning of the war in September 1939 French consulates in Europe were no longer allowed to issue visas, which forced the couple to prolong their stay in Switzerland. After the German invasion of the Low Countries and France in spring of 1940, the Lachs were desperate to leave Europe before the United States entered the war. They first turned to their network of friends. "Es war uns klar geworden, daß wir nun alle persönlichen Beziehungen zu den Freunden in den USA aktivieren mußten, um ein glaubwürdiges Affidavit zu erhalten und noch vor dem Eintritt Amerikas in den Krieg [...] in die Staaten einreisen zu können."[28] [It was clear to us that we now had to activate all our personal relationships to friends in the USA in order to obtain a reliable affidavit to be able to enter the states and before America joined in the war [...].] Although they received an affidavit from Austrian friends who when they left Switzerland promised to help them once in New York, it was deemed insufficient. Consequently, their efforts at the American consulate seemed hopeless. "Bei unserer letzten Vorsprache im amerikanischen Konsulat hörte ich aus der Absage des Konsuls eine gereizte Arroganz heraus. Von ihm hatten wir nichts Gutes zu erwarten."[29]

27   Lachs, Ibid., 222.
28   Lachs, Ibid., 243.
29   Lachs, Ibid., 245.

[At our last interview with the American consulate I could hear a testy arrogance in the denial from the consul. We could expect no good from him.] However, when they were suddenly called back to receive the necessary papers, they asked about the change in heart. At the time they were only told that "eine wichtige Persönlichkeit" [an important personality] had intervened for them in the White House.[30] As ties to a known socialist network were essential in getting out of Vienna, this time the necessary paperwork to emigrate to the United States came from an anonymous source with ties to Austrian socialists. Years later Lachs found out that the American Muriel Buttinger, married to the Austrian socialist Joseph Buttinger, was instrumental in their flight from Europe.

In summary, the personal, professional, political, and ethnic networks with which Lachs interacted in Switzerland did not face the same constraints as the Viennese networks. Moreover, Lachs was able to exercise more agency either as a member of a network or when tapping into other social networks.

Conclusion

Although many non-Jewish acquaintances and friends deserted her and her husband, her long-term ties to Austria played an important part in the networks that helped the Lachs survive in and escape from Vienna. Her reputation as an outstanding teacher and her affiliation with the Socialist Party laid the foundation for saving help. On the other hand, her position as pregnant and Jewish placed her in a vulnerable position, which led to help coming from both non-Jewish and Jewish networks. In Switzerland the personal, professional, political, and ethnic networks with which Lachs interacted did not face the same constraints as the Viennese networks. Moreover, Lachs was able to exercise more agency there, either as a member of a network or when tapping into other social networks.

30   Lachs, Ibid., 246.

When the Lachs left Switzerland in July 1941 and boarded the *Navemar* in Spain for New York, they were faced with one last harrowing situation. Because of the wretched conditions aboard the ship, it acquired many monikers, including pirate ship, hell-ship, and a floating concentration camp. After a description of the journey, Lachs closes *Warum schaust du zurück* (Why look back) with her arrival in the United States. She immediately telegraphs her parents: "Wir haben überlebt, wir sind gerettet."[31] [We've survived, we're saved].

Although her years of exile were not over when she traveled to the United States in July 1941, the months in post-Anschluss Austria and the years in Switzerland had prepared her for the challenges that faced her in the United States. There her efforts to tap into social networks were motivated largely by her identity as wife and mother and as a professional and contributor to the family finances.

31   Lachs, Ibid., 269.

KÄTHE ERICHSEN

10 Exiled Memories: Searching for Home in Sonia Wachstein's Memoir *Hagenberggasse 49*

ABSTRACT
This chapter explores an intertwined reading of exile and gender through the lens of a lesser-known memoir, *Hagenberggasse 49*, written by Sonia Wachstein, an Austrian-Jewish émigrée in exile. Throughout this chapter I reference both the German-language and English-language publication of the text, which are not simply a translation of one or the other but rather in conversation with each other. My literary analysis examines the text(s) as simultaneously conveying lyrical storytelling and historical testimony, through an exiled framework. The status of exile will be examined through internal, external, and borderless representations of exile, questioning what establishes the home and how the displaced person can negotiate the concept of home.

Introduction

At the beginning of *Exile and Creativity*[1] Christine Brooke-Rose compares the state of exile to that of being on an island; in fact, she mentions that growing up bilingual in a French and English household she "used to think that the word *exile* meant "*ex- île*, out of the island." I'd like to keep this quote and the image of exile as an island in mind for the purposes of this reading. The state of exile is often a very physical one, but it is intertwined with psychological and spatiotemporal elements. Regardless, while there may be neither metaphor nor image that can constitute the

---

1   Susan Rubin Suleiman and Christina Brooke-Rose, "Exsul," in *Exile and Creativity: Signposts, Travelers, Outsiders, Backward Glances* (Durham: Duke University Press, 1998), 9.

emotional and physiological boundlessness of exile, I believe Christine Brooke-Rose's image of an island comes close, as the island reminds us of the singularity and loneliness of exile. Although there can be communities of diasporic groups and societies for intellectual exiles that unite people of a shared persecution, exile, too, remains an island of solitude, in which each individual's experience is remarkably singular. In the text *Women in Austria*[2] Helga Embacher gives an important insight into what life was like for Jewish intellectuals before, during, and after the Holocaust, citing that in 1910 "30% of female students in *Gymnasien* (secondary schools) in Vienna came from Jewish families," demonstrating the high intellectual level that Jewish students in Austria maintained. She goes on to show that after 1945 cultural assimilation to dominant, Christian-Austrian society was normalized. She continues,

> to live as a Jew in Austria after the Shoah meant looking away, repressing, and constructing one's own illusions which, nevertheless, continually threatened to collapse. Even those returning to Austria had to maintain a cleavage between themselves who had been expelled and those who had remained.[3]

In this excerpt, Embacher describes the long-lasting exile that Jewish Austrians experienced externally after many became emigres abroad and internally after returning to Austria. This paper seeks to broadly investigate how women are portrayed in exile literature and how exile literature within the context of post-Holocaust narratives often overlooks the female perspective. More specifically, this paper focuses on the Austrian writer, Sonia Wachstein and her memoir, *Hagenberggasse 49*,[4] which

---

2   Helga Embacher, "The Expulsion of 'Female Rationality' from Austria," in *Women in Austria*, ed. Günter Bischof, Anton Pelinka, and Erika Thurner (New Brunswick, NJ: Transaction Publishers, 1998), 6.

3   Ibid., 11.

4   Wachstein's memoir was published in both German and English. While originally published in German under the title *Hagenberggasse 49*, the text was originally written in English and later published in the United States under a different title. Therefore, the German "original" could be considered a work of translation.

details her personal experiences as an Austrian-Jewish woman living through Nazi persecution and explores her multi-layered exiled flight leading her through Austria, England, Italy, Palestine, and ultimately to the United States. Through the form of memoir, she details not only her own perspective but also shares stories of Bernhard Wachstein, her father, a prominent Judaic Studies scholar in Vienna, her brother, Max, a doctor who is imprisoned at Dachau and Buchenwald, and the little-known lawyer, novelist, and playwright Michael Feuerstein[5] who killed himself in 1938 amidst the rise of antisemitism, all while recounting the chaos of being uprooted from one's home. This chapter seeks to respond to the question of what it means to search for the home(land) in the exiled landscape. It uses the genre of memoir to explore how memory and displacement simultaneously express lyrical storytelling and historical testimony. I interpret Wachstein's exile to not only cast her into external exile by forcibly removing her from her country of origin, but also to be internal, complicated by her gender and social discrimination that subject her to exiled experiences in pre-Nazi Austria, Nazi-controlled Austria, and even in the countries she seeks refuge in.

Memoir: Expressions of Lyricality

I argue that Wachstein's memoir expresses a simultaneous act of *poesis* and *techne*. In the article *Interpreting Literary Testimony*, James E. Young argues, "[I]f the diarists' and memoirists' literary testimony is evidence

---

5   Michael Feuerstein was an Austrian-Jewish playwright, novelist, and lawyer. His comedy play, *Ein Süsses Geheimnis (1927)*, successfully toured Austria and the crownlands and was made into a film in 1931. The manuscript is housed by the Dramatisk Bibliotek in Copenhagen. His only known novel, *der Jünglinge,* was published in 1902 and translated by me as part of archival research for the treatment of a film in development with Waystone Productions, LLC that will feature his play. The manuscript is housed by Harvard University. The translation and original text currently remain unpublished.

of anything else, it is of the writing act itself. That is, even if the narrative cannot document events, or constitute perfect factuality, it can document the actuality of writer and text," demonstrating the act of *poesis* this intimate form of writing allows for. Martin Heidegger expands on the notion of *poesis* and its roots in *techne* in the essay "The Question Concerning Technology" arguing,

> There was a time when it was not technology alone that bore the name *techne*. Once that revealing that brings forth truth into the splendor of radiant appearing also was called *techne* and the poesis of the fine arts also was called *techne*.[6]

It is important to note that the form of Wachstein's memoir itself demonstrates a process of *techne* as she dictated her story to her niece, Muki W. Fairchild, when her eyesight had deteriorated, and she could no longer write. Moreover, through this writing process, the oral history of her memoir demonstrates a form of recording and preserving history that is arguably closer to the lived experience of displacement and exile as it reflects a dynamic style of storytelling. The vocal oration of a narrative not only demonstrates a process of *techne* but also reflects an extension of being that extends beyond the author's individually lived experience and lends itself to the echoes of many victims' preserved and lost voices. It should be noted that while Sonia Wachstein, a Jewish-Austrian who survived the Holocaust, records her own and her family's experiences of persecution and internment, her memoir extends past the genre of Holocaust testimony. Furthermore, it can be read as literature of exile with a female lens to the experience of exile. One should not forget the complicated relationship that a Jewish-Austrian had to negotiate under the Annexation of Austria, for the two identities could not be separated from one another. In *Reclaiming Heimat*, Jacqueline Vansant discusses Jean Amery's perspective of negotiating the spatiotemporal relationship to exile as a Jewish-Austrian émigré, who has written extensively on his experience.

---

6   Martin Heidegger, *The Question Concerning Technology*, trans. William Lovitt (New York: Garland Publishing, 1977), 34.

The loss of *Heimat* or total severing of linguistic, spatial, and temporal connections to an Austrian "we" resulted in what Amery labels *Heimweh* (homesickness). Elaborating a pathology of exile, Amery very explicitly ties possession of *Heimat* to selfhood. The first time Amery uses *Heimweh* he equates it with "self-alienation," connecting his estrangement to his lost past. As a result, he tried to forget his memories of Austria's history and its landscape. However, because these were so integral to his self-image, a consequence was a diminished sense of self.[7]

This sense of defamiliarization of the home as a physical landscape and as a nostalgic memory can be seen throughout the sentimental pages of Sonia Wachstein's memoir, *Hagenberggasse 49*, in which Wachstein traces her briefly serendipitous childhood amidst the remnants of the Austro-Hungarian Empire, her shaky adolescence in Nazi-controlled Austria, her exodus to England during the war and her ultimate arrival to the East Coast of the United States—what would ultimately become her third home in exile.

Forms and Images of Exile: Internal Displacement

I argue that Sonia Wachstein's entire memoir could be read as a story of exile, even before she is cast out of her homeland and into the bound-lessness of emigration. At first glance, the chapters of her memoir seem to convey a sense of chronological logic, beginning with the address of her childhood home[8] details of her education, independent travels to Italy and England, the death of her father, her trip to Palestine, the year 1938, her exiled flight to England, and ultimately her arrival to the United States. Though Wachstein details her travels to Italy, England, and even Palestine prior to her forced emigration from Austria, these earlier travel accounts not only show a young woman exploring the world but also serve

---

7 Jacqueline Vansant, *Reclaiming Heimat: Trauma and Mourning in Memoirs by Jewish Austrian Reémigrés* (Detroit: Wayne State University Press, 2001), 39.

8 The address of Wachstein's family home in Austria shares the same name with the title of the German-language publication of her memoir: *Hagenberggasse 49*.

as a precursor to her subsequent journey as a refugee fleeing from Nazi-controlled Austria. These travels show a woman who already is experiencing a sort of social exile, as she recounts the judgment she receives from her father and the patriarchal culture she was raised in, for traveling, oftentimes solo, as a woman abroad. While she looks back on these memories of traveling in her youth prior to the Annexation of Austria from a chronological perspective, they also have a dream-like, even nostalgic quality to them that disrupts the chronological order in which Wachstein seeks to categorize her life of exile, revealing the non-linear state of exile. What is altogether striking about Wachstein's recollections is that prior to her exile, and even afterwards, she illustrates the continuous experiences of antisemitism in her life that beg the exiled question: if one is not accepted within their own homeland where exactly are they accepted? An example of such anxiety around authenticating one's bloodline to assimilate within the ethnonationalist nation-state can be witnessed in the first chapter of Wachstein's memoir in which she recollects on her memories of trying to comprehend the so-called "Jewish Problem[9]" [Judenfrage] as a child growing up in Vienna.

> The "Jewish Problem" was then a mystery to us. I remember walking in the neighborhood with Max when he was just two years old; his coloring was dark, while I was blonde. Children would scream "black Jew" or "dirty Jew" at him, or yell evil senseless rhymes at us—Then I did not understand the effect of those words on my brother, although I can now imagine how much anger and hurt they caused him.[10]

This passage is just one of many in the memoir that recounts Sonia Wachstein's recollection at an early age of being subjected to bullying and internal exile in her childhood memories of society in Austria, where her and her brother were socially alienated by their non-Jewish peers. Wachstein often describes herself as an assimilated Austrian but notes

---

9   The "Jewish Problem" or "Jewish Question" is philosophically extensively theorized on by Wachstein's father, Bernhard Wachstein, in the text *Diskussion über die Judenfrage: Das Neue Gesicht des Antisemitismus*, 1934. The text is referenced in a footnote in Wachstein's memoir.

10   Sonia Wachstein, *Too Deep Were Our Roots: A Viennese Jewish Memoir of the Years between the Two World Wars* (New York: Harbor Electronic Publishing, 2001), 38.

that her father's public position as a prominent Jewish writer and gene-
alogist often exposed her to bullying by her peers and made her an easy
target for investigation. She also recounts the arrest of her brother, Max,
by the Gestapo in 1938, and his imprisonment in Dachau.

> After a while they informed me that Max had been sent to Dachau. I tried to restrain
> myself but began to cry. Even before Austria was occupied, Dachau had become the
> symbol of all horror and atrocity. "Why are you carrying on like that?" one of the
> men said. "Dachau is not a bad place."[11]

Wachstein, not being given the reason for her brother's arrest believed it
to be punishment for having a sexual relationship with his "Aryan" girl-
friend Edith,[12] and only learns years after his release from Dachau and
Buchenwald that he was suspected to be a communist. The prior fear of
race laws separating "Aryan" Austrians from Jewish Austrians demonstrates the personal anxieties that many Jewish Austrians faced in persecution and exile within their own country, culture, and homeland. In *Exile
and Everyday Life*, Janine Barker explores the émigré experience through
the narrative of Henry Rothschild's and George Mosse's negotiations of
defining their double identity as both German and Jewish persons. The
author remarks on their experience of antisemitism between the years of
1923 and 1934 writing:

> The reconciliation between being Jewish and being German was a relatively easy one
> in the inter-war period, at least for the Jews themselves, and that their perceived oth-
> erness was not profoundly felt. It is difficult to imagine then, in the space of a few
> years, how it would have been to be removed physically, emotionally, and mentally
> from a society that had previously formed part of one's identity.[13]

---

11   Sonia Wachstein, *Too Deep Were Our Roots,* 169.
12   Edith Emory wrote an autobiography about her life in exile, as she fled Austria
     as a communist. In certain chapters and sections of the text she elaborates on the
     Wachstein family, whom she was closely affiliated with and about Max, whose child
     she was pregnant with before undergoing an abortion upon receiving the news
     that he had been sent to Dachau. See Edith Emery, *A Twentieth Century Life: An
     Autobiography* (Artemis, 1995).
13   Andrea Hammel and Anthony Grenville, eds, *Exile and Everyday Life* (Leiden:
     Koninklijke Brill, 2015), 49.

This demonstrates how due to existing antisemitic othering, the origins of exile begin within the home country, creating an internal experience of exile prior to casting out the othered person into external exile. While during her earlier years Wachstein was socially ostracized, after the Annexation of Austria she experienced political exile. Additionally, well before she fled to London, her brother's forced deportation and imprisonment in Dachau would lead her to witness Jewish Austrians around her as subjected to legalized internal displacement and exile.

Exile and Metaphysical Pain Manifested in the Body

I argue that not only being spatially and emotionally removed from one's homeland creates a chasm in the partial loss of one's identity but also that it produces a form of permanent metaphysical pain. Walter Benjamin discusses pain and pleasure in a metaphysical sense in his essays in *Toward the Critique of Violence*, stating that "pain alone among all somatic feelings is, for human beings, like a navigable river with waters that never dry up, leading them into the see … in truth, pain is a connection between worlds and can be permanent."[14] Based on the analysis of pain being a connector between two worlds, it is evident that the emotional and psychological toil Sonia Wachstein experienced through her permanent loss of homeland manifested itself in a psychological and physical form. While expressions of this pain do not constitute the pages of her memoir, they are further evidence in private writings[15] of family members detailing Wachstein's life, etched onto the body through the cosmetic procedures that Wachstein underwent after arriving in the United States, such as rhinoplasty. The loss of homeland illustrated through the body is further

---

14   Walter Benjamin, Peter D. Fenves, and Julia Ng, eds, *Toward the Critique of Violence: Critical Edition* (Stanford, CA: Stanford University Press, 2021), 103.

15   These "private writings" are made up of essays that were written by a niece of Sonia Wachstein. While I am not at liberty to quote them directly, I did have access to them while conducting archival research into her life.

expressed by Jacqueline Vansant, who argues "If we consider specific representations of the trauma and mourning of the loss of Heimat, two related constellations emerge: The body and Austria are recurrent 'sites' onto which the memoirists inscribe the complex processes of trauma and mourning,"[16] illuminating the physical connection between body and temporal-spatiality that can be witnessed through the form of the memoir. Moreover, as a child being surrounded by playwrights, such as her father's friend and playwright, Michael Feuerstein, and charismatic actresses, like Hansi Niese, Wachstein becomes fixated at a young age with physical appearance and with becoming an actress, detailing in her memoir,

> I found myself entirely unattractive and maybe I was. Favorable remarks about a child's looks were entirely discouraged in our culture. I had my father's high color and deep red cheeks, which I found the very opposite of my ideal of delicate, pale, fragile womanhood.[17]

Throughout her memoir, she recounts at a young age being drawn to the stage but being discouraged by those around her such as her scholarly father and other figures of authority in her life, such as Richard Beer-Hofmann,[18] who described Wachstein after her audition as "too young" and "ungraceful." Additionally, it is crucial to mention that while she lived much of her life and even died under the name of Sonia Wachstein, she was born with the first name Sophie,[19] named after her maternal aunt, who died at a young age. While this name change could have been a choice of preference, I argue it begs the question of identity and how one's name, homeland, and language are crucial to the essence of one's self-identification. Furthermore, the above excerpt illustrates how Wachstein's physical insecurities may have contributed to a degraded sense of self that

16 Vansant, *Reclaiming Heimat*, 83.
17 Wachstein, *Too Deep Were Our Roots*, 63.
18 Former director of the Vienna National Burgtheater.
19 This name change occurred after Sonia Wachstein's immigration to the United States, and it is never directly discussed within the pages of her memoir, rather mentioned in an unpublished essay written by a relative about her life and listed in Aryanization documents located at the Austrian State Archives.

manifested itself in the physical body heightened through the traumatic experience of exile.

Social Alienation in Internal Exile: Expressions within the Form of Memoir

Wachstein's memoir goes on to express alienation by her peers due to her persecuted subject position during her university years in Vienna, which were marred by rioting and pogroms against Jewish students. Wachstein went on to earn a Ph.D. in philosophy with a focus on eighteenth-century Viennese National Theater and taught at several schools.[20] Before exile from Austria, her road to higher education was filled with instances of continued antisemitism, creating a systemic framework of internal exile outlining her adolescence. In recollections of her university years, she reveals:

> [O]n a certain day I would enter the University and immediately sense trouble in the air. I tried to ignore it, but it was impossible. Masses of students would occupy the entry halls. Then, organized into smaller groups, they would break into lecture halls, screaming, "Out with the Jews, the lecture is over."[21]

This memory illuminates the experience of internal exile for Wachstein and other Jews that permeated the structures of academia. She goes on to recollect that the so-called "color" of a student's hair or physical appearance ended in their violent removal from the classroom, demonstrating the unruly and unjust authentication process that developed based on public stereotyping which was later backed by law after the Annexation of Austria. These recollections reveal Sonia Wachstein's own memories of living in internal exile prior to the Annexation, as these moments of

20   Most notably, Sonia Wachstein was a teacher at the Chajes Gymnasium, the only Jewish school in Vienna, which remained open until 1939.
21   Wachstein, *Too Deep Were Our Roots*, 85.

public antisemitism take place often prior to the Annexation, foreshadowing how displays of racism would later become affirmed by a legal framework that segregated and imprisoned Jewish Austrians. In the text, such recollections allude to a range of exile testimonies that were never recorded or have been lost, thus creating a continuum of exile made possible by the form of memoir. Jacqueline Vansant, who explores the role of memory embedded within memoir, writes:

> If the memoir writers attempt to document memory with the inclusion of photographs, official documents, and letters, they also point to the limitations of such documentary material. Because of the nature of the National Socialist terror, the Jewish genocide, exile, and the destruction of the war, documents of their lives as well as those of others have been eradicated. Thus, memory becomes important "evidence" and a virtual archive.[22]

This process of threading the connectivity between memory and memoir demonstrates the collective quality of such documents, often speaking to the experiences of not only one individual but rather a larger group of shared experience and in this case, shared experiences of antisemitism and shared exile. To further elaborate on the shared experiences of exile as recorded in memoirs, it entails also a form of healing trauma as the memoir comes closest to the resummoning of the moment that is etched in time. Vansant ascertains:

> The memoirists' descriptions often bring to mind what psychologists have termed a "flashbulb memory"—a memory of "a novel and shocking event." Whether the memoirists remember the events exactly as they happened is not essential: the vividness of the memories conveys an emotional truth.[23]

This further showcases how the genre of memoir, intertwined with memory and trauma, serves as a unique form of writing that allows for an assemblage of emotive memory that lives in the present. Moreover, this returns to the earlier mention of Heidegger's notion of *techne*. In relation to the dictated memoir, here it can be observed how the memoir's form,

---

22   Vansant, *Reclaiming Heimat*, 75.
23   Vansant, *Reclaiming Heimat*, 69.

tied closely to memory making and memory recording, illustrates a form of *techne* or artistic creation that is tied to the very act of the writing process itself.

Exile in Conversation with Gender

In this next section, I will investigate the relationship of gender and exile, focusing on how Wachstein's subject position as a woman played to both her advantage and disadvantage within internal exile in Austria and later in external exile. Brinson and Hammel's *Exile and Gender: Literature and the Press* discusses the relationship between gender and biography from the perspective of several different essays dealing with biographies and memoirs of German and Austrian victims and survivors of the Holocaust. It is significant to consider the role of gender within exile literature as women's experiences of exile mainly became a topic of interest in the mid-1980s[24] when the lives of women in exile were reconstructed and made visible within the canon of exile literature that had traditionally been represented and structured by male perspectives. Within the field of Holocaust Studies, gender traditionally was a subject that was largely seen as secondary and often ignored altogether since it was believed that one's minority subject position as Jewish superseded the gendered experience. Andrea Hammel expands on this lack of recognition for a gendered experience in the Holocaust citing:

> Questions of gender were seen as irrelevant, even irreverent; however, from the early 1990s studies appeared that contradicted this view. These studies emphasized that the experience of women and girls during the time of National Socialist persecution and the Holocaust was different from the experience of men and boys and that therefore studies that investigated gender were important and women survivors' voices needed to be heard, studied and commemorated.[25]

---

24   See: Chapter 1: "Exemplary Lives"? Thoughts on Exile, Gender and Life-Writing, *Exile and Gender: Literature and the Press*, 10.

25   Hammel and Grenville, eds, *Exile and Everyday Life*, 19.

Andrea Hammel demonstrates using a series of texts from memoirs written by child survivors of the *Kindertransports* that women tend to frame their memoirs differently than men, framing their relationships with other women, children, the household, and gendered abuse they suffered such as physical and sexual abuse. Within the same chapter the author references the research of Marion Kaplan[26] who uses memoirs for her study of German-speaking Jewish people in the 1930s and 1940s, arguing:

> Gender mattered as people reflected upon their lives. There is a relationship between gender and memory. Women and men concentrate on different recollections. As one might expect, women's memories tend to center on family and friends, schools and neighborhoods, while men's tend to focus on the business or the political environment. Do they remember differently, or did their original experiences, gendered as they were, provide for the different perspectives they offer?[27]

It is important to recognize that Holocaust memoirs serve as literary narratives as well as historical narratives and while Sonia Wachstein's memoir is not a story specifically of the *Kindertransports*, her narrative blurs categories of genre, as it intertwines a gendered experience with forced emigration. Wachstein's memoir in many ways is representative of the gender experience that Marion Kaplun argues, considering how much time within the text Wachstein allows for describing the genealogical origins of her family, photographic details from her childhood and hometown of Vienna, and navigating the sexism at the university, and in her own household. Experiences such as these appear throughout Wachstein's memoir, for example, when she recalls meeting a male acquaintance at his apartment on a Sunday afternoon and being scolded by her father for meeting a man alone, remarking how "I was aghast at such narrow-mindedness and felt superior to my father[28]" or recalling her brother's blatant sexism when discussing her university years and how women made up half of the

---

26 See Chapter 1: "Exemplary Lives"? Thoughts on Exile, Gender and Life-Writing, *Exile and Gender: Literature and the Press*, 10.

27 Hammel and Grenville, eds, *Exile and Everyday Life*, 24.

28 Wachstein, *Too Deep Were Our Roots*, 74–8.

class in the first year of medical school and his response that women were not suitable for careers as physicians and "even those who finished were inferior.[29]" Wachstein recalls how she dealt with frequent conversations such as these by referencing successful female figures from history, such as Madame Curie as an example of women's intellectual capacities, but nevertheless continued to challenge ingrained notions of sexism from the dominant male society she was raised in and categorized by. Wachstein illustrates throughout her memoir how she had to negotiate her travels prior to her flight from Austria since her position as a woman affected her mobility. For instance, when she traveled to Italy with a university colleague, her father attempted to prevent her from leaving, causing a great deal of guilt for going against his wishes, which ultimately affected her relationship with him. "He was still angry when I left, and I think my guilty feelings about disobeying him never left me completely, even when I undertook numerous journeys long after his death."[30] Her feelings of guilt and sense of "disobedience" demonstrate Wachstein's difficulties as a modern, young woman trying to negotiate her position among dominating men and among a patriarchal society that was becoming more aggressive and fascist by the day. While exile literature is often relayed through legal segregation, which ultimately Sonia Wachstein and her family are subjected to, early on in her memoir, it is evident that she feels socially exiled as a young woman who attempts to carve out an independent, feminist identity for herself against the mainstream, patriarchal culture she is a product of. Thus, these experiences of challenging sexism and imposed limits of her movement as a woman serve a greater purpose of interpreting less studied gendered experiences within Holocaust and exile literature.

Wachstein's recollections of her experiences focus not only on her family dynamic, schooling, and personal life but also describe historical facts regarding the annexation of Austria, legalization of pogroms, and segregation against Jewish Austrians. The inclusion of these topics demonstrates her interest in politics and the political future and ultimately allows her

---

29   Ibid.
30   Wachstein, *Too Deep Were Our Roots*, 79.

strength to choose a future for herself and leave her country. Wachstein writes of the methodical annihilation of Jewish Austrians, noting at the start of the Annexation, there was a semblance of legality such as owners having to sign over their properties as opposed to them simply being re-possessed by the government. She discusses these methodical measures of the dehumanization of Jewish Austrians by referencing specific dates and statistics such as when the Aryanization of business took place in 1938:

> For the roughly 180,000 Jews in Austria, most of whom lived in Vienna, life had turned around one hundred and eighty degrees. From one day to another, Jews had lost all human and civil rights. They were now subject to crimes directed at them that went unpunished: physical force, murder, robbery, intrusion into their homes, and loss of property, livelihoods, and positions.[31]

This demonstrates how Wachstein's memoir offers historical testimony of the exiled experience through an inclusion of historical data, which documents the dehumanization that she witnessed, and analyzes the raw data of historical facts.[32] By combining historical facts with her own experience, she intertwines historical testimony with lyrical storytelling. Her memoir, aesthetic in form, with inclusions of photographs, song lyrics, and transcribed personal letters, allows her narrative to convey a poetic quality to the reader that differs from a strictly testimonial perspective.

Forms and Images of Exile: External (Dis)placement

Towards the end of her memoir, Wachstein decides to permanently leave Austria in October of 1938, fearing for her life and the life of her

---

31   Wachstein, *Too Deep Were Our Roots*, 161.

32   This can be seen throughout the text and notably in footnotes where Wachstein provides statistical data. See Footnote 17 in the English-language text, "In 1936, 67.2 percent of the dentists, 47.2 percent of physicians, and 62 percent of the lawyers in Vienna were Jewish." Wachstein, *Too Deep Were Our Roots*, 212.

mother, who decides to temporarily stay.[33] She travels alone from Vienna to Berlin hoping to secure her brother's release but is unsuccessful in receiving any concrete answers about his imprisonment, or possible release. From Berlin she travels to England to stay with a friend and embark on a new life. Yet, while her freedom of movement and her rights in London, England, are less constricted than in Nazi-controlled Austria, she reflects on feeling displaced in England:

> Living in England as a tolerated guest—as an exile from my own country of birth—was very different from being there on vacation. The city in which I had wandered around as a tourist and had so admired and loved now seemed strange and forbidding. There was always the thought that the English government had given us hospitality but expected us to move on.[34]

Wachstein reflects on her feelings of displacement as an emigrée and draws the reader into the subconscious of a person in exile, framing the image of the city once visited before emigration as now a desolate place of disassociation in exile. In the next few pages, Wachstein goes on to explain how her refugee status in England felt unwelcome due to the stamp in her passport that forbade her from working. She recollects how she was forced to rely on friends in England to provide for her housing and living expenses until she was able to legally acquire a work permit and job from the Jewish Refugee Committee a year later in 1939 to work with *Kindertransports* arriving in England. Ultimately it is in this first country of exile that Wachstein is reunited with her brother. Max joined her after his release from Buchenwald in 1939 and they both emigrate to the United States in 1943, where they remain for the duration of their lives. In the last pages of her memoir, she contemplates what it would

33   Marie Wachstein stays temporarily in Vienna before her house is fully Aryanized and she ultimately escapes to the United States by ship passage through Portugal. Extensive documents pertaining to the aryanization of her home are located at the Austrian State Archives in Vienna. She is able to remain in her home at Hagenberggasse 49, while the home is split into two separate properties and she dwells in half of it with an Aryan in-law of hers until 1941, when she flees to England to join her daughter.

34   Wachstein, *Too Deep Were Our Roots*, 186.

be like to return to Austria after the war. Wachstein states, "I could not conceive of this plan or understand how I would be emotionally ready to live in Austria again,[35]" demonstrating the deep-seeded trauma that Wachstein held towards her homeland and the distrust that never disappeared. In *Reclaiming Heimat*, Vansant writes about the linguistic, spatial, and temporal links that connect and disconnect exiled memoirists from their home:

> The memoirists salvage traumatic memories through body memories and emotional associations with place to convey a sense of loss, which has remained with them. Their experiences and their memories of these experiences permanently change their spatial identity and their relationship to their Austrian surroundings. Because being thrown out of an Austrian "we" transformed their spatial semiotic competency, they experience emotionally "saturated" places with a sense of temporal simultaneity.[36]

This sense of spatial disconnect between the self and the country is echoed throughout the pages of Wachstein's memoir and is restated even in the last lines of her memoir in which she writes of her arrival all alone in New York, "I imagined that the tall, grey towers were welcoming us, and telling me what I could not then believe, that Manhattan would be my third home.[37]" In the original German publication, she uses the term *Heimat*, demonstrating her deep psychological desire to have a place, temporal and spatial, to call home. Yet, Wachstein's specific wording of "what would be my third home" aligns Austria, England, and the United States as separate homelands, that arguably cannot exist in unison. Moreover, Wachstein's decision not to return to her original home(land) in Austria signifies the separation between herself and the place she once called home due to her persecuted subject position as a Jewish-Austrian. Her memoirs make it clear that amidst her displacement and the aftermath of the Holocaust, there is no clear separation between the Austria of her youth and postwar Austria. "The temporal link to a pre-*Anschluss* history appears the easiest to reestablish. Yet even these configurations

35   Wachstein, *Too Deep Were Our Roots*, 209.
36   Vansant, *Reclaiming Heimat*, 151.
37   Wachstein, *Too Deep Were Our Roots*, 210.

of their past illustrate the tension between various subject positions."[38] This further demonstrates that even if Wachstein were to attempt to end her transatlantic exile and return to Austria, it would still be a location that in a spatiotemporal sense would be implicated in the same country that thrust her into exile. Moreover, the timeline of her exile cannot be specifically pinpointed to a date or a location. While she feels exiled in her youth by antisemitic slurs shouted at her and her brother by their "Aryan" peers that segregate her into an internal exile, she also uses the term "exile" in the English publication when describing her home life.[39] "We ran up to my father's study in the attic, complaining about our exile. He was sitting at his desk, deeply engrossed in his research. Being a voluntary exile from these gatherings, he showed no sympathy."[40] While in this momentary recollection she is simply separated from an adult gathering, her specific wording highlights the solitude and dissociation she felt at a young age within a Viennese society that shunned her for being Jewish. Her family did not support her dreams of being an actress and patriarchal figures like her father[41] and brother made her feel socially inadequate due to her gender. This foreshadows her impending exile that would thrust her across the geographical borders and spatiotemporal boundlessness of life as an émigrée.

---

38   Vansant, *Reclaiming Heimat*, 52.
39   While the text exists in two separate forms (German and English edition), both narratives were constructed in a multilingual framework. Originally, the text was dictated to Wachstein's niece, Muki W. Fairchild, and preliminary drafts were constructed by Sonia in a combination of English and German. Muki spent countless hours with her aunt, attempting to edit the text, but was ultimately only allowed to be dictated to by her aunt. Ultimately, the text was published in English, but American publishers took little interest in her story. It was then translated into German by her cousin, Dorothea Winkler, and published for the first time in German by a Viennese publisher. Only after its publication in 1996 was the original English text published in the United States in 2001 by a separate publisher.
40   Wachstein, *Too Deep Were Our Roots*, 28.
41   While Wachstein's relationship to her father is indeed complicated by gender and gender norms in twentieth-century Austria, she does ultimately dedicate her memoir to her father, Bernhard Wachstein.

Conclusion

Sonia Wachstein draws the reader into the psychological and spatial constraints of a woman in internal and external exile. While her story alone cannot speak to the entirety of the canon of exile and Holocaust literature, by writing her story as a memoir and dictating the narrative to her niece, she memorializes an experience that speaks to both historical testimony and lyrical narrative. Wachstein brings the reader to the marrow of her memoir. In the antisemitic accounts that she narrates from the experience of name-calling to the loss of basic human rights, she demonstrates that even at home whether that home be her homeland in Austria, her refuge land of England, or her self-proclaimed third home of the United States, she exists in a boundless state of exile. As a woman in exile her narrative provides a unique perspective within exile literature. Wachstein gives a female perspective that is often overshadowed and dominated by canonical male perspectives. Wachstein's story is one that has been overlooked for far too long as it was a story that was almost never published. Dictated in English to her niece, Muki W. Fairchild, it sat on the shelves of her New York apartment, lacking interest from American publishers, who cast her narrative and memories aside. It wasn't until her cousin Dorothea Winkler encouraged her to allow it to be translated into German that it was published in 1991 by a small printing house in Vienna. In fact, it may have never reached an English-speaking audience if it hadn't been for the interest of her neighbor in New York, James Monaco, that her original story was republished. Furthermore, it speaks volumes that Wachstein's memoir is now out of print in both English and German. While she cemented her boundless exile into print, today her story is widely unknown within Austria and the United States, demonstrating the very scholarly barriers[42] that obscure Wachstein's story—the story of not only a vibrant,

---

42　*Haggenberggase 49* dwells solely in archives and university research libraries today. My research was conducted by sourcing the English-language text through a university library and the German-language text through the United States Holocaust Memorial Museum at the Shapell Center Reading Room.

novice actress but also of a teacher, traveler, survivor, and an intersectional Austrian-Jewish woman in exile. Sonia Wachstein went on to live a successful life in the United States, despite her many years in external exile. She continued to teach German and English at various institutions and universities for the rest of her life, but her main passion became psychology as she dedicated her career to becoming a child social worker and publishing a great deal of literature within this field. Much of her life's work and personal diaries which help to gain a wider perspective on her life, can be found at the Leo Baeck Institute in New York. Interestingly, current research is being done on Sonia Wachstein's life and her descendants in a documentary film, *The Archives*, in-production with Ein Süsses Geheimnis, LLC. Her memoir and explorations into her interest in theater will be featured as the basis for the narrative film, *A Sweet Secret*, in-development with Waystone Productions.

CHRISTINA WIEDER

11 Künstlerinnen über_setzen: Visuelle Netzwerke des Exils in Argentinien

ABSTRACT

This article examines the cinematic works of the exiled artists Hedy Crilla (1898–1984) and Irena Dodal (1900–89). Using selected film segments, this paper examines cultural translation and, in particular, appropriation and resignation within translation processes in exile. Special attention will be paid to which figures (e.g. the New Woman) were integrated and translated in their exile works and which political implementations went hand in hand with this. The works of Hedy Crilla and Irena Dodal are also analyzed as a form of self-translation, which is read as an attempt to make their country of origin and exile visible and to counteract the fragmentation of their work and biography caused by the experience of flight.

Kontrastreiche Belichtung, dynamische Bewegungen und montagenhafte Schnitte, die eine Beschleunigung andeuten, sowie atmosphärische Musik kombiniert mit einer modernen Formsprache—dies sind nur einige Gemeinsamkeiten, die die beiden Filme *Ideas in Search for Light* (R: Irena Dodal, CS/FR 1938) und *Barrios y Teatros de Buenos Aires* [Stadtteile und Theater von Buenos Aires] (R: Hedy Crilla, ARG 1962) aufweisen (Abb. 10 und 11). Zwischen den beiden Produktionen liegen vierundzwanzig Jahre, die für die Regisseurinnen von Flucht und Verfolgung geprägt waren. Dieser Aufsatz bespricht, wie die Erfahrung des Exils, das die beiden Frauen nach Buenos Aires brachte, unzählige Versuche der Übersetzung, sowie Bestrebungen nach Vernetzung in der neuen Umgebung hervorbrachte, die sich maßgeblich im Raum des Visuellen bzw. innerhalb der Kunstproduktion von Irena Dodal (1900–1989) und Hedy Crilla (1898–1984) abbildeten.[1]

---

1 Wie viele Frauenleben im Exil sind auch jene von Hedy Crilla und Irena Dodal von diversen Namenswechseln begleitet. Um daraus resultierende biografische

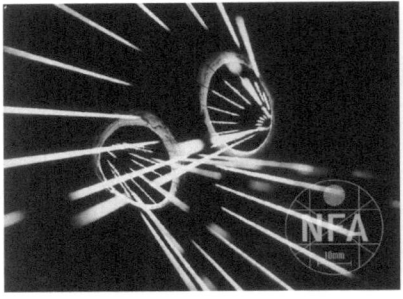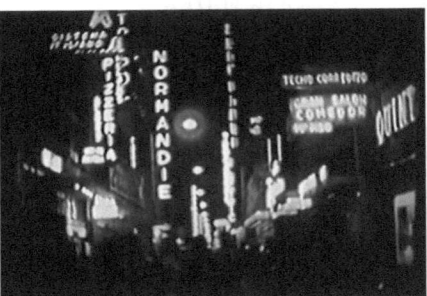

Abb. 10–11. Links: Still aus *Ideas in Search for Light* (R: Irena Dodal, FR 1938).
Rechts: Still aus *Barrios y Teatros de Buenos Aires* (R: Hedy Crilla, ARG 1962).

Obgleich die beiden Filme unterschiedliche Genres bedienen—*Ideas
in Search for Light* ist ein Experimentalfilm im Kurzformat und *Barrios y
Teatros de Buenos Aires* weist einen dokumentarischen Charakter auf—gab
es keine nachweisbare persönliche Bekanntschaft zwischen den beiden
Regisseurinnen. Die Filme wurden auf unterschiedlichen Kontinenten
produziert, und dennoch verbindet sie das gemeinsame Bestreben, Aspekte
des modernen Kunstschaffens in ein neues Umfeld zu übersetzen und damit
auch eine spezifische Vorstellung von Emanzipation einzuführen, welche für
die beiden Frauen von zentraler Bedeutung in ihrer frühen künstlerischen
Sozialisation war. Doch auf welchen Ebenen des Filmschaffens lassen sich
solche emanzipativen Bestrebungen erkennen und wie lassen sich diese
charakterisieren? Wie manifestiert sich die Erfahrung des Exils visuell im
Schaffen dieser Frauen und welche Bedeutung kommt Übersetzung in
einem transnationalen Kontext zu? Durch die Analyse der Arbeiten von
Irena Dodal und Hedy Crilla soll gezeigt werden, inwiefern der Ansatz
der kulturellen Übersetzung für die Erforschung von Erfahrungen von
Frauen im Exil gewinnbringend sein kann. Wie ich im Folgenden argumen-
tiere, erlaubt der Ansatz der kulturellen Übersetzung erstens, das Exil als

---

Unklarheiten zu vermeiden, werde ich im Folgenden jene Namen verwenden, die
sie selbst im argentinischen Exil für sich wählten, allerdings Variationen in der biografischen Vorstellung kurz erwähnen.

transnationales Phänomen zu fassen, das keine linearen Bewegungsmuster aufweist, sondern vielmehr durch eine Vielzahl von Netzwerken, parallelen und teils sogar asynchronen Entwicklungen gezeichnet ist. Indem kulturelle Kontexte im Herkunfts- und im Aufnahmeland als gleichermaßen relevant für Übersetzungsprozesse erachtet werden, tritt der Ansatz damit zugleich selektiven Rezeptionen von Exilkünstler*innen entgegen, welche sich entweder auf die Phase vor dem Exil oder aber auf jene im Aufnahmeland fokussieren.[2] Zweitens erlaubt der Fokus auf Übersetzung das Schaffen von Frauen im Exil verstärkt sichtbar zu machen, denn das Hinterfragen von etablierten Hierarchien—seien dies Geschlechterhierarchien oder aber Hierarchien zwischen Kulturen—ist ein essenzieller Bestandteil von Übersetzungsprozessen und eröffnet damit eine erweiterte Perspektive, die insbesondere für Frauenleben im Exil neue Erkenntnisse bringt.

Durch die Linse der *Neuen Frau*

Hedy Crilla (geb. Hedwig Schlichter, später auch Krilla) wurde am 26. September 1898 in Wien geboren, sie war das dritte von vier Kindern und wuchs in einer wohlsituierten Familie im sechsten Wiener Gemeindebezirk auf. Der Vater war Arzt, die Mutter Hausfrau, wie in vielen Wiener jüdischen Familien spielten religiöse Praktiken kaum eine Rolle in ihrer Sozialisation. Für Crilla wurde ihre jüdische Zugehörigkeit erst relativ später durch die Flucht zu einem zentralen Faktor ihrer Selbstidentifikation. Sie besuchte die bekannte Wiener Mädchenschule von Eugenie Schwarzwald und beschloss später, entgegen des Wunsches

---

2 Zur Herausforderung, von Migration und Exil geprägte Biografien zu beschreiben, ohne sie ihrer Fragmentiertheit zu berauben, sie gleichzeitig aber auch nicht allein darauf zu reduzieren, siehe: Levke Harders, „Migration und Biographie. Mobile Leben beschreiben", in *Biographien und Migrationen/Biographies and Migrations*, *ÖZG 29*, Hrsg. Johanna Gehmacher, Klara Löffler, und Katharina Prager (2018), 3, S. 17–36.

der Familie, einem Schauspielstudium nachzugehen. Nach zwei Semestern an der Akademie für Musik und darstellende Kunst in Wien (heute Universität für Musik und darstellende Kunst) folgten einige unstete Anstellungen an diversen Theatern in der Weimarer Republik und Österreich sowie kleinere Filmauftritte und Beteiligungen in experimentellen Spielstätten, u.a. in der von Berthold Viertel gegründeten „Truppe", einem genossenschaftlich organisierten Theater, das sich auf gesellschaftskritische Stücke konzentrierte. Als ihr später als Jüdin die Mitgliedschaft zur Reichstheater- bzw. Reichsfilmkammer verweigert wurde, schloss sie sich dem von Leopold Jessner begründeten Tournee Ensemble an, mit dem sie 1934 durch Europa tourte. Einer vorübergehenden Rückkehr nach Berlin folgte ein Zwischenstopp in Wien und 1937 bereits die Entscheidung, nach Frankreich ins Exil zu gehen. Dort war Crilla an diversen Filmprojekten der jüdischen Exilgemeinde beteiligt, dennoch sollte es ihr nicht gelingen, langfristig Fuß zu fassen. Nach politisch und beruflich ebenso wie emotional herausfordernden Jahren in Paris folgte Crilla 1941 dem Ruf ihrer beiden Schwestern und ihres Bruders, die sich alle bereits in Argentinien aufhielten, und entschied sich schließlich nach Buenos Aires zu gehen. Dort fand sie erst im von Paul Walter Jacob gegründeten Exiltheater, der Freien Deutschen Bühne, ein Engagement, sollte aber zugleich in französischen Theatertruppen, im argentinischen Film sowie als Schauspiellehrerin für Kinder an der Sociedad Hebraica, einer jüdischen Kulturvereinigung, die maßgeblich an der Flüchtlingsbetreuung beteiligt war, tätig sein. Ab den 1950er Jahren machte sie sich stetig mehr einen Namen als Schauspiellehrerin an freien Theatern, arbeitete intensiv mit der *Stanislavsky Methode*[3] und absolvierte

---

3   Die *Stanislavky Methode* beschreibt einen von Konstantin Stanislavsky entwickelten Schauspielansatz, der primär auf der Erkundung persönlicher Erfahrungswelten von Schauspieler*innen basiert. Durch Rückgriff auf individuelle Erinnerungen und die Aktivierung ihres emotionalen Gedächtnisses sollten diese dem Spiel eine realistischere Note verleihen. Schauspieler*innen würden demnach nicht bloß eine Bühnenfigur adaptieren, sondern diese als Erweiterung ihrer eigenen emotionalen Biografie verkörpern. In den USA fand die Methode durch die Arbeit Lee Strasbergs Anfang der 1930er Jahre vermehrt Anerkennung und wurde vor allem im New Yorker Group Theater praktiziert.

neben zahlreichen Theaterarbeiten immer wieder kleinere Auftritte im argentinischen Film. Bis ins hohe Alter war Crilla als Schauspiellehrerin, Schauspielerin und Regisseurin tätig und prägte nachhaltig die argentinische Film- und Theaterszene.[4]

Irena Dodal (geb. Rosneróva, später Leschneróva/Dodalóva) kam am 29. November 1900 in der tschechoslowakischen Kleinstadt Ledeč nad Sázavou zur Welt. Wenig später übersiedelte die Familie nach Brno, wo der Vater eine Stelle als Leiter eines jüdischen Waisenhauses antrat. Dort besuchte Dodal einige Jahre eine Mädchenschule, später noch die deutsche Handelsschule, nach deren Abschluss sie eine Ausbildung als Opernsängerin begann. Nach kurzer Tätigkeit am Deutschen Brünner Theater absolvierte sie einen mehrmonatigen Auslandsaufenthalt in Deutschland, kehrte allerdings in die Tschechoslowakei zurück, wo sie in Prag einen neuen Lebensmittelpunkt fand. Gemeinsam mit ihrer Mutter und ihrem Bruder bezog Dodal eine Wohnung im Stadtteil Žižkov. Anfang der 1930er Jahre lernte sie schließlich den Filmemacher Karel Dodal kennen, den sie 1935 heiratete. Schon davor hatten die beiden das gemeinsame Trickfilmstudio IRE Film gegründet, das das Ziel verfolgte, einen „neuen, künstlerischen, europäischen Typ des Zeichenfilms (zu) schaffen".[5] IRE Film konzentrierte sich auf Werbeproduktionen, folgte dabei aber klar künstlerischen Ansprüchen und setzte auf diese Weise neue ästhetische Parameter für die wirtschaftliche und experimentelle Trickfilmproduktion in der jungen Tschechoslowakei. Mit dem Ziel die vielfältige Filmproduktion Europas besser kennenzulernen, unternahmen Irena und Karel Dodal diverse Studienreisen nach Italien, Österreich, Frankreich und Deutschland. Sie machten sich auf diesem Wege mit avantgardistischen Projekten vertraut

---

4   Für weiterführende Informationen zu Hedy Crilla, siehe: Cora Roca, *Días de Teatro. Hedy Crilla* (Madrid: Alianza Editorial, 2000); Christina Wieder, *Visuelle Transformationen. Das Exil der jüdischen Künstlerinnen Grete Stern, Hedy Crilla und Irena Dodal in Argentinien*, phil. Diss. Universität Wien, 2023, S. 46–61, S. 128–37.

5   o.A., *Besuch bei Frau Irena: Hurvínek contra Mickey Mouse. Die Avantgarde des Zeichenfilms.—Das einzige Trickfilm-Atelier der Republik*, undatiert, Nachlass Irena Dodalová, National Film Archive, Prag.

und integrierten diese in ihr eigenes Schaffen. Bedingt durch die politischen Entwicklungen planten Karel und Irena Dodal bereits 1938 Prag zu
verlassen. Sie gingen vorübergehend nach Paris, doch aufgrund familiärer
Umstände sah sich Irena Dodal gezwungen, in die Tschechoslowakei zurückzukehren. Es gelang ihr 1939, als Prag bereits von nationalsozialistischen Truppen besetzt war, noch das Filmequipment an ihren Ehemann
für die geplante Emigration in die USA zu schicken, allerdings sollte ihr
selbst die Ausreise nicht mehr gelingen. Vorübergehend untergetaucht
in einem Vorort von Prag wurde sie 1941 denunziert und gemeinsam mit
ihrer Mutter ins Ghetto Theresienstadt verschleppt. Trotz inhumaner
Bedingungen setzte sie in Theresienstadt einige künstlerische Projekte
fort, zudem war sie an der Produktion des nationalsozialistischen Films
Theresienstadt 1942 beteiligt.[6] Noch vor Mai 1945 gelang es Dodal über
einen Rot-Kreuz-Transport in die Schweiz zu kommen und wenig später
in die USA zu reisen, wo es zu einer Wiedervereinigung mit Karel Dodal
kam. Wenig erfolgreich betrieben die beiden dort erneut ein Filmstudio,
das allerdings bald in Konkurs gehen sollte. Die Einladung des argentinischen Bildungsministers Oscar Ivanissevich bot daraufhin eine gelegene
Möglichkeit, um in Argentinien beruflich und privat neu zu beginnen. Nach
einigen Jahren der Tätigkeit für das peronistische Bildungsministerium als
Herstellerin von Bildungstrickfilmen, begann Irena Dodal in den frühen
1950er Jahren mit eigenen Produktionen und kehrte zum avantgardistischen
Experimentalfilm zurück. Karel Dodal verließ wenig später Argentinien
um in die USA zurückzukehren. Irena Dodal sollte bis an ihr Lebensende
in Argentinien bleiben und kleinere Filmprojekte umsetzen sowie als
Theaterlehrerin tätig sein.[7]

6   Zur Produktion des Films und den Umständen im Ghetto Theresienstadt, siehe: Eva
     Strusková, „Film Ghetto Theresienstadt: Die Suche nach Zusammenhängen", in
     *„Der Letzte der Ungerechten". Der Judenälteste Benjamin Murmelstein in Filmen
     1942–1975*, Hrsg. Ronny Loewy und Katharina Rauschenberger (Frankfurt/
     Main: Campus, 2011), S. 125–158.
7   Zu Irena und Karel Dodal, insbesondere den Jahren in der Tschechoslowakei,
     siehe: Eva Strusková, *The Dodals: Pioneers of Czech Animated Film* (Prag: NFA,
     2013); außerdem für Argentinien: Wieder, Visuelle Transformationen, S. 137–146.

So unterschiedlich die Werdegänge von Hedy Crilla und Irena Dodal auch scheinen, so weisen ihre Biografien dennoch einige Gemeinsamkeiten auf und geben Auskunft über die Erfahrungen des Exils, die sich auch in ihrem künstlerischen Schaffen manifestieren. Beide Frauen waren Repräsentantinnen einer Frauengeneration, die um 1900 geboren Zugang zu einer breiten Bildung und damit auch zu emanzipativen Ideen hatten. Die bis zur Flucht relativ sichere finanzielle Lage der Familien hatte ihnen zudem ermöglicht, in durchaus prekäre Berufsfelder einzutreten sowie sich künstlerisch fortzubilden. Wie die Kunsthistorikerin Isabelle Graw argumentiert, ist es insbesondere auf die weitreichende akademisch-künstlerische Bildung zurückzuführen, die Frauen ab Ende des 19. Jahrhunderts erfuhren, dass sie sich ab den 1920er und 1930er Jahren zunehmend des Prinzips der künstlerischen Aneignung bedienten.[8] Nicht nur eigneten sich Frauen künstlerisches Wissen und Strategien an, auch machten sie sich insbesondere traditionell männlich besetzte Formen und Darstellungsweisen zu eigen, wie beispielsweise Selbstbildnisse und -porträts.[9] Auf diese Weise schufen sich Künstlerinnen zugleich Möglichkeiten zur Mitgestaltung kulturpolitischer Diskurse. Dies taten Hedy Crilla und Irena Dodal—ebenso wie viele andere Frauen ihrer Generation—nicht zuletzt als Jüdinnen mit spezifischen Erfahrungen und dem Anliegen, diesen eine Öffentlichkeit zu geben.[10]

Ausgestattet mit dem Selbstbewusstsein der *Neuen Frau*—einer Figur, die vielfach in der Populärkultur auftauchte und ab den 1920er Jahren zu einem medialen Ideal mit gesellschaftlicher Vorbildwirkung wurde[11]—

---

8   Vgl. Isabelle Graw, *Die bessere Hälfte. Künstlerinnen des 19. und 20. Jahrhunderts* (Köln: DuMont, 2003), S. 33–38.

9   Zu Selbstbildnissen von Frauen in der Moderne, vgl. Gerda Breuer und Elina Knorpp, Hrsg., *Gespiegeltes Ich. Fotografische Selbstbildnisse von Künstlerinnen und Fotografinnen in den 1920er Jahren* (Berlin: Nicolai Verlag, 2014); Nadja Köffler, *Vivian Maier und der gespiegelte Blick: fotografische Positionen zu Frauenbildern im Selbstporträt* (Bielefeld: Transcript, 2019).

10 Vgl. Lisa Silverman, *Becoming Austrians: Jews and Culture between the World Wars* (Oxford: Oxford University Press, 2012), S. 3–27.

11 Zur *Neuen Frau* in medialen Kontexten, vgl. Ute Eskildsen, „Die Kamera als Instrument der Selbstbestimmung", in *Fotografieren hieß teilnehmen: Fotografinnen*

sollten Hedy Crilla und Irena Dodal ihre emanzipativen Bestrebungen auch im Exil weiter vorantreiben und für Sichtbarkeit und Mitgestaltung kämpfen. Schließlich sahen sie sich in Argentinien erneut damit konfrontiert, dass traditionelle Frauenbilder intensiv verbreitet wurden, welche sie auf den privaten Raum, Hausarbeit und die Erziehung von Kindern reduzieren wollte. Insbesondere in den Jahren des Peronismus ist eine ambivalente Entwicklung im Bereich der Frauenpolitik zu verzeichnen, die zwar einerseits durch die Einführung des Frauenwahlrechts im Jahr 1947 eine Demokratisierung vermuten ließ, andererseits durch den intensiven Einsatz von visuellen Medien zu Propagandazwecken aber ein (Re-)Etablierung traditioneller Rollenbilder forcierte. Wie bereits angedeutet, ließ sich das Emanzipationsideal von Crilla und Dodal nur schwer mit einer solchen konservativen Frauenpolitik vereinbaren, weshalb sie ihre Kunst nutzen, um alternative Weiblichkeitsentwürfe in den Diskurs einzuführen.

Aneignung, Resignifikation und Übersetzung im Exil

Dass im Exil stets Übersetzungsprozesse laufen—sprachliche, kulturelle und visuelle—wird seiner transkulturellen und multilingualen Bedingtheit zugeschrieben und wurde bereits in diversen wissenschaftlichen Studien untersucht.[12] Zwar konzentrieren sich diese Forschungsarbeiten weitgehend auf textuelle Übersetzungsabläufe, allerdings berücksichtigen

---

der Weimarer Republik, Hrsg. Ute Eskildes (Düsseldorf: Richter, 1994), S. 13–25; Gabriele Jatho und Rainer Rother, Hrsg., *City Girls. Frauenbilder im Stummfilm* (Berlin: Bertz+Fischer, 2007); Elizabeth Otto and Vanessa Rocco, Hrsg., *The New Woman International: Representations in Photography and Film from the 1870s through the 1960s* (Ann Arbor: University of Michigan Press, 2011).

12   Exemplarisch: Anne Benteler, *Sprache im Exil. Mehrsprachigkeit und Übersetzung als literarisches Verfahren bei Hilde Domin, Mascha Kaléko und Werner Lansburgh* (Stuttgart: J. B. Metzler, 2019; Aleksey Tashinskiy, Julija Boguna, und Tomasz Rozmysłowicz, Hrsg., *Translation und Exil (1933–1945) I: Namen und Orte. Recherchen zur Geschichte des Übersetzens* (Berlin: Frank & Timme, 2022).

einige auch kulturelle Dimensionen von Übersetzung und wenige Einzelstudien sogar visuelle Strategien.[13] Dass Übersetzung darüber hinaus mit der Aneignung spezifischer Merkmale einer Kultur, sowie auch von traditionell männlich besetzten, gesellschaftlichen Räumen einhergeht bzw. Aneignung schon als Bedingung für eine folgende Übersetzung zu verstehen ist, betonen Maud Anne Bracke, Penelope Morris und Emily Ryder in ihrer Studie *Translating Feminism: Transfer, Transgression, Transformation (1950s–1980s)*. Die Autorinnen adaptieren darin das Konzept der Aneignung und erweitern es durch jenes der Resignifikation, um Übersetzung als feministische Praxis zu beschreiben und der Frage nachzugehen, wie unterschiedliche Feminismen sich in transnationalen Kontexten transformieren. Sie argumentieren, dass „(s)uch approaches critically question well-established hierarchies between languages, cultures and societies on a global scale".[14] Auf diesem Wege würden sie zudem den etablierten Kanon daraufhin befragen, wie er sich durch „cultural and gender biases"[15] bestimme und Übersetzungsstrategien fokussieren, die einer sprachlichen und kulturellen Hierarchisierung entgegenwirken.

Wie ich im Folgenden zeige, muss auch die visuelle Übersetzungstätigkeit von Hedy Crilla und Irena Dodal als ein solches Hinterfragen, sowie ein damit einhergehender Versuch der Erweiterung des Kanons betrachtet werden. Schließlich nutzen sie ihre Kunst nicht nur, um sich von der geltenden Norm im peronistischen Argentinien abzusetzen, sondern auch um sich selbst, als marginalisierte Subjekte im Exil und künstlerisch tätige Frauen mit jüdischer Fluchterfahrung, darin einzuschreiben. Bevor ich

---

13 Vgl. Birgit Mersmann, *Über die Grenzen des Bildes. Kulturelle Differenz und transkulturelle Dynamik im globalen Feld der Kunst* (Bielefeld: Transcript, 2021); Birgit Mersmann und Alexandra Schneider, Hrsg., *Transmission Image: Visual Translation and Cultural Agency* (Newcastle: Cambridge Scholar Publishing, 2009); Claudia Benthien und Gabriele Klein, Hrsg., *Übersetzen und Rahmen. Praktiken medialer Transformationen* (Leiden: Wilhelm Fink, 2017).

14 Maud Anne Bracke, Penelope Morris, und Emily Ryder, "Introduction. Translating Feminism: Transfer, Transgression, Transformation (1950s–1980s)", *Gender & History* 30 (2018): 1, S. 214–25, S. 215.

15 Ibid.

diesen Punkt aber durch die Analyse ausgewählter Filmbeispiele weiter ausarbeite, soll noch kurz auf spezifisch visuelle Strategien der Übersetzung eingegangen werden.

Stärker noch als bei kulturellen Ansätzen der Übersetzung stellt sich bei visuellen Übersetzungsprozessen die Frage nach dem Original, das es zu übersetzen gilt. Folgt man hier den Überlegungen Walter Benjamins, der mit seinem Aufsatz „Die Aufgabe des Übersetzers" (1923) zentrale Vorarbeit für spätere kulturelle Übersetzungstheorien leistete, ist die Übersetzung als „zweite(r) Text, den die Übersetzung produziert, nicht als Abbild desselben Textes in einer anderen Sprache"[16] zu verstehen. Dies bedeutet, dass Original und Übersetzung als zwei separate Texte in Erscheinung treten, die nicht zuletzt durch ihren jeweiligen kulturellen Entstehungskontext determiniert sind. Benjamin plädiert deshalb dafür, das „Wesentliche" eines Textes— gleiches gilt natürlich für Bilder—ins Zentrum zu rücken und damit die essenzielle Aussage zu transportieren, ohne dabei das Original der Übersetzung überzuordnen.[17] Auch hier wiederholt sich also das Postulat von Bracke, Morris und Ryder, kulturelle Hierarchisierungen zu hinterfragen und vermehrt den Austausch gleichberechtigter kultureller Begegnungen zu fokussieren. Dass zudem Bilder selbst ein konkretes Mitteilungsbedürfnis in sich tragen, bringen Birgit Mersmann und Alexandra Schneider pointiert zum Ausdruck:

> Images are not produced in a no-man's land, and they do not circulate without purpose—as is often stressed in the context of the globalization debate. Images are directional forces; image transmissions also entail a transference of power. When we speak of "migrating" images, we have to be aware that these simultaneously emigrate and immigrate.[18]

16 Gudrun Rath, *Zwischenzonen. Theorie und Fiktionen der Übersetzung* (Wien: Turia+Kant, 2013), 7.

17 Walter Benjamin, „Die Aufgabe des Übersetzers (1923)", in *Walter Benjamin, Gesammelte Schriften, IV/1*, Hrsg. Rolf Tiedemann (Frankfurt/Main: Suhrkamp, 1972), S. 9–21, S. 9.

18 Birgit Mersmann und Alexandra Schneider, Hrsg., "Introduction", in *Transmission Image*, S. 1–9, S. 1 f.

Die spezifische Medialität visueller Erzeugnisse berücksichtigend, platzieren sie damit Bilder an der Schnittstelle von „cross-cultural encounters"[19] und damit zugleich an jenen transnationalen Zwischenzonen, an denen Übersetzung begleitet von Prozessen der Aneignung und Resignifikation stattfinden kann. Sie betonen außerdem ein weiteres Mal, dass Migration und Flucht von Individuen ebenso wenig wie von Bildern als lineare Bewegungen zu verstehen sind, sondern wiederum in einer netzwerkartigen Struktur auftreten.

Sichtbarkeit und (Selbst-)Übersetzung

Wie ich anhand der Filmarbeiten von Irena Dodal und Hedy Crilla zeige, handelt es sich bei diesen nicht nur um Übersetzungen eines spezifischen, (national-)kulturellen Wissens und den damit verbundenen Emanzipationsvorstellungen der Regisseurinnen. Es sind zugleich Formen der Selbstübersetzung, die das eigene Schaffen in ihren von Exilerfahrungen geprägten Biografien sichtbar machen. Damit sind sie als Versuch zu verstehen, sich einerseits in den neuen Kontext des Aufnahmelandes einzuschreiben und andererseits der bereits erwähnten selektiven Rezeption entgegenzuwirken, indem sie durch Übersetzung die Schaffensphasen vor und nach der Flucht durch ihr eigenes Schaffen miteinander verbinden. In der folgenden Analyse werde ich Irena Dodals *Ideas in Search for Light* mit ihrem späteren Werk *Apollon Musagete* (ARG 1952) in Verbindung bringen und zweitgenanntes als Übersetzung des ersten lesen. Damit wird *Apollon Musagete* zugleich zu einer Selbstübersetzung des eigenen Werks. Auch Hedy Crillas *Barrios y Teatros de Buenos Aires* wird als eine Form der Selbstübersetzung interpretiert, mit der zahlreiche weitere Übersetzungsprozesse kultureller

---

19   Ibid., S. 2.

und visueller Natur einhergehen—allerdings ohne sich dabei so stark wie
Dodal an einem Original zu orientieren.

Rein formal gleichen sich *Ideas in Search for Light* und *Apollon
Musagete* stark, sie weisen eine ähnliche dramaturgische Struktur, eine
vergleichbare Länge und das Grundthema von musikalisch untermauerten
Bewegungsabläufen auf. Eine tragende Rolle kommt dabei dem Einsatz von
Licht zu, der die Bewegungsmuster bzw. die Tanzschritte dramaturgisch
unterstützt und als politischer Hoffnungsträger inszeniert wird. Während
Ideas in Search for Light noch zwischen Prag und Paris produziert wurde,
allerdings bereits als frühes Exilwerk Dodals zu bezeichnen ist, ist *Apollon
Musagete* schon in Buenos Aires entstanden und integriert unterschiedliche Aspekte der argentinischen Kunstszene—so wurde der Film im bekannten Teatro Colón, einem prestigeträchtigen Theater, gedreht und mit
dort engagierten Tänzer*innen besetzt. Dies kann bereits als ein zentraler
Versuch der Aneignung und Beschäftigung mit der neuen Lokalität der
Übersetzerin gelesen werden.[20] Lokalität wird jedoch schon in *Ideas in
Search for Light* zentral behandelt, denn die Eingangssequenz verortet
die Produktion in einem transnationalen Zusammenhang und spricht ihr
durch den Verweis auf die Städte „Prague–Paris–New York" (Abb. 12)
einen kosmopolitischen Charakter zu. Dieser kosmopolitische Charakter,
der zugleich ein künstlerisches Vernetzungsanliegen betont und auf eine
visuelle Netzwerkstruktur Dodals Schaffen schließen lässt, wird zudem
dadurch unterstrichen, dass der Film im dramaturgischen Aufbau dem zu
Beginn des 20. Jahrhunderts beliebten Genre der Stadtsymphonien folgt.
Solche Stadtsymphonien wurden für Berlin, Paris, New York bis hin zu
Sao Paulo und Buenos Aires kreiert, zeugen also von einem internationa-
listischen Verständnis und waren ein beliebtes Format, um die städtische
Moderne mit den darin kursierenden Figuren vorzustellen. Bereits das
Genre, das sich in den 1930er Jahren in fast sämtlichen Metropolen und
Weltregionen wiederfindet, ist damit Ausdruck einer netzwerkartigen
Struktur des Kunstschaffens, die sich im Visuellen abbildet. Auch die *Neue*

20   Wie Bracke, Morris und Ryder argumentieren, ist die Berücksichtigung der
      Lokalität ein zentraler Faktor in Übersetzungsprozesse, vgl. Bracke/Morris/
      Ryder: Introduction. S. 223.

Frau war eine jener Figuren, die in den Stadtsymphonien als hoffnungsvolle Figur auftritt, mit der oftmals das Versprechen der Demokratisierung und Emanzipation einherging.

Vergleicht man nun *Ideas in Search for Light* mit dem späteren *Apollon Musagete*, der Dodals Schaffensphase in Buenos Aires entstammt, sticht insbesondere ein Merkmal hervor: In der visuellen Übersetzung ihrer Suche nach Licht durch *Apollon Musagete* verschwinden die Bezüge auf spezifische Orte. Es ist nicht mehr Prag, Paris oder New York, in denen sie oder ihre Protagonisten sich frei und gestaltend bewegen können. Vielmehr handelt es sich um einen luftleeren Raum, der möglicherweise aufgrund Dodals eigene Exilerfahrung keine genaue geografische Verortung zulässt. Innerhalb dieses Vakuums—welches darüber hinaus als Anspielung auf die Situation

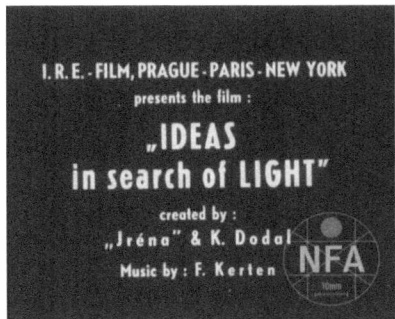
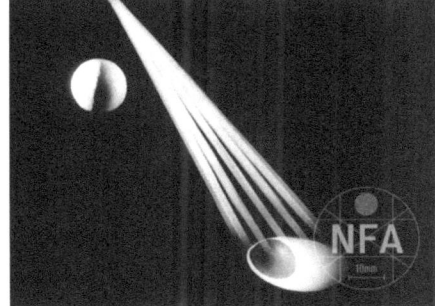
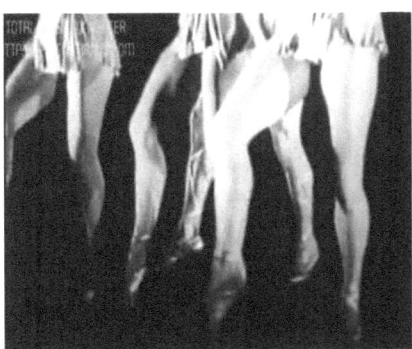
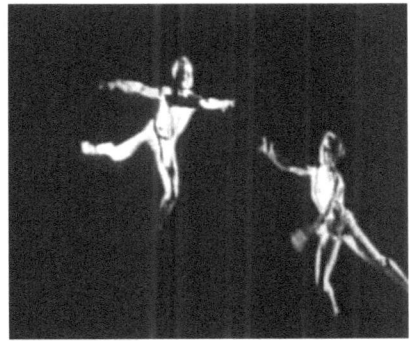

Abb. 12–15.   Oben: Stills aus *Ideas in Search for Light* (R: Irena Dodal, CS/FR 1938).
Unten: Stills aus *Apollon Musagete* (R: Irena Dodal, ARG 1952).

von Frauen im Peronismus ebenso wie auf ihre spezifische Erfahrung des Exils gelesen werden kann—treten jedoch weibliche Körper hervor, sich überlappende Gliedmaßen (Abb. 13–16), die zugleich eine Übersetzung Irenas Emanzipationsideals darstellen sowie als Anleitung zur Handlung, als Form der *agency* verstanden werden können.

Irena Dodals Übersetzungstätigkeit findet damit auf zwei Ebenen statt: Erstens übersetzt sie ein hoffnungsvoll demokratisches Prinzip, indem die Stadt—ehemals Prag, Paris und New York und später auch Buenos Aires—als Handlungsraum verstanden wird, der insbesondere für Frauen emanzipative Räume eröffnet. Schließlich adaptiert sie erneut das Genre der Stadtsymphonien, in dem die *Neue Frau* eine wiederkehrende Figur darstellt, die nicht zuletzt Irena Dodals Generation maßgeblich beeinflusste. Es kann darüber hinaus davon ausgegangen werden, dass sich Dodal selbst als Vertreterin der *Neuen Frau* verstand, schließlich war sie gebildet, durch ihr künstlerisches Schaffen ökonomisch unabhängig, sie war im Trend der Zeit und sexuell selbstbestimmt—sie erfüllte damit die essentiellen Charakteristika dieser modernen Figur, die jedoch aus den Darstellungen der peronistischen Propaganda weitgehend ausgeschlossen wurde. Zweitens—und dies schließt auch an vorab erörterten Punkt an—übersetzte Dodal ihr eigenes Werk, das bedingt durch ihre Flucht, die Erfahrungen im Ghetto Theresienstadt und das Exil Fragmentierung erlebte und damit drohte, in Vergessenheit zu geraten. Die visuelle Übersetzung von *Ideas in Search for Light* in Form von *Apollon Musagete* ist also mehr als eine autobiografische Referenz, sie ist eine Adaptierung ihres eigenen Stoffs, der durch Aneignung und Resignifikation an die neue Umgebung angepasst wurde. Selbstübersetzung im Falle von Irena Dodal ist damit auch eine Form der Selbstdarstellung, die wiederum als Resultat ihrer künstlerischen Sozialisation im frühen 20. Jahrhundert gelesen werden kann. Schließlich eigneten sich junge Künstlerinnen ab den 1920er Jahren mehr und mehr Strategien an, um das männlich dominierte Genre des Selbstporträts emanzipatorisch umzudeuten. Anschließend an die Argumentation der Kultur- und Literaturwissenschaftlerin Elisabeth Bronfen kann Selbstübersetzung dementsprechend ebenso wie das Selbstporträt als Strategie gedeutet werden, die nicht nur dokumentiert, dass es eine Künstlerin in der Vergangenheit bereits gegeben hatte und sie zudem in der Gegenwart des

Exils agiert, sondern auch mit Blick auf die Zukunft, „daß es sie gegeben haben wird".[21]

Eine ähnliche Form der Selbstübersetzung findet sich bei Hedy Crillas *Barrios y Teatros de Buenos Aires*, ein Film, der wiederum unterschiedliche Seiten ihres Selbst übersetzt, allerdings nicht primär mit dem Anliegen, ein argentinisches Publikum zu adressieren, sondern ein europäisches in den 1960er Jahren. Der Film ist eine Produktion aus dem Jahr 1962 und wie der Titel bereits vermuten lässt, gibt er dokumentarisch Einblick in die Theater und Stadtteile von Buenos Aires. Hedy Crilla agierte in dem Film in unterschiedlichen Rollen, als Produzentin, Regisseurin, Autorin. Außerdem tritt sie selbst als Schauspielerin auf. Als Teil einer Gruppe von Schauspieler*innen, die alle aus dem Ensemble von *La Mascara*— einem Freien Theater, in dem Crilla unterrichtete—stammen, erkundet sie im Film die Theater und Viertel der Stadt. Der Opening Shot zeigt Buenos Aires in der Horizontalen im Morgengrauen, die Dächer, die Straßen, die Weitläufigkeit. Daran anknüpfend wird die Gruppe von Schauspieler*innen von oben fokussiert und anschließend springt der Schnitt zu Großaufnahmen der Gesichter. Wiederum folgt der Film also dem Genre der Stadtsymphonien und begleitet die Gruppe von morgens bis abends auf ihrem Weg durch Theater, Parks und Gassen. Wie vorab erwähnt, ist allerdings bemerkenswert, dass der Film nicht für ein argentinisches, sondern für ein europäisches Publikum produziert wurde. Denn er sollte 1962 während Crillas Europa-Reise in Wien gezeigt werden. Hedy Crilla reiste in diesem Jahr das erste Mal seit ihrer Flucht nach Europa und besuchte u.a. ihre Geburtsstadt, wo sie im Zuge eines Vortrags am Theaterhistorischen Institut den Film präsentierte. Der Film ist damit mehr als eine reine Selbstübersetzung, er ist ein Versuch der Rückübersetzung und Sichtbarmachung dessen, was die Schauspielerin und Regisseurin in den Jahren des Exils in Buenos Aires erschaffen hatte, ihrer Rollen, die sie spielte—als Regisseurin, Lehrerin und Schauspielerin—und ihrer Funktion im Prozess der Modernisierung des argentinischen Theaters.

21   Elisabeth Bronfen, „Frauen sehen Frauen sehen Frauen", in *Frauen sehen Frauen. Eine Bildgeschichte der Frauen-Photographie*, Hrsg. Lothar Schirmer (München: Schirmer Mosel, 2020), S. 9–28, S. 21.

Es überrascht deshalb kaum, dass Crilla Buenos Aires als moderne, dynamische und technisch versierte Metropole von kosmopolitischem Charakter präsentiert (Abb. 17–19), schließlich nahm sie an, auf diesem Wege ihren eigenen Verdiensten Nachdruck verleihen zu können. In gewisser Weise zeigt Crilla Buenos Aires als Gesamtkunstwerk, die Architektur der Stadt, ihre Theater, die darin ausgestellte Kunst sowie sich selbst—ebenfalls als Kunstfigur—, die ihre Umgebung kreativ gestaltet (Abb. 20–22). Sie präsentiert sich neben ihren Schüler*innen als Figur, die sich quasi organisch im urbanen Umfeld von Buenos Aires bewegt, mit jenem Selbstbewusstsein und emanzipativen Gestus, wie sie von der *Neue Frau* in den Medien der 1920er und 1930er Jahre vorgelebt wurden. Zwar ist über die weitere Rezeption des Films nichts bekannt, allerdings kann aufgrund fehlender Unterlagen davon ausgegangen werden, dass er wenig erfolgreich blieb und das österreichische Publikum in den 1960er Jahren nicht breitenwirksam anzusprechen vermochte. Schließlich lag ihm ein Kunstverständnis zugrunde, das Crilla vor ihrer Flucht kennengelernt hatte und das durch die Jahre der nationalsozialistischen Kulturpolitik weitestgehend zerstört war. Obgleich Teile dieses demokratischen Moderneverständnisses im Exil überleben und sich transformieren und weiterentwickeln konnten, bildete es nicht mehr die Grundlage für Aneignung und Resignifikation im zentraleuropäischen Kontext, um damit eine zielgerichtete Übersetzung leisten zu können. Hinzu kam eine zutiefst eurozentristische Grundhaltung, die die argentinische Kunstproduktion keineswegs als gleichwertig ansah. Österreich war schließlich nach 1945 weitgehend zur nationalisierten und restriktiven Kulturpolitik der Vorkriegsjahre—die sich nicht unwesentlich auf die Kulturpolitik des Austrofaschismus bezog[22] und durch die Rückbesinnung auf die Selbstpositionierung als große Kulturnation auszeichnete—zurückgekehrt. Letztendlich wurden auch emanzipative Entwürfe wie die *Neue Frau* durch die Rekatholisierung des Landes weitgehend aus dem öffentlichen Raum verdrängt.[23] Crilla stieß mit ihrem

22   Vgl. Klaus Kastberger, „Wien 1950/1960. Eine österreichische Avantgarde," in *Die fünfziger Jahre: Kunst und Kunstverständnis in Wien*, Hrsg. Berthold Ecker (Wien: Springer, 2010), S. 35–46.

23   Vgl. Irene Bandhauer-Schöffmann und Claire Duchen, Hrsg., *Nach dem Krieg. Frauenleben und Geschlechterkonstruktionen in Europa nach dem Zweiten Weltkrieg* (= Forum Frauengeschichte, Band 23) (Herbolzheim: Centaurus Verlag, 2000).

Anliegen der Sichtbarmachung ihres Schaffens im Exil in Wien kaum auf Interesse und ihr Versuch der Selbstübersetzung, der wiederum als Reaktion auf die Bruchstückhaftigkeit ihrer biografischen Erzählung zu verstehen ist, muss demnach als gescheitert erklärt werden. Weder gelang es ihr, trotz vorab laufender Korrespondenzen langfristige Kontakte zu Wiener Theatern zu knüpfen, noch wurde ihr Film abgesehen von der Aufführung im Theaterhistorischen Institut in Wien an weiteren Stellen gezeigt oder öffentlich besprochen. Die Schauspielerin kehrte nach Buenos Aires zurück, ohne in Wien je wieder künstlerisch Anschluss zu finden. Die Anerkennung ihrer künstlerischen Verdienste blieb ihr bis heute verwehrt.

Die visuellen Nachleben des Exils

Wie anhand der Arbeiten von Hedy Crilla und Irena Dodal gezeigt wurde, entwickelten diese Frauen unterschiedliche Strategien der visuellen und kulturellen Übersetzung und Selbstübersetzung innerhalb ihres Werks—z.B. indem sie ihre eigenen Filmarbeiten übersetzten, sich selbst innerhalb ihres Schaffens in unterschiedlichen Rollen inszenierten oder sich auf frühere Kontexte des Schaffens vor ihrer Flucht bezogen, ohne aber dabei zu vergessen, ihre jeweilige Lokalität zu reflektieren. Auf diese Weise stellen die Übersetzungsversuche von Crilla und Dodal stets auch eine Verbindung zu ihrer vom Exil geprägten Biografie her, die durch Flucht und Vertreibung einen bruchstückhaften Charakter aufweisen. Das Übersetzungsanliegen dieser Künstlerinnen kann demnach als Versuch gedeutet werden, diese Fragmentierung ihrer Biografie und ihres Werks nicht noch weiter fortzuschreiben und durch Selbstdarstellungen und -übersetzungen ihr Werk in Vergangenheit, Gegenwart und Zukunft sichtbar zu machen. Sie taten dies mit dem Selbstbewusstsein der *Neuen Frau*, einer Figur, die insbesondere in den visuellen Medien der 1920er und 1930er Jahre als Idealvorstellung auftauchte und ebenso von Crilla und Dodal durch ihre Bezüge auf deren städtische Verortung übersetzt und in neue Kontexte eingeschrieben wurde. Übersetzung, dies haben die Arbeiten von Crilla und Dodal gezeigt, ist ein Prozess, der

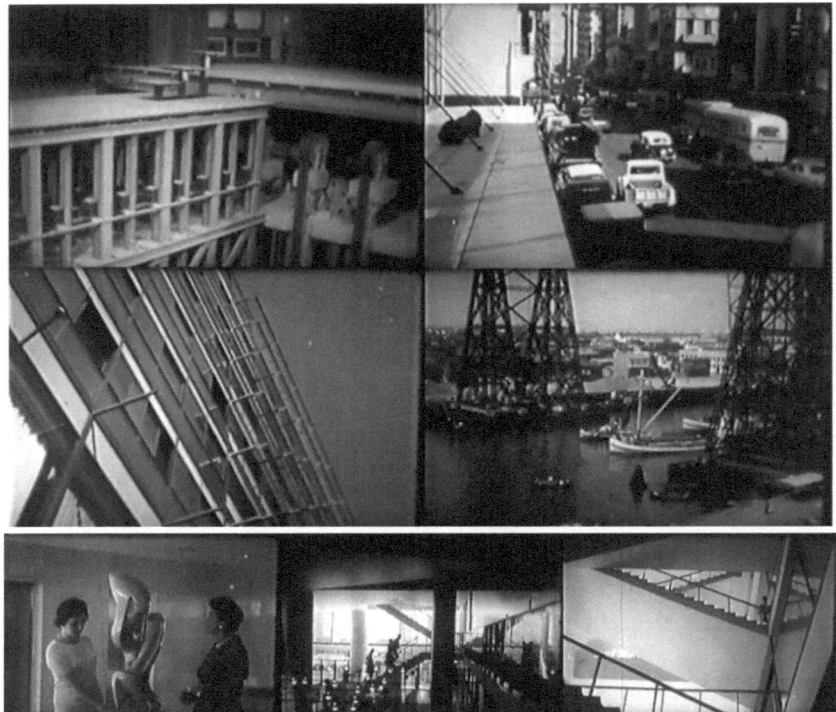

Abb. 16–22. Stills aus *Barrios y Teatros de Buenos Aires* (R: Hedy Crilla, ARG 1962).

mit Aneignung und Resignifikation einhergeht und der insbesondere
in Form der Selbstübersetzung Akteurinnen mit Handlungsmacht aus-
stattet. Die beiden Künstlerinnen erkundeten diese Handlungsmacht
nicht nur, um visuelle Verbindungen zwischen ihren früheren Arbeiten
und ihrem Werk im Exil herzustellen und damit eine transkulturelle
Vernetzung ihres Kunstschaffens weiter vorantreiben, sondern auch, um
dem Vergessen ihres künstlerischen und emanzipatorischen Wirkens
in ihren Herkunftsländern entgegenzuwirken. Sie legten durch ihre
Selbstübersetzungsbestrebungen also eigeninitiativ den Grundstein, um
ihr von Transnationalität geprägtes Werk in seiner Gesamtheit erfassen
zu können. Schließlich wollten sie auch im Exil nicht nur passiv in einem
bereits prädeterminierten visuellen Netzwerk verharren, sondern es aktiv

mitgestalten, indem sie emanzipatorische Ideen kulturell und visuell übersetzen. Diese Arbeiten bilden also nicht zuletzt selbst ein visuelles Netzwerk, das europäische und argentinische kulturelle Kontexte miteinander verknüpft und zugleich exiliertes Kunstschaffen auf einer bildlichen Ebene zusammenführt.

MARGRIT FRÖLICH

12 More Than a Brand Name: Lenya

ABSTRACT

When Lotte Lenya arrived in New York in 1935, together with her husband, the Jewish composer Kurt Weill, after they had fled from Nazi Germany, their artistic careers were broken. In Berlin at the end of the 1920s, Kurt Weill had been a steady musical collaborator with Bertolt Brecht. Lotte Lenya was a star performer in some of Brecht's plays, best known for her role as Jenny in the legendary theater production of the *Threepenny Opera* (1928). There was no guarantee that Lenya and Weill would succeed in the United States, irrespective of their celebrity status in Europe. This chapter explores the factors that affected Lenya's career in America. It examines why Lenya failed to establish herself at first, only to reemerge, against all odds, after Kurt Weill's death. It discusses how she became a cult figure: a genial interpreter of the works of Brecht and Weill, but also a musical and film star.

Who will not remember forever the switchblade sticking out from the tip of the black lace-up medium high heel shoe? Venom-coated, the tiny steely dagger embedded in the shoe, is meant to kill James Bond. The footwear belongs to none other than the actress and singer Lotte Lenya, a living icon of Berlin's avant-garde musical theater of the late 1920s. In *From Russia with Love*, the second in the series of Bond films, released in 1963, she plays Colonel Rosa Klebb, former head of the Soviet secret service who defected and joined SPECTRE, the globally operating criminal organization in the movie. Lenya was the first female villain in the James Bond film series. With her short copper-colored hair parted on the side and flat against her head, wearing a uniform covered with awards and decorations above the left breast pocket, her demeanor emanates an air of severity, if not cruelty. The character's lesbianism, more pronounced in Ian Fleming's book than in the film, is implied in a scene, in which Rosa Klebb recruits the beautiful female Russian embassy clerk Tatiana Romanova for a mission that requires Tatiana to act as bait and seduce James Bond in a honeypot operation.

Explaining the task, Klebb casually places her hand on Tatiana's leg. In the final showdown scene, after the original plan to take down James Bond failed, Klebb appears in the disguise of a chambermaid in the hotel room in Venice, where Bond and Tatiana are lodging, and attempts to steal a Lektor decoding machine now in the possession of Bond that SPECTRE wants to sell back to the Soviets. Bond and Klebb battle with each other, and she nearly succeeds in killing him with the switchblade in her shoe, but is fatally shot by Tatiana, who has fallen in love with James Bond.

The lush blockbuster spy thriller from the Cold War era was Lenya's most famous role in a film, immortalizing her in the popular memory as "the lady with the knife in her shoes," albeit viewers of the Bond film may or may not have known who Lotte Lenya was. Many accomplished actors to this day would love to be cast as a villain in a Bond film. How did it happen that Lenya was chosen to play in such a high-profile movie that turned out to be one of the most celebrated James Bond films of all times? After all, Lenya was nearly 65 years of age at the time, and her career had been stalled after she arrived in New York in 1935, together with her husband, the Jewish composer Kurt Weill. In this chapter, I will explore the impact of exile on Lotte Lenya's artistic development, focusing on her experiences in the United States, and discuss the following questions: what factors affected Lenya's performing career in American exile, and to what extent did gender, age, and especially her non-native English impinge upon it? I will examine the dynamics that enabled Lenya to relaunch her career after Kurt Weill's premature death in 1950, and what accounted for her stunning success in the 1950s and 1960s. Examining these questions will give us further insight into how Lenya's artistic sensibilities brought together European modernism with commercial American culture in productive ways.

Breakthrough in Berlin, 1928

Lotte Lenya, born in 1898 as Karoline Wilhelmine Charlotte Blamauer into a poor Viennese family with a violent father, made history with her performance in the legendary production of *The Threepenny Opera*.[1] The musical opera, a collaboration between Bertolt Brecht and Kurt Weill, which Brecht's long-term associate Elisabeth Hauptmann had adapted from John Gay's early eighteenth-century *Beggars Opera*, became a surprise sensation after its premiere on August 31, 1928, at the Theater am Schiffbauerdamm in Berlin. Lenya's breathtaking performance in the role of Jenny, a prostitute, who for money and out of jealousy betrays her lover, the gangster Mack the Knife, to the police, catalyzed epochal excitement.[2] Lenya brought an unusual simplicity and a simultaneous ingenuity to the stage, her eroticism mesmerized audiences.

The stunning success of *The Threepenny Opera* put Lenya on the map of Berlin's theater world. She subsequently performed in a number of works by other authors, for instance, in Lion Feuchtwanger's *Die Petroleuminseln* (*The Oil Islands*) (1928), for which Kurt Weill wrote the music; in Paul Kornfeld's stage adaptation of Feuchtwanger's novel *Jew Süß*, directed by Leopold Jessner (1930); in Frank Wedekind's *Frühlings Erwachen* (*Spring Awakening*) (1929); and in Marie-Luise Fleisser's *Pioniere in Ingolstadt* (*Pioneers in Ingolstadt*) (1929), to name a few. She also starred in *Aufstieg und Fall der Stadt Mahagonny* (*Rise and Fall of the City of Mahagonny*) (1931), developed from an earlier shorter "Songspiel" (1927), another collaboration with Brecht and Weill. In G. W. Pabst's film adaptation of *The Threepenny Opera* (*Die 3-Groschen-Oper*) (1931), one of the first German sound films, Lenya played the role of prostitute Jenny, as she did in the original stage production. She sang the song of Pirate Jenny, which in the original theater production was performed by the character of Polly Peachum. The song became Lenya's signature song.

Kurt Weill's music was tailor-made for Lenya's voice that Weill had praised in these words: "[W]hen I feel this longing for you, I think most

---

1   Her stage name "Lenya" was derived from her Austrian nickname "Linnerl," tweaked with a Russian sounding twist.

2   Adding to *The Threepenny Opera*'s popularity was the release of an audio record in 1930, which included most numbers from the stage production interpreted by members of the original cast.

of all of the sound of your voice, which I love like a very force of nature, like an element."[3] Lenya's soprano voice, untrained, and not beautiful in a conventional sense, but rich in modulation, almost like the voice of a child, radiated both delicacy and roughness, an unsentimental coolness, when expressing somber realities of human and social existence. The seductiveness of Lenya's performance in *The Threepenny Opera* and its epochal cultural impact has been compared to that of Marlene Dietrich as Lola-Lola in the 1930 musical film drama *The Blue Angel*.[4] The same night when *The Blue Angel* premiered in Berlin on April 1, 1930, Dietrich boarded a train to head for Hollywood, a contract with Paramount Pictures in her hands. Dietrich starred in American films such as *Morocco* (1930), *Dishonored* (1931), *Shanghai Express* (1932), *Blonde Venus* (1932), and *The Scarlett Empress* (1934), all directed by the established Hollywood film director Josef von Sternberg, who had directed *The Blue Angel* for Paramount's sister studio Ufa in Berlin, and with whom she created her highly stylized screen image.[5] In March 1934, Weill, struggling in exile near Paris, was happy to receive a telegram from Marlene Dietrich in which she asked: "Would you be interested in coming here and working with Sternberg and me on a musical film."[6] These plans never materialized. For Lenya and Weill there was no guarantee that they would succeed in the United States, irrespective of their celebrity status in Europe.

3   Lys Symonette and Kim H. Kowalke, eds, *Speak Low (When You Speak Love): The Letters of Kurt Weill and Lotte Lenya* (London: Hamish Hamilton, 1996), No. 15 (July 1926?), 48.

4   Günther Rühle, "Der Auftritt der Jenny: Lotte Lenya wird achtzig Jahre alt," in *Frankfurter Allgemeine Zeitung*, October 14, 1978.

5   Karin Wieland, *Dietrich & Riefenstahl, and a Century in Two Lives* (New York: Liveright Publications, 2015), 171–257.

6   Symonette and Kowalke, eds, *Speak Low*, No. 67 (March 3–6, 1934), 115.

Starting a New Life: New York, 1935

Lotte Lenya and Kurt Weill, the divorced and soon-to-be-remarried couple, arrived in New York on September 10, 1935, full of enthusiasm for American culture.[7] A dress rehearsal of George Gershwin's *Porgy and Bess* they attended inspired Weill to reach for the creative musical possibilities America offered. More than most European émigrés, he eagerly plunged into American life. Over the next fifteen years, Weill's American musical career blossomed, and he launched a string of successful musical projects, composing for Broadway and Hollywood. These works included, among others, *Johnny Johnson* (1936), *Knickerbocker Holiday* (1938), *Lady in the Dark* (1940), *One Touch of Venus* (1943), *Street Scene* (1946), *Love Life* (1947/48), *Down in the Valley* (1948), and *Lost in the Stars* (1949). He also wrote the music for Fritz Lang's film *You and Me*, Weill's first Hollywood movie, released in 1938 by Paramount Pictures. By contrast, Lenya's American career did not amount to much.

---

7   The relationship between Weill and Lenya had become increasingly complicated, and Lenya, who was having an affair with the tenor Otto Pasetti, filed for divorce on June 23, 1933, when both she and Weill had already left Germany. The divorce was granted by a Berlin court on September 18, 1933. The tone of the correspondence between Weill and Lenya continued to be loving and tender throughout this period. Lenya's biographer Donald Spoto therefore suggests that the divorce may have been a tactical maneuver so that Lenya, who returned to Berlin in August of 1933, could sell Weill's house and retrieve his possessions without raising the suspicion of the German authorities. Pasetti, however, embezzled part of Weill's money, and the affair with Lenya ended. In 1935, Weill, against the advice of his friends, invited Lenya to come with him to New York. Only two days before the scheduled departure on September 4, 1935, Lenya arrived in Paris. The couple, although officially divorced, traveled to New York as Mr. and Mrs. Kurt Weill. On January 19, 1937, they remarried in North Castle in the State of New York. Donald Spoto, *Lenya: A Life*, Boston, Toronto, London: Little, Brown and Company, 1989, 110, 113–14, 120, 131–2; see also Lenya's own account: David Farneth, *Lenya: The Legend: A Pictorial Autobiography* (Woodstock: The Overlock Presse, 1998), 79, 95–6. Jens Rosteck argues that Lenya's motivation to file for divorce remains enigmatic. Jens Rostock, *Zwei auf einer Insel: Lenya und Kurt Weil* (Berlin: Propyläen, 1999), 156/161, 186–9, 210–11.

On December 17, 1935, the New York League of Composers sponsored an evening dedicated to Weill's works. Yet the concert, attended by New York's musical world, with Lenya singing highlights from works Weill had composed in Berlin and during his exile in Paris, was unsuccessful, as half of the audience left during the intermission.[8] The hype *The Threepenny Opera* had generated across Germany and Europe had never reached the United States. A Broadway production of the work in April 1933 had flopped due to a bad translation and a weak production.

The concert at the League of Composers showed that Lenya's talent did not easily transfer to American audiences. The American composer Marc Blitzstein, however, who had studied with Arnold Schoenberg, and who three decades later played a decisive role in catapulting Lenya to stardom with his new adaption of *The Threepenny Opera*, praised Lenya's American debut. He captured Lenya's unusual qualities as a performer and detected the difficulties she would have in carving out an American career. Blitzstein wrote that Lenya

> is too special a talent, I am afraid, for a wide American appeal; but she has magnetism and a raw lovely voice like a boy-soprano. Her stylized gestures seem strange because of her natural warmth; but in the strangeness lies the slight enigma which is her charm.[9]

Lotte Lenya's Career Trouble in America

Lenya and Weill had lived in the United States for almost a decade, yet Lenya still took note of the different styles of American musical shows and her own approach. After seeing the popular American singer Gertrude Niesen in a Broadway show in June of 1944, Lenya praised her to Weill:

---

8   Jürgen Schebera, *Kurt Weill* (Reinbek: Rowohlt, 2000), 104.
9   Marc Blitzstein, "New York Medley, Winter 1935," in *Modern Music* 13/2 (January–February 1936), 36, cited in Howard Pollack, *Marc Blitzstein: His Life, His Work, His World* (Oxford: Oxford University Press, 2012), 156.

Sings beautifully with a very deep voice and completely relaxed and like a fish in clear water. (…) You know how excited I can get, when I see something good on the stage. But I saw also, how very, very different it is, when they sing songs. I don't think I ever can learn that. Or somebody would have to teach me.[10]

Lenya's first role in an American theater production was in *The Eternal Road*, a Jewish oratorio based on biblical motives. This project had brought Weill and Lenya to the United States in 1935. Weill, the son of a Jewish cantor from Dessau who was familiar with the Jewish liturgical music, had been contracted to compose the music. The pageant, directed by Max Reinhardt, with the original text written by Franz Werfel, was postponed at least ten times before it finally opened on January 7, 1937, in the Manhattan Opera House. The small part that Weill had secured for Lenya got more and more reduced in the process.[11] Lenya played Miriam, the sister of Moses, performing a song Weill had written for her. Not surprisingly her performance in the giant spectacle, with over two hundred performers involved, went unnoticed by the press.

Lenya's severe difficulties with the English language hampered her American career.[12] Cheryl Crawford, a theater producer and director who knew the couple from their association with the Group Theatre collective in New York,[13] observed that Lenya did not show much professional ambition, at least not publicly, which let Crawford to assume that Lenya "seemed content without being a big star."[14] For Weill, who enjoyed the opportunities coming his way, although he experienced occasional setbacks, especially in Hollywood, it was not simple to secure parts for Lenya. The American music conductor Maurice Abravanel remembers when he encouraged Weill to write an opera, Weill replied: "First I must write something

10 Symonette and Kowalke, eds, *Speak Low*, No. 310 (June 26, 1944), 371. After 1935, Weill and Lenya gradually began to communicate in English; occasional grammatical errors or stylistic awkwardness reflect the wording of the original letters.

11 Spoto, *Lenya: A Life*, 124.

12 Sanders, *The Days Grow Short*, 338.

13 Schebera, *Kurt Weill*, 105–6.

14 Spoto, *Lenya: A Life*, 129.

for Lenya."[15] However, as a composer Weill had to write the musical score and did not have leeway to add characters that Lenya was suited to play. The more deeply his projects were rooted in an American narrative setting, the slimmer such chances became. Yet Weill, although he was ambitious to shape his own success, tried to promote Lenya whenever he got the chance. In a letter dated April 2, 1937, Weill sent from Hollywood to Lenya in New York, he wrote:

> Just now, Elisabeth Meyer (…) called and asked me if I knew of a European actress (with an accent) for a role at Selznik [sic] International. Of course, I recommended you right away. (…) I told them you were the Luise Rainer type, and just as good an actress: for certain things even better. (…) If they like your pictures, they'll have you come out for a *test*. I don't know if anything will come of it, but in general I'm convinced you have a good chance.[16]

When Lenya considered having her teeth modified in order to comply with Hollywood female beauty ideals, Weill talked her out of it, arguing that

> it doesn't make sense to undergo such a strenuous ordeal for the vague possibility of a movie. Regardless of the movies, I don't even know whether it would be right for your face, because your teeth lend character to your face just as they are and certainly enhance your personality on stage.[17]

Nothing transpired for Lenya, and after *The Eternal Road* ended in May 1937, she did not get cast as an actress until 1941, neither in Hollywood nor on Broadway.

At least Marc Blitzstein cast Lenya for his radio opera *I've got the Tune*. Commissioned by CBS Radio, the thirty-minute production was broadcast live on October 24, 1937, in the radio station's experimental series, the Columbia Workshop.[18] Blitzstein's radio opera, dedicated to Orson

---

15   Maurice Abravanel, cited in Ronald Sanders, *The Days Grow Short: The Life of Kurt Weill* (New York: Holt, Rinehart and Winston, 1980), 338.

16   Symonette and Kowalke, eds, *Speak Low*, No. 177 (April 2, 1937), 227.

17   Ibid., No. 188 (May 17?, 1937), 241.

18   Pollack, *Marc Blitzstein*, 199–205.

Welles, who originally was supposed to play a part in it, stands out for its artistic ambition and radiogenic qualities, and it was reviewed positively in musical journals. In Blitzstein's lyrical radio opera, Lenya plays "The Suicide." The sadness of the song she performs is touching, her tender high-pitched voice captivating, while the song's complex melody gives evidence of Lenya's musical talent.[19]

Ups and Downs in America

The following year, starting in April 1938, Lenya had a month-long engagement at the fashionable New York nightclub Le Ruban Bleu, where Cole Porter and Marlene Dietrich attended some of her performances. "Last night Marlene (…) just showed up," Lenya wrote to Weill in Hollywood.

> She looked marvelous and was unbelievably nice to me (…), she said quite loudly, *"how wonderful,"* and applauded like crazy (…). She brought me over to her table. Well you should have seen all the others.[20]

Lenya's repertoire at the nightclub included, in addition to songs by Weill, also a song Marc Blitzstein had written for her, "Few Little English," which was popular with the audiences at the nightclub. It is a humorous song about a gangster bride from Europe who lives with a Chicago gangster and tricks her lover's rival, as well as the FBI, by pretending that she doesn't speak enough English.[21] Lenya's heavy German accent perfectly matched the song's narrative. Lenya quickly grew tired of performing in the nightclub. "If nightclubs were my only ambition, I would be totally content," she wrote to Weill. "But thank God, I've got other fish to fry."[22] Summing up her experience at the nightclub, she concludes: "It didn't do

---

19   Marc Blitzstein "I've Got the Tune," <https://www.youtube.com/watch?v=IMH8 9xEy5XE> (18:05–22:30) (last accessed June 1, 2023).

20   Symonette and Kowalke, eds, *Speak Low*, No. 201 (April 28, 1938), 257.

21   Pollack, *Marc Blitzstein*, 156–7.

22   Symonette and Kowalke, eds, *Speak Low*, No. 207 (May 8, 1938), 264.

me any harm, and I've learned a lot, but so far it hasn't done me any good, and I hated it more than any previous work."[23]

It took three additional years until Lenya appeared on a theater stage again. The American writer, Maxwell Anderson, Lenya's and Weill's neighbor and friend in New City in Rockland County, New York, where they made their home, helped out. Anderson had successfully collaborated with Weill on the musical comedy *Knickerbocker Holiday* (1938) and out of friendship he added a small role for Lenya to his play *Candle in the Wind*. In this drama about the Nazi invasion of France, with Helen Hays in the leading role, Lenya played an Austrian maid named Cissie.[24] When the show opened in October 1941 at the Shubert Theatre on Broadway under the direction of Alfred Lunt the *New York Times* theater critic Brooks Atkinson wrote: "Lotte Lenya plays the part of a continental servant with the patient weariness of experience."[25] After its New York run, Lenya went on tour with the production through the American Midwest and parts of the south until May of 1942. Weill encouraged his wife: "There is no doubt in my mind that you can be a terrific success in this country if we only get the right play."[26] Lenya replied: "(…) I discovered my love for acting again. I had forgotten how much of an actress I am all those years sitting still."[27]

In 1943, the first music album Lenya recorded in the United States was released. It included six Weill songs, newly arranged by the composer, which she sang in three different languages, English, French, and German.[28] That same year, Lenya also participated in an ambitious concert program entitled "We fight back!" along with many other German-speaking émigrés. The concert, intended to support the war effort, took place at Hunter College on April 3, 1943, and was broadcast by Voice of America. Lenya made a mark singing a Brecht poem, "Und was bekam des Soldaten Weib?

23   Ibid.
24   Alfred S. Shivers, *Maxwell Anderson* (Boston: Twayne Publishers, 1976), 56–7; Farneth, *Lenya: The Legend*, 101.
25   Symonette and Kowalke, eds, *Speak Low*, 274.
26   Ibid., No. 232 (February 12, 1942), 292.
27   Ibid., No. 233 (February 13, 1942), 293.
28   Farneth, *Lotte Lenya: The Legend*, 104.

("What Did the Soldier's Wife Receive?"). Weill had written the music and accompanied Lenya on the piano.[29]

Another acting opportunity came Lenya's way in July 1944, when Weill announced to his wife: "I am going to have a showdown with Ira today about you."[30] At the time, Weill was working in Los Angeles, on a play entitled *The Firebrand of Florence*, together with Edwin Justus Mayer and Ira Gershwin. Weill wanted Lenya to get cast in the production: "I told him (…) that I had been waiting to find a part for you for years, that I was sure this is the part and that I am determined to have you play it."[31] Excited about the project, Weill wrote to his wife:

> The whole thing looks quite exciting and it looks as if it could develop into one of the most interesting projects I worked on. It probably will become almost an opera because I hear music almost all the way through, except for the comedy part.[32]

In this drama set in Florence in 1535 about the sculptor Benvenuto Cellini, Weill wanted Lenya to play the part of the Duchess. He fought with producers and his collaborators to get his wish granted, writing to Lenya: "You know I wouldn't do it if I wouldn't be convinced that you are ideal for the part."[33] Lenya, who depended on her husband to promote her, assured him of her reliability as an actress: "As soon as my feet hit the stage—I am safe as you know. I just have to get there."[34]

Given the high hopes Weill had for the production and for Lenya playing the Duchess, it must have been devastating, when the production, which opened on March 22, 1945, at the Alvin Theatre on Broadway, flopped.[35] It was Weill's only failure on Broadway. On the last day of the show, Weill, back in Hollywood, wrote to Lenya at home: "I am sad when

---

29   Ibid., 104: James K. Lyon, *Bertolt Brecht in America* (Princeton: Princeton University Press, 1980), 274.

30   Symonette and Kowalke, eds, *Speak Low*, No. 325 (July 17, 1944), 392.

31   Ibid., No. 326 (July 17, 1944), 393.

32   Ibid., No. 315 (July 3, 1944), 378.

33   Ibid., No. 325 (July 17, 1944), 393.

34   Ibid., No. 318 (July 7, 1944), 381.

35   Farneth, *Lotte Lenya: The Legend*, 105.

I think about it, but I know it's no use getting upset again."[36] Lenya had been perceived by many critics as miscast and was torn up by the press. Weill tried to console his wife, telling her about friends, "who loved your performance," admitting to her that "the show was killed by the production. (…) The only thing I regret is that you were involved in it (…)."[37] The casting for the production had not worked out as hoped, Weill couldn't get their friend Moss Hart to direct the piece, and some performers turned out weaker than expected.[38] Instead of the Vienna-born Hollywood actor Walter Slezak whom Weill had wanted for the role of the Duke, the British actor Melville Cooper was cast. Cooper was ill-suited for the role and did not harmonize with Lenya, therefore the performance lacked the seductiveness it required.[39] After the disastrous outcome, Lenya withdrew from acting, insisting: "Kurt, no, listen to me. This was the last time you try to write for me in this country. Just forget about me. I'll do whatever you need for your comfort."[40] Five years later when Weill's musical work, *Lost in the Stars*, was still running on Broadway, and his music for a musical play based on Huckleberry Finn was yet to be completed, he suddenly died of a heart attack, at age 50, on April 3, 1950.

Emerging from Obscurity, 1950 and After

After Kurt Weill's death, Lenya's career took an unexpected turn. The driving force behind her stunning revival was George Davis, who became Lenya's second husband. "He is the one who really started my second career," she said.[41] When Weill died, Lenya fell into a deep

36   Symonette and Kowalke, eds, *Speak Low*, No. 372 (April 28, 1945), 454.
37   Ibid., No. 368, April 14, 1945, 450.
38   Ibid., 447; Philip Furia, *Ira Gershwin: The Art of the Lyricist* (New York: Oxford University Press, 1996), 191.
39   Farneth, *Lotte Lenya: The Legend*, 105.
40   Ibid.
41   Ibid., 128.

depression: "After Kurt died, I really sank to the bottom of the ocean," she admitted.[42] When Brecht, six years later, died of a heart attack in East Berlin, and Lenya sent her condolences to his widow, the actress Helene Weigel, she recalled her experience after her husband's death: "Als Weill so plötzlich starb, konnte ich auch so gar keinen Sinn mehr in meinem weiteren Dasein sehen. Es dauert lange, bis man wieder zu sich kommt, aber es geschieht." ["When Weill died so suddenly I also couldn't see any meaning anymore in my further existence. It takes a long time until you more or less come around again, but it happens."][43] George Davis helped Lenya to overcome her depression.

Upon Davis's urging, Lenya gave her first public performance in a tribute concert to her late husband, Kurt Weill, ten months after Weill's death, in Manhattan's Town Hall, on February 3, 1951. But it was not easy to coax Lenya to perform Weill's music when she was still mourning his death. Ernst Josef Aufricht, who in 1928 had produced *The Threepenny Opera* at his Theater am Schiffbauerdamm in Berlin, and who also was in charge of the concert in Manhattan, remembers: "Nach langer und intensiver Probenarbeit rief mich Lenya am Morgen der Premiere heulend an und verlangte kategorisch, den Abend abzusagen, ich mache sie und Kurt lächerlich." ["After long and intensive rehearsals, Lenya called me on the morning of the premiere, crying, and she insisted categorically that I should cancel the evening because I would expose her and Weill to ridicule."][44] The contrary happened. The Manhattan Town Hall was sold out, when Lenya, in the middle part of the concert, performed songs from *The Threepenny Opera*. The newspaper reviews were glowing, and the concert was repeated three times.

Aufricht offers a description of George Davis, the man behind Lenya's success:

---

42   Ibid., 127.

43   Letter by Lotte Lenya to Helene Weigel, August 21, 1956, Akademie der Künste, Berlin, Bertolt Brecht-Archiv 886/39.

44   Ernst Josef Aufricht, *Und der Haifisch, der hat Zähne: Aufzeichnungen eines Theaterdirektors* (Berlin: Alexander Verlag, 2018), (1998), 251.

Ein kleiner rundlicher Mann gratulierte der Lenya. George Davis, amerikanischer
Schriftsteller und Journalist, grauhaarig, mit einem kindlichen Gesicht und verträum-
ten Augen, beeindruckte jeden, der ihn näher kannte durch seine Bescheidenheit, seine
Intelligenz und einen untrüglichen Sinn für Qualität.

["A short plump man congratulated Lenya. George Davis, American writer and journalist, grey-haired, with a childlike face and dreamy eyes, impressed everyone who knew
him better with his modesty, his intelligence, and an unmistakable sense for quality."][45]

Davis was a gay man and considered a highly gifted editor, who had discovered the talents of writers like Truman Capote and Carson McCullers.
"George was the architect of the entire Lenya enterprise in the 1950s," the
cartoon artist Milton Cardiff, who knew both Lenya and Davis, said in
an interview. Davis was also skilled in making the necessary professional
moves on Lenya's behalf. "He contacted those who would make a deal
for a recording and for productions, and it was done."[46] Lenya and Davis
were married on July 7, 1951. Davis had been a friend of Lenya and Weill
since 1936, and he genuinely appreciated Weill's music. He offered Lenya
companionship and friendship at an extremely difficult time in her life,
and gave her strength, while she provided him with material stability he
lacked, since he failed to maintain steady employment.

Promoting Kurt Weill's legacy henceforth became Lenya's life mission. As Weill's widow, she also had to manage his estate. This included
dealing with complex copyright issues, performance rights, royalty payments, legal obligations and disputes, as well as negotiations with music
publishers.[47] Lenya devoted herself diligently to these tasks, struggling
with Helene Weigel and the heirs of the Brecht estate, as well as the li-
cense holders of the works of Brecht and Weill; in 1962 she formed the
Kurt Weill Foundation for Music.[48] As a result of Lenya's efforts, a renaissance of Weill's music took place in the United States. Lenya's mission

45   Ibid., 252.
46   Milton Caniff, cited in Spoto, *Lenya: A Life*, 211.
47   Farneth, *Lenya: The Legend*, 166–8; 205–9.
48   Jürgen Hillesheim, *Lotte Lenya und Bertolt Brecht: Das wilde Leben zweier
     Aufsteiger* (Darmstadt: wbg, 2022), 229, 233, 252–5, 267–70; Farneth, *Lenya: The
     Legend*, 160–1. Arguments between Weill and Brecht about the legal status of their
     shared property, in particular *The Threepenny Opera*, started, when both men were

to promote Weill's work extended also to Germany. In 1955, she traveled for the first time in nearly twenty years to Germany, together with Davis, who had arranged a recording session for Lenya in Hamburg. The released record became an instantaneous hit and received distribution also in the United States. From 1955 onward Lenya frequently returned to Germany for concerts, performances, and recordings, and she was lauded as a living symbol of Weimar culture.[49]

Rising to Stardom, New York 1954

Lenya became a star with the fabled 1954 New York production of *The Threepenny Opera*, based on a new English adaption by the American composer Marc Blitzstein.[50] Two years earlier, on June 14, 1952, Blitzstein's translation was first presented in a concert version at Brandeis University, with Leonard Bernstein conducting and Lenya singing, while Blitzstein acted as narrator. The campus audience responded enthusiastically. In an interview she gave decades later, Lenya recounted how a large audience of university students sitting on the campus ground chanted the popular song about Mack the Knife, the *Moritat*. Lenya performed the songs of the prostitute Jenny, the character she had embodied two-and-half decades earlier in Berlin, now with a deeper and husky voice, unlike the almost childlike soprano of her early years, singing in English.

---

still alive. Pamela Katz, *The Partnership: Brecht, Weill, Three Women, and Germany on the Brink* (New York: Anchor Books, 2015), 357, 363–9.

49   During one of her travels in Germany, Lenya recorded a one hour-long radio program with Theodor W. Adorno in the Frankfurt radio station, broadcast in 1960, which was inspired by the fascination emanating from 1920s Weimar culture, being rediscovered by a new generation in postwar Germany.
        "Adorno/Lenya: Die Zwanziger Jahre. Legende und Ärgernis. Diskussion mit Lotte Lenya und Adolf Frisé," Akademie der Künste, Berlin, Adorno-Archiv, TWAA TA 082; <https://www.youtube.com/watch?v=x8PnTxZTMsM> (last accessed June 1, 2023).

50   Pollack, *Marc Blitzstein*, 350–64.

A full stage production in New York was launched when two emerging
male producers, Stanley Chase and Carmen Capalbo approached Lenya and
Blitzstein, and legal approval was negotiated with Brecht. Notwithstanding
their limited experience, Chase and Capalbo won Lenya over because they
assured her they would stay faithful to Weill's score and the original work.
A letter by Leon Kellman of the William Morris Agency to the publisher
Peter Suhrkamp in Frankfurt, to whom Brecht had transferred the rights
to his works, pitched the request for approval as follows:

> Now a talented theatrical company of young people desires to produce this work
> on stage. This would be done in the Theatre de Lys in New York City, which is one
> of several so-called "off-Broadway" theatres, where groups of younger people have
> been doing outstanding work and presenting worthy productions. Prices are low,
> but the quality of the presentations is of high standard, since the people are young
> professionals. (…) Several actors and directors who are now important, first came
> to prominence in these theatres. (…) Mrs. Weill and Mr. Blitzstein believe that it
> would be a fine thing for this group to present the work, and that this might lead to
> productions elsewhere (…).[51]

Everyone in the cast, including Lenya, received $5 per week during the
rehearsal phase and $25 base payment after the show opened.[52]

The Threepenny Opera premiered on March 10, 1954, at the Theatre de
Lys on Christopher Street in Manhattan, with Carmen Capalbo directing.
Lenya's initial concern that audiences would not come downtown to the
off-Broadway site in Greenwich Village, proved unfounded. *The Threepenny
Opera* became a sensational hit, topping all expectations. Lenya was 55 years
old at the time of the premiere. Except for her, all of the actors were relatively young and unknown. Initially, she had been self-conscious about
her age but was persuaded by Capalbo, Blitzstein, and Davis, to play the
role of Jenny like she did a quarter of a century before in Berlin. The press
raved about Lenya's stage performance, which also earned her a Tony award.
The Threepenny Opera ran for a total of almost seven years, until December

---

51   Letter from Leon Kellman (William Morris Agency) to Peter Suhrkamp,
     November 11, 1953, Akademie der Künste, Berlin, Bertolt Brecht-Archiv 582/03.
52   Pollack, *Marc Blitzstein*, 358.

1961, with a record number of over 2,600 performances. When Lenya left the show after two years,

> they were all heartbroken and horrified. They said, "Miss Lenya, look—we'll have to close the show." I said, "You will not. Don't be silly. This is a marvelous work, and it would be a very poor sign for Brecht and Weill if its success depended on the minor role. If Jenny ever becomes a major role, then there's something goddamn wrong with the whole production."[53]

Lenya had ignited the renaissance of this seminal work, but she was then eager to pass on the torch to a young generation of American artists who had found a fresh approach to it, while they were enthusiastic about Lenya's involvement.

Adding to Lenya's picture-book revival with *The Threepenny Opera* was also her participation in a recording session with Louis Armstrong and his band in 1955, when Armstrong recorded a Dixieland-style version of the song "Mack the Knife." In his rendition for Columbia Records, he explicitly throws in Lenya's name; and in one of the two takes, not published until after Lenya's death, she and Armstrong sing together. Armstrong's 1955 recording brought the famous song from *The Threepenny Opera* to prominence, giving it an even far wider public exposure than Lenya's stage performance achieved. Ever since, the song has been picked up and popularized by a number of famous singers, including Bobby Darin, Ella Fitzgerald, Marianne Faithful, and many others.

Lenya's star was shining bright when she suffered yet another blow to her personal life: on November 25, 1957, during a trip to Germany, George Davis died of a heart attack, at age 51, like Kurt Weill seven years before him. Once again, Lenya experienced a profound crisis, now that the devoted architect of her late fame was gone. Yet it seems that Lenya, who needed the encouragement and the promoting genius of George Davis to overcome the inner barriers that impeded her from pitching herself, had found the strength and was famous enough to carry on by herself.

---

53   Farneth, *Lenya: The Legend*, 134.

Lenya's Magnetism

After her legendary comeback in the 1954 New York adaptation of *The Threepenny Opera*, Lenya celebrated a string of successes in her professional life, giving concerts and completing recordings of Kurt Weill's music. This continued throughout the 1950s and 1960s. Lenya was lauded, for instance, for her guest performance in *The Seven Deadly Sins*, staged by the New York City Ballet in 1958 under the direction of George Balanchine, who already in 1933 had choreographed the same work by Brecht and Weill in Paris.[54] Lenya's first concert in 1965 at the prestigious Carnegie Hall in New York became a raving success. Three years earlier, on January 3, 1962, Lenya starred in a show entitled *Brecht on Brecht*, again in the *Theatre de Lys* in lower Manhattan. The Hungarian-born Jewish writer and theater director George Tabori had put the show together. A cast of six people, with Lotte Lenya in their midst, presented a selection of poems, songs, and scenes.

The music critic Everett Helm saw the show in New York, where it completed a run of 200 performances, before it went on to London. He describes how he perceived Lenya, giving us a sense of what accounted for her magnetism both in 1954 and in 1928, when she first came to fame with the role of Jenny in *The Dreigroschenoper*:

> I watched her closely as she came unobtrusively onto the stage and sat almost indifferently on her stool while the others performed. Then, as her turn came to recite or sing, the transformation took place. The passivity of her former mood was gone in an instant: without doing much more than changing posture or taking two steps, she had become a magnet for all the eyes. And from that moment until her number ended, she had every member of the audience in the palm of her hand, hanging on every gesture, every word, every change of expression. It was as if she had turned

---

54 *The Seven Deadly Sins*, by Kurt Weill and Bertolt Brecht, and choreographed by George Balanchine, opened in Paris in June of 1933. Lenya starred as Anna I, alongside the dancer Tilly Losch. Whereas the cool music was dismissed by the critics, the performance of the two women was praised by French critics and audiences. The Paris production marked the end of the successful collaboration between Weill, Lenya, and Brecht, which had lasted four years.

on a "concentration machine" from which nobody could escape. Her number over, she turned it off again. (…) This ability to switch from complete participation to a state of complete non-involvement is, I am convinced, one of the secrets of Lenya's success. (…) I doubt whether this is a conscious process on her part. But it helps to explain why she is as breathtaking today as she was (…)[55]

Paradoxically it was Lenya's performance style and her appearance, deemed unsuitable for the tastes of American mainstream audiences in the 1930s and 1940s, which became the very foundation of her late fame. The obituary George Tabori wrote after Lenya's death gives us a sense of what accounted for the secret of her success:

> Lenyas persona, besser bekannt als Seeräuberjenny, war die wahre Mutter des Coolen: ein Opfer ohne Mitleid oder Selbstmitleid, das darauf wartet, dass seine Kumpel in den Hafen segeln und die Köpfe der Unterdrücker abhauen, während sie mit der entzückten Stimme eines kleinen Mädchens "Hoppla" ruft.

> [Lenya's persona, better known as Pirate Jenny, was the true mother of Cool: a victim without pity or self-pity, who is waiting for her buddies to sail into the harbor and cut off the heads of the oppressors, while she cries with the delighted voice of a little girl, "Oops."][56]

According to Tabori it was the duality of prostitute and little girl that shaped Lenya's public image, even in her advanced age, and made her,

> wenigstens für einige von uns, sehr viel attraktiver als die andere große deutsche Legende, Marlene Dietrich, die von Hollywood in eine reine Kunstfigur umgemodelt wurde, indem man alles ausradierte, was sie wirklich war (…)

> [at least for some of us, much more attractive than the other great German legend, Marlene Dietrich, who had been remodeled into a purely artificial character by Hollywood, erasing everything she really was (…).][57]

With Lenya it was quite the opposite, as Tabori observed: "Der Lenya konnte niemand etwas ausradieren," ["Nobody could erase anything from

55   Everett Helm, "Lenya," *Musical America* LXXXII, no. 5 (1962): 22–3.
56   George Tabori, "Die Letzte der großen alten Huren: Noch ein Abschied—George Tabori über Lotte Lenya," in *Theater heute*, 3/1982, 53.
57   Tabori, "Die Letzte der großen alten Huren."

Lenya."][58] Vouching for Lenya's unpretentiousness and her lack of vanity, he recalls the allure in Lenya that enchanted him, together with an entire generation of rebellious minds:

> Ich bewunderte sie wie ein Fan, (…), aber diese Bewunderung wurde von allen geteilt, die die Sechziger Jahre bestimmt haben: den Studenten, den Schwarzen, den Schwulen, den Junkies, den Revoluzzern—allesamt Piraten, die davon träumten, das Schiff mit acht Segeln miteinander zu teilen und die Köpfe zu fällen.[59]

> [I admired her like a fan (…), but this admiration was shared by everyone who shaped the 1960s—students, blacks, gays, junkies, revolutionaries—all of whom were pirates who dreamed of sharing with one another the boat with eight sails and chop off heads.]

Weimar Revisited: *Cabaret*, 1966

A high point of Lenya's American career was her Broadway performance in the musical *Cabaret* in 1966, which increased her popularity even further. With music by John Kander, song texts by Fred Ebb, and the text of the play by Joe Masteroff, *Cabaret* premiered on October 10, 1966, in a pre-Broadway tryout in Boston's Shubert Theatre. A month later it opened in New York's Broadhurst Theatre, where it stayed for three years and 1,165 performances, most of them with Lenya. *Cabaret* was based on a stage drama by John Van Druten, entitled *I Am a Camera* (1951), which itself was inspired by Christopher Isherwood's Berlin novels, *Goodbye to Berlin* (1939) and *The Last of Mr Norris* (1935). In these two novels Isherwood describes the decadence and turmoil of Berlin culture during the final phase of the Weimar Republic. *Cabaret* centers on Sally Bowles, a nightclub dancer in the KitKat club, who begins a short-lived, ill-fated romance with the American writer, Cliff Bradshaw. Bradshaw is one of

---

58 Ibid.
59 Tabori, "Die Letzte der großen alten Huren." The wording "… the boat with eight sails and chop off heads …" is a reference to the lyrics of the song of Pirate Jenny from Brecht and Weill's *The Threepenny Opera*.

the guests in Fräulein Schneider's pension. Lotte Lenya plays the role of Fräulein Schneider. Advanced in age, Fräulein Schneider is courted by Herr Schulz, a vegetable dealer who expresses his love by giving a pine-apple, the most exotic fruit in Germany at the time, to her as a gift. Hence the pineapple song, one of the four songs Lenya performs in the musical. Fräulein Schneider and Herr Schulz celebrate their engagement, but their happiness is destroyed when Herr Schulz is confronted with fierce anti-semitism by one of the lodgers, and Fräulein Schneider complies to the pressure and calls off the planned wedding with her Jewish bridegroom.[60] It seems that this musical that celebrated Lenya's artistic roots in Weimar culture was well-suited for her talent, which included a lightness and del-icacy, as well as a seductiveness, shining particularly when situated within a plot of social ghastliness, the roughness of a dive-bar or other louche settings.

Lenya's Film Career

After Davis's death Lenya took on roles that brought her into her own beyond the legacy of Weill. "When I do a film that has nothing to do with Kurt Weill, then I am happy," she said in an interview. "I am on my own. In a Kurt Weill work I am as nervous as a cat. A burden falls on my shoulders. I feel a crushing responsibility."[61] Lenya was offered to play in a number of films, and she eagerly accepted those roles, relishing the op-portunity to act in a film. She did not mind that she was cast to play, in her own words, "these ugly women," ugly not in a physical sense, but in terms of viciousness and lack of virtue. The first film in which Lenya per-formed, thirty years after she had starred in Pabst's film adaptation of *The Threepenny Opera*, was *The Roman Spring of Mrs Stone* (1961). Directed

60   In the 1972 movie with Liza Minelli, which was based on the Broadway musical, this part of the plot is missing, and so are the characters Fräulein Schneider and Herr Schulz.
61   Lotte Lenya, cited in Spoto, *Lenya: A Life*, 268.

by José Quintero and based on a novel by Tennessee Williams, Lenya played alongside Vivian Leigh and Warren Beatty. Critics were enthusiastic about her performance and agreed that she almost stole the show. Lenya's character, Contessa Magda Terribili-Gonzalez, is a procurer who runs a number of handsome gigolos, offering them to lonesome ladies who pay handsomely and take 50% of the revenue. The role earned Lenya an Oscar nomination for best supporting actress.

Lenya's next film role was as Rosa Klebb in the James Bond film *From Russia with Love* (1963).[62] It was followed by *The Appointment*, a film directed by Sydney Lumet, starring Omar Sharif and Anouk Aimée in leading roles. Here Lenya played Emma Valadier, an antiques store dealer, who discreetly manages a group of highly prized prostitutes. *Semi-Tough* was yet another film, in which Lenya got a part. In this comedy directed by Michael Richie, with Burt Reynolds as leading actor, Lenya played a tough massage therapist. She further participated in an adaption of Tennessee Williams' play *Ten Blocks on the Camino Real* (1966) for American television, and she played in an episode of *Trio for Lovers* (1974), which was part of the Daytime 90 series on CBS. By the 1970s, Lenya was invited to popular shows that aired on American television, such as the legendary Dick Cavett show on ABC (1975). At the end of the interview in which Lenya talked about Weimar Germany, the host joined Lenya in singing together with her in German the Bilbao-song from *Happy-End*, yet another Brecht/Weill collaboration.

By contrast to her picture-book professional successes, her personal life was riddled by a sequence of shocks. In 1962, Lenya married for a third time. Her third husband, the American painter Russell Detwiler, was gay, 27 years younger than Lenya, and an alcoholic. When he died seven years later in 1969, due to an accident induced by his alcohol abuse, Lenya was in the middle of preparing a Weill concert at Lincoln Center. After Detwiler's

---

62   Hillesheim reads Lenya's participation in this anticommunist Cold War era Hollywood production as a provocative statement on Lenya's part, considering that Lenya, the world-renowned interpreter of songs by Brecht and Weill, relished in embodying a persiflage of a female Soviet Political Commissar. Hillesheim, *Lotte Lenya und Bertolt Brecht*, 264–5.

death, she fell into another depression and canceled all activities for about a year. A fourth marriage which Lenya kept secret even from most of her friends with the filmmaker Richard Siemanowski, yet another gay man and an alcoholic, ended 1973, after two years, in divorce.

Conclusion

When Lenya died of cancer on November 27, 1981, in New York, she had reached celebrity status, and she had become a cult figure eternally associated with the libertarian German culture of the 1920s which in the 1950s began to inspire American audiences. Lenya, whose interpretations of Brecht and Weill songs have become iconic, championed Weill's work on both sides of the Atlantic through her live performances and studio recordings. She also moved beyond the legacy of Weill and in the 1960s became a star in her own right, for instance, with her lauded Broadway performance as Fräulein Schneider in *Cabaret*, or as the memorable Rosa Klebb in the James Bond film *From Russia with Love*. Yet initially, in the 1930s and 1940s, Lenya's career as an actress, like the careers of many German-speaking émigré actresses and actors in America, was hampered by her troubles with the English language, and she was living in relative obscurity. Her performance style in combination with her heavy Austrian-German accent, and her appearance were not compatible with either Broadway or Hollywood, and her special talent and enigmatic charm that Marc Blitzstein in 1935 had described seemed unsuited to American mass appeal. While Kurt Weill was still alive, Lenya did not make efforts on her own to advance her career.[63] This may have been in part the result of her realizing that her chances in American theater and film were slim. But her reluctance to network with agents, theater producers, or directors in order to secure a role in a play indicates that Lenya,

---

63   Spoto, *Lenya: A Life*, 162, 166.

for reasons we do not fully understand, relied on Weill to promote her, instead of taking her career into her own hands.

After Weill's premature death in 1950 Lenya's career took an unexpected turn. She emerged from obscurity and stepped into the limelight. It took the support of George Davis, her second husband, for Lenya to succeed. Whereas Weill, although loyally dedicated to promote his wife whenever he could, was an artist who also had his own musical career to tend to, George Davis was adept in activating the relevant professional contacts and forging deals on Lenya's behalf. With much success, Davis committed himself to resuscitating Lenya's career, even though initially against her own resistance.

Lenya embraced her unexpected stardom late in life and enjoyed her success in film, theater, and music. Her chief motivation was not so much to advance her career for her own sake but a desire to serve as a catalyst for the memory of Weill's music to stay alive. With the support of George Davis, who shared her devotion to Weill's music, Lenya accomplished this purpose. Along the way, she also helped emerging artists achieve successes, as evidenced by her involvement with the 1954 New York production of *The Threepenny Opera*. Two years before she died, Lenya met the Canadian soprano singer Teresa Stratas at the Metropolitan Opera in New York where in a production of *Rise and Fall of the City of Mahagonny* Stratas performed the role of Jenny that Lenya had played in 1931 in Berlin. On January 4, 1980, Lenya, who was then already struggling with cancer, attended the legendary concert at the Whitney Museum, where Stratas performed a number of largely unknown Weill songs for which Lenya, captivated by the singer's talent, had given her the score.[64] Being recognized and endorsed by Kurt Weills's widow to carry on the legacy of the composer's music contributed significantly to the fame of Teresa Strata.

Lotte Lenya will be associated eternally with the works created by Brecht and Weill in Weimar Germany. The fact that the Alabama-song (*Moon of Alabama*) from the musical opera *Rise and Fall of the City of Mahagonny*, for instance, was covered by internationally renowned artists such as Jim Morrison of The Doors, David Bowie, Nina Simone, Nina

64   Farneth, *Lotte Lenya: The Legend*, 210; 213.

Hagen, and others, gives evidence of Lenya's splendid achievement of her mission and how, in addition to that, some of Weill's works were absorbed by popular culture.

In this way, Lenya owed her fame in America to her first two husbands. Kurt Weil provided the music material and her second husband George Davis opened the way into the performing arts. Both, Kurt Weill and George Davis, gave their unflagging support and ignited Lenya's success in America. Yet ultimately, it was Lenya's unique voice and performance style that prompted the Kurt Weill renaissance in the 1950s, in the United States and abroad, and posthumously earned him the recognition as one of the most important composers of the twentieth century. By devoting her artistic spirit and energy to keeping Weill's legacy alive, Lenya, with her signature role as Pirate Jenny, became a cult figure with an allure that resonates with contemporary sensibilities.

CAMILLE JENN-GASTAL

13 Die deutsch-jüdische Musikwissenschaftlerin Anneliese Landau: Von der „deutsch-jüdischen Symbiose" zur Integration in der Neuen Welt

ABSTRACT

This essay represents an examination about how the German Jewish musicologist Annelise Landau had to struggle in her exile after she came to New York in 1940, how she began a new life, resumed her academic career as a female musicologist and completed the mission for making German Jewish composers known to the American public.

Als Anneliese Landau am 1. Januar 1940 den nordamerikanischen Boden in Boston betrat, ließ sie ihre Eltern, eine verlorene Heimat, eine verschollene Kultur, schließlich eine vielversprechende, zwangsläufig unterbrochene Karriere als Musikwissenschaftlerin, hinter sich zurück. Wie alle anderen deutsch-jüdischen Künstler und Intellektuellen war sie seit dem 5. März 1933 auf zunehmend unerträgliche Weise von den Nazis belästigt, schikaniert, verleumdet, ausgegrenzt, gedemütigt, und dann zensiert, ausgebürgert und entrechtet worden.

Ihr damaliges Leben in Deutschland kannte drei Phasen, die für das Schicksal vieler deutsch-jüdischer Intellektuellen und Künstler jener Generation kennzeichnend waren: Stationen der Ausbildung und des Studiums; Beginn einer vielversprechenden Karriere als Akademikerin; Ausgrenzung und Ghettoisierung durch die Nazis. Anstatt Karriere in Deutschland, floh sie 1939 nach London, und 1940 nach Amerika. Dank ihres großen Mutes und Hartnäckigkeit gelang es ihr, nach vielen Schwierigkeiten Fuß zu fassen, so dass sie ihren Lebensunterhalt in ihrem Fachgebiet als Musikwissenschaftlerin bestreiten konnte.[1]

---

1   Bis 2017 waren Landaus Aufzeichnungen als unveröffentlichte Manuskripte im Archiv der Akademie der Künste in Berlin zu lesen; seit 2017 gibt es

Die Verwurzelung in der Musik

1903 in Halle geboren, stammte Anneliese Landau aus einer wohlhabenden jüdischen Familie des liberalen Bürgertums der Mittelklasse.[2] Nach dem Besuch der „Frauenschule" konnte sie sich mit Unterstützung der liberal gesinnten Eltern von den herkömmlichen Verhältnissen emanzipieren und ließ sich 1923 an der Universität Halle immatrikulieren. Sieben Jahre davor hatte sie den Besuch der Synagoge aufgegeben und verfolgte nun den Weg der Emanzipation, der persönlichen Entfaltung und der akademischen Ausbildung. Was sie im Leben am meisten begeisterte und über alles liebte, war die Musik, die ihr so wichtig und unentbehrlich war „wie das Atmen."[3] Durch ihre Erziehung war Landau in der musikalischen, romantischen und postromantischen Tradition der deutschen Kultur verwurzelt. Ihre erste akademische Arbeit war eine Analyse der Liederreihe *Die schöne Müllerin* von Schubert (1823). Sie besuchte die Seminare von Hans Joachim Moser, der eindeutig antisemitisch gesinnt war, und von Arnold Schering, dem sie nach Berlin folgte, als er dort eine Professur erhielt. In Berlin schrieb Landau dann ihre Promotion über Conradin Kreutzers Kunstlieder (1780–1849) auf dem Gebiet der klassisch-romantischen Tradition. Den Doktortitel erhielt sie im Juli 1929. Bald darauf wurde ihre Promotionsarbeit unter dem Titel: *Das einstimmige Kunstlied Conradin Kreuzers und seine Stellung zum zeitgenössischen Lied in Schwaben* 1930 bei Breitkopf und Härtel veröffentlicht.

---

eine Veröffentlichung von Daniela Reinhold und der Akademie der Künste Berlin: die Zusammensetzung der zwei auf Englisch verfassten autobiographischen Texte: *Bridges to the Past* (circa 1975 geschrieben), und: *Pictures you wanted to see—People you wanted to hear* (circa 1987 fertig geschrieben), die ihren Neffen Liesel und George Paechter gewidmet sind. Die Zitate des vorliegenden Beitrags sind der folgenden Veröffentlichung entnommen (*Von Berlin nach Los Angeles. Die Musikwissenschaftlerin Anneliese Landau*, Berlin: Hentrich & Hentrich, 2017) und werden in den Anmerkungen mit „AL" und Seitennummer notiert.

2　　Damals Alte Promenade 6, jetzt Universitätsring 6.

3　　AL 22: „Musik wurde für mich so selbstverständlich wie das Atmen".

Solange der Antisemitismus in Deutschland nicht offiziell zur
Bedrohung wurde, war für Landau das „Jüdisch-Sein" kein Problem. Trotz
des unterschwelligen Erlebnisses des Antisemitismus, gab es bei ihr, wie bei
den meisten ihrer jüdischen Kollegen und Freunde, keine Infragestellung
(auch kein Hinterfragen) der eigenen „Identität." Es gehörte zu ihrem
Lebensalltag, dass sie über all die Jahre des langen Studiums mit antisemitisch gesinnten Gelehrten, Akademikern, Musikern kohabitieren und sich
manchmal wehren musste. So hatte sie zum Beispiel den Mut, 1929 Moser
als Mitglied der Jury ihrer Promotionsprüfung abzulehnen. Trotz manchmal
bedrückender Stimmung konnte sie sich also in Deutschland und Berlin
entfalten. Zu ihren nahen Freunden gehörten unter anderen das Ehepaar
Beidler,[4] sowie Klaus Pringsheim.[5] Sie pflegte eine Zusammenarbeit mit
Bruno Walter, Alfred Einstein, Siegfried Ochs und vielen anderen deutsch-
jüdischen Künstlern und teilte mit ihnen die Verehrung von romantischen
Komponisten (Johann Sebastian Bach, Mendelssohn-Bartholdy), postromantischen Komponisten (Mahler), und natürlich Wagners Musik.
Auch interessierte sie sich für die neue atonale Musik Arnold Schönbergs,
hatte Kontakte mit Paul Hindemith, war von den neuen Medien, wie dem
Rundfunk, begeistert.

Knapp vier Jahre nach ihrer akademischen Ausbildung versuchte
Landau sich einen Platz in der Welt der Musikwissenschaft und in der
Kulturwelt Berlins zu schaffen. Sie schrieb wichtige Beiträge für Jahrbücher,
wie das *Händeljahrbuch* 1930–1931 und *Bach-Jahrbuch* 1930, und leistete
1932 Pionierarbeit, indem sie Musiksendungen im Rundfunk moderierte.[6]

---

4   Franz Wilhelm Beidler war ein Sohn von Isolde Wagner und ein Enkelkind
      von Richard Wagner, er war mit einer jüdischen Frau verheiratet. Beide waren
      Mitglieder der SPD. Das Paar emigrierte in die Schweiz und ließ sich in Zürich
      nieder.
5   Klaus Pringsheim (1883–1972) war Dirigent und Komponist und Katia Manns
      Zwillingsbruder.
6   Für den Berliner Rundfunk, die Deutsche Welle (auch „University oft the
      air" genannt) arbeitete Landau erstmals am 22. November 1930 und dann ab
      dem 19.6.1931 mit einer Sendung: „Frauenstunde". Ihre erste Sendung war der
      Komponistin Emilie Zumsteeg (1796–1857) gewidmet, dann folgten z. B.: „Die
      Musik und Goethe", „Fanny Hensel".

Während dieser Zeit veröffentlichte sie bibliographische Arbeiten für Alfred Einstein und leistete damit anspruchsvolle wissenschaftliche Arbeit.[7] Zu jener Zeit war die eigentliche Schwierigkeit in der Öffentlichkeit und in der beruflichen Umwelt nicht so sehr ihr „Jüdisch-Sein", sondern das „Frau-Sein." „Einstein versuchte, mir zu helfen und mich als Lehrling beim *Berliner Tageblatt* oder der *Vossischen Zeitung* unterzubringen, aber „keiner wollte eine Frau nehmen![8]" Unter Musikwissenschaftlern war eine promovierte Frau zu jener Zeit noch eine Rarität. Eine Ausnahme waren Elsa Blumenfeldt, die 1903 in Wien promovierte, sowie Bertha Antonia Wallner (Promotion 1910, München) und auch Kathi Meyer-Baer (Promotion 1916, Leipzig). Die Emanzipierung deutsch-jüdischer Frauen erfolgte aufgrund individueller Initiativen und fügte sich in keine umfassende organisierte Bewegung ein. Im Jahre 1933 gab es in Deutschland 33 promovierte Frauen. 1,2 % aller akademischen Stellen waren von Frauen besetzt.[9] Hinzu kommt die Tatsache, dass trotz des Gesetzes zur Emanzipation der Juden, das seit 1869 den deutschen Bürgern jüdischer Herkunft alle Studiengänge erlaubte, die akademische Laufbahn für deutsch-jüdische Wissenschaftler faktisch erschwert wurde. Aus diesem Grund konnte sich beispielsweise Alfred Einstein zu seiner Zeit nicht habilitieren lassen.

Außerdem besaß unter allen akademischen Disziplinen die Musikwissenschaft am Anfang des 20. Jahrhunderts und dann insbesondere in den dreißiger Jahren einen besonderen Status: In der Musik sollten (vermeintlich) typische „germanische" Eigenschaften erkannt werden. Es wurde „deutsche" Musik mit seinen eigenen quasi „essentiellen" Qualitäten verherrlicht. Zu einer solchen Essentialisierung der Musik trug Richard Wagners Pamphlet *Das Judenthum in der Musik* weitgehend bei.[10] Wagners

---

7   Alfred Einstein war bis 1933 Leiter der Zeitschrift für Musikwissenschaft. Zu Landaus bibliographischen Arbeiten, siehe AL 58, 59.

8   AL 61.

9   Eva Rieger, *Frau, Musik und Männerherrschaft. Zum Ausschluss der deutschen Frau aus der Musikpädagogie, Musikwissenschaft und Musikausübung* (Kassel: Furore Verlag, 2021), 302 S.

10   Dieser Text, der ursprünglich als Antwort in einer literarischen Kontroverse mit Giacomo Meyerbeer gedacht war, enthielt Passagen, die die eindeutig antisemitische Gesinnung Richard Wagners verriet und ihren Beitrag zu einem ungehemmten aggressiven Antisemitismus lieferte: Richard Wagner, *Judenthum in der Musik*

Äußerungen reflektieren den starken Antisemitismus in der Gesellschaft. Auf das Gebiet der Musik übertragen nehmen sie einen essentialistischen, rassistischen Charakter an. Doch konnte Landau sich und ihre universalistischen Musikauffassungen trotz dieser generell verbreiteten Tendenzen behaupten und mit ihrem Wissen und Können Avantgarde-Arbeit leisten. Dies geschah beispielsweise durch ihre Tätigkeit im Berliner Rundfunk, und anlässlich von Konferenzen, bei denen sie ohne Notizen frei vortrug, und ein modernes, damals unbekanntes Format erfand. Ihre Vorträge wurden einer von ihr ausgesuchten Thematik gewidmet (Kunstlied, Kammermusik, Oper und Operette), sowie durch Zwischenspiele von Musikstücken illustriert und „live" interpretiert. Landau lud dazu renommierte Musikinterpreten ein (zum Beispiel: Wolfgang Rosé am Klavier, Friedrich Lechner als Sänger). Neben ihrer Tätigkeit im Bereich der Musik, engagierte sich Landau auch politisch, indem sie 1929 der SPD beitrat (nach einer Zeit der Vertretung für Klaus Pringsheim in der SPD-Zeitung *Vorwärts*). Für ein Mitglied des assimilierten aufgeklärten Judentums war dies keine Besonderheit, aber für eine Frau war dies ein zusätzlicher Akt der Selbständigkeit und zeugte von autonomen Denken und individuellem Lebensstil. Während der Weimarer Republik zeigte Landau viel sozial-politische Eigenständigkeit und berufliche Initiative. Auf die Einladung Alfred Einsteins hin kollaborierte sie ab 1930 an der *Zeitschrift für Musikwissenschaft*. Auf diese Weise arbeitete sie allein und selbstständig am Aufbau ihrer Karriere, mit den Mitteln des „Selfmanagement" (wie sie Jahre später ihre Vorgehensweise bezeichnete).

Beginn der Nazizeit

Als Landau 1933 die Teilnahme am Berliner Rundfunk und an der *Zeitschrift für Musikwissenschaft* verweigert und sie dann 1935 als „staatenlos" erklärt wurde, erwachte in ihr das Bewusstsein eines Auftrags

---

(Leipzig: 1869) (2. Ausgabe nach der ersten unter dem Pseudonym „K. Freigedank" in Zürich für die *Neue Zeitschrift für Musik*).

ethischer Natur. Im *Kulturbund deutscher Juden*, der bereits im Juli 1933 in Berlin gegründet wurde, hatte ihr Kurt Singer die Leitung der musikpädagogischen Abteilung anvertraut.[11]

So gab Landau von nun an ausschließlich im Rahmen des *Kulturbunds* musikhistorische Vorträge. Bald darauf ging sie auf Tournee durch Deutschland, wo sie ein wissbegieriges, ausschließlich jüdisches Publikum mit lebhaften Vorträgen über Mozart, Chopin, Bach, Händel und Themen, wie „Die Kammermusik es Rokokosalons", „Musik des alten Wiens", „musikalische Reisebilder", und dann zunehmend mit Vorträgen über „jüdische Musiker" begeisterte.[12] Auch wurde sie mit Einführungen zu den Konzerten und Opernvorstellungen des *Kulturbunds* beauftragt und schrieb Artikel für jüdische Zeitungen (*CV-Zeitung, Jüdische Rundschau, Jüdisches Gemeindeblatt*) über junge, damals unbekannte jüdische Komponisten, wie etwa Berthold Goldschmidt, Gerhard Goldschlag, Edvard Moritz, Bernhard Heiden, Werner Seelig-Bass, sowie Lieder von Max Kowalski.

In Nazideutschland stand der Kulturbund verwaltungsmäßig unter der Autorität Hans Hinkels. Die Organisation war abhängig vom „preußischen Theater-Ausschuss." Die Programme mussten systematisch und mindestens einen Monat vor der Vorstellung den Behörden, der Gestapo vorgelegt werden, damit wurden die Inhalte streng zensiert, so dass es beispielsweise bei Landaus Vortrag am 30. Januar 1937 zu der zynischen Absurdität führte, dass sie überhaupt nichts mehr öffentlich aussprechen durfte:

> Der schlimmste Abend kam, als ich im Bachsaal, der eine Kapazität von fast 1.200 Plätzen hatte, sprechen sollte. In dem Manuskript, das ich zurückhielt, war fast alles gestrichen worden. Mir blieben nur einige Ankündigungen der Stücke, die meine Künstler spielen würden. (…) Dementsprechend ging ich mit dem Manuskript in der Hand auf die Bühne, (…) kündigte den Titel des Programms an, (…) und wendete Seite um Seite um, sehr langsam, ohne etwas zu sagen oder aufzuschauen,

---

11   Zum Kulturbund: Gabriele Fritsch-Vivié, *Gegen alle Widerstände. Der jüdische Kulturbund 1933–1941* (Berlin: Hentrich & Hentrich, 2013), 273 S. Akademie der Künste, Hrsg., *Geschlossene Vorstellung. Der jüdische Kulturbund in Deutschland 1933–1941* (Berlin: Hentrich & Hentrich, 1992), 454 S.

12   Der erste in dieser Reihe fand am 19. Okt. 1936 in Berlin statt. Auch verfasste sie Artikel im Mitteilungsblatt des Kulturbundes: z. B. „Der Jude als Musiker", KB Monatsblätter, Okt. 1933.

bis ich zu einer Zeile im Manuskript kam, die nicht gestrichen war und die so allein, aus dem Kontext gelöst, keinen Sinn ergab. Ich las sie und dann wendete ich erneut lautlos die Seiten. (…) Es war ein kurzer Abend und ich erhielt donnernden Applaus. Alle verstanden und gingen traurig und still nach Hause. Wir wussten, dass es das Ende war. So konnte ich nicht weitermachen, die Gestapo hatte gewonnen.[13]

Ab 1934 durfte sie nur noch über jüdische Komponisten und Musiker berichten, zudem mussten alle ihre Vorträge vom „Reichskulturverwalter" Hans Hinkel in allen Einzelheiten genehmigt werden. Unter diesen Umständen blieb für Landau nur noch die Mission übrig, die jüdischen Familien fürs Weiterleben und für Kultur zu motivieren. In ihren Artikeln und Vorträgen warb Landau fortan für Musikerziehung und „Hausmusik." Zwischen 1936 und 1939 war es Landau möglich ihre Arbeit, trotz zunehmender Bedrückung und Bedrohungen, zu intensivieren, indem sie sich an der *Musikschule Holländer* beteiligte, im *Jüdischen Frauenbund*, sowie an der jüdischen Volkshochschule (*Jüdisches Lehrhaus*) tätig war.[14] Jene Jahre zwischen 1933 und 1938 waren paradoxerweise ihre intensivsten Jahre des beruflichen Engagements und als Landau auf ihr eigenes Leben zurückblickte, erkannte sie, dass sie in Nazi-Deutschland in dieser Hinsicht glücklich war![15] Am 7. März 1939 hielt sie ihren Abschiedsvortrag „Ungetanzte Tänze" vor einem überfüllten Saal.

---

13 AL 85.

14 Die *Private Jüdische Musikschule Hollaender* wurde im Frühjahr 1936 von den ehemaligen Eigentümern des *Stern'schen Konservatoriums*, Kurt Holländer und Susanne Landsberg-Holländer, gegründet.

15 AL, z. B. 83–84 : „Die Welt schien wieder perfekt zu sein. Es war nicht für lange. Aber für drei Jahre waren wir eine glückliche Familie, die zusammen die Theaterstücke, Konzerte und Vorträge des Kulturbunds besuchte. Ich konnte meine Vorträge mit meinen Eltern besprechen, und nach meinen Vorträgen genossen wir eine Tasse Kaffee in dem kleinen Café in der Nähe des Theaters, wo sich unsere Mitglieder und Künstler um die kleinen Tische drängten".

Der jüdische Kulturbund

Einhergehend mit der immer fortschreitenden Unterdrückung und Ausgrenzung durch das Nazi-Regime gibt es bei vielen deutsch-jüdischen Künstlern und Intellektuellen, die damals nicht emigriert waren, eine Wende im eigenen Selbstverständnis. Der Zweck des *Kulturbundes*, der anfänglich darin bestand, dem verlorenen Broterwerb seiner *Kulturbund*-Mitglieder in Deutschland einen erneuten „Sinn" zu geben, sowie das Publikum seelisch zu unterstützen, wurde bald zum Auftrag als Befürworter und Vertreter der Ethik und unpervertier-ter Werte (Werte der Aufklärung und der Haskala) aufzutreten. Diese Wende wurde auf dem Kongress vom 5. bis 7. September 1936, auf dem sämtliche regionale jüdische Kulturbünde in Berlin zusammentrafen, er-arbeitet. Auf der Konferenz betonte Kurt Singer den Zusammenhang zwischen „Jüdisch-Sein" und einer jüdischen Musik, die grundsätzlich vokal und dem Gesang des Chasans in der Synagoge nahe stand. Weitere Komponisten der Zeit unterstrichen ihrerseits den sowohl sephardischen als auch ostjüdischen Charakter einer als „jüdisch" bezeichneten Musik, die also religiöse und folkloristische Charakteristika annahm.[16] Vorträge befassten sich ausschließlich mit einer „Judaisierung" der Programme des *Kulturbunds*, um jüdische Kultur und Musik zu fördern und auf-zuwerten.[17] Die Konsequenz für Landau war, dass sich ihre Auftritte beeindruckend vermehrten, sowohl in Berlin als auch in der Provinz. Diese Tourneen, die stets nach dem gleichen Muster verliefen und nun ausschließlich jüdische Thematiken und Musik behandelten, erreichten Ende 1937 einen Höhepunkt mit 450 Veranstaltungen.

So sehr Anneliese Landau in ihren musikalisch-historischen Auffassungen diesen Standpunkten nahe stand, so war sie doch mehr am Kunstlied als am Volkslied interessiert. Sie konzentrierte ihre Vorträge auf jüdische Musiker, wie beispielsweise Meyerbeer, Offenbach, Mahler, Schönberg, und D. Milhaud, die ihrer Ansicht nach einen Beitrag zum

---

16   So, z. B., der *Winawer Chor.*
17   *Gegen alle Widerstände,* 111–112.

universellen Schaffen leisteten, und warb um zeitgenössische jüdische Komponisten, unter denen einige, wie Heinrich Schalit, Ernst Bloch, Wolfgang Korngold, Oskar Guttmann, in den dreißiger Jahren schon sehr bekannt waren. Im Gegensatz zum *Kulturbund* behauptete sie allerdings, dass es „kein rein jüdisches Kunstlied" gebe[18] und argumentiert:

> Dieses subjektive Jahrhundert[19] schafft sich erst seine eigene, neue rein lyrische Ausdrucksform im Kunstlied und die jüdischen Komponisten haben auch Lieder geschrieben: Ruben Goldmann, Ignaz Brüll, Meyerbeer. Auch Offenbach schrieb Lieder. Die Lieder haben gar nichts mit dem Judentum Ihres Komponisten zu tun. Sie wachsen aus der Atmosphäre ihrer Zeit und tragen die Atmosphäre ihres Landes, in dem sie geschrieben werden.[20]

Während der letzten Jahre des Lebens und Wirkens in Nazi-Deutschland zog Landau, wohl auch auf Grund ihrer eigenen Erfahrung, die Schlussfolgerung, dass deutsche Menschen und deutsche Kultur grundsätzlich rassistisch und antisemitisch sind.[21] 1939 wandte sie sich von den Deutschen endgültig ab und ging nicht—wie sie behauptete—ins Exil, sondern in die Emigration. Diese Einstellung prägte ihre spätere berufliche Entwicklung in der Emigration. Im Folgenden soll darauf eingegangen werden, inwieweit dies ein Abschied Landaus von der „deutschen" Kultur war. Ihr Bemühen und Hauptbeschäftigung innerhalb des *Kulturbunds,* nämlich jüdische Komponisten bekannt zu machen, jüdische Musik zu fördern und die Eigenarten jüdischer Kompositionen hervorzuheben, sollte auch Teil ihrer Mission in den USA werden. Für Landau bedeutete dies aber auch, dass eine Hervorhebung des spezifisch Jüdischen in der deutschen Musik auf keinen Fall gleichzeitig bedeuten kann, dass man Musik ohne den deutsch-klassischen Beitrag auffassen könne. Solch ein endgültiger Bruch mit der deutschen Kultur sei unmöglich, darauf werde ich im nächsten Abschnitt zurückkommen.

18 *Geschlossene Vorstellung*, 291.
19 Das 19. Jahrhundert.
20 Siehe Anm. 19.
21 AL 37 : „Heute weiß ich, dass der Antisemitismus im deutschen Wesen tief verwurzelt ist, er war schon immer da, lange vor Hitler".

Emigration und Stationen eines neuen Lebens

Nach einem Zwischenaufenthalt in London fuhr Landau auf dem Schiff „Nova Scotia" weiter nach Nordamerika und kam am 1. Januar 1940 in Boston an. „Dort wurden wir mit riesigen Hakenkreuzen begrüßt, die zusammen mit den Worten „Tötet alle Juden!" auf die Säulen der Anlegestelle gemalt waren."[22] Gleich nach ihrer Ankunft wurde Landau zusätzlich, als Migrantin aus Deutschland, mit den unfreundlichen Worten der Vertreterin des Council of Jewish Women konfrontiert, die sie mit den Worten begrüßte, „Sie verstehen kein Jiddisch, was für eine Jüdin sind Sie? Sind Sie überhaupt Jüdin?"[23] So anekdotisch diese zwei knappen Beobachtungen von Landau auch sein mögen, so weisen sie doch auf die Fremden- und Judenfeindlichkeit, die es in den USA gab. Rechtsradikale, rassistische und antisemitische Attacken begleiteten Landau über die vier Jahre ihrer Integration in den USA:

> Die Zeitungen der Zeit waren voll mit rechtsorientierten Leserbriefen, die die Immigranten beschuldigten, Amerikanern die Arbeitsplätze wegzunehmen. Es war eine ähnliche Propaganda, wie ich sie in Deutschland erlebt hatte, nur die Bezeichnungen hatten gewechselt: in Nazi-Deutschland war es „der Jude", der die leitenden Positionen auf jedem Gebiet okkupierte, hier in Amerika war es „der jüdische Immigrant", der mit Amerikanern um dieselbe Stellung konkurrierte.[24]

Mit Bitterkeit musste Landau feststellen, dass sie als Immigrantin kein Recht auf eine Einstellung in staatlichen Institutionen hatte.[25] Von Anfang an beschloss Landau, dass sie nicht wieder nach Deutschland zurückkehren würde und dass der Weg nach Amerika für sie kein Exil, sondern eine Immigration ist. Noch im Jahre 1978 schrieb sie ihr biographisches Resümee betreffend an F. Oppenheimer, der sie für das Projekt eines Lexikons des Judentums gewonnen hatte:

22   AL 121.
23   AL 122.
24   AL 149.
25   AL 150.

Bitte streichen Sie überall aus: „im Exil". Keiner ist im Exil, es sei denn der orthodoxe Glaube, dass alle Juden in der Diaspora, im Exil sind, die nicht in Jerusalem sind. Wer sich „im Exil" fühlte, ist nach Deutschland wieder zurückgegangen (…). Alle andern haben hier ihren Wirkungskreis gefunden, und fühlen sich hier verwurzelt.[26]

Sofort nach ihrer Ankunft in den USA erkannte Landau, „Keiner hatte auf mich in Amerika gewartet, um mir ein traumhaftes Angebot zu machen."[27] Die Liste ihrer angeblichen Benachteiligungen in der neuen Welt ist lang. Landau fühlte sich als Migrantin, als Jüdin (allerdings von den amerikanischen Juden des Nicht-jüdisch-Seins verdächtigt), als Deutschsprechende und in Deutschland geborene mit starkem Akzent (die Hoffnung auf Rundfunksendungen musste sie wegen ihres starken deutschen Akzents aufgeben) und, schließlich, als Frau und als Akademikerin. Anders als ihre männlichen Kollegen, und auch anders als professionelle Musiker, die Musikinterpreten waren und in Deutschland bereits einen Ruf genossen (um nur die Bekanntesten, auch ihr bekannten zu nennen: Toscanini, Klemperer, Kleiber, Walter …), für die es keine Sprachbarriere gab, war es für Landau unmöglich, ihre akademische Laufbahn als Musikwissenschaftlerin sofort wieder aufzunehmen. Ihr damals noch rudimentäre Englisch machte es unmöglich, schnell wieder an die akademische Laufbahn anzuknüpfen: Bereits im Sommer 1941 gab es wegen der Flut der akademischen Flüchtlinge aus Deutschland und Europa ein Gesetz, das allen öffentlichen Institutionen verbot, den ausländischen Akademikern eine Stellung anzubieten.[28] Um ihren Lebensunterhalt zu bestreiten, nahm Landau in New York eine Stelle als Gesellschafterin in einer wohlhabenden Familie an, über mehrere Sommer arbeitete sie als Betreuerin in Sommercamps für Jugendliche,[29] wo sie immerhin ihr Englisch deutlich verbessern konnte und freundliche Kontakte zu Jugendlichen und Mitarbeitern hatte.

26 AL 9–10.
27 AL 128.
28 AL 150.
29 AL 134–135, 137.

Dank des Wiedersehens mit ehemaligen Kollegen oder Zuhörern aus Deutschland,[30] knüpfte sie mit der Zeit neue berufliche Kontakte. Einerseits erhielt sie lebensnotwendige Kontakte und Verbindungen über jüdische Organisationen, andererseits bekam sie die Möglichkeit ihre musikwissenschaftliche Vorträge wieder aufzunehmen und somit den 1938 unterbrochenen Faden der Kulturbund-Konferenzen über Musik und jüdische Komponisten wieder aufzunehmen. Diese Vorträge gab sie aber erstmals unentgeltlich.

Landaus Vortragsorte und Veröffentlichungen geben Einblick in die unentwegte Bemühung ihren Beruf auch in den USA zu verwirklichen, sie bezeichnete dies als ihre ersten „Selbstmanagement-Versuche.“ Unter anderem gab sie Vorträge im *Friendship House* in New York City, am *Institute of Jewish Learning* in Newark, und im Herbst 1941 in der Carnegie Hall. In diesen Monaten bekam sie ihr erstes Honorar für einen Artikel, den sie für die *National Federation of Temple Sisterhoods* schrieb und im Frühling 1942 veröffentlichte sie ihren ersten Artikel in einer Musikzeitschrift. Auf Vorträge in der *B'nai B'rith Loge New York* folgten Tourneen in verschiedenen Städten und Staaten (New York, Connecticut), und später 1943–1944 in vielen anderen Staaten der USA.[31] Indem Anneliese Landau ihren zur Zeit des *Kulturbundes* in Deutschland geschriebenen Artikel zur *Verbotenen Musik („Forbidden Music“) in den Diktaturen der Achsenmächte* auf Englisch im *Army Emergency Relief Fund* vortrug, vollzog sie eine Art Widerstandsakt. Der Widerstand galt nicht nur den im Titel erwähnten Diktaturen, sondern auch (auf einer persönlichen Ebene) dem Unternehmen die deutsch-jüdische Kultur in Deutschland auslöschen zu wollen. Durch ihre Arbeit in Amerika hatte Landau auch die Möglichkeit, bereits vorgetragene Beiträge zu jüdischen Komponisten erneut vorzustellen, indem sie etwa ihren Berlin Vortrag *Ungetanzte Tänze* am 20.1.1943 im *Jewish North Center* in New York vortrug. Auf diese Weise engagierte sie sich für Flüchtlingsorganisationen, für Solidarität, und gab moralische Unterstützung für deutsche und österreichische jüdische Exilierte.

---

30 Viele Persönlichkeiten, Künstler, und Rabbis kannte sie aus der Zeit des Kulturbunds: AL 147.
31 AL 171–172.

Durch ihre erneuten Vortragsserien in Amerika—wie zum Beispiel ihr Austin Texas Vortrag über „*Broadway Goes Classical*"—gewann Landau die Möglichkeit in ihrer eigenen Karriere als Musikwissenschaftlerin voranzukommen.[32] Dies kostete viel Zeit und Energie, war aber in der Tat ein Karrieredurchbruch, ohne jede akademische Unterstützung und ohne Hilfe von Seite der Musiker oder der ehemaligen Kollegen. Es war eine gelungene Aktion der Selbstentfaltung und des Neuerwachens durch die Wiederaufnahme und das Wiederbeleben der ihr am Herzen liegenden Thematiken. Auf diese Weise musste sie außerhalb von Deutschland nicht von der Musik und ihrer Karriere Abschied nehmen. Im Gegenteil durch ihre Immigration konnte sie die ehemalige *Kulturbund* Mission erweitern und nicht nur den jüdischen Beitrag zur Musik unterstreichen, sondern auch für die jungen zeitgenössischen jüdischen Musiker und Komponisten, unter denen viele im Exil lebten, werben und sie bekannt machen.[33]

Landau in Los Angeles

Durch ihre Vorträge wurde Landau in den kultivierten Kreisen und liberalen jüdischen Gemeinden immer bekannter. Im September 1944 verließ sie endgültig New York, um eine Stelle als Musikleiterin der *Jewish Centers Association* in Los Angeles anzunehmen.[34] Trotz anfänglicher Enttäuschung veranstaltete sie Kurse für Erwachsene, gründete Musikkurse für Jugendliche und arbeitete an der Gründung und dem Aufbau einer Schallplattenbibliothek. Die erbärmliche Situation der öffentlichen Musik in Los Angeles spornte sie zu Projekten an. In Los Angeles gab es damals nur ein einziges Plattengeschäft; es gab auch keine Philharmonie, sondern nur eine einzige Konzertassoziation, die *Beymer Concerts*, die Kammermusikkonzerte veranstaltete und deren Ziel es war jüdische Musik einem breiten Publikum näher zu bringen. Hier gelang

---

32   AL 172.
33   So z. B. die Veranstaltung *Musicians in the Making*, AL 198.
34   AL 179.

es Landau, ihren Auftrag als Musikerzieherin und als Werberin um jüdische Komponisten miteinander zu vereinigen. Sie nahm Kontakte zu exilierten deutsch-jüdischen, sowie zeitgenössischen Komponisten auf und organisierte eine Konzertveranstaltung mit dem Namen *International Composers Concert*, das zu einem großen Ereignis wurde. Am 25. April 1945 wurden Werke von Ernst Toch, Erich Wolfgang Korngold, Arnold Schönberg, Darius Milhaud, Louis Gruenberg, Mario Castelnovo-Tedesko in Los Angeles vorgespielt. Mit der Zeit konnte sie durch ihre ehrgeizigen Projekte das Interesse für Musik im *Center* und bei der lokalen Bevölkerung erwecken und entwickeln.

Jedoch eine Schwierigkeit, ja ein Hindernis in der Durchsetzung ihrer Projekte, bildete die Einstellung der Leitung im *Jüdischen Center*. Sie wollten ausschließlich „jüdische Musik", von jüdischen Komponisten komponierte Musik, oder jiddische Volksmusik fördern. Landau sah dies nicht so und kommentiert, „Ich musste sie davon überzeugen, dass man ohne die Auseinandersetzung mit Bach, Beethoven, Mozart und Brahms keine Musik beurteilen könne, weder jüdische noch nicht-jüdische."[35] So zog Landau auf kohärente Weise die einzig logische Schlussfolgerung, „Eine grundlegende Musikerziehung durch Hören und immer wieder Hören musste der Anfang sein."[36]

Für Landau war es zeitlebens wichtig, dass Musik jedem Menschen angehöre. Musik ist für alle Menschen geschaffen. Sie behauptete zwar, dass „das Werk eines Komponisten das Spiegelbild des kulturellen Hintergrunds seiner Zeit" sei,[37] aber die Musik auch einen universellen Status und Sinn habe, und dass dabei die deutschen Komponisten nicht wegzudenken seien. Dies bildet den Grundtenor von Landaus Musikansichten und gehört zu ihren philosophisch-ethischen Prinzipien bei der Ausführung ihres Berufs. Mit diesen Ansätzen steckte sie viel Energie in den Aufbau einer Musikerziehung in Los Angeles, die ohne den Bezug auf das deutsche Musikerbe nicht möglich geworden wäre.[38] Die Arbeit für jüdische

35   AL 181.
36   *Idem, ibid.*
37   AL 126.
38   AL 181–191.

Musikorganisationen, an der sie ein Leben lang teilnahm, brachte ihr aus diesem Grund auch immer wieder eine tiefe Enttäuschung, da die parteilich verschlossenen jüdischen Kreise, mit denen sie in den letzten Jahren ihrer Karriere in Los Angeles zu tun hatte, diesen universellen Aspekt der Musik nicht immer mit ihr teilten.[39]

Trotz ihrer vielseitigen Musikarbeit blieb Landau in ihrem tiefsten Inneren ihrer ersten Liebe, dem Kunstlied, treu:

> Ich wollte allen die Augen öffnen für die Schönheit des kleinsten Juwels in der Welt des Klanges, der Melodie unseres Lebens, die uns von Kindheit an formt, für das Lied, (…) Lieder mit oder ohne Worte als Quelle von Kammermusik und Orchesterwerken, die kleinste Einheit und gleichzeitig die größte.[40]

Gegen Ende ihrer Karriere gelang es ihr im Jahr 1980 bei einem amerikanischen Verlag ihr Buch *The Lied. The Unfolding of its Style* zu veröffentlichen. Hiermit beendete sie, was sie selbst als ihre eigentliche „Mission" betrachtete. Nach all den Jahren der professionellen Ausgrenzung, des brutalen Antisemitismus in Deutschland, und der Abhängigkeit von jüdischen Gemeindezentren während ihres langjährigen Integrationsprozesses in Amerika, fühlte sie sich endlich „befreit." Nun konnte sie „Komponisten und Interpreten auf ihren Geburtsort und ihre nationale Herkunft hin … untersuchen."[41] Musik war für sie lebenswichtig, universell und das Wichtigste überhaupt auf der Welt. Ihrer Ansicht nach hatte das „Jüdisch-Sein" im Grunde damit nichts zu tun. Am Ende ihrer Karriere hatte sie endlich ein Leben als freier Mensch.

39   AL 214.
40   AL 214.
41   AL 215.

Schlussbemerkung

In der amerikanischen Emigration gelang es Anneliese Landau, professio-
nell Fuß zu fassen und ihre Tätigkeit als Musikwissenschaftlerin fortzuset-
zen, wenngleich auch in einem begrenzten Rahmen. Wie auch schon in
Deutschland arbeitete sie für jüdische Organisationen und führte deren
„Mission" durch. Es galt den jüdischen Kreisen in Los Angeles, sowie der
amerikanischen Öffentlichkeit die zeitgenössischen Kompositionen der
im Exil lebenden deutsch-jüdischen Künstler näher zu bringen. Landau
bemühte sich, das Interesse der jüdischen Gemeinden für zeitgenössische
Musik zu wecken und dabei über konservative kulturelle Auffassungen
hinaus zu gelangen. Zu diesem Zweck setzte Landau zahlreiche pädago-
gische Mittel in Gange: im Rahmen des Jewish Centers in Los Angeles
gelang es ihr, nicht zuletzt durch ihre außerordentliche Kraft und
Energie, Konferenzen, Treffen, Debatten, Seminare, Konzerte, thema-
tische und musikalische Abende zu veranstalten und nicht zuletzt eine
Schallplattenbibliothek mit Werken jüdischer Komponisten der Zeit im
Center selbst zu errichten. In all den Jahren der beruflichen Integration
und des Wirkens in Amerika verfolgte Landau jedoch auch ihr eigenes
Ziel nämlich die jüdischen Kreise und Gemeinden davon zu überzeugen,
dass das Jüdische in der Musik weder auf das Volkslied, noch auf die syn-
agogale Musik beschränkt sei. Sie wollte das Jüdische in der zeitgenössischen Musik bekannt, hörbar und sichtbar machen.

Als weibliche, alleinstehende Emigrantin ohne Familienbande musste
Landau soziale und berufliche Isolierung durchbrechen. Auf der einen Seite
war ihr, wegen ihrer anfänglich begrenzten englischen Sprachkenntnisse,
eine akademische Karriere als Emigrantin versperrt. Auf der anderen Seite
aber war sie ab 1940 in Amerika als nicht verheiratete, alleinstehende Frau
ohne Familie auch vollkommen frei ihren eigenen Berufsweg nachzugehen.
Sie war offen für neue berufliche Erfahrungen und unbekannte Wege. Diese
Freiheit und Offenheit, kombiniert mit ihrem kräftigen, energievollen,
mutigen Temperament, führte sie nach Jahren eines prekären beruflichen
Status zu der Übernahme der Leitung der Jewish Centers Association in
Los Angeles. Dank ihrer selbstständigen, kompromisslosen und mutigen

Art konnte sie dort Neuerungen im musikalischen und kulturellen Leben der amerikanisch-jüdischen Gemeinde durchsetzen und deutsch-jüdische Komponisten aus dem Vergessen retten. Die vielen politischen und sozialen Hindernisse konnten Anneliese Landau nicht davon abhalten, ihre Musikleidenschaft bis zu ihrem Lebensende umzusetzen.

KATRIN SIPPEL

14 The "Conquest" of Public Space: Female Refugees in Portugal in the 1930s and 1940s

ABSTRACT

In this chapter, I will investigate the refugee presence in Portugal in the 1930s and early 1940s with a special focus on female refugees. The Portuguese Estado Novo regime had kept the country in a kind of "splendid isolation." The society was conservative with strict social rules, especially for women as far as dress, behavior, and the use of public space were concerned. There was more focus on female refugees than their male counterparts. The government saw Portugal as a country of transit, not exile, and most refugees did not want to stay in a place they perceived as poor and backward. Thus, they dressed and behaved as if at home and thereby inducing cultural changes and conflicts.

Women in Portugal in the Late 1930s and Early 1940s

During the 1930s and 1940s, cultural conservatism reigned in Portugal with the motto and three pillars of the corporatist authoritarian *Estado Novo* [New State] regime, established by António de Oliveira Salazar in 1930: *Deus, Pátria, Família* [God, Fatherland, Family]. The family was seen as the "nucleus of society." Healthy, happy, united, and disciplined families were synonymous with a strong, cohesive, and obedient nation.[1] When speaking about his country's colonial politics Salazar, who had been appointed prime minister in 1932, coined the famous phrase *orgulhosamente sós* [proudly alone]. During his dictatorship the

---

1   Isabel Alves Ferreira, "Mocidade Portuguesa Feminina: um ideal educativo," *Do Estado Novo ao 25 de Abril. Revista de História das ideias* no. 16 (1994): 193–233, 207.

Iberian country lived in a kind of "splendid isolation."[2] The author José Rodrigues Miguéis, a republican who went into political exile in 1935 and lived in New York,[3] wrote: "O mundo ficava longe" [The world was far away].[4] Salazarism venerated women at home and glorified motherhood.[5] Professional activity by women was frowned upon by the regime, fearing it would lead to the disintegration of families.[6] Minimum wage was lower for women, and female teachers were not allowed to wear makeup, and they had to ask the Ministry of Education for permission to marry.[7]

Women were socially and politically pushed back into the home. Only widows, divorcees, and women whose husbands lived abroad were allowed to vote, provided they had a secondary school degree or a university education.[8] Laws established during the First Republic in 1910 that benefited women (stating they could not be forced to return to the marital home and had the possibility of a divorce with equality shares) were abolished.[9]

2   António José Telo, "Introducção," in *Ericeira, 50 anos depois. Os refugiados estrangeiros da 2a Guerra Mundial*, ed. José Caré Júnior (Ericeira: Mar de Letras, ³1998), 11–21, 12.

3   Reinaldo Francisco Silva, "José Rodrigues Miguéis," in *Portuguese Writers: Dictionary of Literary Biography*, ed. Monica Rector and Fred M. Clark, vol. CCLXXXVII (Farmington Hill: Gale Research Inc., 2003), 170–5, 170–1.

4   Maria João Martins, "Sob céus estranhos. O quotidiano em Lisboa durante a Segunda Guerra Mundial," in *Tempo de guerra. Portugal, Cascais, Estoril e os Refugiados* (Cascais/Vila Real de Sto Antonio: Câmara Municipal, 2004), 52. All translations are my own unless otherwise noted.

5   Anne Cova and António Costa Pinto, "Women under Salazar's Dictatorship," *Portuguese Journal of Social Science* 1, no. 2 (2002): 129–46, 129.

6   António de Oliveira Salazar, *Comment on relève un état* (Paris: Flammarion, 1937), 39. Cited after Carvalho de Karina Matos Marques, "Holocausto e exílio. O refugiado no corpo social português e brasileiro," in *Abril, Revista do Núcleo de Estudos de Literatura Portuguesa e Africana da UFF* 5, no. 11 (2003): 100–15, 104.

7   Irene Flunser Pimentel and Helena Pereira de Melo, *Mulheres Portuguesas* (Clube do Autor, 2015), 221, 240; Ellen W. Sapega, *Consensus and Debate in Salazar's Portugal: Visual and Literary Negotiations of the National Text, 1933–1948*. Penn State Romance Studies vol. 8 (University Park, 2008), 95n 13; cited after Marion Kaplan, *Hitler's Jewish Refugees: Hope and Anxiety in Portugal* (New Haven: Yale University Press, 2020), 94.

8   Kaplan, *Hitler's Jewish Refugees*, 94.

9   Cova and Costa Pinto, "Women under Salazar's Dictatorship," 131.

Most women had little formal education, in fact, in 1930, about 70% of women in Portugal were illiterate compared to 53% of men.[10] Laws and social structures made sure that women were held within a certain societal place. According to the 1933 *Estado Novo* constitution, the husband was the head of the family who had the authority and the wife was the heart.[11] Wives were supposed to "maintain the cleanliness, tidiness and joy of the home [...] make it cozy and comfortable and present to the husband the deference and obedience that are his right as head of family."[12] Even religion enforced the place of women in society. A papal encyclical of that time states that "nature" had foreseen women to give birth to children and do household tasks. Not unsurprisingly, the so-called "female nature" was used as an argument against professional activity by women.[13]

The discourse of domesticity was one of the principles of the *Estado Novo* ideology. The private area of the home was reserved for women, to justify that men had the privilege of using public space.[14] Some *Estado Novo* politicians even compared housekeeping to governance, arguing that women and men held equally important but separate places in society.[15] Through this gender discourse, women were supposed to become the anchors of the regime, they were considered bastions of family and fatherland.[16]

Salazar himself held very firm views about the role of women, as expressed in a 1932 interview. "Has man ever complained about having to work, day after day, for his wife's keep, to shield her from the storms

10 Cova and Costa Pinto, "Women under Salazar's Dictatorship," 132, 137.

11 Cova and Costa Pinto, "Women under Salazar's Dictatorship," 130.

12 Helena Neves and Mario Calado, *O Estado Novo e as Mulheres. O género como investimento ideológico e de mobilização* (Lisbon: Biblioteca Museu da República e Resistência, 2011), 10. Cited after Ana Gabriela Macedo, "Resiliência criativa no feminino e re-significação da história em contraponto com a ‚manipulação de género' do Esto Novo," *Diacrítica. Revista do Centro de Estudos Humanísticos* 34, no. 2 (2020), 77–91, 80.

13 Cova and Costa Pinto, "Women under Salazar's Dictatorship," 129.

14 Ana Gabriela Macedo and Ana Luisa Amaral, *Dicionário da Crítica Feminista* (Porto: Afrontamento, 2005), 43–5 cited after Macedo: "Resiliência criativa," 81.

15 Cova and Costa Pinto, "Women under Salazar's Dictatorship", 129.

16 Macedo, "Resiliência criativa," 81.

outside? [...] Woman's liberty [...] but do men have the absolute liberty she asks for herself?"[17] He claims that, "men fight in the life outside, on the street, and women defend this life, hold it in her arms, in the inside of the home [...] I do not know who, in the end, has the higher, more beautiful and useful role."[18] This assessment was reflected throughout Portuguese culture. An illustration from the 1938 series *A lição de Salazar* [Salazar's lesson] was often reproduced in murals and schoolbooks at the time.[19] The woman in the painting *Deus-Patria-Família* is framed by the chimney, the man by the door that opens into the world.

Refugees who came to Portugal during those years, however, experienced gender separation differently and saw it more critically. In their writings, refugees who fled Nazi Germany mention and describe the subaltern situation of women in Portugal. In her semi-autobiographical novel *Under Strange Skies*,[20] Ilse Losa from Germany, who fled to the country as a young woman and made it her home, illustrates the subaltern position of many Portuguese women by providing scenes of small bourgeois family life in the 1940s. The characters in her book include a couple, their 11-year-old daughter, the wife's mother, and her unmarried sister. The sister is a milliner and earns a substantial part of the household income. Yet, it is only the man of the family who can grant the women permission to go to the theater or the cinema. Losa comments, "At most, they were allowed to attend mass on their own."[21] Husband and wife lead a strictly gender-structured life, even at home; the wife serves her husband lunch and dinner while standing behind his chair, and she only eats after he has finished.[22]

17   António Ferro, *Entrevistas de António Ferro a Salazar* (Lisbon: Parceria A.M. Pereira, 2004), 91, cited after Macedo, "Resiliência criativa," 83.

18   Ferro, *Entrevistas*, 90.

19   Nova História de Portugal, Dir. Joel Serrão e A.H. de Oliveira Marques. Vol. XII: Portugal e o Estado Novo. Coordenação de Fernando Rosas (Lisbon: Editorial Presença, 1992), 448.

20   The first publication was in Portuguese in 1962, the title *Sob céus estranhos* has been a success and reissued by artists and scholars.

21   Ilse Losa, *Unter fremden Himmeln* (Freiburg: Beck & Glückler, 1991), 64.

22   Losa, *Unter fremden Himmeln*, 64.

Gendered Roles for Young Portuguese Girls

In order to secure the role of women in society, an important statal organization prepared Portuguese girls for their future roles as wives and
mothers. Membership in the female youth group Mocidade Portuguesa
Feminina (MPF) was mandatory for all girls between 7 and 14 and voluntary until the age of 21, or 25 for students.[23] The MPF organized courses
in household management, childcare, and "sciences of motherhood" to
make sure that through love, work, and Christian spirit the girls would
uphold the basis of the Estado Novo. Through state-guided instruction,
girls had to learn obedience, order, devotion, the spirit of sacrifice, hu-
mility, love for work, charity, and devotion to God and the nation. They
were familiarized with the five pillars of the MPF, which are (1) moral and
religious education (faith and Christian virtues), (2) nationalist education (love for the nation), (3) family and household education, (4) physical education (order and discipline), and (5) studies and culture (arts,
literature, science).[24] The cult of the Immaculate Virgin, the Patron of
Portugal, was also of great importance.[25] MPF girls were reminded to be
sensible, chaste, and restrained in their relationships with boys. While
love was important, the bond of marriage had to be consolidated by
children—the more, the better.[26] Wives and mothers were supposed to be
obedient, loyal, docile, tender, vigilant, and ready to sacrifice everything
for their family.[27] They ought to be educated in order to avoid monotony
in the marriage, but it was also believed that girls should not have a know-
it-all attitude, since men do not like women who show themselves to be
superior—the wife had to know her place.[28]

---

23 Isabel Alves Ferreira, "Mocidade Portuguesa Feminina: um ideal educativo," in
    Do Estado Novo ao 25 de Abril, Revista de História das ideias 16, (Universidade de
    Coimbra, 1994), 193–233, 193–4.
24 Alves Ferreira, "Mocidade Portuguesa Feminina," 222.
25 Ibid., 198.
26 Ibid., 208.
27 Ibid., 209.
28 Ibid., 221.

The spiritual and emotional appearance of girls was also promoted
through the organization. Girls were to learn that spiritual beauty was what
mattered most for an MPF member. As appearance reflected inner beauty,
however, female readers of the group's magazine were constantly reminded
to dress, do their hair, and behave in society in a simple and modest manner.
Luxury and flamboyance were discouraged as were arrogance, vanity, and
makeup. A girl had to look modest but was also encouraged not to neglect her appearance.[29] Aside from a modest dress code, the magazine also
recommended physical exercise to maintain a slender figure. Girls were
encouraged to add elegance to their movements and stay resistant to illness.
Among the exercises suggested was going for walks with the baby carriage
and running around with small children. Horseback riding (sidesaddle),
fencing, volleyball, basketball, tennis, swimming, cycling, skating, and
walking were considered physically and morally healthy. Developing too
much muscle, however, was not considered feminine.[30]

Refugees in Portugal

After Hitler's rise to power in Germany in 1933, the first refugees began
to arrive in Portugal. More followed after the annexation of Austria, the
November pogroms in 1938, and above all after the capitulation of France
in June 1940. The number of refugees who passed through Portugal is
estimated at 60,000–80,000 persons.[31] About 90–95% of refugees in
Portugal were Jewish or persecuted as Jewish following the Nuremberg
Laws.[32]

29   Ibid., 199–200.
30   Maria Benedita, "Desportos. Elasticidade, Resistência, Saúde e Beleza do Corpo,"
     Boletim da M.P.F. 75–6 (July/August 1945): 7.
31   Irene Flunser Pimentel, "Portugal and the Holocaust," in *Portuguese Jews, New
     Christians, and "New Jews": A Tribute to Roberto Bachmann* = The Iberian Religious
     World, vol. IV, ed. Claude B Stuczynski and Bruno Feitler (Leiden: Brill, 2018),
     441–55, 453.
32   Patrik von zur Mühlen, *Fluchtweg Spanien-Portugal* (Bonn: Dietz, 1992), 115.

Throughout the war, the *Estado Novo* maintained its neutrality, pursuing a seesaw policy between the Allies and the Axis powers.[33] Its asylum policy was liberal in the years before World War II, very restrictive after it began, and more generous again when the Allies' victory became foreseeable.[34] The Portuguese regime never saw the country as a place of exile or asylum for refugees from National Socialism.[35] The foreigners were perceived as a threat to the integrity of the Portuguese people.[36] They were also suspected of being "potential enemies of the Portuguese authoritarian regime" importing communist ideas that could be incompatible with the "national spirit" in Portugal and lead to social tensions.[37] Strict selection upon entering the country and constant supervision during their stay were implemented to guarantee that they would not endanger the stability of the *Estado Novo*.[38]

Salazarism dissociated itself from racial-biological antisemitism.[39] The refugees were welcomed warmly by the population. There are frequent stories of "Portuguese kindness," examples of help by locals, train conductors lending money without taking jewelry as security, landlords refusing the payment of the rent, and so forth.[40] Artists, intellectuals, politicians, affluent people or those with contacts in foreign countries were often able

33 Michael L. Marrus, *Unwanted: European Refugees in the Twentieth Century* (New York: Oxford University Press, 1985), 263.

34 Ansgar Schäfer, "Hindernisse auf dem Weg in die Freiheit. Der portugiesische Staat und die Deutsche Emigration," *Exil* 1 (1993): 39.

35 Esther Mucznik, *Portugueses no Holocausto. Histórias das vítimas dos campos de concentração, dos cônsules que salvaram vidas e dos resistentes que lutaram contra o nazismo* (Lisbon: Esfera dos Livros, 2012), 86.

36 Carvalho de Matos Marques, "Holocausto e exílio," 101.

37 Avraham Milgram, "Portugal, the Consuls, and the Jewish Refugees, 1938–1941," in *Yad Vashem Studies*, vol. XXVII (Jerusalem 1999), 123–56, 126.

38 Schäfer, "Hindernisse," 39.

39 Ursula Prutsch, *Iberische Diktaturen. Portugal unter Salazar, Spanien unter Franco* (Vienna: Studienverlag, 2012), 77.

40 See for example Friedrich Torberg, "Eine tolle, tolle Zeit," *Briefe und Dokumente aus den Jahren der Flucht* 1938–1941 (Munich: Langen Müller, 1989), 124, or Friederike Maria Zweig, *Spiegelungen des Lebens* (Vienna: Hans Deutsch Verlag, 1964), 230–1.

to leave Portugal after a few weeks. Less famous refugees without financial means could not afford the high price of a ship passage and had to try to acquire further funds. At times this turned into a nightmare as immigration visas for their destinations expired and they had to apply anew. Refugees who were caught in this vicious cycle of obtaining the right papers were obliged to stay in Portugal for many months and even years.[41]

Émigrés usually have the choice between two options: to endure the exile experience and hope for a return to the old homeland or look for a new homeland in the host country through integration.[42] In Portugal, most refugees opted for a third condition: they regarded their stays merely as a period of transit, as did the Portuguese authorities. Portugal was too close to fascist Spain, so many feared a German invasion. Most refugees perceived the country as impoverished and backward. The socioeconomic differences were overwhelming and did not make it attractive as a country of exile. Therefore, the émigrés did not care about adapting to local customs or trying to blend in with the host society. Instead, they hoped to find an exile country that offered more freedom such as the United States. Regarding their dress code, social life, and pastimes, refugees continued to behave as if they were in their own homeland.

Women and Portuguese Fashion

Bourgeois women in Portugal had to wear gloves, hats, and stockings at all times of the year unless they wanted to break the rules of good manners.[43]

41   Von zur Mühlen, *Fluchtweg Spanien-Portugal*, 158–9.
42   Horst Weber, "Exilforschung und Musikgeschichtsschreibung," in *Geächtet, verboten, vertrieben. Österreichische Musiker 1934–1938–1945*, ed. Hartmut Krones (Vienna: Schriften des Wissenschaftszentrums Arnold Schönberg, 1, 2013), 259–84, 274–6.
43   Alexandra Weber Ramos Reis Gameiro, "*A Moda* e as Modistas em Portugal durante o Estado Novo—As mudanças do pós-guerra 1945–1974." Ph.D. diss., Universidade de Lisboa, 2017, 158. Thanks to Xenia Ribeiro from the Museu Nacional do Traje for sending me this thesis.

The colors deemed appropriate for them were rather dark and somber. This clashed noticeably with the dress code of refugee women who went outside without hats, gloves, and stockings and wore sleeveless blouses or dresses of much lighter and flashier colors,[44] some even wore trousers.[45] Refugees kept their hair open, in ponytails, pinned up, or with scarves around their heads, mainly because they lacked money for the hair-dresser.[46] The changes in fashion brought by refugees were noted in the press. An article in the *Mundo Gráfico* magazine entitled *Lisboa a capital da moda* (*Lisbon the Capital of Fashion*) states, "Lisbon became the capital of fashion with the war […] you don't have to look for dresses in Paris anymore. They come by train—naturally on their living models."[47] Over a short period of time, Portugal became infiltrated by Western fashion.

Fashion at the beach soon became a problem for refugee women as they were not familiar with local laws and conservative social rules. Some refugees wore two-piece bathing suits, bikinis *avant la lettre*, which were considered scandalous[48] and fascinating, as the crowds flocked to Monte do Estoril to watch the scantily clad women.[49] The different fashion statements by the refugee women were countered by the Portuguese Ministry of the Interior who established a *decreto-lei* [decree] with detailed rules on how to dress at the beach. This was posted in the beach resorts.[50] Male bathing suits had to cover the torso and especially the nipples;[51] women had to wear bathing suits with an overskirt. The cleavage should not be "exaggerated."

44   Madalena Braz Teixeira, "The Refugee," in *A Moda do Século. 1900–2000* (Lisbon: Museu Nacional do Traje/Instituto Português de Museus, 2000), 117–20, 119.

45   Braz Teixeira, *The Refugee*, 119.

46   Christa Heinrich, "Zuflucht Portugal. Exilstation am Rande Europas," in *Filmexil 16* (Berlin: Filmmuseum Berlin, 2002), 4–33, 23; Heine Teixeira, Lisboa, símbolo de esperança, 675–6.

47   "Lisboa a capital da moda," in *Mundo Gráfico*, 1, Lisbon, October 15, 1940, 7.

48   Heinrich, *Zuflucht Portugal*, 23.

49   Marina Pignatelli, "Os refugiados judeus em Portugal: memórias de exílio," in *Arquivo Maaravi. Revista Digital de Estudos Judaicos da UFMG*, v. 11 n. 21, Universidade Federal de Minas Gerais, ed. (Belo Horizonte: 2017), 1–21, 15.

50   Weber, *A Moda*, 74.

51   "Algumas normas para o uso de fato de banho," *MI, Gabinete do Ministro* 518, no. 76 (1941).

Bathing suits that became transparent in the water were prohibited. Girls up to 10 and boys up to 12 years were exempt from these norms, except in cases of precocious development.[52] Marta Feuchtwanger is one of the refugee women who was taken by surprise as she came into conflict with the law. In a 1976 oral history interview, she remembers walking from Lisbon to Estoril in order to save money:

> I had my French swimming suit, which was in two parts, like all the French swimming suits. This road [...] went along [...] the Tejo estuary [...] and I decided to take a swim because in how long I didn't have a bath anymore. So I began to [..] undress [...]. And then a man came. I thought at first he comes because he is interested in me as a woman, but it was not the case: that would have been much easier. He was from the police. He said it's a crime against the moral that I have a double bath suit instead of a single bath suit; [...] this is not allowed, and he has to arrest me. I said, "But I didn't know." I spoke a little French, a little Spanish, so I found out I did something which I shouldn't do. "Is there a fine?" And I understood that he said yes. I said, "How much?" I had about five dollars or so, and I wanted to give it to him. But he didn't take it. [Afterwards, Marta Feuchtwanger was accused of having wanted to bribe the officer].[53]

This episode shows how refugee women were held to the same standards as the local women. They had to adhere to local rules and regulations even though those were not always known to them. For women who were not sure whether their bathing suits were in compliance with the law, the MPF commercialized its own line of officially approved bathing suits.[54] Not very successfully, as it seems, because time and again, articles in the MPF magazine warned its members of the two-part bathing suit or praised girls and women who dressed properly.[55]

---

52 Decreto-Lei no. 31: 247, *Diário do Govêrno*, I série, no. 102: 5 Maio 1941, 397.

53 Marta Feuchtwanger, *An Émigré Life: Munich, Berlin, Sanary, Pacific Palisades*, interview by Lawrence M. Weschler, 7/1975. Vol. 3 (Los Angeles, CA: UCLA Oral History Program and the Feuchtwanger Fund of the University of Southern California, 1976), <https://archive.org/details/emigrelifeoralhio4feuc>.

54 Susana Lobo, "O corpo na praia: a cultura balnear em Portugal no século XX," *O Corpo. Revista de História das ideias* 33 (Coimbra: Almedina, 2012): 261–76, 275.

55 Irene Flunser Pimentel, *Judeus em Portugal durante a II Guerra Mundial: em fuga de Hitler e do Holocausto* (Lisbon: Esfera dos Livros, 2008), 171.

The Use of Public Space

"The right to the city is gendered. [...] the 'public' realm is perceived as the white middle—or upper class heterosexual male domain."[56] This gender division in the public sphere was particularly true for Portugal in the 1940s when most refugees arrived. When the American heiress, gallerist, and art collector Peggy Guggenheim had to flee from German-occupied France, she also spent some time in Portugal before returning to the United States. Guggenheim was shocked about the public invisibility of Portuguese women. The only visible women, she noted, were peasants offering their goods in the market and whores.[57] Author Friederike Zweig-Winternitz, Stefan Zweig's ex-wife, observed that "[t]he nobler a woman, the more hidden she was, and probably still is today, because this remains a country of the past."[58] Salamon Dembitzer, a journalist and author from Cracovia who had lived in Berlin until 1933, and in Benelux before his flight, described Porto's Praça da Liberdade square as "full of vivid small dark men with diligently brushed and oiled hair and shining shoes. The square was "frauenleer" [devoid of women], the few women who appeared there caused a stir and admiration, because some had short hair like men and smoked cigarettes."[59] These eyewitness accounts of exiles describe vividly how the conservative gender politics of the host country were noticed and became part of a cross-cultural discord.

For the younger generation the gender divide was particularly troublesome as they felt severely limited in their freedom to be independent and take part in public life. Margit Morawetz, a banker's daughter from Prague who was 18 years old when she came to Portugal, remarked that

---

56 Samantha Wilkinson, "Identity and Place," in *The Routledge Handbook of Place*, ed. Tim Edensor, Ares Kalandides, and Uma Kothari (New York: Routledge, 2020), 218–23, 221.

57 Guggenheim, *Out of This Century*, 242.

58 Friederike Maria Zweig, *Spiegelungen des Lebens* (Vienna: Hans Deutsch Verlag, 1964), 232.

59 Salamon Dembitzer, *Visum nach Amerika. Geschichte einer Flucht* (Bonn: Weidle, 2009), 190–1.

young middle-class women were not permitted to go out onto the street unchaperoned. She was horrified that her landlady's daughter "spent most of her day on the windowsill."[60] For others, such as the 17-year-old Denise Hahn from France, it was a quick realization that women could not simply enjoy a visit to a public park. When Denise went to a Porto Park with her sisters, they "quickly understood that this was unacceptable behavior for proper folks. "[61] Ruth Arons shares a similar experience of harsh public rules and a society that keeps each other under strict surveillance. The family had recently arrived from Berlin in the mid-1930s. Her mother came to pick her up from school and, while waiting, sat down on a bench on the Avenida—something apparently considered indecent. The next day, a schoolmate asked Ruth why her mother had been sitting on a bench, and without a hat![62] At that time, only prostitutes did not cover their heads in Lisbon.[63] The risk of being considered a prostitute when frequenting the public space is also featured in Ilse Losa's novel in which a German refugee complains about Porto, "A girl cannot go out into the street after dinner unless she wants to be taken for a whore."[64]

Women and Cafés

The cafés in Portugal had traditionally been meeting points for men. Sigmund Freud's granddaughter Sophie Freud, for instance, recalls that the *leitarias*—which served milk and cakes—were the only places women could go unaccompanied for afternoon tea.[65] Ilse Losa's description of

---

60 Margit Meissner, *Margit's Story* (Rockville: Schreiber Publishing, 2003), 122.
61 Her testimony can be found on the website of the Sousa Mendes Foundation: <http://sousamendesfoundation.org/family/hahn>
62 João Martins, "Sob céus estranhos," 59.
63 Kaplan, *Hitler's Jewish Refugees*, 96.
64 Losa, *Unter fremden Himmeln*, 54.
65 Sophie Freud, *Im Schatten der Familie Freud. Meine Mutter erlebt das 20. Jahrhundert,* (Berlin: Claassen Verlag, 2006), 314.

a café in Porto confirms how the presence of women was seen as scandalous, "As was customary at that time, no female element was present, except two heavily made-up whores …."[66] Hence when female exiles arrived from other countries where it had been normal to go to cafés in their hometowns, they quickly learned that this was not customary in their host country. It was not unusual that they felt uncomfortable such as young Yvette Davidoff from Vienna who on her first day went with her mother to a café in Lisbon and reports:

> … and suddenly there was a queue of men staring at us! And my mother said: "There will be a demonstration!" Later, they were told by locals: "Don't go to cafés, you can't do that here, it's only for men". … [W]e could not do anything, not even go to the cinema on our own! You don't do that here![67]

While initially refugee women suffered due to social restrictions, over time a gradual change emerged as more and more refugees arrived and took part in public life. After the first shock was experienced by the Portuguese and the refugees, more women began to attend cafes and moved into the public space. Writer Arthur Koestler describes central Lisbon Rossio square in his autobiographical novel *Arrival and Departure* and reveals how the gradual transition of a gender-integrated public space led to a breaking down of strict societal rules, at least in the behavior of the exiles who did not follow official rules. Koestler writes, "Most of the tables were occupied by men, the swarthy natives of Neutralia, with butterfly-ties and padded shoulders […] Some of the tables were occupied by mixed groups of men and women […] obviously foreigners, exiles in transit […]."[68] This change in the public space did not go unnoticed and a different gendered atmosphere slowly took hold in Portuguese society and even affected the names of public places such as the *Pastelaria Suiça*.[69] This popular meeting

---

66 Losa, *Unter fremden Himmeln*, 71.

67 Marina Pignatelli, "Os refugiados judeus em Portugal: memórias de exílio," *Arquivo Maaravi. Revista Digital de Estudos Judaicos da UFMG* 11, no. 21 (2017): 1–21, 16.

68 Arthur Koestler, *Arrival and Departure* (London: Jonathan Cape, 1946), 14–15.

69 The pastry shop and café on the Rossio near the train station, established in 1922, much to the chagrin of locals and visitors, closed permanently in 2018.

point of refugees in central Lisbon was now called *"Bompernasse"* by the Portuguese, because one could see "good legs" there [*"bom"* for good, *"pernas"* for legs].[70] In time, the changes brought about by the refugee women affected a major social shift and made it possible for women to be welcomed into public places. In May 1941, an article for the magazine *Mundo Gráfico* mentioned the female presence in the cafés in a rather favorable way, commenting on how the women turned the public square into a pleasant space. It states, "The women ornament the cafés and make them nicer places. There are more sweets on the tables, fewer cups with spirits, more perfume in the air and less waste on the floor."[71]

Locals and Refugees

For the most part, Portuguese society struggled with the changes that were introduced through the exiles and wished to hold on to their previous values. "Cá faz-se assim" [here we do it this way] was a typical expression of locals who saw the foreigners as people from "outside," in contrast to the "people from here." Not unsurprisingly, the locals discovered many faults with the foreigners. For the locals, the female refugees were "shameless hussies who went to the cafés as if they were men."[72] Townspeople felt unsettled by the different cultural attitudes of the foreigners, they voiced their outrage after observing them. In Ericeira, a small beach town and place of *residência fixa,* [assigned residence] to which refugees were sent due to lack of accommodation in Lisbon, elderly ladies went on "excursions" to watch refugee women. For the ladies it seemed to have been a pastime activity that carried a sense of scandal and fascination for the

---

70   Flunser Pimentel, *Judeus em Portugal,* 168.
71   Rodrigo De Mello, "As Mulheres e os 'Cafés,'" in *Mundo Gráfico* 16 (Lisbon, May 30, 1941), 12.
72   Flunser Pimentel, *Judeus em Portugal,* 170.

spectators.[73] In an effort to hold on to previous values, the ladies passed a stern judgment. The parson described the foreign women as dishonest, the men as assassins of Jesus, urging the locals to stay away from them.[74] Nonetheless, there were also activities where both groups came together. The ladies' choice practiced by the refugee women at dances caused quite a stir,[75] as the local chronicler remembers the first party of locals and refugees together. He writes, "Everybody came. They wanted to see the foreigners and dance with the women. When the foreign women asked the Portuguese men to dance, one thing was sure: nothing like this had ever been seen in Ericeira."[76]

The unsettling newness of foreign behavior was not only observed but also carried at times severe ramifications for the locals. In the beach resort Figueira da Foz, for instance, the breakup of a Portuguese family was witnessed with great concern. A Portuguese father of four, on holiday with his family, had left his wife and children for a Dutch refugee girl. According to the screenwriter Jan Lustig, she was arrested at the dinner table, "The emigrant that has violated the country's decency falls under the whore laws. She is deported to Curia [another place of assigned residence]. It is ensured that she will never see the man again."[77] In Eugen Tillinger's report, the consequences sound even more dangerous, "She is in Caxias prison waiting for a visa to return to her country."[78] Salamon Dembitzer

73 José Caré Júnior, *Ericeira, 50 anos depois. Os refugiados estrangeiros da 2a Guerra Mundial* (Ericeira: Mar de Letras, [3]1998), 34–5.

74 Fritz Teppich, *Um refugiado na Ericeira* (Ericeira: Mar de Letras, 1999), 28, 30–1, cited after: Flunser Pimentel, *Judeus em Portugal*, 245.

75 Caré Júnior, *Ericeira, 50 anos depois*, 43–5.

76 Christa Heinrich, "Von Integration konnte man nicht reden—eher von Zusammenleben ...," "Über das Leben in Ericeira—*residencia fixa* für viele vor den Nazis Geflüchtete," in *Zeitschrift für Kulturaustausch* 44, no. 1 (1994), special issue *Ein Blick aus weiter Ferne? Zu den Kulturbeziehungen zwischen Deutschland und Portugal, Teil 1*: 67–9, 68.

77 Jan Lustig, *Ein Rosenkranz von Glücksfällen. Protokoll einer Flucht* (Bonn: Weidle, 2001), 92–3.

78 Ana Vicente, *Arcádia. Notícia de uma família anglo-portuguesa* (Lisbon: Gótica, 2006), 180. Unfortunately, the mentioned article cannot be found in the *Daily Mirror* archive.

also mentioned that same event, "A female refugee has been arrested because a married Portuguese has fallen in love with her."[79] This was not an
isolated incident. Lustig also mentions the arrest of two other young refugee
girls who had worn short trousers on Figueira beach and been seen with
a gentleman in a cabriolet. They, too, were accused of disturbing public
morality and prostitution.[80] The reprimands and public outcry seem to
have occurred mostly toward women, men were left largely undisturbed.
To the author's knowledge, no male refugee was arrested in Portugal due
to their attire or behavior. There seem to have been, however, complaints
that they often did not wear hats,[81] and wore open shirts without ties.[82]
Ruth Arons recalled that depending on age, class, and sometimes gender,
the Portuguese found the refugee women's behavior either outrageous or
fascinating.[83] This left refugee women at a greater risk of suffering from
gender politics in Portugal.

Changes in Portuguese Society

Renée Liberman, who had come to Caldas da Rainha as a refugee girl
from Luxemburg and married a local doctor, said in a later interview:

> It is funny, because Portuguese women in those days stayed at home, learned to sew,
> to speak French and to play the piano, little more [...] First love was via the window!
> I thought that was a joke, I had never seen anything like it. [...] I think that Caldas
> modernized itself quicker than other places, because of the foreigners.[84]

---

79   Dembitzer, *Visum nach Amerika*, 245.
80   Lustig, *Ein Rosenkranz von Glücksfällen*, 104–5.
81   Weber Ramos Reis Gameiro, *A Moda*, 154.
82   Telo, *Introducção*, 19.
83   Helena Ferro de Gouveia, "Lisbon. From Refuge to Home," *Deutsche Welle*,
      29.12.2012 dw.de/lisbon-from-refuge-to-home/a-16410819, cited after Kaplan,
      Hitler's Jewish Refugees, 97.
84   Dulce Soure and Marina Ximenes, "Das Caldas da Rainha e a II Guerra Mundial,"
      in *Marcas da II Guerra em Caldas da Rainha*. Catálogo da exposição 1/10–15/

Liberman points out that Portuguese society became impacted by the different gender behavior and the public space slowly began to change. This is confirmed by Ilse Losa who witnessed that "all of a sudden, one could see Portuguese girls from the so-called old Lusitanian families [traditional upper class families with pedigree] sit in the cafés with feigned nonchalance and a hairstyle *à la Refugié*, smoking and arguing loudly or loiter in the foyers during intervals of theater performances."[85] Even the media noticed and began to write about this change as it cautioned about the impending danger to Portuguese society. Eugen Tillinger wrote in the *Daily Mirror* in 1940:

> [...] Lisbon clerical circles are worried about the "bad influence" that many lady refugees coming from Paris, Brussels and Warsaw may have on Portuguese morals. They note that the Portuguese women are wearing more and more makeup and that, which is worse, they are copying fashions in hats and shoes worn by the foreign ladies. On top of this, they are starting to smoke in public.[86]

The media points to the slow decline of Portuguese women who copy not only refugee fashion but also begin to imitate their careless public behavior. Columnist Maria Joana[87] complained to her readers in the *Boletim da MPF* about the beach at Figueira da Foz, where "so much nudity without shame is exhibited in very inconvenient bathing suits ..." stating that one could hardly tell the difference between foreigners and Portuguese anymore.[88] While the authorities attempted to curtail foreign influence, Ramalho points out that their attempt to "hold back these

---

11/98, ed. Dulce Soure und Marina Ximenes (Caldas da Rainha: Osíris Galeria Municipal, 1998), 25–9, 29.

85   Losa, *Unter fremden Himmeln*, 83.

86   Cited after Vicente: Arcádia, 180. Unfortunately, the mentioned article cannot be found in the *Daily Mirror* archive.

87   Surname Mendes Leal: she was the director of the Boletim and, from 1947 to 1972, of its sucessor, *Menina e Moça*. Isabel M. R. Mendes Drumond Braga und Paulo Drumond Braga, "A Mocidade Portuguesa Feminina e a formação culinária em Menina e Moça (1947–62)," *Cadernos Pagu* (39/2012): 201–26, 205.

88   Maria Joana, "Carta Aberta—Queridas raparigas," *Boletim da MPF* 17 (September 1940): 5.

modern touches" was in vain. Before the end of the war, the change could not be stopped. Portuguese women dared to remove their stockings, and mothers began to visit café terraces with their husbands to protect them against other beautiful women.[89] This points not only to a gradual societal change but also to a convenient way for Portuguese women to enter the public space. At times this caused a gender rift as some Portuguese men were not at all pleased and complained that their daughters and wives imitated the refugees' dress and hairstyles.[90]

For many Portuguese women, the refugees brought a welcome change. Madalena Braz Teixeira writes, "The refugee was an example and constant influence on Portuguese women and helped them change their mentalities. They helped transform the Portuguese bourgeoisie that gradually integrated these new ways of living in society."[91] In time, more and more support arose to give women more rights. According to António José Telo, the government should not have been afraid of the refugees' (leftist) political activities. The long-term effect on habits and the national mentality was most certainly much greater than any political activity.[92] Writer and contemporary witness Alexandre Babo agreed with this assessment as he described the new standard of living.[93] Historian Madalena Braz Teixeira called it a "transformation and modernisation of mentalities."[94] The refugees began to be seen as a symbol of modernity. Rather than being shaped by foreign political activism, it was the refugees' day-to-day behaviors that proved to have a much greater long-term effect on Portuguese culture and national sensibilities.[95]

The changes occurred quite quickly after the arrival of a large number of refugees in 1940: An article in the magazine *Mundo Gráfico* of May 1941 describes the times when cafés were places exclusively for men as "long long

---

89   Magalhães Ramalho, *Lisbon,* 44.
90   Heine Teixeira, *Lisboa, símbolo de esperança,* 676.
91   Braz Teixeira, *The Refugee,* 119.
92   Telo, *Introducção,* 18.
93   Alexandre Babo, *Recordações de um Caminheiro* (Lisbon: Escritor, 1993), 143, cited after Flunser, Pimentel *Judeus em Portugal,* 364.
94   Braz Teixeira, *The Refugee,* 117.
95   Telo, *Introducção,* 18; Braz Teixeira, *The Refugee,* 119.

ago".[96] In May 1943, the magazine presented a double page with photographs entitled *Avenida,* showing women on café terraces, with skirts that end above the knees, and stockingless legs.[97] The caption of a photograph in the article reads, "Portuguese women are already used to not wearing hats. This new habit reveals us new hairstyles.[98] The Avenida at that time was called "*a praia de Lisboa*" [the beach of Lisbon] referring to the fact that it was fashionable not to wear stockings. The caption of a photograph showing a woman sewing while sitting on a bench states that this woman does not care about making a bad impression—at least sitting on a bench on the Avenida was not considered very indecent any more.

Final Remarks

The example of Portugal shows that the relationship between refugees and host society is not a one-way street to acculturation. Refugees in Portugal caused changes in the host society, while there is little evidence of influence going in the other direction. Especially refugee women, who behaved and dressed like they did in their home country, induced changes in Portuguese society, as far as dress, use of public space, and behavior are concerned, making Portugal a place bit more liberal during the years of their presence. Marion Kaplan asks in her article, "Did gender matter during the Holocaust?" and terms refugee experience in Portugal, "a *flattening of gender roles*, as men and women stood in consulate lines, applied to aid organizations … had lost homes, homelands, and their places in society."[99] While one can agree that for refugees gender roles were "flattened" during their experience of escape and exile, in the case of Portugal refugees it is clear that gender mattered and caused great turmoil.

---

96   *Mundo Gráfico* 16, May 30, 1941.
97   "Avenida 1943," in *Mundo Gráfico* 64 (May 30, 1943): 16–17, 30.
98   "Lisboa a capital da moda," in *Mundo Gráfico* 1 (October 15, 1940): 7.
99   Marion Kaplan, "Did Gender Matter during the Holocaust?," *Jewish Social Studies* 24, no. 2 (Indiana University Press, Winter 2019): 37–56, 56.

Confronted with a very conservative host society, refugee women experienced a period of high scrutiny and social reprimand. Yet, the impact of gradual social change that was introduced by the foreigners, was also felt by local women. On the one hand, they were not used to seeing such different attire and public behavior; on the other hand, the refugees introduced exciting new freedoms. For refugee women it meant that in comparison to male refugees, their behavior was more quickly judged to be inappropriate, with severe consequences, as previously described. Therefore, gender made a big difference to the experience of these refugees. In the final analysis, it is true that while female refugees had less freedom of movement, at the same time, their example made greater agency for local women possible.

PART V

From the Desk of the Feuchtwangers

EDGAR FEUCHTWANGER

15 The Lion Feuchtwanger Diaries: An Insider's View

ABSTRACT

Edgar Feuchtwanger reviews *Lion Feuchtwanger: Ein möglichst intensives Leben, Die Tagebücher*, edited by Nele Holdack, Marje Schuetze-Coburn, and Michaela Ullmann (Berlin: Aufbau Verlag, 2018). This is an insider's view of the diaries, from Edgar Feuchtwanger's present-day perspective as a professional historian. It focuses in particular on the diary entries in which Lion Feuchtwanger records his encounters with Eleanor Roosevelt, Einstein, Stalin, and other leading figures of the international scene. The video version of this paper, including image overlays, is available on YouTube.[1]

Introduction

The only thing worse than being mentioned in someone's intimate diaries is not being mentioned, and in my uncle's diaries[2] the closest I came to a mention was when I was 7, when my father and my half-sister Dorothea paid him a visit in Grunewald on January 5, 1932, having left me behind with my mother in Munich. Had I been allowed to go with them to Lion's newly built villa in that expensive part of Berlin, I admit my principal sentiment would probably have been jealousy rather than admiration— jealousy that my half-sister was getting so much attention.

---

1   <https://youtu.be/n1VMK147thI>.

2   Lion Feuchtwanger, *Ein möglichst intensives Leben. Die Tagebücher*, ed. Nele Holdack, Marje Schuetze-Coburn, and Michaela Ullmann (Berlin: Aufbau Verlag, 2018). All diary entries cited in this article are from that edition.

"Mein Bruder Ludschi und seine vierzehnjährige Tochter da." [My brother Ludschi and his 14-year old daughter are here] Grunewald, January 5, 1932.[3]

But those childish concerns faded long ago, and from my current perspective what fascinates me most in these diaries are my uncle's encounters with Eleanor Roosevelt, Einstein, Stalin, and numerous other leading figures of the international scene. Per se, the diaries are skeletal, compared for example with standard sources such as Victor Klemperer[4] in Dresden in 1940, or Chips Channon's[5] scurrilous accounts of political intrigue in Britain at the time. Nonetheless, as with all diaries which merit publication, the frictional effect of the personal realm rubbing up against historical events works in unexpected ways to bring the period to life. They will be a valuable primary source for future generations.

Since this volume has a gender studies theme, by way of introduction I should also mention my aunt Marta and her role in Lion's life. She clearly enjoyed Lion's glory days as a celebrity international author and public intellectual up to January 30, 1933, and that was how my father and mother portrayed it to me as a child. But, less visibly to us, Marta had to endure Lion's attitudes to gambling and sex workers, which are evident from the diaries. In today's terms these behaviors would probably be designated "compulsive" rather than fully fledged addictions. Nonetheless, it is clear from the diaries that Lion and Marta's so-called open marriage gave rise to all sorts of intense emotional problems which were exacerbated by the circumstances.

In exile in Sanary, Marta and Lion were companions in fate with limited choices, and Marta rose to the challenge by providing Lion with emotional support and continuity. Without her help Lion would not have made it out of occupied Europe alive. Evidently her position became a little

3   Feuchtwanger, *Die Tagebücher*, 278.
4   Victor Klemperer, *Ich will Zeugnis ablegen bis zum letzten, Tagebücher 1933–1945*, ed. Walter Nowojski (Berlin: Aufbau Verlag, 2015).
5   Henry "Chips" Channon, *The Diaries (Volume 2): 1938–1943*, ed. Simon Heffer (London: Hutchinson, 2021).

easier during their American years, as Lion sublimated some of his urges into collecting historic books used as primary sources for his mature works.

Leading Figures of the International Scene

In late 1932, at which point I had just turned 8 and still had to stand on tiptoes to peer out of my window onto Munich's Grillparzerstrasse to spy on Hitler, Lion was living the sort of life of which a young boy of that time could only dream: traveling to London and across the United States to much acclaim, meeting the great and the good, flying in airplanes, and being frequently mentioned on the radio in connection with famous names. I often heard my parents discussing the key dramatis personae and though to my ears at that age they were just names, I was old enough to understand that they were important figures.

Lion's meeting with Eleanor Roosevelt was on January 25, 1933, during an extended U.S. book tour which is recorded in detail and is one of the most interesting parts of the diaries. Lion met her at a dinner in New York:

> Abends das Dinner mit Mrs. Roosevelt. Mein kleines Speech gelingt sehr gut. Ich werde ringsum ausserordentlich geehrt. Mrs. Roosevelt lädt mich ein, sie und ihren Mann zu besuchen.

> [In the evening, dinner with Mrs. Roosevelt. My little speech was a success. I am celebrated everywhere. Mrs. Roosevelt invites me to visit her and her husband.]

> New York, January 25, 1933.[6]

This was shortly before Franklin D. Roosevelt took office on March 4, 1933. She was already a fan of Lion's novels, and they were on common ground ideologically, with a strong commitment to the rights of under-represented groups. The success of *Jud Süss* in the U.S. edition published by the Viking Press[7] was still resonating in the United States and Lion

---

6   Feuchtwanger, *Die Tagebücher*, 313.
7   Lion Feuchtwanger, *Power*, trans. Edwin Muir (New York: Viking Press, 1927).

was often quoted in the American press on the subject of German-Jewish affairs; Eleanor Roosevelt was fresh from her successful involvement in transforming the Todhunter School for girls in Manhattan from a finishing school into a girls' preparatory school modeled on progressive English schools such as Bedales. The dinner was probably a sort of meeting of the minds.

As it turned out, the meeting with Eleanor Roosevelt ultimately saved Lion's life in the summer of 1940. Lion's American publisher Ben Huebsch was able to show her the now well-known photo of Lion behind barbed wire at Les Milles. She was a firm backer of the Emergency Rescue Committee and the photo no doubt helped her fully grasp the urgency of the situation.

She met with Varian Fry on June 25, 1940, before he flew to Europe, and thanks to his efforts and the brave involvement of American Consul Hiram Bingham and the Unitarian minister Waitstill Sharp, Lion and Marta and numerous other prominent Jewish intellectuals and scientists made it to safety.

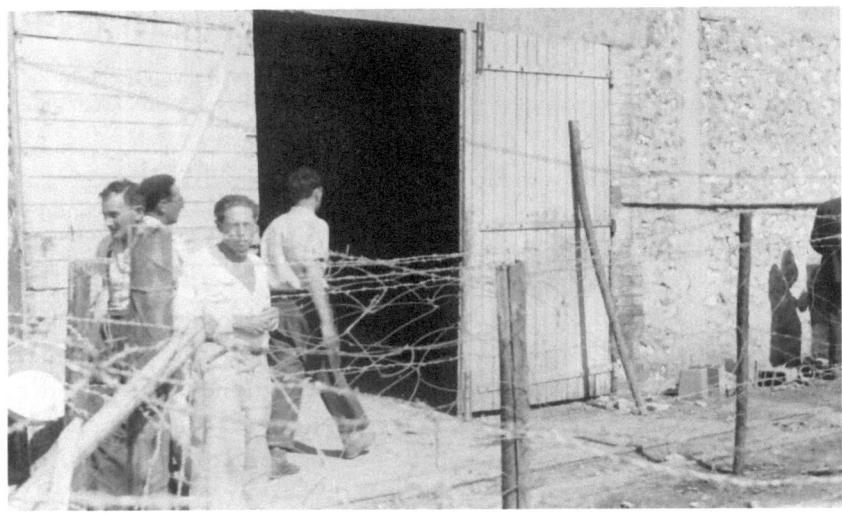

Figure 23. Lion Feuchtwanger in Les Milles, 1940. Unknown photographer. Feuchtwanger Papers, USC Libraries, University of Southern California.

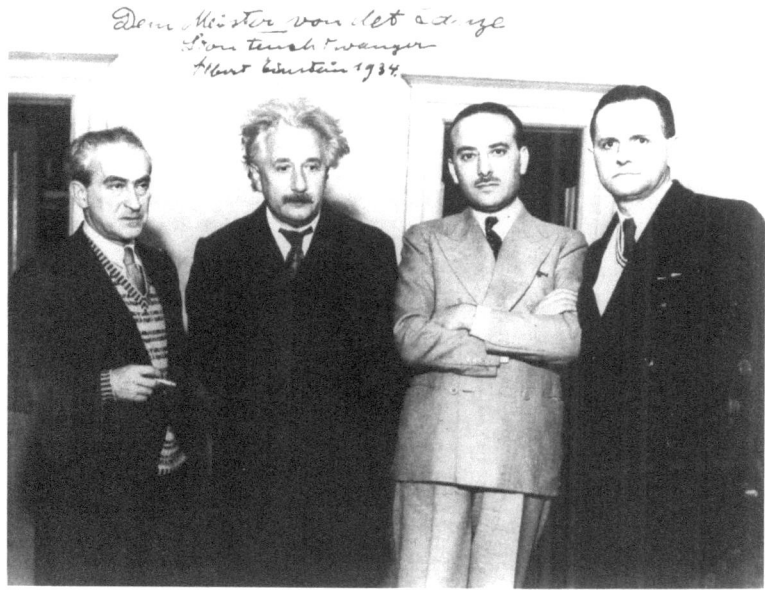

Figure 24. Albert Einstein at the premiere of the Lothar Mendes film *Jew Süss* in New York, 1934. Unknown photographer. Feuchtwanger Papers, USC Libraries, University of Southern California.

During the aforementioned American book tour, Lion met with Albert Einstein in Pasadena, California on January 11, 1932. He writes in his diary, "Abends lange Autofahrt nach Pasadena zu Einstein. Ganz nett. Einstein redet ziemlich wenig und selbstgefällig. Er ist furchtbar saturiert. [Long car journey to Pasadena in the evening to visit Einstein. Very pleasant. Einstein didn't say much and seems self-satisfied. Very smug.]. Pasadena, January 11, 1933."[8] Lion only occasionally wrote about the world of science and technology, but when he did he reached considerable literary heights: with the cold rigor of the *Neue Sachlichkeit*, his short story *Höhenflugrekord*[9] enacts a record-breaking flight into thin air aimed at pushing back the boundaries

8   Feuchtwanger, *Die Tagebücher*, 310.
9   Lion Feuchtwanger, *Höhenflugrekord* (Munich: Drei Masken Verlag, 1929).

of scientific knowledge. It is still well regarded among critics today, and
Marcel Reich-Ranicki, the leading literary critic in postwar Germany, included it in his anthology *Der Kanon*.[10]

Lion's meeting with Einstein presumably left an imprint on the physicist's mind, reminding him of what he had left behind in his native country.
As one of a group of high-profile German-Jewish emigrés from Nazi
Germany, in 1934 Einstein attended the premiere of the Lothar Mendes
film version of *Jud Süss* in New York, giving the film his stamp of approval
by signing his autograph on a photo in dialect: "Dem Meister von det
Janze." [To the master of it all].

The Sanary Years

The diary entries from Lion's Sanary years are extensive, and one gets a
sense of his very strong commitment to the antifascist cause, as an ac-
tivist author caught between the rock and the hard place of fascism
and Stalinism. At the 1935 International Writers' Congress in Defense
of Culture in Paris, he worked tirelessly with Bertolt Brecht, Heinrich
Mann, and many others to warn the international community about to-
talitarianism. Lion writes, "Ich spreche gut, aber alles verpufft infolge
schlechten Arrangements. Unzählige Leute gesprochen. Ganz nett. Die
Russen besonders angenehm zu mir. Babel, A. Tolstoi, auch sonst." [My
speech went well but everything fell flat due to poor arrangements. Spoke
with countless people. Very pleasant. The Russians have been particularly
nice to me. Babel, A. Tolstoi and others.] Paris, June 24, 1935.[11]

Also evident from the diary entries from those years are the interne-
cine tensions among the narrow clique of intellectuals in Sanary, including
Lion's feelings when Eva Herrmann, with whom he was in a liaison, breaks
the news that she is also at the same time romantically involved with Aldous
Huxley.

10   Marcel Reich-Ranicki, *Der Kanon* (Frankfurt/Main: Insel Verlag, 2003).
11   Feuchtwanger, *Die Tagebücher*, 372.

The diary entries from the Moscow visit have been covered in admirable detail by Anne Hartmann in her recent monograph[12] and need not be touched upon here. All I can add from my insider's perspective is this: of course, Lion was very wrong indeed about Stalin, but one has to remember that the situation at the time was desperate, as it seemed as though the Western powers were not going to put up any resistance. Moreover, Lions healthy cynicism did not entirely desert him. When my aunt Bella came to visit us in Munich in 1937 she told us that Lion had stopped off to see her on his way back from the Moscow trip. Bella said Lion was well aware that there were Potemkin villages and that the golden taps in his hotel often produced no water.[13] Allegedly Lion had said to Stalin: "How much pleasure does it give you that there's a picture of you on every toilet seat in Russia," to which Stalin apparently replied, "That's how things work here." It seems to me that throughout his life Lion was a man of the Enlightenment and reason, and that somehow came into conflict with his powerful imagination.

After November 1938 and "*Kristallnacht*," Lion showed his best side, that of a generous, supportive, committed family member. As is clear from the following diary entries, Lion helped pay for my father's release from Dachau:

> Mitteilung dass meine Brüder Ludschi und Fritz im Konzentrationslager sind.

> [Message that my brothers Ludschi and Fritz are in concentration camp. November 28, 1938.]

> Schritte genommen, um Ludschi aus dem Konzentrationslager zu befreien.

> [Took action to get Ludschi out of concentration camp. December 1, 1938.]

---

12   Anne Hartmann, *"Ich kam, ich sah, ich werde schreiben," Lion Feuchtwanger in Moskau 1937. Eine Dokumentation* (Göttingen: Wallstein Verlag, 2017).

13   Bella was deported from Prague to Theresienstadt on 8 May 1943. From there she was deported to Auschwitz on 22 June 1943. She died in Auschwitz on 12 September 1943 (see Arolsen Archives records: <https://www.feuchtwanger.com/AA1.pdf>). According to evidence in the Feuchtwanger Memorial Library, she died of typhus.

Unangenehmes Telegramm in Sachen meines Bruders. Ich soll viel Geld zahlen.

[Unpleasant telegram regarding my brother. I will have to pay a large sum of money. December 22, 1938.]

Viel Geld für meinen Bruder Ludschi geschickt.

[Sent a large sum of money for my brother Ludschi. January 3. 1939.] [14]

My father was ultimately able to get out of Dachau in one piece; he, my mother, and I then emigrated to England later in 1939.[15]

---

14   Feuchtwanger, *Die Tagebücher*, 449–51.
15   Edgar Feuchtwanger, *I Was Hitler's Neighbour* (London: Bretwalda Books, 2015).

Notes on Contributors

KÄTHE ERICHSEN is a graduate student at Johns Hopkins University, where she is pursuing a Ph.D. in Modern Languages and Literatures with a focus in German-language poetry and literature of exile as well as a Graduate Certificate in Film and Media Studies at the Center for Advanced Media Studies. Erichsen's primary research interests deal with exile poetics and literature of the twentieth century, women and gender studies, decolonization of the German literary canon, and theories of translation. Her current research extends beyond literary and philosophical inquiries of exile literature and into the materiality of Holocaust documentation at the site of the archive, through her work as a research assistant for a documentary film in pre-production with Waystone Productions.

EDGAR FEUCHTWANGER taught history at the University of Southampton and has published numerous books on German and British history as well as major biographies of Gladstone, Disraeli, Queen Victoria, and Bismarck. In 2003 he was awarded the *Bundesverdienstkreuz Erster Klasse*, and in 2022 he received the OBE (Officer of the Order of the British Empire).

MARGRIT FRÖLICH is a film scholar and a cultural historian. Her research has focused on Weimar culture and film, exile studies, the post-history of the Holocaust, modern German history and culture in a European context, and European intellectual history. From 2012 to 2017 she was DAAD professor of history, culture, and media at the University of California, San Diego. She currently serves as director of studies for film and culture, as well as transatlantic dialogue at the Protestant Academy in Frankfurt, Germany.

ROLAND JAEGER is an independent art historian and literary scholar in Hamburg and Berlin. He was educated in Hamburg ,where he received a

Master of Arts and Ph.D. He researches and publishes on topics related to art, architecture, photography, graphic design, the history of books and publishing houses, and on German-speaking exile 1933–45 in the United States. Jaeger is a founding member of the International Feuchtwanger Society, recipient of a Villa Aurora stipend in 1997, and author and operator of the website <www.feuchtwanger-research.online>. He is also a member of the Historical Commission of the Association of the German Book Trade.

CAMILLE JENN-GASTAL has been a lecturer at the Université de Reims Champagne-Ardenne in France since 2002. Dr. Jenn-Gastal's research interests include modern German literature, translation, the history of ideas, philosophy, and cross-cultural studies.

WILLIAM KATIN has been a lecturer teaching European History at California State University, San Bernardino since earning his Ph.D. at UCLA. His first book entitled *Hostile Takeovers of Large Jewish Companies, 1933–1935; Reassessing Aryanization of Jewish-Owned Firms* was published by Lexington Books in 2020. Beyond the economic aspect of the Holocaust, Dr. Katin's research interests include German-Jewish culture of the Weimar Republic and the Third Reich. His article *Galka Scheyer in the International Art Business* was published by Michael Imhof Verlag in 2022. Katin's *Recognizing Lion Feuchtwanger's Philological Accomplishment in the Light of Victor Klemperer's Language of the Third Reich* also appeared in 2022 in a Peter Lang volume. His *Memel's Jewish Space as German West Meets Yiddish East in East Prussia* will be published by Michael Imhof Verlag.

TANJA KINKEL was born in Bamberg, studied German literature, drama, and mass communication, and was awarded various literary prizes and scholarships in Rome, Los Angeles, and at the script writing class in the Munich University of Television and Film. She is a member of the German PEN Centre and President of the International Feuchtwanger Society, of which she is a founding member. As a guest lecturer, she has worked at universities both within and outside of Germany. She contributed to anthologies, wrote sketches, and has published twenty novels, which have been translated into more than a dozen languages, with globally sold more than seven million copies. Dr. Kinkel is patron of the Federal Association of Child Hospices. In 1992, she founded the children-focused charity "Bread and Books."

BIRGIT MAIER-KATKIN is Associate Professor of German in the Department of Modern Languages and Linguistics at Florida State University. Her research centers on twentieth- and twenty-first-century German literature with a special focus on exile writers, cross-cultural topics, as well as memory, border and human rights studies. Maier-Katkin has published numerous articles, and among them are essays on Lion and Marta Feuchtwanger, Carl Zuckmayer, Anna Seghers, Walter Benjamin, Hannah Arendt, and Yoko Tawada. Her book *Silence and Acts of Memory* examines literature's contribution to historical memory. Currently, she is working on a book about Sino-German cross-cultural relationships with a special focus on Jewish Exiles in Shanghai. In addition to language courses, she teaches seminars on German literature and culture with a concentration on Human Rights and transcultural themes.

HELGA SCHRECKENBERGER is Professor of German at the University of Vermont. Research interests focus on contemporary Austrian literature, and exile and migration Studies. Her publications have covered Arthur Schnitzler, Gerhard Roth, Lilian Faschinger, Ingeborg Bachmann, Erich Maria Remarque, Adrienne Thomas, Erika Mann, and Egon Schwarz. Schrenkenberger is the editor of *Ästhetiken des Exils* (2003), *Alchemie des Exils/Exil als schöpferischer Impuls* (2005), and *Networks of Refugees from Nazi Germany: Continuities, Reorientations, and Collaborations in Exile* (2016).

MARJE SCHUETZE-COBURN is Associate Dean for Faculty Affairs and Feuchtwanger Librarian of the USC Libraries. She has written articles about Lion Feuchtwanger and his collection and created several exhibits related to the émigré community in Los Angeles. Schuetze-Coburn has co-edited two publications about Lion Feuchtwanger and

German-speaking exiles in Southern California with Michaela Ullmann, and Nele Holdak including *Lion Feuchtwanger: bin ich deutscher oder jüdischer Schriftsteller? Betrachtungen eines Kosmopoliten* (Berlin: Aufbau Verlag, 2023), *Lion Feuchtwanger: ein Möglichst Intensives Leben—Die Tagebücher* (Berlin: Aufbau Verlag, 2018), and with Bill Dotson and Michaela Ullmann *Against the Eternal Yesterday: Essays Commemorating the Legacy of Lion Feuchtwanger* (Los Angeles: USC Libraries, 2009).

KATRIN SIPPEL, MA, studied History, Spanish, Interdisciplinary Communication and Latin American Studies at the Universities of Vienna, Klagenfurt, and Granada (Spain). She works in Vienna as a freelance historian, exile researcher, translator, and interpreter (English, French, Spanish) and is Secretary General of the öge (Austrian Society for Exile Studies). She has published on the Jewish community in Vienna before and after 1938, Austrian resistance members in France, and refugees in Portugal. Most recent publications: "And without a hat! Refugees in the Transit Country Portugal after 1938." In Bastiaan Willems, Michal Pálacz (eds), *Transnational History of Forced Migrants in Europe: Unwilling Nomads in the Age of the Two World Wars* (London: Bloomsbury Academic, 2022) "Ich gebe Ihnen mein Ehrenwort als Offizier der früheren oesterreichisch-ungarischen Armee." Zwangsaufenthalt und Inhaftierung von Flüchtlingen in Portugal zur Zeit des Zweiten Weltkriegs. In Gabriele Anderl, ed., *Hinter verschlossenen Toren. Internierung von Geflüchteten von den 1930er Jahren bis in die Gegenwart* (Vienna: Verlag der Theodor Kramer Gesellschaft, 2023).

HEIKE SPECHT studied History and German Literature in Erlangen and Munich. Her Ph.D. thesis, "Die Feuchtwangers. Familie, Tradition und jüdisches Selbstverständnis," won the Hochschulpreis der Landeshauptstadt München. Specht worked for several years as a senior editor at Random House in Munich, now she lives in Zurich. Her latest book *Die Ersten ihrer Art. Frauen verändern die Welt* about female political leaders in the last 100 years was published this spring. Currently, she works on a history of the Feuchtwangers told through the women of the family.

FRANK STERN is Professor for Visual and Cultural Studies at Vienna University. He has previously taught at Tel Aviv University, Ben-Gurion University, and Beer-Sheva, and was a visiting professor at Columbia University, Georgetown University, Humboldt University Berlin, and others. He is Vice-President of the International Feuchtwanger Society, General Editor of the Feuchtwanger Studies series, and President of the Jewish Film Club Vienna. He has done research and publications on German and German-Jewish history and visual culture, film and media, exile and Jewish studies. His ongoing research is on the role of exiles in British Palestine and Israeli cinema.

MICHAELA ULLMANN is Head of Instruction and Assessment and Feuchtwanger Projects Coordinator at USC Libraries, where she served for many years as Exile Studies Librarian and oversaw the Feuchtwanger Memorial Library. Ullmann's research specializations are in German-speaking intellectuals and artists who fled Nazi Germany and came to Los Angeles in the 1930s and early 1940s. At the California Rare Book School, Michaela regularly teaches the course Critical Special Collections Pedagogy. Ullmann has published widely on Lion Feuchtwanger and other German-speaking exiles. Ullmann holds an M.A. in Cultural Anthropology and Archaeology from University of Bonn (Germany), and an M.A. in Library and Information Sciences from San José State University.

JACQUELINE VANSANT, Professor Emerita of German at the University of Michigan-Dearborn, has centered her scholarly work on the constructions of ethnicities, gender, and identities in post-World War II and contemporary Austrian literature, memoirs, and films as well as the image of Austria in Hollywood films and exile studies. Her publications include *Against the Horizon: Feminism and Postwar Austrian Women Writers* (1998), *Reclaiming "Heimat": Trauma and Mourning in Memoirs by Jewish Austrian Reémigrés* (2001), and *Austria Made in Hollywood* (2019).

CHRISTINA WIEDER, historian and cultural scientist, is a postdoctoral researcher at the University of Applied Arts in Vienna. In her Ph.D. project,

"Visual transformations. The exile of the Jewish artists Grete Stern, Hedy Crilla and Irena Dodal," she focused on artistic representations of exile and forms of cultural translation in Argentina. From 2015 to 2021, she was part of the research group "Visual Contemporary and Cultural History" and lecturer at the Institute of Contemporary History at the University of Vienna. Together with Klaudija Sabo, she directed the documentary film "Die Zweite Reihe des Wiener Filmexils." Wieder was a Junior Fellow at the International Research Center for Cultural Studies (IFK Vienna) and a visiting researcher at the Institute for Cultural Studies at Humboldt University in Berlin, at the Instituto de Artes del Espectáculo in Buenos Aires, and at the Cinémathèque française.

FRANZISKA WOLF is Honorary Faculty Research Fellow at the Faculty of Medieval and Modern Languages at Oxford. Her Ph.D. thesis provides an analysis of the depiction of minority discrimination in Germany by comparing Feuchtwanger's *Wartesaal* trilogy with Abbas Khider's novels *Der falsche Inder* (2008) and *Ohrfeige* (2016), arguing that these writings can be studied comparatively through the notion of "world literature." Her doctoral research was funded by the German Academic Exchange Service (DAAD), the College of Arts and Law at the University of Birmingham, and the Institute of Languages, Cultures and Societies (ILCS, formerly IMLR) at the School of Advanced Studies, University of London, through a Sylvia Naish Visiting Scholarship. Her research interests include exile literature, migrant literature, postcolonialism, and psychoanalysis.

Index

Feuchtwanger Studies

General Editor: Frank Stern

This series focuses on the life and work of the internationally celebrated German writer Lion Feuchtwanger (1884–1958), whose works have been translated into many languages. Of particular interest are topics such as Feuchtwanger's role as a critic of Weimar Germany and the rise of Nazism, his years of exile in France (1933–40) and in the United States (1940–58), his achievements as a proponent of the historical novel, and his reception both in Germany and in the wider world. The series presents Feuchtwanger in the context of his times, paying special attention to his years in Southern California and his relationships with other leading cultural figures of the era.

With Feuchtwanger at its core, the series explores the multinational literary and intellectual network that resulted from German and Austrian exile under Nationalism Socialism: from Paris to Vienna, Los Angeles to London, Buenos Aires to Tel Aviv, and New York to Moscow. Contributions present cutting-edge research elaborating on the intricate relations of literary locations, emotional spaces and biographies characteristic of these important writers, artists and filmmakers. Books in the series will be of interest to those working in German studies, exile studies, Jewish studies, gender studies and film studies.

Volumes in the series include selections of refereed and reworked papers from the biennial conferences of the International Feuchtwanger Society as well as specially commissioned monographs relating to Marta and Lion Feuchtwanger, their circle and contemporaries.

Printed by
CPI books GmbH, Leck